To Sayo,

for all the times your smile gave me life when I ran out of coffee.

I
Responsibilities

LETHI

Lethi crept out of the bed, quiet as a thief, trying not to wake up Marlé. The empty decanter and drink-drained cut glasses on the dressing room table were a remnant and reminder of the night that had passed.

He ran a hand through his hair and pinched the bridge of his nose. *Reckless.*

He was a lieutenant now, the youngest in the Palmaine Army. He had responsibilities and drunken nights with Marlé were not one of them.

His trousers and uniform jacket were bunched in a shameful tangle only a few steps from Marlé's bed. He suppressed a smile, remembering the moment she had told him to undress. How quickly he had ripped his uniform off.

He touched the pendant at his neck. A four-point star suspended on a rope of gold. The closest thing he had to a mother. Inwardly he recited from the *Holy Book of Palman. For the Son sees our hearts and brings peace to those who resist evil.*

He drew his trousers up to his hips and buttoned his jacket. The soreness from the thick scar across his neck resurfaced as he fastened his gorget patch to the buttons under his chin. *Where is my rifle?*

'Did I bring it with me?' he said, under his breath. *I must have.*

He scanned the room. It was dark, but he could see the gun's silhouette. Leaning against the far wall, like an irritated travel companion waiting for him to get ready.

'Where are you going?' came a voice from behind him.

He glanced back. *Marlé.* Her voice was sweet as pine honey. She held the bedcovers up to her neck with one hand, almost as a threat. The smile on her lips said she meant to make good on her implied challenge. Her eyes carried the sure knowledge that she could make him come alive again with a drop of the bedcovers.

'I said, where are you going?'

A sliver of morning light leaked through her curtains, illuminating her grape-dark skin for the slightest moment and it made Lethi's heartbeat faster.

'You know I can't stay,' he said, sliding his rifle sling over his shoulder.

'But I want you to stay,' she said, lowering the bedcover ever so slightly. An inch from abandoning modesty.

He lifted his chin. 'I can't.'

'Last night, you said I could have anything I wanted.'

'That was last night.'

Her smile widened. 'Fine. I know you will always come back to me.'

'Is that so?'

She gave a soft nod. 'You are in love with me, Lethi, and I wonder when you will finally say it.'

He strode towards her and crouched low. 'I might be a reckless soldier and a degenerate gambler, but I'd never take such a ghastly risk as loving you.'

She threw back her head and laughed. The sweetness of the

noise filled the room and Lethi found himself leaning towards her. That close, he could smell the powdery musk of her perfume. Every cord of muscle in his body pulsed with the desire to kiss her.

Her laughter cut off sharply and her dark eyes were on him again. She traced a finger over the deep scar across his neck and inclined her head towards his. Then, as he parted his lips to touch hers, she grabbed him by the chin. 'Be gone then, soldier man, but come back to me.'

Lethi's breath caught in his chest as she shoved him back. It almost hurt to be diverted from their kiss in that way.

'Shave before you come back to me,' she said, massaging the dark stubble on his chin. 'Like the first time.'

Lethi smiled and bowed as he rose to leave.

She gave him a long look. 'I know your secret, soldier man.'

Lethi went completely still.

'I can see it in the thickness of your hair. The bridge of your nose. The smell on your skin when you sweat. The colour of your eyes by candlelight.'

Lethi could only stare, mouth agape.

She leaned forward and whispered in his ear. 'You can dress like them and style your hair just so, but you can't fool me. I have seen the dancing truth of you. When you talk in your sleep, you speak Odu.'

Lethi's breath caught in his gullet and for a moment it was as though he had been punched in the throat. He took a stumbling step, remastering himself as he drew back from her. 'I don't know what you're talking about,' he muttered.

Even to his own ears it was unconvincing.

She gave a knowing smile. 'Of course you don't.' She leaned back in her bed and let out her breath. 'Till we see each other again, my lost soldier.'

'Till we see each other again.'

Lethi slipped out of the door, down the narrow staircase and through the arched doorway. The sudden glare of the sun made him shield his eyes. *How late is it?*

His grey saddlehorse was hitched to a lantern post, and he mounted without ceremony, directing the horse towards the northernmost of the six villages they had been working through for the best part of a year. His fire team would be waiting for him.

When he arrived, the air in the village still carried the smell of death and gun smoke. People ran or hid at the sight of his uniform as he rode through. He parted the crowd with all the gentle authority of a ship's prow parting the ocean face.

One particular woman stared at him as though he was a walking, breathing pile of crap. 'What are you looking at?' Lethi said, in the Common Tongue.

She spat on the floor in disgust. 'How do you sleep at night?'

He tapped his rifle casually. 'With one eye open.'

Her snarl disappeared at the sight of his gun, and she backtracked into the shadow of a mudbrick shack with the rest.

A scream nearby drew Lethi's attention. He rode towards the sound. Banasco, a burly man with a receding hairline, stood in front of a cluster of shackled captives with black sacks over their heads. Beside him stood Dareem; a thin, bald man with a thick beard and a cattle prod in hand.

'How many did you find?' Lethi asked.

The two men turned to him and saluted.

'Seven, sir,' said Banasco. 'Attem is still searching the village, but these seven for sure are from the Black Hammer Clan.'

Lethi studied the captured men. One of them, by his size, looked little more than a child. Lethi removed his hood. It *was* a boy, not more than fourteen if Lethi guessed right. All the same, the boy's brown-eyed stare was pure murder. Young or not, he wanted to do Lethi violence.

'Quite young,' Lethi said.

Banasco shrugged. 'What shall we do with them?'

Lethi thumbed his chin. Their orders were to kill all members of the Black Hammer Clan, but their campaign through Guyarica had been a long one and whatever remnant there was of the Black Hammer would be dead before the end of the year. In truth, their work was as close to done as it could possibly get.

'How many did we catch in that last village?' he asked.

'Twelve,' Banasco said.

Lethi scratched his neck. 'Leave the boy. Hang the rest somewhere everyone in the village will see.'

Banasco didn't move. 'Leave the boy?'

Lethi froze. The man was lurking dangerously close to insubordination and for a young lieutenant that could be the beginning of the end. He drew himself up to his full height and spoke low. 'If you *ever* make me repeat myself again, I'll have you flogged naked in front of the natives.'

For one, eternal moment a tense silence had its way and Banasco just stared. Then he let out a breath and bowed his head. 'Of course, sir.' He turned to Dareem. 'You heard the lieutenant. See that they're hanged.'

Dareem scowled. 'I hung the last batch. The Lieutenant said *you* should hang them.'

'Chain of command,' Banasco said, smirking.

'I'll just wait for Roadie to get back. He enjoys it,' Dareem said.

'Take your squabbling elsewhere,' Lethi snapped.

The two soldiers saluted and dragged the prisoners away.

Two men appeared in the distance. Attem and Roadie. Attem was a dark Darosan man, with tribal marks on his cheeks and shoulder-length locs. He was the only native on their team, and without him they would have been lost in Guyarica. The man could smell sedition in a sweetshop. As good at hunting the Black Hammer Clan as a veteran cat culling a rat infestation. Within hours of them landing in a village, Attem would find a way to flush the clan out from the deepest, darkest holes. The team would spend hours searching a house, then Attem would arrive and fish out three insurgents from a cupboard as though he had told them to wait for him there.

The other man, Roadie, was of Northern Palmaine vintage – pale as the first sheet of snow. Even in the blistering heat, it was plain he came from a place where the sun never shone. Frighteningly skinny, he had the skeletal hands and stern-faced stare of a man that had seen death and spurned its summons. It was said of Roadie that he had seen more corpses than cooked meals. A good man to have on your side to be sure, but a dangerous one too. Hardly ate, never seemed to sleep, never hesitated to draw his blade.

Attem gave a casual salute. The man always had an easy bearing. Other Lieutenants had said he was too easy for a native, but their loss was Lethi's gain. Native or no, he was the best tracker Lethi had ever seen.

'The village is clean, sir,' said Attem.

On the matter of hiding rebels, Attem's word was as good as certainty.

'Good,' said Lethi.

'That's the last of the villages in Guyarica. Sir, we could sweep out east to the river to make sure, but I think we have routed the Black Hammer in this land.'

Lethi thought the same thing, though he had hoped not to

hear it so soon. It meant this part of their mission was over, and there had been great pride in doing it so well.

'I am minded to agree with you, Attem.'

Attem nodded and wet his lips. 'If I may ask, sir, what is next?'

In truth, Attem certainly could not ask. A man of his rank asking his lieutenant any question was an act of shuddering audacity. But what did rank mean now? What good was there in withholding that information when their early success was largely based on Attem's tracking skills.

'We wait for instruction from the Crown,' said Lethi. 'Then I expect we move on west.'

Attem clicked his tongue. 'West?'

'To Basmine.'

Roadie leaned back suddenly and gripped his knife as though the word alone was sure to bring danger.

'Sir...' Attem started. 'Basmine is not like this place. It is far larger, dense as a rock. If the Black Hammer Clan have gone as far as Basmine then—'

'Attem,' Lethi said, putting a hand on Attem's shoulder. 'We will have our orders.'

Attem swallowed and let out a heavy breath. A sigh heavy with the resigned irritation of a guilty criminal receiving his death sentence.

'Give me a week to tell my people, see my family,' Attem said. 'I am an Odu man.'

It was a fair request. Richly deserved. Lethi nodded. 'Four days.'

Attem hissed but made no further complaint.

Roadie gestured to the boy prisoner, still kneeling in the dust, and inclined his head. It was his way of asking, 'Should I kill him?'

Lethi shook his head and waved off Attem and Roadie in dismissal. They saluted and moved in the direction of the rest of the fire team. They would call him a hero for what he had done in Guyarica. A light in the darkness. *And what ugly heroes we make.*

Lethi turned his attention to the boy. Though silent, his jaw was clenched tight, and a trail of tears had run down his dust-soaked cheeks. Lethi sank to his haunches and pulled six gold coins from his jacket pocket. 'Take this and start over somewhere.'

The boy made no move to collect the coins.

Lethi shrugged and dropped the coins on the floor. 'Suit yourself.'

He straightened and walked towards the rest of his team.

'Omaku,' said the boy.

Lethi narrowed his eyes. He had heard the curse before, along their campaign. It was an Odu word. It meant something along the lines of 'I will find joy when you die'.

When Lethi first heard it, it had unnerved him, but the Palmaine Army had been long in Guyarica, and the word had lost its power.

He smiled at the boy. 'Find joy some other way.'

2

Godsblood

RUMI

The young man walked with the slow hesitation of a panther on the prowl. His teeth were clenched tight with the same sort of predatory anticipation. The vaulted theatre was teeming with people and all eyes seemed trained on him.

'That's him,' someone whispered.

He walked with his back straight, uncomfortable with the attention but maintaining his soldier's bearing. The single black cowrie that served as a pendant for his necklace seemed to grow warm as he moved under the attention of their stares.

'The Old Dog Never Dies!' someone shouted.

He raised a hand in salute. It was a gesture of respect, when said in that way. An homage to his mother who had once worn those words.

Another shouted a name. 'Ajanla Erenteyo.'

He turned at the sound of it. It was not his true name but one he wore as a sort of mask. *Ajanla Erenteyo*. The one who killed the Priest of Vultures. It was like they were talking about someone else. His true name – that he had only just come to know – carried a story that most would struggle to believe.

A voice sounded from behind him. 'You're getting good at this.'

He glanced over his shoulder. A woman with fire-red hair

and a high-necked grand-boubou, gave him a teasing smile. Though it felt strange, when he looked at her, he could think only of a sword.

'Zarcanis,' he breathed.

She smiled. 'Hello, Rumi. Keep this up and people might actually believe you are who they say you are.'

Rumi didn't have to ask what she meant. The Eredo was preparing for war and it meant that the people needed symbols. Stories. Symbols like Zarcanis who had gone toe-to-toe with a godhunter and told others to leave her to it. Symbols like Alangba who had faced down twenty Obair and won. Like Ladan who had lost a hand to save his friend. *Renike.* Renike, barely fifteen, who had faced a nightmare and stood her ground. People who had fought in the Battle of the Thatcher and won. It was why Rumi walked like he was strong, even when he wanted to be anything but strong.

The truth was, there had been no victory won at the Thatcher. The hundreds who were now in shallow graves were a testimony to the silent truth. When the battle ended there were tears of sorrow, not of joy. They had lost more than they ever could claim to have won. Basmine was still under the control of the Palmaine, and across the protectorate they were still whipping native boys bloody for whistling at night. It was survival, not a triumph.

The fighting, they all knew, was far from over and nothing stirs people to fight like a story. A myth. Something to believe in. To hope for. So they let the stories grow till they had sprouted legs and walked on their own.

It occurred to Rumi that stories had a way of shape-shifting as they travelled. In the Eredo they called him Ajanla Erenteyo, but the Priest of Vultures had called him the Son of Despair. His mother had called him Voltaine and now he was meant to understand that his true name was Omo-Xango – a descendant of a god; Xango the agbara of thunder. It was a lot for anyone to hold together all at once.

In the aftermath of the battle, a good number of capable Seedlings were made Sulis. More at one time than ever before. The Eredo needed shadowwielders if it was to succeed in its unimaginable task, so they were quickening the process of making them. Every day, new recruits were given the Bloods and being taught to wield the shadow.

Rumi had not called his own shadow since the battle. Had not returned to sparring. He wasn't ready. He had not fortified his mind enough to even attempt to call it again. To call the shadow was to confront the deepest truths of the mind. To face the deepest gripes of the unconscious. There were truths lurking at the back of Rumi's mind that he dared not confront. Truths too clear and sharp to acknowledge.

They reached the meeting room and a tall, bearded man gave an affirming nod. The muscles on his arms would look obscene on any statue and yet here he stood, a full picture of brawn. He had the look in his eyes of a man who had to fight to the death to earn his morning bread. Alive and intense.

'Ajanla Erenteyo,' he said.

Rumi smiled. 'Strogus the doorkeeper.'

Strogus held the door open. 'Take a deep breath. Your crowd awaits.'

Rumi breathed in as he stepped into the meeting room. The huge chamber could have been a theatre of its own. Rock lanterns had been carved into the stalactite canopy and the large roundtable at the centre of the room dominated the space. Every man or woman one would expect at a war council meeting was in attendance. Lord Mandla, the leader of the

Eredo; his six chiefs who served as trusted advisers; the Captain Shadowwielders who trained everyone in the Shadow Order; the First, Second and Third Rangers of the Chainbreakers – the Eredo's expeditionary force. All sat with grave, contemplative faces.

Rumi searched high and low, but there was no sign of Nataré. No sign of any of the sentries, for that matter. They were still at their posts, no doubt – guarding the broken walls.

He took a seat away from the round table, in one of the more inconspicuous parts of the room. He thought of his father, still recovering in the botanical ward from his injuries at the Thatcher. At the battle, his father, Griff, had released an explosion of shadow that Rumi could scarcely believe. They had their name back now and what a name it was: *Xango*.

Rumi scratched his neck. *What does it mean to be the descendant of a god?* It certainly didn't give him any godly power. It was said that when Xango called thunder by its name, the thunder would answer; when Rumi called a dog by its name, he was usually ignored. Though he had moments of great strength in the shadow, Rumi was not one of the best shadowwielders. Neither was he a great conjurer, nor did he have the ingenuity of someone like Sameer. In short summation – aside from as a musician, he had seldom shown any true skill in anything. All in all, he was pretty sheggin' pathetic for a godling. And yet, here he stood – in a room full of heroes, with a name that stood as high as all the others. He felt like an impostor and thief.

A strong tower of a man stepped up to the roundtable – it was Telemi, Lord Mandla's bodyguard. He raised his hand, cleared his throat and all the talking stopped. Lord Mandla, the beating heart and thinking mind of the Eredo, rose to his feet in the silence. He wore the woven raffia headdress of an aminague, which made him look more ominous and final than he already was.

'Welcome,' Mandla said. He cast a quick glance over the room like a shepherd silently counting his flock. 'We are all here in the context of terror. Thirteen days ago, our gates were broken and we fought an enemy most believed only existed in scare stories. Our grave sites are full, our martyrs have made their stand, and the nights of mourning have not ended. But the truth remains: we are in the teeth of terrible jeopardy. The nation that they call Basmine, and all its precious people, remain in the hands of an oppressive foreign power. With the battle at the Thatcher, forces beyond our imagination have now been made aware of our existence, of our strength. They have broken our wards and left us completely exposed. As a people – as a reality – we face extinction. But I did not call this meeting to dress the wounds of our defeats. We will dress them until we die. I called this meeting to tell you that the future imagined in the dreams of generations past is in our reach.'

Rumi sat up as though suddenly called to attention.

'Our story is not at its end,' Mandla said. 'It is at its beginning. The Palmaine king has covenanted with Palman and the godhunters may break down our door, but we have something they never will: the evidence of the Skyfather's hand.'

Rumi glanced at the door.

Mandla locked eyes with Rumi, his stare seeming to hold him in place. Rumi was certain that Mandla was going to name him as the evidence of the Skyfather's hand. Make him some symbol of salvation. His heart kettle-drummed his ribs. Mandla shifted his stare to the tall doors at the far end of the room.

'We know the truth. We know the mission of their missionaries. We know the silent violence of their loud lies. We know their civilisation is not civilised and we see through the disguise.

This year we break the mask. This year we show them that there is a nation. This year we show them that Dara lives. The old blood is back.'

The doors creaked slowly open as Chainbreakers spilled into the room. They moved with perfect synchronicity, forming an honour guard.

A woman strode imperiously forward. She wore a beaded crown that covered her face and a golden iborun shawl of glimmering damask. Her fly-whisk was made with the stark-white hairs of Shinala tail. One by one, the crowd bowed in total salute.

Mandla cleared his throat. 'Old blood has returned. The circle of time spins anew. All hail the Golden Eagle; all hail the Golden Eagle! Queen Falina Almarak, daughter of King Olu Almarak, blood of the ancestors and rightful ruler of our nation. Ka-Biyesi O!'

Rumi pressed his face to the floor in the highest possible salute. Even to one not born in the Eredo, it was a compelling spectacle.

It was death to look a monarch in the face when they wore the crown. Yet Rumi's gaze lifted to peek up at her. He stole a quick glance up as the woman took her seat at the centre of the roundtable. *A queen*. No less than King Olu's daughter. *Now that is a story*.

A voice boomed behind Rumi as he came to his feet. 'Long may she reign.'

He glanced over his shoulder. A small-boned Kuba stood with arms folded across his chest.

Rumi smiled. 'Sameer.'

Sameer grinned. 'Ajanla Erenteyo. I hear you killed two hundred Obair with one hand tied behind your back. I hear you blink twice for a good night's rest. I hear your shadow is like a rolling ocean wave and a mighty east wind.'

Rumi touched his chin. 'Funny that. I hear you are so clever you tricked Ilesha out of his only good pair of sandals. I hear you read two books every hour and recite them all from memory before you go to sleep. I hear you never use a clock because you count time in your head.'

A third figure appeared; an albino man, big as a bricklifter, with scarred knuckles and golden eyebrows. He grinned. 'I hear you...'

They waited for a moment, but Ahwazi just gave a confused look.

'You ruined it, Ahwazi,' Rumi said with a laugh.

Ahwazi scratched his chin. 'I had something but it just slipped my mind. What was it?'

Sameer turned to Rumi as they sat down. 'Is it true you haven't touched your shadow since it happened?'

Rumi nodded. 'That one's true.'

Sameer let out a breath and nodded his understanding. 'It all got a bit much in that battle.'

Rumi frowned. 'It did.'

A small silence ensued before Ahwazi snapped his fingers in realisation. 'That was it. I heard you... Shege, that wasn't it either.'

Rumi laughed and turned to Sameer. 'I was told only Suli could attend this meeting.'

He smiled. 'That's why I am here.'

Rumi gave him an appraising look. 'They raised you to Suli?'

Sameer nodded. 'We just found out this morning.'

Rumi blinked. 'Ahwazi, you too?'

Ahwazi nodded. 'Honour in battle. A good many Seedlings were raised today.'

'I am glad to hear it,' Rumi said.

Sameer took a moment to wipe his thick spectacles. 'Everything has changed now. Our gates were knocked down. Our wards were broken. We can no longer pretend that there isn't a world out there that is desperate for our participation.'

Ahwazi rolled his shoulders. 'And what a participation it will be.'

'What do you think happens next?' Rumi asked.

Now Sameer rolled his shoulders. 'I can't say for sure' – he gestured to the now-seated queen – 'but she stands at the centre of it.'

Rumi lowered his gaze. 'Long may she reign.'

'Long may she reign,' Sameer added.

Ahwazi raised his chin, his voice suddenly serious. 'I remember now, and I actually did hear this one.'

Rumi smiled. 'We are listening.'

Ahwazi put a hand on each of their shoulders and spoke. 'I heard your father shouted the name of a god to call his shadow. I heard the blood of a god runs through your veins.'

The laughter stopped.

3

The Golden Eagle

FALINA

Falina could barely see anything beyond the crown's beaded veil. It was a miracle she had made it to her seat without tripping over, and now she wanted nothing more than to take the crown off and have someone rub peppermint oil into her scalp. Maka Naki pulled her chair out and bowed low, his face almost pressed to the ground. He'd been different since the battle. Fewer smiles, hardly any jokes, no interest in her bottom. They were all different since that day.

She glanced across the table at Alangba and managed a smile, though he could not see it past the beaded veil. Alangba had put his life on the line for her against unimaginable odds. Having someone give so much of themselves to see you safe; all because they believed that you were something important, something worth fighting for. It changes you. That was why she was here. That was why she wore the crown. Alangba's words flashed through her head: 'duty comes before death'.

A part of her did not want to be there. In a way, knowing they were all survivors of that carnival of death made the guilt stronger. Who were they to live and hold meetings when so many had died? At the same time, being around them gave her a sense of belonging that she had never had before. In Palmaine, she'd felt like a flower cut from the cluster; in the Eredo she was a seed replanted. They had been to the hellmouth together and here they were – fighting. 'One Nation,' Mandla had said. One speech from Mandla would have a fish fixing to fly. *I don't have what he has – I'm no leader.*

Her sister Adelina should have been the one to wear this crown. She would have carried it well – *but she jumped from the slave ships. And now the coward wears the crown.*

Falina drew in breath, nodded to the gathered crowd and spoke in perfect Mushiain. '*Ejide.*'

At her command, men and women rose from their bows to take their seats.

Mandla cleared his throat. 'Your Majesty, we have called this meeting to seek your approval on the recommendation of the chiefs.'

Falina raised an eyebrow. 'And what is that recommendation?'

Mandla lifted his raffia headdress and met her gaze. 'War, Your Majesty.'

Falina's knees kissed as her entire body went tense. What she had seen was just a battle, and now the call was for war. It was no surprise to hear Mandla say it, but the word still hit like a punch.

She drew in a breath. 'Are we not safe here? Can we not rebuild our walls? Fortify ourselves?'

Mandla's expression did not change. 'Our wards were the work of ancient magic that cannot be restored. Our walls and gates will be rebuilt, but it will take time. Worse still, some of the prisoners we held have escaped, Zaminu amongst them. The man is no fool – he knows we are here and will certainly try to find us. We will fortify as best we can, and perhaps we might be safe again, but we will never have peace. The Palmaine strangle our land, dominate our brothers and sisters, and we sit quiet while the blood song plays.' He shook his head. 'A bird in a cage may be safe but it will know no peace until it can fly. After all that we have seen, all that we have lost, I believe that the time to dance has come. We've hidden long enough.'

There were murmurs of strong approval amongst the crowd. Any idle spectator saw that there could only be one choice now. Mandla had laid the truth out plainly – to hide now would be an act of loud cowardice. There was one thing Falina knew for sure about the Kasinabe – cowardice to them was a sin as grave as treason.

Falina's jaw tightened as she lifted her gaze to the crowd. 'So, it is war, then.'

The crowd didn't cheer, didn't grumble, didn't even murmur in surprise. Her declaration of war was regarded with the solemn silence of a gardener trimming the hedges – war was nothing new to them, it was what they had always known would come, what they were built for.

Mandla bowed low. 'Long may you reign and may your victory be permanent.'

Falina tilted her neck slightly under the weight of the beaded crown. 'How do we begin our preparation?'

'First, by raising your war chiefs, Your Majesty,' Mandla said.

'Who are the candidates?'

'The Six Chiefs remain at your service, Your Majesty, but for this campaign we will need at least two more.'

Falina rubbed her neck. 'Who would you recommend?'

'On the field of battle, there is none greater or of more varied experience than Zarcanis the Viper.'

A tall, lithe woman with red hair rose to her feet. Falina made a show of inspecting the woman. From the set of her shoulders and the subtle cords of muscle under her high-necked boubou, it was plain this was a warrior. Her dress was simple and she had a deviously casual bearing that complemented the blank, inexpressive look on her face.

Falina parted her veil with one hand. If she was going to go to war alongside this woman, she wanted them to be face-to-face when they agreed to it. The crowd gasped, but this was not a time for ceremony. 'Zarcanis the Viper?'

'Some people call me that,' the woman said.

Falina produced a golden kola nut from the ornamental satchel at her hip. 'What do others call you?'

Zarcanis stared at the golden kola nut like it was a dire threat, then picked it up and broke it. She studied Falina for a moment, then leaned forward to whisper in her ear.

'Zaiyana Daishen,' she said.

'A Guyarican name?' Falina said.

'It is where I was born.'

Falina nodded and spoke low. 'Will you be my war chief, Zaiyana Daishen?'

The woman dropped to one knee and in an instant, her inexpressive stare seemed to fall to pieces. Emotion sat plain and heavy in her eyes. 'I served under your father. The greatest man I have ever known. I also have the unhappy misfortune of becoming an expert in war. Seeing you here now is, for me, an inward liberation. It would be an honour and a privilege to be your war chief... My Queen. I will live and die for you.'

Falina raised her chin. 'The honour and the privilege is mine.' She turned to address the crowd. 'Brave warrior. I name you Chief.'

From the muted cheers and gruff sounds of approval it was plain that Zarcanis was respected more than she was liked. A good trait to have in a war chief, her father had always said. Walade the Widowmaker was widely hated and feared in her father's army, and yet no one inspired more discipline and battle vigour than him.

She glanced up at Alangba. 'And your second recommendation?' she asked.

Mandla scratched his chin. 'I would recommend one of the Chainbreakers, perhaps—'

'Alangba,' Falina said sharply.

A metallic clang filled the air as Alangba dropped his spear.

The crowd turned towards him as he drew in a breath and knelt. 'Your Majesty, I... I am afraid I cannot accept.'

Falina gave him a confused look.

Alangba lowered his chin. 'I am no more than a dogfighter. If it is to be one of the Chainbreakers then there is no man amongst us with the strategy and experience to match the First Ranger, Okafor.' He gestured to Okafor – a tall, bald man standing just behind him. 'I am none to query you, Your Majesty, but I ask that you consider the First Ranger in my stead.'

None to query me? He had queried her to irritation onboard the *Black Crocodile* but now played the part of the courtly subject. She smiled and shifted her gaze to the tall, burly man stood behind Alangba. Falina knew what it was. Alangba was only Third Ranger and for him to be raised ahead of his superiors was an affront to the chain of command. They already had a leader, and who was she to change that?

She cleared her throat. 'Okafor, First Ranger, will you accept this office?'

The First Ranger dropped to one knee. 'With all honour and pride, Your Majesty.'

Mandla walked over to where the First Ranger knelt and placed a hand on the man's shoulder. 'So it's settled then; our preparation begins. The season of sowing and tilling is over, now comes the harvest.'

Falina gave Mandla a long look and spoke low, so that only those around their table could hear. 'How do we define victory in this matter? What is our aim?'

Mandla drew in breath. 'Our aim is to drive the Palmaine from our land. Take back power. To free all of Basmine.'

'Even if I am to imagine that what you say is possible, I cannot imagine what would happen after we have achieved it. How do you think the other native tribes will react to a Kasinabe army storming their capital and taking control?'

Mandla gave a knowing nod but said nothing.

Karile cleared her throat. 'The queen is right. They watched the Palmaine kill us before, they will happily watch them finish the work. They see us as a greater evil than the Palmaine ever were.'

'It is true,' Gaitan agreed.

Falina glanced up at Mandla, his face completely expressionless as he listened. 'You have a plan?' she asked.

He nodded once. 'I do.'

The Queen inclined her head. 'What is it? What do you propose that we do?'

He glanced over at Alangba. 'The people of Basmine are in chains. The door to their freedom is in plain sight, but they won't knock until they believe they have paid for entry. My plan is simple, we send them the Chainbreakers. Pay the price in blood for all to see. Shatter the chains on the minds of our people.'

4
New Seeds

RENIKE

Renike sucked in a deep breath as she stared up at the moon crescent table. There were eight people seated before her. Six of them Renike had met before – Mandla, Lungelo, Karile, Kwesi, Kovi and Gaitan were all white-cap chiefs. The men and women who ran everything about the Eredo from the bakery to the blacksmiths. Of the two others at the table, one was instantly recognisable. *Zarcanis the Viper.*

Zarcanis wore an Odeshi collar around her neck and had her hair tied back into a thick, red braid. Even sitting down, she looked big. Renike knew that the Viper had trained Rumi. The story was that she had walked alone to face down the Priest of Vultures – *a warrior straight from storybook.* When Renike met her gaze, Zarcanis had an expression close to amusement.

The unfamiliar face was that of a tall, bald man with a worryingly long neck who wore the green robes of a Chainbreaker.

Behind the chiefs were several others standing by the wall. Some faces were familiar to her, others were not. These, she knew, were the trainers.

At the centre of the table were six gourdlets, an empty calabash and a plate of kola nuts.

'Please step forward,' Mandla said, gesturing towards the circle of sand, near the centre of the room. Renike met his gaze as she obliged.

Mandla raised a kola nut so all could see and spoke with the power and clarity of a bugle. 'We may exchange kola nut.'

A ceremony of exchange began, with each person in the room breaking and eating of the kola nut. Some chose to introduce themselves once the nuts were broken and gave Renike names she knew she would have to learn again in the days to come.

When the agreement was sealed, Mandla cleared his throat. 'Who are you and what is your petition?' he asked.

Renike raised her chin. 'My name is Renike Denaiya of Odu and I am here to be admitted into the Shadow Order.'

Karile smiled wide and gave an approving nod.

'How old are you?' Mandla asked.

'Fifteen,' she said. 'In two weeks.'

'Young for the Shadow Order,' Kwesi offered.

Zarcanis cleared her throat. 'But not unprecedented.'

Karile nodded. 'Agreed.'

Gaitan scrubbed his beard. 'I hear you and your friends stopped an Obair.'

Renike answered honestly. 'We were fortunate. Dara was on our side.'

Gaitan smiled. 'Who are we to question one so favoured of the Skyfather?'

Karile lent her voice to his. 'She is good iron. Strong, resilient, teachable. She will make a story we cannot believe.'

Mandla gave a firm nod. 'Are there any objections?'

Lungelo cleared his throat noisily but no objection came.

Mandla gave Renike a studying look. 'Daughter of Odu, do you accept the Bloods?'

Renike lowered her eyes. 'I do.'

'And do you promise to keep the immortal secrets of the Bloods and all its manifestations?

'I do.'

Mandla's jaw tightened as he raised one of the six gourdlets. 'Blood of the leopard,' he said, pouring the contents into the calabash. 'Blood of the bull... Blood of the eagle... Blood of the lion... Blood of the tree.' He hesitated. 'Blood of the agbara.'

He emptied the last gourdlet into the calabash and offered it to Renike. 'Drink,' he said.

The moment she had prepared for. Renike shut her eyes and drained the calabash in a single gulp. The sharp metallic pang of old blood made her wince as the taste hit her tongue.

She straightened and set her jaw. *Now here comes the worst part.*

Gaitan kicked a bucket out. It slid across the floor and came to a stop at her feet. 'In case you need to vomit,' he said.

Mandla stretched out his hand and whistled. A small, white dove flew into view and settled on his palm. He glanced up at her and spoke.

Renike barely heard what he said. All she could hear was the urgent thump of her fast-beating heart. She took the bird in her hand and formed a tight fist. She felt the bones break as it let out a dying whisper then she took her first bite, squirming as the feathers tickled her gullet. More than once, she wanted to retch, but she held herself still, refusing to even glance at the bucket. Bite by sickening bite, she ate the bird whole.

A thick silence fell upon the room and Renike wondered for a moment whether she had done something wrong.

'Did I do it?' she asked. Her voice produced visible clouds of mist as she spoke. The room had suddenly gone quite cold.

'Did I—'

Power seized her by the throat as tendrils of billowing shadow circled like a thick wind.

Her heart slowed to a solemn beat. Breathless, she reached out for the swirling blackness. The shadow beckoned her, even as it moved to meet her. *Here it goes.*

Her eyes snapped open as she touched the shadow, her entire body shaken by a reverberating tremor of power. Without meaning to, she let out a deep, guttural scream. It sounded like it had come from somebody else. Something old, instinctive and ancient. All calm was lost. Her spine flexed and she stared at the ceiling as wave after wave of awesome power swelled within her body.

Her emotions formed a line and took their turn on her mind. Anger, fear, joy, sadness, love, hate and, above all, grief. The sorrow struck her like a steel mallet but when it hit, there was no pain. Everything was shockingly clear and the power to do and undo rested in her hands. She tried to speak, but all that came out was wordless babble. All awareness of time and place faded away. There was only shadow.

A bell rang somewhere in the distance and Renike opened her eyes. She was back in the great hall and all the chiefs and shadowwielders were watching her, tense with worry.

'She's back,' Karile said, with a smile, and everyone seemed to relax.

Her shadow fell from her fingers and settled into a thick, black pool. The power had disappeared and Renike's mind returned to her.

Finally, she vomited.

Karile crouched to place a hand on her back and whispered. 'Well done. That was a strong binding. Very strong.'

Renike coughed and wiped her mouth. 'I barely knew what was happening.'

'A part of you did,' Karile explained. 'So you will get better with it as you learn.'

Renike let out a ragged cough and rose gingerly to her feet.

Her breathing was slow, her vision blurry. A light breeze would have toppled her over.

Karile grabbed her by the shoulders, steadying her. 'Breathe.' She glanced up at Mandla. 'Who will train her?'

Mandla cleared his throat and glanced at Zarcanis, then another woman – Xhosa.

Xhosa bowed and brought her forehead to her knee. 'I would gladly take her on, Lord Mandla.'

Renike let out a breath. She had heard about Xhosa – a good trainer, who was loved by all whom she taught. She was a woman too and knew how to bring the best out of women shadowwielders. There could be few better options than her.

Renike glanced at Zarcanis, but the trainer seemed more interested in the length of her nail – avoiding Renike's gaze entirely.

Mandla cleared his throat. 'Thank you, Xhosa, but I believe the Viper would serve better in this instance.'

Zarcanis raised an eyebrow in surprise. 'Me?'

Mandla nodded. 'You worked well with Rumi; I believe you will work well with her also.'

'I had Yomiku then. He's...' She hesitated. 'We lost him. I don't think it works to train a single Seedling on her own.'

Mandla nodded. 'I agree. That's why you will be training another.'

Telemi drew open the door again and a young Kuba woman walked into the room. Renike winced as she saw who it was. The girl had a scar on her cheek that was carved in the shape of an eye. Though barely sixteen, she had the thick muscle of a man ten years older and walked with a subtle slouch that signalled she was unafraid and ready. *N'Goné*.

Zarcanis gave N'Goné an appraising look, which was quickly followed by a subtle nod of wordless approval.

Mandla lowered his chin. 'Zarcanis, meet N'Goné.'

5
A Prayer

NATARÉ

Nataré raised her bow and pulled the string back. She gritted her teeth, fingers raw as she tried to keep her aim steady under the strain of the draw-weight. Something had moved in the darkness – she was sure of it. Tall as a man but thin as a blade. *A monster.* She waited, patient as the night owl, for the creature to reveal itself. Her heart was pounding at her ribs, her stomach tight as a knot, her shoulders throbbing as she held the bow-string. She hadn't planned on killing anyone tonight but plans could so quickly change.

'One more move,' she whispered, ready to fire.

A moment passed and nothing happened. Her breath produced a small cloud of vapour as she lowered her bow ever so slightly. Another moment passed – still nothing. The light danced across a tree and cast an unsettling shadow.

Nataré dropped her bow. *Maybe it was nothing.* This was her fourth night of patrol, which was unusual for even the most seasoned sentries. Her lips were dry and cracked and her eyes a deep red from sleepless nights and restless days. It was difficult to stay alert for two nights in a row, let alone four. *Definitely nothing.* She let out a resigned breath and kept on walking – she was seeing things again.

A large tree appeared ahead, casting in darkness half the path before her. She winced as she drew close – it still carried the scent of death. She didn't need to see the smashed-in bark or the reddish-brown branches to know that people had died there but she stared all the same, unable to take her eyes away from the scene of someone's last stand. She wondered how many had been killed here. Innocent people who had not known she would bring creatures of the night to the Eredo. Her one selfish act – keeping the ghost stone – had allowed the Priest of Vultures and his army of Obair to find them.

She glanced up at the gnarled tree and let out a breath. The bark was carved in the image of an old, haggard face with thick arched brows. For some reason, when bloodwood trees were carved with faces, they were always made to look like very old, disapproving people. *Maybe that is how the gods see us – as foolish children making all the mistakes they know to avoid.*

She closed her eyes as a gust of wind shuffled her night shawl. *May the dead rest well.*

Nataré had been through many things. She had been held captive by witch doctors and been rescued. For too long, the memory of it had made her feel vulnerable and alone – easy prey. There was a time, long gone, when she looked over each shoulder while she walked, and her heartbeat rattled her chest after dark. She had been a slave to fear, and it had dominated her life. Getting through those moments was done with constant affirmation; five words had changed her life, changed her perspective and given her a new identity. *I am the knife edge.*

She spoke the words to herself now as she stared into the scowling tree.

A voice from behind broke her focus – someone had called her name. Not her real name, but the one she gave most people whom she only halfway wanted to know.

'Kayalli,' he called out again.

She stopped for a moment, heaving in a breath as she glanced over her shoulder. The man standing behind her was tall enough to touch the highest branches of the tree, with a thick beard that curled into his moustache. He took three quick steps to close the distance between them and leaned forward, panting hard.

'I haven't seen you in a while,' the man said.

She grimaced. 'There's been a lot going on, Strogus.'

Strogus nodded. 'True.'

There was a brief silence as he stared at the ground.

'I heard you've gone four nights on patrol without relief; that you have refused to take a break,' Strogus said. 'You look like you haven't slept in days.'

Nataré glanced up at him. 'Is it a crime to work now?'

Strogus scratched the top of his ear. 'You can't blame yourself for what happened here. He would have found us no matter what. *No matter what.*'

Nataré's jaw stiffened as she resisted the sudden urge to cry. 'You can go now, Strogus.'

'Kayalli, please, just—'

'I led him right to us. *Right* to us. I kept the ghost stone because I was selfish. Because I was seduced by its power and wanted to keep it for myself. I was told more than once what the dangers were, and still I kept it. How can you say I can't blame myself?'

'Everyone makes mistakes,' Strogus said.

'People died because of my mistake,' she hissed.

The skies overhead groaned as misty droplets of rain fell.

Strogus frowned. 'They came for Ajanla. He carries just as much blame as you. You don't have to carry this alone.' He reached out, perhaps to touch her shoulder, but she pulled away.

'I'll carry it how I please.'

He froze and gave her a long, knowing look. Then turned

on his heel and snorted out an irritated breath. 'Do as you like then.'

Nataré watched him leave, her entire body stiff with irritation. Strogus could be a kind man but he was not given to it easily. The chip he carried on his shoulder was boulder big and he wasted no time in counting a person amongst his enemies. He was hard all the way through – not like Rumi.

As soon as she had that thought, she regretted it. She had tried not to remember Rumi. How he had come to her aid when she was closest to death. It wasn't just that he'd showed her that he cared. It was that she cared so much too. Something about him drew her out from all her secret places. How could he carry part of the blame? All he had done was live.

Nataré turned back to the tree and it almost looked like the carved eyes had turned angry.

Nataré laughed. *Even the gods are growing tired of me.*

Nataré's mother had prayed often. Once before she slept and once as soon as she was awake. In times of turmoil her mother had even thrown their cowries into the river. It hadn't stopped most of their lives going to shege. The gods, she had learned, were like parents – just as likely to ignore you as they were to save you.

The wind murmured as the rain thickened to cold drizzle. She glanced up at the tree again and her mother's words flashed through her mind – *Prayer is not about selfish want. It is about admitting you are not enough.*

Nataré didn't leave. Instead, she stared at the tree as the eyes in the carved face seemed to widen. Without allowing herself to think, she dropped to her knees. Drawing her sword, she made a small cut along the back of her forearm. She thumbed the wound and pressed the tree with her blood – just as her mother had taught her. Glancing up, she spoke aloud: 'Gods of my ancestors, Dara, Father of All, hear my prayer. I've never asked you for much and when I have, you haven't answered. I'm not resentful about that – I don't want sympathy. I probably haven't deserved to have my prayers heard. I'm … far from holy. I haven't always followed the Way. I've never given you great gifts or true praise. In any way that matters to you, I have fallen painfully short.' She hesitated. 'But my mother always told me I was a child of the Skyfather and that if I prayed honestly enough, you would listen. That's why I am here. I have done something unforgivable. Something that cost the blood of innocents. I am not here to ask for forgiveness – I don't deserve it. I don't need it. What I am asking for, is a chance – just one. A chance at redemption. A chance to save more lives than I have ever been responsible for losing. Give me that, Dara' – she glanced down at the thin line of blood across her forearm – 'and I will give you everything.'

6

Back to the Dance

RUMI

The botanical ward was deathly quiet. In the days since the battle, it had been inundated with the dead and dying. The walls of the ward had seen more horror in the last week than perhaps ever before.

Griff lay perfectly still, the slow rise and fall of his chest the only evidence that he was still alive. The ward was running low on Oké water from the summit of Erin-Olu and so he was only allowed a few drops a day. Oké water was known as a panacea. It healed many wounds, relieved pain and blotted out illness. Without it, many would die.

'Keep fighting,' Rumi whispered to his father.

The door hissed behind and a botanical stepped inside. She wore a white kaftan with gloves wrought of fabric and shadow. She looked Rumi up and down, appraising him, then raised her chin.

'You're the son, I expect.'

Rumi nodded. 'Yes I am.'

She blinked and strode up to his bedside. Raising a hand, she summoned her shadow and it formed a thin cloud of mist over Griff's unconscious form. 'They call me Uroma.'

Rumi raised an eyebrow and leaned forward. 'Ajanla Erenteyo.'

He had never seen the botanicals work this way.

She pressed her shadow close to a wound along Griff's stomach and inclined her ear as though to listen.

'What are you doing?' Rumi asked.

She ignored him, leaning closer. When she was satisfied with what she'd heard, she straightened and gave Rumi the exasperated look of the long-suffering parent to the clueless child.

'It is called shadow's tongue,' she said with a sigh. 'The shadow speaks to all things. Even to parts of the body.' She touched his forearm, still crisscrossed with scars. 'What would your arm say to me, if it had words you could understand?'

Rumi looked over his scabs and scars along his forearm and frowned. 'It will tell you that it wanted me to stop.'

Uroma smiled. 'Actually, it says you should try the other arm once in a while.'

Rumi laughed. 'Can you truly hear from each part of the body?'

She touched her chin. 'Not words in the same way we are speaking now, but something akin to emotions. With time and experience you learn to understand what the body is saying. It is why we are botanicals. We speak with the shadow's tongue – the language of emotions. We know where the pain is and what the body wants us to do.'

'What does Griff's body want you to do?'

She frowned. 'The one thing we will never do to a warrior.'

Rumi studied his father's motionless face. Kasinabe creed dictated that a warrior be given the choice between the courage to die and the courage to live, and no one else could make that decision in his stead.

The botanical examined the wound across Griff's chest and seemed to satisfy herself. 'If we had more Oké water, we could have done more for him – without it we are limited in what we can do. But he is fighting hard.'

'Is something being done to get more water?'

'A band of Truetrees left for the summit of Erin-Olu over a week ago. We await their return.'

'Over a week ago? Shouldn't they have been back by now?'

Uroma's expression did not change. 'We await their imminent return.'

With that, she left Rumi alone again, with nothing but Griff's ragged breath for company.

Rumi lowered his head and touched his cowrie necklace as he whispered a solemn prayer. When he was done, he squeezed Griff's hand, turned on his heel and left the ward.

From there it was only a short walk to Zarcanis's practice room. Rumi had always wondered if they kept Zarcanis close to the botanical ward because she sent more people there than anyone else.

Though it had only been a few days, the high ceilings and thick stone walls of the practice room appeared to Rumi as long-lost friends who had only now returned to his life.

He went down into a split, stretching his arms wide. The routine was done slowly and carefully, in the way Zarcanis had always insisted. He let out small breaths as he dropped into a low squat and arched his back, feeling the tension clench the roots of his spinal cord.

The shrill sound of shifting wind carried to his ear as someone stepped into the room. Turning onto his hands, he glanced up. Zarcanis stood in the doorway with her blade in hand.

'You're not doing it right,' she said. 'You should be able to go lower than that by now.'

She took two quick steps and pressed him deeper into the squat. He let out a sharp breath and winced.

'Much better,' she said with a grin, pulling him up to his feet. 'So, the Old Dog finally returns.'

Rumi brushed down the sleeve of his kaftan. 'It's been... difficult to come back here. Since—'

Her face was level and expectant, but Rumi had no way to finish his sentence.

Zarcanis cleared her throat. 'Are you ready to come back?'

Rumi nodded. 'I think I am.'

Zarcanis met his gaze. 'Why?'

'What?'

'Why are you here? Why do you want to continue to learn the shadow? When I first met you, I could see that deep desire in you. You wanted something and believed that shadowdancing would lead you to it. You trained like an animal. Never gave up. You surpassed every expectation I had because you pushed yourself further than anyone could have reasonably expected.' She drew in a breath. 'But now you've had your revenge. You have done what you came here for. Your fire is gone.'

Rumi shook his head. 'No, it isn't.'

'You're barely sweating, which means you're half-arsing it, Rumi. I'm sure there are a bunch of other trainers who would love to have you, but I've got no use for someone who doesn't give everything. Maybe just focus on your music – that is your true gift. You will never be as good a fighter as you are a musician. Especially if you don't give everything.'

'I will give everything,' Rumi insisted.

'Why?'

'Because my brother is still out there in the Originate somewhere. Because our people live under the thumb of the Palmaine.' He hesitated. 'But most of all because I owe it to you.'

She gave him a confused look. 'To me?'

Rumi drew in a deep breath. 'We lost Yomiku because of me. I—'

She raised a hand, cutting him off.

Rumi's vision blurred as his eyes were touched by the faintest kiss of tears. It had been his rash actions that had led to Yomiku's death. That was part of why it had taken him so long to return. Facing that wall of incredible guilt. Seeing Zarcanis there, knowing it was now a place forever changed. A broken memento of a time when to walk the fighting pit was to tread on Yomiku's blood and sweat. Rumi's cheeks flattened as he took it all in – that deep knowing that Yomiku was a braver, better fighter than he had ever been and that he had let the man down.

Zarcanis seemed to read his mind. 'A fight is a hellish place – one where we act on the purest form of instinct. We make gambles and sometimes we lose. Sometimes we run when we should stand. Sometimes we stand when we should run. But yesterday is gone forever. You can't build anything with regret and now, more than ever, I need you to build, Irumide.'

Rumi shivered at the use of his full name. Zarcanis had never used it before. Hearing it from her felt deeply personal.

He straightened and ran a palm over the scars crisscrossed along his forearm. 'So let's build then.'

Zarcanis put her fists on her hips. 'The rules haven't changed. I know your bravado is fragile. I will break it over and over again until you lose it completely.'

He walked over to the wall and picked up a safespear. 'I wouldn't have it any other way.'

'I will push you hard. Probe your every emotion until I know the truth of it.'

'That is what I came here for.'

He threw the safespear directly at her. Her hand shot out like a toad's tongue as she snatched it out of the air.

Rumi smiled. 'Shall we dance?'

Zarcanis's grin was deep as she shifted effortlessly into form.

'Oh yes.' She lifted the safespear and twirled it through the air in much the same way that a conductor would call an orchestra to attention. Call the Viper anything in the world but never call her dull.

'It's time to drop the good boy act again, Rumi, embrace all your darkness — we are here to beat the shege out of one another.'

Rumi lowered his head and for the first time since the battle, he called his shadow. He no longer needed to cut himself to call it forth — now he had his true name. With a single word, an explosion of black mist surrounded him as he drank deep from the well of sudden power. Long-lost emotion flooded his throat as he tried to control the sweltering shadow. That was what the shadow did — before it allowed you to taste the fullness of its power, it made sure you acknowledged all your hidden emotions. Rumi groped for the edge of the wall, utterly overwhelmed by the incredible urgency of it. It throbbed like a second pulse. Guilt, pain and regret pummelled his mind, but he was ready for it — he stood his ground and took a hold of the shadow.

Zarcanis's voice rose over the noise of his thumping heart. 'You are struggling with the shadow. And yet, you say you are a Suli?'

She frowned as she circled him. With a whisper, her shadow was called. A powerful shiver of discomfort swept across the room. Rumi's shadow was a swirling black wind, Zarcanis's a neat, flowing cape. Her control of the shadow was second to none, but she wasn't just good, she was casually good. What others had to grit their teeth and scream for, she blinked and shrugged for. In the art of violence, there was no greater practitioner — he had seen Zarcanis peel Obair three times her size like oranges, her face plain and pitiless as the sea.

'The shadow wrestles with you because you have not allowed

it to have its say. If you are feeling grief, don't call it anger because the shadow will not be satisfied. Speak the truth to yourself, Rumi. What are you feeling?'

Rumi narrowed his eyes and spoke in a hoarse voice. 'Guilt... Shame... Fear.'

She tilted her neck until he heard a soft click and her eyes snapped open. 'Good,' she said, rolling her shoulder. 'Fear of what?'

Rumi's grip on the safespear tightened. 'Of not being enough for what is to come.'

Zarcanis arched her back in a stretch. 'You are certainly not enough but tomorrow starts today. I'll make something of you. I hope you've been working on your craft because I have certainly been working on mine.'

Rumi had no time for a clever retort as she came at him like the east wind. Her safespear missed his shoulder by a hair. Without hesitation, she twisted the weapon sideways and knocked Rumi across the side of his head.

Zarcanis licked her teeth. 'That'll be a bruise then.'

Bristling, Rumi rolled his shoulders and came at her with nothing held back. He struck with *snake shoots venom* and darted aside as Zarcanis countered with *shepherd holds the crook*.

'You're slower than I remember,' Zarcanis said, with a smile he knew was meant to rile him up.

Rumi grinned. 'Using my pride against me won't work any more.'

She bent a knee and arched her back in *leopard stalks its prey*. 'So, you are no longer an empty vessel. Good.' She lashed out in the shadow, quick and powerful.

Her safespear struck him square in the chest and he staggered back, heart thumping. *She is too fast.*

'Your pride always confused me,' she said, moving – nimble as a spider – into a protective stance. 'I used to wonder what gave you such haughty pride. Then I saw how you were with your father – how angry you were with him. You saw him as a coward because he abandoned your family at the hardest hour. You clung to your pride fiercely because it protected you from the darkest truth – that you are a coward in disguise. We despise in others what we most fear in ourselves. It wasn't until you accepted you were a coward that you were able to find bravery and strength.'

Rumi smiled. 'I may be a coward in disguise, but that doesn't mean I won't put a hurting on you if you let me.'

Her eyes narrowed to slits. Playtime was over. 'So, I won't let you,' she said gently, 'but you knew that.'

They sparred for about half an hour. Rumi could not be sure if she was taking it easy on him or if he truly had improved, but more than once, he came close to scoring a clean hit. There was freedom in the fighting this time and that made everything much easier than it had been in the past – his shadow was no longer a complete enemy.

'You are beginning to learn,' she said, when their session had come to an end. 'Using the shadow is no different to any other sort of energy. Like so many other things in the world, energy is disordered. It desires focus and is better used when it is concentrated. The ant has no cares, crawling under the naked sun, but with a magnifying glass, I can melt that ant with the same sun. The more you can focus on the strongest emotions of your shadow, the better you can use them.'

Rumi nodded his understanding. 'I've always wondered,' he said, meeting Zarcanis's gaze. 'What emotion do you focus on in the shadow?'

Zarcanis's eyes narrowed dangerously. Rumi instinctively stepped back out of easy striking distance. For a long moment, his whole body was tense as he waited for the strike to come, but the moment passed. She snorted, raised her chin and went to her desk. She retrieved a book and handed it to him.

Rumi read the title aloud. '*Letters from the Fires of Hell*, by Kuda Kamo.'

Zarcanis nodded. 'It is the sequel to his first book. He was imprisoned in a labour camp in Palmaine for eleven years. He wrote this while inside.'

Rumi tucked the book underarm. 'I look forward to reading it.'

Zarcanis turned to the door. 'Good session today. Be better tomorrow.'

'We're done?'

Zarcanis nodded. 'I have been given new Seedlings to train. They will be here any moment.'

'Who?' Rumi asked.

The door slipped open and a young woman stepped inside. Rumi let out a silent breath. If ever there was an illustration of what time in the Eredo could do to a person, it was Renike. The innocent, skinny slip of a girl who had arrived alongside him was gone. Now there stood a young, dark-eyed woman touched with a promise of danger. Rumi wasn't sure how he felt about it. The once-sun-brightened veil of their time in Alara had been pulled away and now he saw the world for what it was – a place where the Renike of old could not survive. This was who she'd had to become and there was no running from that.

'Renike,' Rumi breathed.

She offered him a kola nut and he broke off a piece. 'They call me Rain now.'

Rumi nodded his understanding. It was customary for all Seedlings to be given new names to protect themselves from mindwalking. True names had the power to grant access to the mind.

'A fitting name,' Rumi said. 'Rain cannot be stopped, and it comes with a promise of sun.'

Renike grinned. 'I like that.'

Another girl stepped into the room – she was Kuba and harder-faced than any woman of her age ought to be. She had a thick scar on one cheek in the shape of an eye and looked like she could hold her own in a bare-fisted bar fight amongst the lowest of the low. Rumi had seen the scar-faced girl before – braiding Renike's hair after the battle.

'This is my friend,' Renike said. 'They call her Nagode.'

Nagode offered Rumi a kola nut and he broke it with her. 'My real name is N'Goné,' she said.

'Good to meet you,' Rumi said, shaking her hand.

Zarcanis sighed in exasperation. 'Enough. This is a fighting pit, not a dinner table. Here we learn the warrior's way.'

N'Goné gave a grim nod and wrapped her arms around her ankles in a deep stretch.

'Good,' Zarcanis said, turning to the girls. 'You two will be the first women I have ever trained. I hope you do not see shadowdancing as a man's walk because if you do, you won't last very long here. Shadowdancing is our gift just as much as it is theirs – you are not trespassing on tradition. Within these walls we do not ignore the shared history of all the great shadow-dancers who were born as we were. There was the darkman but there was also Adunola.'

Rumi quivered at the mention of his mother's name.

Zarcanis touched N'Goné's shoulder, summoning her up from her stretch. 'There was Walade the Widowmaker but there was also Adelina, Princess of Shadow. Your stories could be the ones to transform a nation – do not cut corners. I will not let you.'

Rumi glanced at the two girls, already in awe of Zarcanis.

They looked at her with all the quiet devotion of a zealot at the sight of a miracle. Young or old, the Viper had that effect on everyone.

She pointed at Renike. 'You are a pretty little flower – are you sure you are ready for this work?'

Renike met her gaze. 'I am not a flower. I am an iroko tree.'

Zarcanis grinned and nodded as she spun a safespear along her wrist. 'If you are anything like me, your chest might get in the way of your underarm swings as you grow older. I will teach you how to use that to your advantage. Subtle adjustments in the forms that turn all your challenges into triumphs. But first, I will need you bendy.' Pushing N'Goné into a deep, thigh-splitting stretch, she said, 'You think you know a thing about stretching – you have no sheggin' idea.'

Zarcanis turned and folded Renike into a stretch, causing her to let out a sharp gasp.

'Nothing easy here. The shadow, as you should know, is a manifestation of all the hidden aspects of yourself that are buried under your own lying ideas. If you want to be a great shadow-dancer, you must acknowledge all your deceptions, embrace your dark side and become the true you. All the emotion you run from, all your fear and pain, is a source of untapped potential – but you must integrate it.' She pushed N'Goné deeper into the stretch. 'Rumi tried to run from his love and grief. Tried to become a hard man. It didn't work. He didn't come into himself until he acknowledged that love was at the very centre of his being. To be a shadowwielder, you must be your whole, authentic self. This is where you become whole again. I have no time for the pretty half of you.'

Rumi smiled and gave Renike an affirming nod as N'Goné let out a yelp of pain. 'Welcome to the Shadow Order.'

7

The Land Where the First Man Trod

LETHI

Lethi touched the pendant of the four-point star as the sea mist brushed the nape of his neck. The smell of fish was thick in the air and the clouds above were dark with the promise of rain. Any minute now, the heavens would open. Stray cats prowled the dockside, sniffing at the air, hopeful to make breakfast of a passer-by's benevolence. Ahead stood the proud statue of Governor-General Zaminu Alharan, portrayed in stark, greywhite limestone. In one hand the statue held the *Holy Book of Palman*, in the other he held a ceremonial sabre with a decorated cross-guard.

Pinned to Zaminu's chest was the four-point star – which represented the power of the governor-general as an ordained holy minister of Palman – and the great lion sigil of the Palmaine crown. The statue had been horribly defaced. Red paint had been smeared across the hands to give the impression that blood dripped from the holy book and sabre. The word 'Demon' had been marked across the front of the statue's uniform in deep black ink.

Banasco cleared his throat. 'One thing about the Black Hammer Clan, they know how to get their message across.'

Lethi gave an unimpressed frown. 'A little too on the nose for my taste – but I suppose with a name like the "Black Hammer Clan", subtlety is not quite what they're going for.'

Another blast of cool breeze sent a shiver up Lethi's spine as a wave smashed against the dockside. The clouds groaned and flexed – their final warning.

'Where are they?' Dareem asked, pulling his thin coat tight around his shoulders.

'They are coming,' Lethi said.

A carriage was supposed to have been ready for them as soon as they disembarked from the ship but they had been waiting for a good half hour and no one had arrived.

Attem stood with the tense readiness of a hunting hound ready for release. The masseter muscle at his jaw tightened as though he were chewing, but he said nothing.

Lethi turned from the sea towards the town. He had heard Basmine was big, but this was far beyond anything he could have imagined. The dock ran as far as the eye could see and was filled to the brim with boats and ships. The docks were alive with the bustle of street hawkers. Tiny stalls dotted across the pier were manned by men and women who had the hard-faced, paper-thin smiles of veteran hagglers. People stood almost shoulder-to-shoulder, such that it seemed as though they were one sinuous wave of human flesh. Never before had Lethi seen quite so many people in just one place. *What a responsibility to be the stewards of this land.*

A cock-eyed hawker shoved past them with a bucket of fish and shouted, 'Fresh catch,' at the very top of his lungs.

Though they were dressed in full uniform, no one seemed to pay them any mind. In Guyarica, people paid attention when soldiers were around – here in Basmine, they were less relevant than a bucket of mackerel.

Banasco gave Lethi a worried look that sent a question swimming through his mind. *Did we make a mistake coming here?*

Lethi threw back his shoulders and raised his chin. 'We'll be fine.' He had meant to sound confident, but against the warning howl of the sea, his voice was pitifully small.

A man ahead had a voice that carried on the wind. He was dressed in priestly robes that looked like they hadn't been washed since the day they were first sewn. He lifted a golden four-point star in his right hand and hefted the Palman holy book in his left. 'Are you ready to hear the truth?' he shouted.

No one paid him any mind.

'Beware, for the Son of Despair commeth! He commeth, and there will be no shelter for the sinner. Turn to the Light now, surrender to Palman and be saved!'

Lethi's concentration was broken as a little boy barged into him. As he gathered himself, some long-forgotten instinct told Lethi that his pocket had just been picked. Seizing the boy by the wrist he dragged him close. 'You'd steal from an officer in the King's Army?'

The little boy's eyes flared with pure terror. He opened his mouth to speak but for a long moment no words came out.

'I'm... I'm sorry,' the boy finally mumbled in the Common Tongue. 'Please, don't kill me.'

Lethi blinked and loosened his grip on the boy's wrist. 'Give it to me,' he said, holding out his palm.

The boy slid the pocketbook back into his hand, along with a bundle of thread, four cowries and two full golden crowns. Lethi stared down at the plunder, a little impressed, then turned back to the boy.

'Should I take care of him, sir?' came a voice from behind. Lethi knew immediately that it was Roadie and furthermore knew what 'take care' meant to him. Lethi shook his head and turned to the boy. 'Get out of here.'

The boy wasted no time getting gone, sprinting as though his shadow gave chase.

Banasco shook his head in disappointment, muttering a little too loud. 'Too lenient.'

A hot splash of anger rose within at that. Every day, Banasco took another step closer to insubordination and Lethi was going to have to deal with it soon.

A sudden flash of lightning was seconded by a clap of thunder and the rain finally began to fall. Within moments their uniforms were soaked through, making them even more of a pathetic spectacle.

'Repent!' cried the street preacher. 'He commeth! The Son of Despair commeth!'

They stood there in the bucketing rain for what felt like a small eternity, looking like overgrown children with no parent to reclaim them.

At last came the clatter of horse hooves. Lethi glanced up. *Finally.* Four powerful, thoroughbred stallions led a large carriage painted in royal Palmaine blue.

The carriage came to a stop barely a few yards ahead as the wheelman dismounted. For a native, he was markedly well dressed and walked with the self-importance of one who was used to having his word obeyed.

He pulled his hood back and glanced down at Lethi's gorget patch, then up at his face. 'You're the lieutenant?'

Lethi rolled his shoulders. 'Yes, I am.'

The wheelman raised an eyebrow. 'You seem a little young to be a Lieutenant.'

Lethi straightened and tilted his chin slightly to show the

deep scar across the bottom of his neck. He gave the native a withering look and breathed out through his nose. 'Am I correct in saying you are a wheelman?'

The wheelman blinked, then glanced down at Lethi's rifle and seemed to finally satisfy himself.

'My apologies. In you get, sir,' he said, holding the carriage door open.

Lethi got in first, followed by the four men who formed his fire team.

It was blissfully warm inside the carriage chamber. Red-hot coals danced in the teeth of a latticed foot-warmer and the doors were thick with cotton padding. Attem looked around the carriage with palpable suspicion, plainly unaccustomed to riding in such luxury. His fingers flexed and twitched the way they did when he wanted to grab his spear.

'Relax,' Lethi said, 'we're fine.'

The warmth of the carriage helped to warm up, if not entirely dry, their clothes as they drove over the Citadel cobblestones. The Citadel was an entirely different proposition to the dockside. The buildings had the grand posturing of strong foundations and best-available limestone. The people walked with casual, unaffected automation, dressed in bright, vibrant colours. Watching them was like watching the insides of a kaleidoscopic clock. Little metallic cogs and screws in the engine of a booming metropolis. The Citadel was the domain of the wealthy. Of bankers, merchants and nobility. Of those who, through business or bloodline, had made worries about money a thing of the distant past. Lethi glanced at Attem, wondering what the native thought about this brazen display of wealth, barely a stone's throw from the dockside where pockets were picked for a slim chance of bread. But this was Basmine – a place where splendour and squalor sat side by side.

Before long, they fell under the shadow of a tower ahead. Lethi glanced through the window and his heart lurched in his chest. He had heard about the House of Palman. Seen half a hundred paintings of it. Nothing could have prepared him for the startling magnificence of the building he saw now.

He let out a shuddering breath. 'Shege.'

Banasco too could only stare, his mouth stretched wide in utter disbelief.

Of their team of five, Attem, who had grown up in Basmine, was the only one who didn't seem stunned. With arms folded across his chest, Attem wore a dour, pitiless expression.

'It's like in the stories,' Dareem said, staring up at the giant of a building.

An understatement, Lethi thought. The stories were not half as grand as this.

Banasco sniffed and touched his chest. 'Makes you remember what we are all fighting for. Makes it all worth it.'

Lethi nodded his agreement, touching the pendant at his neck. 'The star in the sky. The Son who broke the noose.'

They arrived at last at a high-walled compound surrounded by rifle-wielding consular guard. The gates parted as their carriage approached and they rode past a succession of flower gardens before coming to a halt at the edge of a large fountain depicting an angel staring up to the heavens with palms outstretched in supplication. Lethi stared at the door – still half-amazed. *The House of Palman. Holy Ground.*

They were escorted inside by a uniformed steward. In some ways, the interior of the House of Palman was even more impressive than the façade. The ceilings were illuminated by candlelight chandeliers and painted with murals that depicted scenes from Palman scripture. The carpet was a deep royal claret, woven with multiple four-point stars. It reminded Lethi, as they walked, of the deep connection between beauty and power – how the ability to attract always came with the ability to corrupt. How the powerful wielded beautiful things as signals of conquest.

'Through there,' the steward said, pointing at two double doors.

Lethi moved and the team shifted to follow. The steward raised a hand, halting them. 'Only the Lieutenant.'

Banasco made a disgusted noise but stood back with the rest of the team. Lethi stepped into the room alone. The sun was shining outside again and seemed to send its best light through the stained-glass windows, casting angelic shadows on the spotless marble floor.

Three men sat ahead, watching him as he entered.

The first of them was instantly recognisable; not an hour had passed since Lethi had stood face-to-face with his statue. Governor-General Zaminu dressed in the full uniform of his former rank.

Another man was seated just in front of Zaminu – a Kuba man, whose uniform was much the same as Zaminu's, though ill-fitted for the native. Lethi surmised this was the current governor-general – a man called Blaise Paru. Even now, seated as he was, he looked like a puppet with Zaminu pulling the strings just behind him.

The third man was the most disconcerting of the trio. Seated at the centre, he wore the hooded robes of a Palmaine priest. As Lethi walked forward, the man pulled his hood back to reveal eyes that looked like they had been plucked from a demon. Lethi let out an undignified yelp and raised a hand.

'Apologies, Your Eminence,' he said, mastering himself again.

It was the Bishop of Basmine. Perhaps the most powerful man on the continent. Something about the man made Lethi feel like vomiting. For a man who was regarded as the representative of God in Basmine, nothing about the bishop offered any hope of salvation. Those dark eyes seemed to see beyond mere flesh and bone, and it made Lethi uneasy. Against all good sense, he wanted to leave.

'Your Eminence,' he said, bowing to the bishop. 'My lords,' he said, glancing at the past and present governors-general. 'I am Lieutenant Lethi Altayir of Barnham Wood.'

The Bishop of Basmine regarded him with a look that seemed touched with disgust and Lethi had the feeling again that the bishop could bypass skin with his stare. For a long, pregnant moment, no one said anything at all.

The silence travelled quickly from brief, to awkward, to oppressive before the bishop finally cleared his throat to speak. 'We have been keeping an eye on you. We had reports on all your work in Guyarica.'

Lethi gave half a bow and let out a relieved breath. 'We hope to repeat the same success in Basmine, Your Eminence.'

Zaminu squinted. 'Guyarica is barely a township in comparison to Basmine. If all the people of Guyarica were to arrive on Basmine shores tomorrow, they would find room and board within a mile of the dockside. Your work on that island was good, but that isn't why we brought you here.'

Lethi raised an eyebrow. 'I was told—'

'Forget what you were told,' Zaminu snapped. 'We do the telling in this country.'

The bishop raised his chin. 'I understand your father and uncle were distinguished soldiers. Your father rose as high as general, is that right?'

The vein at Lethi's neck pulsed. 'That is correct, Your Eminence.'

Zaminu's grin was like an ugly knife wound. It was a little uncomfortable to look at. The former governor-general scratched idly at his collarbone. 'I heard of your father. He could have been governor-general. A brilliant soldier.'

The bishop nodded. 'Your older brother died in war too – right here in Basmine.'

Lethi gave a silent wince at the mention of his brother. He wondered, for a moment, where his brother's remains had ended up. 'That's correct,' he said.

The bishop leaned forward. 'All that loss. So why have you remained in service? Surely with your connections you could be somewhere else by now – far away from violence.'

Lethi heaved in a sharp breath and fixed the bishop with a hard look. 'There was something my grandfather always used to say – kneel once for the king and stand forever in the kingdom. I stand for the kingdom, Your Eminence. Service is in my blood and bone. Every man of age in my family has wielded a sword in defence of our country because we believe that all the Palmaine are who we say we are. The light in the darkness. The flower in the desert. The glove through which God's hand is felt.'

The bishop nodded vociferously. It was true Lethi had risen to lieutenant the 'old way' but no one got anywhere in the army without learning the benefit of a bit of boot-licking along the way. When it came to kissing arses, Lethi had done his own respectable share. He knew when it was time to pucker up.

'Who was your mother?' Zaminu asked.

Lethi went still as his toes curled up in his boots. He tried his best to appear calm, but his insides were mutinous.

He cleared his throat. 'I never met her.'

Zaminu clicked his tongue and leaned back into his chair. He seemed to ponder on that for a moment before he spoke again. 'Do you know why we brought you here, soldier?'

Lethi let out a breath, glad to be clear of the topic of his mother. 'I cannot be sure, my lord. If it is not for my work in Guyarica, then what else?'

The bishop quirked up an eyebrow. 'We brought you here because we need someone who can work quietly. Someone who is talented but low-ranking. Who won't warrant attention while we attend to other, more important, matters.'

Lethi blinked, stung a little to be called 'low-ranking'. He was rather proud of his position as a lieutenant. But in rooms such as this, there was no space for the wounded pride of ants.

'I am forever at your service, Your Eminence.'

Zaminu brushed the comment aside. 'You have two tasks. The first is to destroy the Black Hammer Clan. They have become a nuisance we can no longer abide.'

Lethi rolled his shoulder wondering if the Black Hammer Clan – more an idea than an institution – could ever truly be destroyed. But of course, this wasn't the time for philosophy. He gave them what he knew they wanted to hear. 'Understood, my lord.'

The bishop met his gaze. 'The second task is of a more delicate nature.'

Lethi leaned forward and spoke low. 'I am listening.'

'How well do you know the *Holy Book of Palman*?' the bishop asked.

Lethi scratched his nose. 'Moderately well,' he answered honestly.

The bishop drew in breath. 'Do you know the prophecy of the Son of Despair?'

Lethi shook his head. 'I am afraid not, Your Eminence.'

The bishop made a disgusted noise in his throat. 'The end of our holy book speaks of a figure known as the "Son of Despair" said to be born in the land the first man trod. It is said that the Son of Despair will cast down the holy place and declare himself Lord of All. This singular act will trigger what is called the Tribulation of Gods — a period of great turmoil all over the world.'

Lethi raised an eyebrow, unsure of what to make of the scripture. 'So... you believe this "Son of Despair" is coming?'

The bishop flashed his teeth. 'We believe the Son of Despair is here in Basmine. The scripture says he will stand at the head of an army of four tribes. Our scholars have long believed this means that the Son of Despair is a rebel leader who will storm the Citadel and destroy the House of Palman.'

Lethi stifled a laugh. 'Will the natives be bringing longer spears than last time?'

No one laughed with him.

'This is serious,' Zaminu hissed. 'The natives have *other* weapons.'

Lethi furrowed his brow, confused. 'No native tribe has the power to challenge the Palmaine Army. Not one.'

Zaminu sniffed. 'Perhaps one tribe can't, but all four, working together — that is an entirely different proposition.'

'The natives will never work together,' Lethi said. 'They hate each other more than they hate us. And besides, there are only three tribes now. The Kasinabe are gone.'

Zaminu looked away. 'I too once believed they were — now I know for sure that they are very much alive.'

Lethi shot him a disbelieving look. 'My Lord, even if we do imagine that the tribes can unite, even if we accept that the Kasinabe still exist, there is no greater force than the King's Army in all the world. From the Ghonjai to the God-Eye, we have faced them all and won.'

'The King's Army is scattered across the world, fighting on many fronts. We are vulnerable.'

Lethi combed through the stubble on his chin. 'So, we reinforce our numbers.'

Zaminu glanced at the bishop and gave a slight nod. 'We are working on that. What we need to know now is if you have the stomach for a fight.'

Lethi glanced up at the ceiling and drew in a deep breath. 'Yes. I do.'

The bishop's face was expressionless as he tapped gently against his desk. 'One more thing.'

Lethi blinked. 'What is it?'

'I hear you have a native amongst your team,' the bishop said.

Lethi nodded. 'Yes, I do. Attem, he is our best tracker – perhaps the most critical asset to our success in Guyarica.'

'Don't over-egg it, boy,' Zaminu said with a scornful look.

'Have you heard what they call me here?' the bishop said.

Lethi knew. Everyone knew. It was the sort of thing that mothers had begun to tell truant children when they spurned their prayers – 'The Eye of the Light sees all.'

Lethi nodded. 'The Eye of the Light.'

The bishop smiled. 'I quite like it. It gives me a certain...' He hesitated. 'Mystique.'

Lethi looked away as the bishop tried to meet his gaze.

'You see, the natives might look a little like us, but we must not forget that we are vastly different, in much the same way the whippet dog is different from the mastiff. We are not the same breed. The typical Darosan is a happy, thriftless, excitable person; lacking in self-control, discipline and foresight; naturally courageous; full of personal vanity, with little of veracity. In brief, the virtues and defects of the native are those of attractive children. And so, it is the Palmaine duty to adopt the role of father to this bastardly people. Bring them out of the darkness and into the light. Keep your native well leashed.'

Lethi, who had heard this precise sentiment a hundred times before, knew there was no merit in offering a response.

'Tell me, Lieutenant, would I be correct in saying you enjoy the company of native women?'

Lethi's stomach turned sideways as his jaw tightened. Every effort to hide the guilt from his face was a shameless effort in vain. 'No,' Lethi blurted out.

The bishop grinned. 'The Eye of the Light sees all. I have heard you are as enduring in battle as you are in the brothel.'

Lethi could only stare.

Zaminu laughed. 'Do not be so ashamed, we have all been tempted at one time or another. The flesh is weak and wanting – that is why it must be fortified. We will fortify you here, Lieutenant.'

He brought his fingers to his lips and whistled sharply. The door cracked open behind them and a man stepped inside. He was tall, thick-shouldered and his skin was the dull yellow of ripe plantain. He wore a deep navy damask kaftan, with tiger-eye buttons along the shoulder seam. His trousers were the same shade of blue and about his neck was a glistening gold medallion fashioned in the shape of an eye. He grinned, and a flush of grim familiarity struck Lethi like a slap. A child born of a Palmaine man and a native woman.

'Meet my son, Azamon,' Zaminu said. 'The head of the Meladroni.'

The word sent a tremor of recognition up Lethi's spine. *The Meladroni.* Zaminu's Temple Knights.

An officer of the Meladroni had the authority of the bishop, which meant they could kill a man without trial and say it was the will of Palman. That Zaminu had sired a child with a native woman was shock enough, but to know he had made him head of the Meladroni was a double decking.

Azamon met Lethi's eye and gave him a nod of acknowledgement. Lethi looked back but said nothing, his mouth dry as desert sand.

With no response forthcoming, the bishop continued. 'Tomorrow, your hunt for the Black Hammer Clan begins. Then you find the Son of Despair.'

8

No Longer a Slave

RUMI

The whistle of the night wind made it seem as though the trees were breathing. Rumi tugged at the shoulders of his kaftan, bracing himself against the cool breeze. Perhaps the Thatcher would always be a cold place now. It once had seemed to embody the strength of the Eredo; now it was a monument to their greatest loss. A battleground filled with battered corpses.

In the days following the battle, Rumi had spent hours with the other members of the Shadow Order, finding the dead, writing their names down, and burying them in the Darani way. They didn't have the time, clay or wood to make coffins – most were wrapped in ceremonial shawls and prayed for by the most pious person available. Rumi himself had sent at least a dozen people to rest with his own parting words of prayer. Being back on the Thatcher now was a reminder of the bitter battle fought on its soil and the battles which still lay ahead.

A stab of sharp hunger hit him and he glanced over his shoulder. It wasn't his own hunger.

'There you are,' he breathed, reaching into his satchel.

A lionhound stepped out from the shadows, its tongue lolling from a slack jaw that bared a row of knife-sharp teeth. They stared at each other for an elongated moment, Rumi's heart pounding as the strength of the bond pulsed through his veins.

He pulled a thick cut of meat from his satchel, dangling it in the air.

'Hungry?'

The lionhound blinked and gave him a halfway irritated look as though to say, 'You know I am'.

He dropped the meat and the lionhound leaped on it before it touched the floor. For a dog that big, Rumi was taken aback by how sharp his movement was. As the lionhound set to work on the meat, Rumi combed a hand through his coat and stroked the back of his ears.

'Good boy.'

Rumi still hadn't given him a name. Zarcanis had once said that naming a thing was not an act of imagination but one of investigation. 'When Dara gives a thing life, he speaks a name.' You had to find the name Dara chose.

'I think I am going to call you Rusty,' Rumi said, stroking his neck.

The lionhound turned on him again with another disgusted look.

Rumi frowned. 'Fine, not Rusty then.'

The lionhound bared its teeth.

'If you're going to be so opinionated about your name, then at least give me an idea of what you would like,' Rumi hissed.

The lionhound gulped down the last scrap of meat and chewed at the air for a moment to make sure the deed was done. Fixing Rumi with a stare, its emotion filled the bond. *Restlessness. Confusion. Readiness. Love.*

Rumi let the emotions wash over him as he looked directly into the eyes of his lionhound. The name came to him as the wave comes to the shore. Slowly, patiently, knowing it will not be refused.

Rumi closed his eyes as he spoke the name aloud. 'Hagen.'

The lionhound's ears shot up erect and it rolled its shoulders in strong response.

Rumi smiled. 'Hagen it is, then.' He reached into his satchel. 'More meat?'

Hagen growled his approval. Rumi laughed as he turned the satchel over and let all the meat fall out. Hagen gave a bark of pure excitement and began to gorge.

'Should I be jealous?' came a voice.

Rumi turned. Nataré stood with arms folded across her chest. Her scent carried on the wind and something stirred within when it hit him.

She was, even in the deadened light, shockingly pretty to him. If a master painter had been asked to match her beauty on canvas, he would fail at every attempt. Her hips, lips and brows were full. Her eyes knew no mentor in brightness. When she looked up at Rumi, she smiled. It was infectious. From the look of her, it was clear she had not got much sleep in the recent past and had likely helped herself to more than a few gulps of palm wine. Even so, her attractiveness was unrestrained. The silver-blue shine in her eyes and the nonchalant curl to her lips only made him want her more.

'No... No,' Rumi said. 'I came to—'

She put a hand on his chest and the words dried up in his mouth. 'I was only joking.'

Rumi twisted his lips to one side as his heart pounded against her palm. 'Yes, of course.'

Here was the one to truly break his bravado. Every single time. There was no hiding place from her, and it was as scary as it was liberating.

Her hair was no longer in a braid, she had let it grow its own wild way. The pretence of propriety had left the Eredo now.

This was a time to live with the freedom of those who had revolted against death.

His eyes met hers and she looked away. It was time to be brave.

'How is the wall coming along?' he asked.

She blinked. 'We are doing a good job of repairing it. We expect it will be taller than it ever was before.'

Rumi inched closer to her. 'Do you feel safe here?'

Nataré's brows rose as she looked him up and down again, as though seeing him for the first time. She had no hiding place from him, either.

'It's different now,' she said. 'Sleep doesn't come as easy as it used to. I keep thinking I—' She didn't complete the sentence. 'If not for me, so many people would still be here.'

Rumi lowered his gaze. 'You cannot blame yourself. Not for that. I'm just as much to blame.'

'I don't see it that way,' she said.

'Change that, Nataré. Regret can enslave you, trust me. It will have you telling yourself you won't be happy until you've made things right – you miss everything around you because you are so focused on a target that can't be hit.'

'There's not much around me to miss.'

Rumi feigned being struck. 'I won't take that personally.'

She raised a hand. 'No, I don't mean you. I just mean... everything else. There is very little to be hopeful about right now.'

'That isn't the sort of thing I ever thought I would hear you say. I've known you long enough to say that you wouldn't be here without hope. You are the knife-edge. You survived things that most could not even dream of. The Thatcher will not define your story. It hasn't defined mine.'

Her lips curled into a strained semblance of a smile, and she spoke low, as though to herself. 'Why does it sound so much better coming from you?'

Rumi opened his mouth to speak but the words — whatever they were — abandoned him.

Silence had its way for a long moment. With anyone else in the world, Rumi could step into the breach without hesitation but with Nataré he understood that he had to pick his moments — sometimes she was a little skittish. So much of what passed between them was unspoken. He was no poet like Belize — he didn't have the words in him to say what needed saying.

There was a lull in the wind and Rumi became suddenly aware of how close she was. The scent of her sweat set his insides aflame. He could kiss her temple without moving his head. If he took one deep breath, their chests would touch. For a moment, he drew back from her, as though she were a whirlpool that would lead him to shipwreck if he got too close. She smiled, seeing his tactful retreat.

'Walk with me,' she said.

Rumi curled his hand around her elbow and pulled her close.

'We have come close to death. Horribly close,' she began.

Rumi nodded, remembering when Saturday himself had blown smoke in his face. 'We have.'

She met his gaze. 'When you took off on that Shinala in the battle, I...' She hesitated and stole a breath. 'I felt *regret*. I thought maybe that I had held back some things and might never get a chance to let them out.'

Rumi straightened, as his heart beat faster. Behind him, Hagen had gone completely still. Sharp emotion flashed through the bond. *Anticipation. Fear. Excitement.*

Nataré stopped and turned to face him. 'I don't want to hold back any more. I don't want to waste another moment being anything less than my entire self.'

Rumi's chest rose in a held breath. 'Me too,' he whispered.

Their eyes met. 'Rumi, I want you to...'

He looked down at her, ready for whatever she had to say next. 'Yes...'

She hesitated again and gave him a long, appraising look. Then she lowered her head. 'I want you to speak to Lord Mandla for me.'

Rumi's heart sank to his stomach. He gave her a confused look. 'Sorry, what?'

'The Shadow Order,' she said, 'I heard that they might be willing to consider people beyond fighting age now. There's a war coming and they need all the recruits they can get – maybe if you spoke to Mandla, they could consider letting me join. I know I am not Zarcanis reborn, but I hear the shadow is about will. I really think, with the right guidance, I could be a good shadowwielder. Make a real difference.'

Rumi's shoulders drooped. 'The Shadow Order. Of course.'

She gave him a searching look. 'What did you think I was talking about?'

He shook his head. 'Nothing. Never mind.'

She studied him for a moment, seeming unconvinced, but said nothing further.

'I'll talk to Mandla, the first chance I get.'

She blinked, smiled then pulled him into an embrace.

The scent of her filled his nose. Notes of apricot beneath clean, polished wood. He closed his eyes and pulled her close.

'Thank you,' she whispered.

His jaw was tight. 'You're welcome.'

Rumi turned to leave; his mind wandering beyond the walls as Hagen strode ahead. *Talk to Mandla for me.* The words had caught him like an uppercut when he was braced for a hook. *What was I expecting her to say?*

He didn't allow his mind to supply the answer. He had half brought to memory Belize's seventh dialogue.

My one desire, to never part
With her who made gentle, the sea of my heart.

'Stupid,' he muttered to himself as he walked away. Hagen ahead gave a frustrated growl in an act of solidarity. He should have spoken, once and for all. Lay it all bare and take her verdict as it came. He glanced over her shoulder. Nataré was still there, she hadn't moved.

He drew in a breath. The future was an excuse for those who were afraid of the opportunity now. What if the horns sounded tomorrow? What if the undead attacked tonight? Nothing was promised beyond the moments you could touch. *Shege that.*

He turned back towards Nataré, his heart thumping hard. Without thinking, he spoke aloud. 'Why are you letting me go through this alone, when I know you want me too?'

She gasped as though suddenly strangled, her cheeks flattening as her eyes went wide. But Rumi wasn't done.

He stepped closer. 'You know what I was thinking when we fought for our lives here? When I thought I'd die and never see you again?'

She didn't answer.

He inched a little closer still. 'I was thinking what a tragedy it would be to die, without ever knowing what it felt like to kiss you.'

Nataré gaped, scratching her elbow as she looked up at him. She drew in a stuttering breath and then let it out slow. 'Rumi...'

'You only need to tell me once that you don't feel the same. I will take that defeat honourably and never trouble you again, but tonight let it not be said that I was a coward. That I didn't say what I feel. Truly feel.' He raised his chin. 'Nataré, just say I'm alone in this and I will never speak of it again.'

She closed her eyes for a long moment, then stepped close and grabbed the collar of his kaftan. 'You're not alone. You've never been alone.'

He leaned in and let her walk through the door; their lips touched. Heat stronger than fire shot through him from toe to tooth. Exculpating sweetness came after and in that moment he knew there was a paradise. A transcendent place in which freedom was entire. Her lips were soft, her mouth warm as home. A gentle sound of pleasure hummed in her throat. She slipped a hand through the buttons of his kaftan and ripped it open. As buttons fell, she ran her fingers down his bare chest. He cupped her bottom and pulled her towards him and she squeezed the back of his neck. He kicked off a sandal, desperate to feel her bare skin on his. He clawed at her sentry vest.

"Take it off," he whispered.

She rushed to obey, ripping her shirt back as though it was burning her skin.

Hagen made a low sound, just a moment before the unmistakable stomp of footsteps came from somewhere behind them. Rumi bared his teeth and found some sense again.

Someone is coming.

At the height of delirium, Nataré pulled back and blinked at him.

'We should stop,' he said, wanting anything but.

She let out a shuddering breath. 'We should.'

For a moment, he was sure they were going to go at it again, but somehow discipline prevailed.

She grinned and narrowed her eyes. 'Now you can die knowing what it feels like.'

She picked up her vest from the ground and slipped it over her head.

He smiled back. 'I almost died just now.'

They both laughed as the sound of footsteps drew closer.

'Will you come to the Thatcher again tomorrow?' she asked.

He nodded. 'I will.'

'And every night after?'

Rumi's heart stirred. 'I will.'

She grabbed the collar of his kaftan and twisted it, pulling him close. 'I am not as strong as you think I am, Rumi. If we do this and what we have breaks, I cannot promise that I will not break along with it.'

'Then we must not let it break.'

Nataré sighed and there was silence for a time.

'Well... I will try, but if I try and we fail, then I will kill you, Rumi. I did not run to you; you ran to me.'

'A fair bargain,' Rumi said, producing a kola nut.

Hagen's tail thumped the ground with all the boundless exuberance of a child. Deep in the bond, Rumi felt his dog's emotions. *Excitement. Pride. Joy.*

9

A Gateway

RUMI

Rumi scratched behind the lionhound's ears. 'I know, Hagen. I know.'

They were headed back towards the Eredo, still jubilant with the thrum of the kiss. They passed the thick shadow of a tree when a sharp wind sent a sudden chill through the night. Hagen made a startled sound and froze.

Rumi raised an eyebrow. 'Hagen? What is it?'

He stepped past the tree and was struck by a blinding flash of light. He blinked and saw, in his mind, the towering figure of a woman. Yet it was only an apparition, more spirit than flesh.

Rumi raised a hand, preparing to call his shadow. 'What kind of spirit are you?' he asked wearily.

He was caught in a trance. In his mind, the spirit walked fully into the glare of moonlight. It was Aja, the night huntress – agbara of the wilderness. Her skin was the colour of rained-on leaves, her hair like the creeping vines of the banyan tree. Her teeth, porcelain-white and sharp as a panther's. In one hand she held a bow and on her back she carried a quiver with just one arrow. She stared at Hagen, barked like a dog and the lionhound understood.

Rumi was paralysed by some combination of fear and wonder. Aja spoke aloud. 'I am Aja. The wild wind. The night huntress.

Soul of the woodland. Heart of the mangrove. You may read my book.'

The cold wind came again and Aja faded to mist along with it. Rumi's heart was still thumping as he turned to his lion-hound. 'I'll be back soon, Hagen. I need to read the *Sakosaye*, now.'

He returned to his dormitory in haste and retrieved the *Sakosaye* from its hiding pace at the back of his locked cupboard. Reading from the Holy Almanac was only to be done after receiving an instruction from the agbara. Now he had one. Flipping frantically through the index, he found the *Book of Aja* and began to read.

> The forests were mine. The animals, too. For me, there was no deeper joy than to have the forest beneath my feet and the trees looming overhead. I walked amongst the lion, the elephant and the hyena. The birds in the sky sang my name. The fish in the sea called me friend. When the son of man came upon the forest, they knew only to take – never to give. Their work was the slaughter of all manner; of trees, animals, birds and fish. They drove the most beautiful creatures deeper into the forest and encroached upon the land as the weeds encroach upon the harvest. Seeing the ways of humanity, I called all the animals in the world to Erin-Olu. A place where nature could make its stand. A sanctuary from the carnage of civilisation. I bound the trees with old juju. Charms that are almost forgotten in the world. Otite and Damudamu and Amunimuye. To protect the last great forest.
>
> Everything that crawls and flies and forages and swims can be found in Erin-Olu. Every plant that grows and every seed that breaks has known its soil. It was never a place for

humanity – it was always a place for the wild things. But even so, there are those amongst humanity who are more of the wild than of the world. Who were treated not as trespassers but as welcome friends. They learned the ways of the wild – of medicine and cooking and power not found in things.

But power can be a poison to the sons and daughters of men. Some thought of using the secrets of the wild to dominate the world. They became jujumen, jazzmen and witch doctors. Corrupting the secrets of the wild to serve their own selfishness and lust. And so, I transformed Erin-Olu again and set it upon seven levels, each with more powerful charms and creatures than the last. Such was the power at the summit of Erin-Olu that for every person who reached it I offered a gift – I built a gateway. Whoever walks through it may pass directly into the Originate and receive the power to call any name and be sure it would answer.

There were some great people who made it to the summit of Erin-Olu and to them I gave this great gift. When they returned from the Originate, some could speak the name of the cloud and command it to rain. Some could speak the name of the sun and turn daylight to darkness. Others called the names of people and they answered.

But as it is above, so it is beneath. The Originate is a place that informs the Lower World and there were powers from the other side who despised humanity and sought to dominate it. The greatest of these by far was the Son of Dara, Palman who was Azuka. He passed through that gateway and struck me down. I raised my spear to hunt him and he struck me down a second time at Mount Darman, which they now call the God-Eye. There he raised five priests to spread his name and make his kingdom come. The Priest of Vultures, whom they call the Accuser; Pretty Yelloweye, whom they call the Priestess of Cats; the Lord of Horns, whom they call the Broken One; Ntanga, whom they call the Laughing One; and Alabelowo who carries the blade of lies. These five must thou fear most of all, for their love is sworn to Palman alone.

The Son seeks to dominate the world, release Billisi and remake it all in his image. That must not be. The Skyfather must rise again and restore balance to a breaking world, but he cannot do it without the brave. The gateway to the other side remains and he who reaches the summit of Erin-Olu gains a gift long lost to man – the power to call one name forth and be sure it would obey.

Rumi closed the book, his heart pounding, his expression grim-faced. The words resounded in his mind – *to pass directly into the Originate.* He could see Morire's face, patient, innocent and kind.

The Originate was where his brother was. The power was no great draw but the chance to bring back his brother – for that he would brave any peril. Any peril at all.

10

The Bishop and the Baker

LETHI

The sound of music wafted through a half-open door. Lethi peeked through the gap and saw a man playing the Selistre harp. He nudged the door a little further open with his toe and took a closer look. It was a ceremony of some sort. There were others in the room, their heads bowed in reverence as they listened to the artist play. The man was dressed in a silk, wide-sleeved kaftan with a thick golden chain around his neck. The room was a monument to Palman. The ceiling mural showed the story of the miracle on the mountain when Palman resisted his murderous father and condemned him to darkness. A startling exhortation of that most famous Palman imagery: the broken noose, and the triumphant son with the four point star raised aloft. The sight of it sent a shiver down Lethi's spine. He had always sensed that his connection to Palman was a special one – he didn't follow any of the traditional Palman rituals but felt coupled to the religion in a deeper, more intrinsic way. There was something resonant about a god who proudly proclaimed to be above all others. A god whose people had never lost a battle. A god who fought for the light. A god who stood for something.

The painted wall depicted Palman carving an eye into Mount Darman. The God-Eye Demonstration – where the Priests of the Son were first consecrated. Six figures were depicted along the five-panelled stained-glass window. Lethi drew in an astonished breath. *The Priests of the Son.*

Lethi had once heard it said that in the highest echelons of the priesthood, the priests who were ordained by Palman on Mount Darman were considered blessed saints despite the fact that their names were never mentioned in the holy book. He studied the figures one after the other. The first stood with a vulture perched on his shoulder. Next to him was a woman with the yellow-gold eyes of a cat and a face that was the work of God. Then came a man who wore a necklace wrought of horns and stood with a jewel-encrusted walking cane. Another clutched his stomach in laughter, and another carried a blade with words written along the face. The last of them was a man whose eyes were the red of true flame and who carried a gleaming double-axe.

They didn't look much like priests. Were this not the inner sanctuary of a temple, Lethi would have thought them far from religious. Yet who else could they be? Depicted with halos above their crowns, beside a painting of the miracle on the mount. *But the scripture says there were five priests, not six.*

The harpist brought his music to a crescendo and Lethi stepped inside to take a seat.

A tall figure appeared on the stage behind the musician. His chain caught the light, illuminating him for a brief moment. It was the bishop of Basmine. He was dressed in full ceremonial garb including a grated, golden mask that covered his face, but through the gaps, Lethi could see his grin.

'Good afternoon, my children,' the bishop said, stepping into the light.

The congregation chorused its response. 'Good afternoon, Father.'

The bishop smiled and nodded to the artist, who slowly let the music fade to silence.

'Seven. It is the number of completion,' the bishop said, gesturing towards the ceiling mural. 'Seven days. Seven sins. Seven books in our holy scripture. Wherever the counting stops at six, you know that seven brings the completion. And so, it is with a heart of joy and thanksgiving that I invite you to say the seven words that seal our salvation.'

The congregation rose to their feet and Lethi quickly did the same.

The bishop raised his hands. 'I confess Palman is Lord of All.'

'I confess Palman is Lord of All,' the congregation answered.

The chanting went on in that way until Lethi slipped into a trance. He was so consumed by it all that he barely noticed the bishop leave the stage until the deep voice growled behind him.

'Come with me.'

Lethi gave a start as an arm fell on his shoulder.

Lethi saluted and bowed at the waist. 'Your Eminence.'

The bishop removed the mask and bared his teeth. 'With me.'

Lethi followed without hesitation, leaving the congregants still chanting as he and the bishop slipped out from the room.

The bishop stared straight ahead, talking as though he had practised what to say over and over again.

'Azamon has received some information on the hideout of the Black Hammer Clan, here in the Citadel. You are to join his investigation.'

The words sent a shiver up Lethi's spine. He raised an eyebrow. 'Now?'

The bishop gave him an unimpressed look. 'Is there something more urgent than your mission here?'

Lethi frowned. 'No, of course not, Your Eminence.'

The bishop furrowed his brow and gave Lethi an inspecting look. 'What exactly is your plan to deal with the Black Hammer Clan, Lieutenant?'

Lethi scratched at his shoulder. 'There is only one way to deal with a snake in the grass – you sever its head. We need to find the one who leads these men. The natives can be fickle. When we take away the snake head, we can pick off every part of the body until the Black Hammer Clan is no more.'

The bishop gave a small smile. 'So, find the head of the snake.'

Lethi nodded. 'We will, Your Eminence.'

They kept walking and came across a painting along the wall that Lethi hadn't noticed before. It depicted a native man with a cloud-grey bushel of hair, dressed in royal Palmaine blue with the ornamental sword of an officer. Curiously, his uniform bore the old sigil of the Palmaine king. Before Basmine was conquered.

The bishop noticed his curiosity. 'You are wondering who that is?'

Lethi nodded. 'Yes, Your Eminence.'

The bishop smiled. 'That is Sir Kojo Damascus, once the commander of a rebel Odu force called the *amotekun*. For three years he tormented Palmaine forces, evading capture and decimating our troops. He was a master strategist.'

'So why is he wearing Palmaine blue?' Lethi asked.

'When Zaminu came, he brokered peace with him. Gave him control over all the southern lands in exchange for his fealty to the Palmaine crown and a promise to crush any other native rebellions. For ten years he was Warden of the South before he was assassinated. His signature is on the Treaty of Bremain, which brought the war to an end.'

Lethi gave the painting a second look. The man looked proud

in his Palmaine colours. That was the genius of Zaminu – he understood better than anyone that sometimes a handshake is better than a closed fist. He understood the natives down to bone and marrow.

'Very enlightening, Your Eminence.'

The bishop nodded and gestured towards the door. 'You'll find Azamon outside. I expect to hear a success story with my dinner.'

Lethi stepped outside, where two carriages were waiting beside the fountain. The first was occupied by half a dozen men of the consular guard with repeating rifles.

Azamon was inspecting the second carriage. He glanced over his shoulder as Lethi approached. 'Lieutenant,' Azamon said with an easy salute. 'We have the privilege of riding the bishop's carriage today.'

Lethi glanced up at the carriage. At first, he thought the stark-white colouring was strange, then he realised what it was supposed to be. The carriage was made in the image of an eye – a roaming eye that watched Basmine. *The Eye of the Light*.

Lethi tightened the sling on his rifle as he climbed aboard, then Azamon gave the signal and they set off down the cobblestoned road.

'We have been made aware that the Black Hammer Clan has a hideout within the Citadel walls,' Azamon explained.

A shadow fell across Lethi's face as they drove through the temple gates. 'Where?'

'I'm not certain yet, but I have my suspicions,' Azamon said.

They slipped into the Citadel and Azamon gestured for the wheelman to stop. He glanced out of the window, staring at the nearest buildings.

Somehow satisfied that they weren't worth looking into, Azamon waved the wheelman on.

Three more times they stopped and went into buildings to make enquiries. Each time, Lethi got the distinct impression that Azamon knew exactly what they were looking for but enjoyed frightening the locals along the way.

The carriage rolled into a narrow corridor of brick houses and Azamon drew in anticipatory breath.

'Here!' he said suddenly.

Lethi studied the building through the pupil-shaped window. Fronted by a small lawn, the façade was of old, pre-consulate design. The surrounding buildings had the renovated frontage of the newly built, but this one stood like an old, stubborn relic. The house, it was plain to see, was let out in small tenements to people who could not afford to buy a place to live. These were people *in* the Citadel but not *of* the Citadel. Working people; tailors, tradesmen, bakers and butchers.

Lethi pursed his lips. To his mind, it was too-easy a target for Citadel suspicion. This did not seem the work of great espionage, just the time-honoured habit of the rich suspecting the poor whenever there was trouble. Buildings like this were likely the first destination of the city watch whenever there was burglary.

Azamon narrowed his eyes as the carriage door was pulled open. 'I am sure you had your methods in Guyarica, but this is Basmine. We do things a little *differently.*'

Lethi followed him out and was confronted by the thick smell of just-baked bread. *A bakery.*

'They are in there,' Azamon said. 'I can smell it.'

Azamon stared at the dust-beaten sandals at the foot of the door and then, with a low grunt of irritation, he nudged his way in.

There were three people inside who had the look of a family – mother, father and child. From the oak-dark shade of the father's skin, he was a native of the Kuba tribe. The mother, however, had all the parts of an Odu woman. The child was their matrimonial result – an unmistakeably two-tribe boy.

Mother and child were seated at a small wooden table before a plate of flatbread. The father stood behind a counter with loaves of fresh bread in a glass tureen. Behind the man was a beaded curtain, which presumably led to their private rooms.

Along the far wall was a line of large wooden barrels of flour set beside a large, still-burning clay oven; illuminated by the roiling dance of flame.

The baker was a bald man, whose fattened cheeks gave the impression that he ate his own leftover pies at day's end. He smiled a welcome at his new customers.

Lethi's stomach turned a little as he studied the room. He wanted to tell the mother and child to run. To get as far away as they could right *now*.

One glimpse at Azamon's golden medallion and it was as if the baker had been struck by thunder. He fell prostrate with total supplication.

'My Lord,' he gasped. 'You are welcome.'

Chairs scraped the floor as wife and child followed the baker's lead and fell forward in greeting.

Azamon gave no immediate response; instead, he glanced at a load-bearing wall behind the barrels of flour. Pinned to it was an ornamental four-point star.

'So, you walk in the light?' Azamon asked.

The baker raised his chin and gave a desperate nod. When he spoke it was with the reverent pitch of a man who found no difficulty in reciting from the holy book. 'I serve the maker and the unmaker, the eternal king whose reign has neither ended nor begun, the ever-victorious god. Palman, my lord. There is no other *god.*'

The last word he spoke with such surrender that Lethi had no trouble believing him.

There was a thick, stretched-out interval of silence as Azamon closed his eyes. 'So, you know the five laws of Palman?'

The baker cleared his throat. 'Yes, my lord.'

Azamon narrowed his eyes. 'Recite them to me.'

The baker raised the four-fingered salute of the Palman faith and spoke in recitation. 'To lie is forbidden, except to protect the truth. To kill is forbidden, except to protect a life. Resist the lies of the Father and the consort of his followers. Resist the abomination of bloodmagic, for it will defile you. Above all, for the greater good of the faith, all things are permissible.'

'Good,' Azamon said, squeezing the baker's shoulder.

The baker gave a small smile at this gesture of acceptance.

Azamon glanced up at the four-point star again, his hand not leaving the baker's shoulder. 'The consulate has been reliably informed that there are men known as the Black Hammer Clan who have made this their hiding place.'

The baker's retort was thick with disgust. 'Never.'

Azamon raised an eyebrow. 'So, you know of the Black Hammer Clan?'

The baker blinked as though realising what he had said, then shook his head. 'Everyone knows about them.'

Azamon gave some semblance of a smile. 'I am inclined to believe you. You are a god-fearing man and you know the five laws of Palman. You also know, I am sure, the punishment for those who break the laws of Palman.'

'Of course.'

Azamon arched his back in a deep stretch. 'I am sure there

has been some mistake but in the interest of posterity, may we check your establishment?'

A flicker of fear touched the baker's eyes. Only for a moment, but if Lethi had seen it, Azamon had too.

The baker gave a rueful smile and nodded. Insisting they 'wouldn't find anything'.

Lethi glanced at the mother and tried to gesture with his eyes. *Run now!* But she didn't move.

It was like watching a new performance of an old story. Azamon raised two fingers to his lips and let off a sharp whistle. The consular guard flooded into the bakery, moving with the practised accuracy of men who knew what they were looking for and where to find it. After a cursory glance around the room, they stepped behind the beaded curtain.

The baker, to his eternal credit, looked absolutely certain that there was nothing to hide.

'May I?' Azamon asked, pointing to the plate of flatbread at the centre of the table.

The baker nodded. 'It would be our honour.'

Azamon snatched up a piece and stuffed his face, attacking the flatbread as though it was his sworn enemy. The only sounds were of his violent mastication and the trample of boots as the consular searched the bakery.

'Delicious,' Azamon said, wiping his mouth. Lethi tried to signal to the mother again, but she was pointedly ignoring him now.

The baker gave a triumphant smile, as the bishop finished his flatbread. 'It is my greatest honour, my lord.'

One of the consular guards returned and shook his head. 'Nothing.'

Lethi let out a silent breath. *They hid well.*

Azamon just blinked and said, 'Keep looking.'

The baker stiffened as the guard saluted and returned to the search.

Azamon glanced down at the baker's son who was still prostrate before him. 'How old is your son?'

The baker made an uncomfortable sound in his throat and hesitated. 'He'll be eleven years this month.'

Azamon laughed and turned to the boy. Leaning forward, he spoke low. 'Do you know who I am, young man?'

The boy's eyes widened and then closed. 'Y-yes.'

Azamon leaned even closer and spoke at a whisper that was close to silence. 'Who am I?' he asked, touching the boy's hand.

Something about Azamon's touch seemed to cause a sharp change in the boy and he babbled like a market mummer. 'You are the Meladroni. The Roar. The Night and the Knight. You are the Eye of the Light.'

Lethi's stomach twisted as the boy's fear went rabid.

'The shadows flee in the presence of light. Here is your chance,' Azamon said, spreading his arms wide. 'Speak now and prove yourself to the light. Show me that you are not an agent of darkness.'

The baker closed his eyes and lowered his head, his jaw trembling as his hand tightened into a fist.

Azamon pointed at the son and snarled. 'Shame the Father. Speak the truth!'

The sharp snap of wood came again and then the stamp of footsteps as the consular guard moved deeper into the building.

The mother glanced up, her face a picture of fear.

'It's not too late,' Azamon said, staring at the boy. 'The Son is merciful as he is mighty.'

The colour drained from the baker's face at those words. Slowly, he raised his chin, his eyes pink at the edges.

Azamon's voice rose, thunderous. 'The truth will liberate you! Break the chains of the Father! Break the chains!'

The baker's face fell as he spoke in a broken sob. 'Stop.'

Tears filled the little boy's eyes as he crumbled completely. Azamon raised an eyebrow. 'You are going to tell me where they are?'

He gave a slow, silent nod. Lethi was stunned.

Just then, one of the barrels of flour toppled over of its own accord and the lid wheeled off through the room.

Azamon whistled hard. 'They are in the barrels of flour!'

Lethi had his rifle in his hand just as the first man exploded from a wooden barrel. He fired once and the bullet took the man at the side of his eye, spraying gore as his head split at the temple. He went down, clutching his head, his body pulsing. A second man came charging at Azamon with a knife in hand, but the Meladroni was ready; he dodged out of a murderous swipe and caught the man about the wrist, wringing the knife from his grip and kicking the back of his knee so hard he buckled. The man raised a hand in agitation and Azamon fired his rifle – his head exploded. The consular guard swarmed the rest of the barrels – the men inside stood no chance.

After a sharp melee of gunfire, two members of the Black Hammer Clan were pulled from the disguised barrels of flour. The rest were all dead.

The taller of the pair had the lean, polished muscle of a man who knew the ins and outs of a good fight. From the tense set to his shoulders, Lethi did not need to see his eyes to know that they were lidded with hate. His shirtsleeves looked as though they had been cut away. His entire neck was dark with the traditional tattoos of the Darani and scrawled around his bicep in clear, black ink were two words that Lethi had heard many times in Guyarica – Furae Oloola. The immortal words to a song that was as seditious as it was catchy.

The second man was barely twenty, he knelt with shoulders slumped and chin drooped in utter defeat. This was the sort of man that every group had; the follower. The tag-along. The one who didn't have to be there. Beside the dark tattoo of a black hammer on his wrist was the word 'Liberation'.

Azamon glared at the tattoo, his face tight as a closed fist. 'Liberation?' He spat the word out like bitter fruit. 'Liberation from what? Was it not the Palmaine who liberated you from the shackles of barbarism? Illiteracy? The influence of the occult? You killed children for bloodmagic and we showed you the light. What new liberation could you possibly ask of us? We have given you far more than you could ever have had the good sense to ask.'

The young man glanced up at Azamon and gave a feral grin. 'You are only half a man to them. Stop telling yourself you are one of them – they don't think you are.'

Azamon narrowed his eyes and backhanded the man. 'You're pathetic, you know. We gave you everything and instead of embracing it, you blame the Palmaine for every rot in your country.'

The man shook his head. 'We blame the Palmaine for not living up to the ideals they profess to have. You are a nation of hypocrites. You are like the farmer who pretends to nurture the calf, when he knows its final destination is the slaughterhouse. That inward lie is why everything you touch is corrupt. Even your Eye of the Light has touched the dark.'

'Bitterness is what has condemned you.'

The man's expression didn't change. 'I am not bitter against the pale man. I have far too many pains for that. Too many deep contemplations. You flatter yourselves. I am talking about the condition of your heart. A condition that allows you to commit the crimes you commit and then pretend you did not commit them. I am talking about what it does to *you*. You are the ones who need liberation.'

Azamon stared at the man for a long moment, then his expression hardened in a deep scowl. 'Throw them into the oven.'

The consular guard wasted no time in obliging. Lethi's heart jumped as the consular dragged the taller man across the floor.

Azamon's face was blank and pitiless as he chanted. 'And the Son shall strike them down, erase their names, their seed in the land.'

The captive, sensing death as the flame licked out at him, raised his voice and cried out in song. 'Furae Oloola, arise the ever-setting sun. They will never defeat—'

The song was cut off as the man was cast into the flames. All the bravery deserted him as the roaring fire flared to engulf him. He screamed a desperate, feral scream. Like an animal finally caught in the teeth of death. A yelp of pure terror. For a long while, the only thing that could be heard was the screams.

Lethi's heart thudded hard in his chest. *Shege.*

The second captive howled and squirmed as he realised what was happening.

'No! No! Please! No!' he urged as the consular dragged him towards the oven. His legs scratched helplessly against the floor as he tried to stop them. 'Please, no!'

The baker's face was etched with colourless despair as he watched.

Azamon raised a hand and the consular stopped. 'Will you talk, boy?'

The young man turned back, frantic, and nodded like a man possessed. 'Yes, I will tell you everything I know,' he begged. 'Everything!'

Azamon nodded to the consular and the man was dragged away. With him gone, Azamon glanced back at the baker and raised a finger. 'You lied to me.' He raised another finger. 'You consorted with the followers of the father. Twice you broke the laws of Palman.'

The baker bowed and pressed his face to the floor. 'Mercy, my lord,' he begged. 'I have walked in the darkness but now come back to light. I was going to give them up. I swear it by everything I hold dear.'

Azamon's face was a wall of solid ice. 'You have shamed yourself.'

The baker sniffed, stifling a sob. 'I know.' He clasped his hands to beg. 'I plead mercy, my lord. Mercy, for the sake of the Son.'

Azamon gave him a long look and straightened. 'Even one such as you is not beyond mercy.' He extended a hand. The baker took it and trembled with tears. 'But even mercy has a cost.'

Azamon gestured to the child with a terrible smile playing at the corner of his lips. 'Throw him into the oven.'

The baker met Azamon's gaze, his mouth drooped in utter shock. Azamon stepped back as the baker moved to shield his son. The consular intervened, brushing the man aside and pinning him back at gunpoint.

Lethi left the bakery as the boy was dragged towards the oven. He would not watch a child being killed. Rather than beg, the baker's boy started to sing. That same seditious song. *Furae Oloola.*

Lethi reached into his jacket for his pipe, then fumbled in his pocket for a light. His stomach tightening as the baker's boy's voice grew louder.

'Need a light?'

It was Azamon, his face touched with triumph.

Lethi accepted the matchbox and lit his pipe, dragging deep as it came alive with fire. Though the bakery door was closed, they could still hear the muffled screams of the baker's son in the oven. He had stopped singing now.

Azamon acted as though there was no noise at all. 'Do you know how I knew he was lying?'

Lethi narrowed his eyes. 'The flatbread.'

Azamon smiled. 'So you *are* as clever as they say you are. The flatbread was made in the old native way. No one eats that around here except—'

'Soldiers,' Lethi said. 'It keeps longer. I know.'

Azamon nodded. 'Precisely. No Citadel bakery would have that much bread that the locals wouldn't eat.' He studied Lethi. 'You don't seem impressed.'

Lethi scratched the back of his neck. 'It was well done.'

Azamon frowned. 'You think your native tracker could do better?'

Yes, Lethi thought, but he shook his head and said, 'Perhaps.'

Azamon wasn't offended, but rather he seemed intrigued.

Lethi cleared his throat and blew out a thick cloud of smoke. 'I have a question.'

Azamon raised an eyebrow, his expression one of amusement. 'Go on.'

'What did that man mean? The first one you threw into the oven, when he said the Eye of the Light has touched the dark?'

Azamon rolled his shoulders as his lips curled up in that same parody of a smile. 'Who am I to understand the rantings of a madman?'

11

Champion of Paper

RUMI

Chief Karile gestured in the shadow and conjured a stemmed lectern as easily as one would wave to a friend. More and more, Rumi could see that strength in the shadow was a subtle thing; in many ways, it was like riding a Shinala – some gained strength by dominating the shadow and bringing it under their will, but the best shadowwielders knew how to whisper to the shadow and be certain that it would obey. They were completely in step and in tandem with it.

Karile set down her heavy-leathered book and drew in breath. 'Welcome to all our newest Suli,' she said with a smile. 'You have all done exceedingly well to get here.'

There were murmurs of irritation from some of the older Suli who had never bothered to hide the fact they thought too many undeserving Seedlings had been raised up.

Rumi had hoped to see Sameer and Ahwazi in this class but neither of them had shown up. It meant he was the only Suli who sat alone on the series of wooden desks built for two. He hadn't been born in the Eredo – softborn they called him – and that went some way to explaining his isolation, but there was more to it than that. He was Ajanla Erenteyo and the story was that he had killed the Priest of Vultures. The others kept their distance. They had spent the morning in Gaitan's class learning the basic formations for a full-scale battle and no one had said a word to him.

Just as Karile cleared her throat to speak, the door to the lecture hall creaked open. A woman stepped inside. She had a sullen, cynical look that she made no effort to embellish with powder or eyepaint. Her skin was as dark as a room with no lantern at night and her broad shoulders were a thing of strength. Chief Karile cast her a disapproving look as she walked in. She responded with an apologetic smile, but said nothing, moving to find a seat. There was a spare desk at the very back of the room but that would entail a long, quiet walk. The only other empty seat was beside Rumi. Her face fell a little when she noticed this.

Rumi raised his chin, jaw set strong. He wouldn't let her look down on him – he wouldn't let anyone look down on him. Not now.

She hesitated as she reached the desk, then slid into the vacant chair. Her scent was deeply familiar – it reminded him of the shopkeepers who spent long hours at the spice market. Mixtures of ginger and fennel seeds and rosemary. A pleasant smell, he had to admit.

Chief Karile cleared her throat once more. 'Stories,' she began. 'Stories are what divide us from all other creatures. Our ability to tell them to one another and transport our minds to places we have never seen, to envision things that may not even exist.'

'So, imagination?' someone offered.

Karile shook her head. 'No, not imagination. Imagination is iron in the earth; stories are a forged sword. Many creatures have imagination but only humans have stories. All creatures who know the sound of an elephant stampede can raise an alarm, but only humans can believe that the elephants are secretly gods who come to lead them to the afterlife. Stories have power beyond anything you can imagine.'

The woman seated next to Rumi cleared her throat and raised a hand. 'Forgive me, Chief Karile, but I thought we would prioritise lessons that relate to our *current* peril. We are preparing for a real war, not a theoretical one.'

Chief Karile regarded her with a look of disappointed reproach. 'Stories concern our current peril far more than anything you can make with a sword or spear, Miselda. They give us not only the power to speak our imaginations but to speak them as one. Stories bind us together; they are the foundation to every collective victory. Kingdoms are just lines on a map, but you cannot have a nation unless its people believe its stories. They focus our energy, and if we mean to fight the Palmaine then we need to be focused above all.'

Miselda gave no great expression, responding with a soft nod. She said, ''Tis the testimony of the priest doth animate the gods.'

Rumi smiled at that. It was a line from the third of Belize's dialogues. Perhaps the most despised and esoteric of the bunch. It had not escaped his notice that her name was Miselda and that her forearm was riddled with dark lines of shadow rank when she raised her hand. The way she sat – back straight and neck slightly arched – was the coiled posture of an ever-ready fighter. Even at rest, Rumi could see she was primed for violence.

Karile smiled at the reference to the third dialogue. 'Belize spoke the truth. Our faith is the lifeblood of the agbara. It is why our gods would always return to do mighty works. To remind us that they are there and that they are mighty. To keep their stories alive. If there is one thing all gods love, it is human praise. The Palmaine will always attack our books, holy places and rituals because they know that faith is power; they know that stories give people hope.'

'But half our stories aren't true,' Miselda said. 'The Odu believe Xango spoke with the voice of thunder, but some Kuba say it was Kamanu. They cannot both be correct.'

'I did not say all our stories are true. The fly in the honeypot does not contaminate the whole. There is sweetness to be found in both our lies and our truths – they tell us something about ourselves that we cannot ignore. Our greatest task is to destroy the stories of our enemies. The story that we feel more and think less. That we eat our young and worship banal gods. That we are childlike. That we kill for sport and lie with animals. That our agonies are not quite so real. That our love is lewd and joy is fickle. That we are – in every sense – of less consequence and dangerous without supervision. If we are to liberate the people of Basmine we must first kill these stories with our own.'

'And what is our story to be?' Miselda asked.

'That we are, above all else, a thoughtful people. That though we are flawed, we are kind, loving, hard-working and honest. That the future will be brighter when we are free, and our future is worth fighting for.'

Karile's lesson went on to discuss the hazards of the deep shadow. How the most powerful emotions can take a toll on the mind of the shadowwielder. Fear, loss, even love. Shadowwielders were vessels of emotion and even the strongest vessels were prone to crack when the emotions got too powerful. It was why they were only allowed three fighting days a week. Overexposure to the shadow was dangerous – especially after they had pushed themselves so hard in the battle at the Thatcher.

Class finished and Rumi immediately rose to leave. A low voice stopped him in place.

'You're him, aren't you?'

Rumi glanced back at her. It was Miselda; the girl who smelled like ginger.

'They call me Ajanla Erenteyo actually, not *him*.'

She didn't laugh. Instead, she pointed at his chair leg. 'Next time don't place your chair so close. You are encroaching on my space.'

Rumi glanced down at the chair and frowned. 'I—'

But she had turned her back on him before he had time enough to answer. Rumi hissed out an irritated breath and gathered his things.

The next class they had was with Chief Gaitan. He was a giant of a man, impossible to miss even from far away, with a laugh that made the world feel small. Rumi could still remember the way Gaitan had charged through the Thatcher. More like a god in battle than something born of flesh and bone. He dispensed death like daisies at a flower garden.

'Welcome,' he said, his booming voice cutting the chatter to silence. 'As Seedlings, you have all learned a piece of what it means to be a fighter. As a Suli, you must learn what it means to be a soldier. Anyone can fight for themselves but there is a higher calling for those blessed of shadow. You must fight for others. Fight as one.'

Gaitan called his shadow and conjured what looked like a seraiye board in the air. 'Anyone consider themselves a good seraiye player?'

Rumi scanned the room for Sameer but again, he was not there. Miselda stepped forward to accept the challenge.

'I do,' Miselda said.

Gaitan grinned and set the pieces across the board. 'You are white, I'll be black.'

Miselda nodded and called her shadow. It came, billowing like a black mist in howling wind. You could tell by the thickness of it that she had some skill as a shadowwielder.

'Your move,' Gaitan said.

Miselda gestured in shadow and the conjured white leopard stone shifted diagonally across the board.

Gaitan blinked at the aggressive move. 'As a Suli, you are only part of a whole.' He gestured in shadow and the black lion stone rose from the board. 'Like pieces in a game of seraiye. The strategy always comes before the glory.' He moved the black lion stone to counter the leopard and pointed to his head. 'Wars are won here...' He pointed to his bicep. 'Before they are ever won here.'

Miselda moved the hyena stone in line with the lion, committing Gaitan to a defensive move.

Gaitan frowned. 'You must believe in the strategy of your commander and commit to it wholeheartedly.'

He moved the black lion only one pace to the left. It was a mistake — even Rumi could see that.

Miselda didn't grin, as the white lion shifted behind the lines of her opponent.

Gaitan had made a seemingly fatal mistake. The rest of the game seemed a formality.

Gaitan moved the monkey stone in some futile act of defence, but Miselda was a merciless player. She struck out with the white lion and began a brutal assault, moving across the board taking piece after piece. The shadows winked out as Miselda devastated the board.

Gaitan lowered his chin with each piece lost, his confidence seeming to wane as Miselda stormed to a crushing victory.

With only a few pieces left, Miselda closed in on the black lion stone.

Suddenly, Gaitan straightened and let out a relieved sigh. 'You sacrifice anything for the success of your strategy,' he said with a grin.

Rumi blinked and only then did he see the sequence begin to unfold. His eyes widened.

Miselda hadn't seen it yet. She took the lioness stone – a hungry move which had left her left side unguarded.

The trap was so beautifully laid that Rumi let out a stuttering laugh.

Miselda glanced up at the sound and gave him an irritated glare.

'Sorry,' Rumi whispered.

Gaitan gave a nonchalant gesture with his thumb and the last black hyena stone struck the white lion from the board.

Miselda leaned forward, staring at the board again as though some foul trick had been played.

People started to laugh.

Gaitan turned away from the board and back to the class, the game won. 'In war, you play to win. No matter the cost.'

Miselda stared at the board for a long moment, then bowed low, accepting that she had been well beaten. It was a devious little trap Gaitan had pulled – giving everything up for the one good chance to take down the lion stone and win the game. His point needed no further illustration.

When class was over, Miselda confronted Rumi with a warning never to laugh at him again with those 'softborn lips'.

Rumi nearly laughed again when she said it. *Softborn lips*. But his smirk had been enough and Miselda lashed out with shadow. It happened so quickly that Rumi was on the floor before he knew what had struck him. His nostrils were clogged with blood as he glanced up at the ceiling. The gathered Suli gasped as Miselda stood triumphant over Rumi. She would likely be suspended for wrongful use of the shadow, but it was plain she thought it was worth it.

'I knew it was all a lie,' Miselda said with a blank stare. 'You're no great warrior, only a jumped up softborn who shouldn't be here.'

Whispers of gossip flared up as Rumi rose to his feet, still groggy. Like a brought-down statue, his veneer of prestige had been peeled away.

Rumours were everywhere before dinner. Word was that Ajanla Erenteyo had not been the one to slay the Priest of Vultures after all – it had been Zarcanis, but they had propped Ajanla up to sway Kasinabe opinions on the softborn. He was Mandla's project – a paper champion.

At breakfast the next day, Suli suddenly found the courage to glare at him. In class someone asked a pointed question about whether the Suli rank was about merit or about charity. In the corridor, someone shouted 'watering down the Bloods'.

Rumi tried not to let it bother him, but a secret, quiet part of him longed to have his say. To call his shadow and fight without restraint. To beat day and night into a few Suli so they would remember that he had shed more blood and sweat in a day than any of them had in their hardest year. That would, of course, have led to a suspension for wrongful use of shadow and Rumi couldn't afford to have time away from the Order. That night, while the other Suli were asleep, he called his shadow again and practised like a lunatic. When morning came, he was going to see Mandla.

12

An Act of War

ALANGBA

Alangba pushed the door open and stepped inside. Ladan stood at the centre of a fighting pit, teeming with shadow. His skin glistened with sweat as he went through an immaculate routine. *Fox enters the henhouse* flowed effortlessly into *eagle snatches the pike*. Even with the spear in his wrong hand, Ladan was formidable. A beautiful fighter in all the ways it was possible to be. Standing across from him was the ugliest fighter imaginable. No Music – a deaf man, who fought as though violence was his safe place. If fighting was a language, Ladan would be a poet and No Music would be a drunken sailor with a mouth full of profanity. The two circled each other briefly before Ladan lunged across the pit. No Music danced back and aimed for the groin. Ladan winced as the safespear brushed the inside of his leg, and lashed out with *snake shoots venom*. No Music let the spear roll over his shoulder and pulled off an elegant shrug to send his safespear through Ladan's armpit. It was a low move, for Ladan had no hand on his right side. Another opponent might have shown mercy but No Music was not that sort. He would offer Ladan no hiding place when it came to a fight – as true a test of his readiness to fight that anyone could give him.

Wincing, Ladan stepped back into *eagle stands amongst the*

cockerels. No Music reacted, ready to beat night and day out of him with *raging rhinoceros.*

'Careful,' Alangba called out, sensing the fight was at its endgame.

No Music shot out like an arrow, his spear aiming for Ladan's throat – sudden as sickness. Ladan leaned back and in the same motion brought the bottom of his safespear up so it struck No Music directly in the gonads. *A beautiful fighter who knows when to make it ugly.*

Alangba was impressed that No Music didn't cry out. Anyone else would but No Music had a fighter's pride that meant he would never let his opponent know when he was hurt. If he was bleeding out to death, he would still be shouting curses.

With a grunt, No Music staggered back, amazingly still keeping hold of his safespear. Ladan moved to end it, flowing forward with his safespear just to the side. No Music's eyes widened for a brief moment before he did something Alangba would not have imagined possible. He stepped directly into Ladan's path and struck out. The only counter Ladan had was to aim for the face but that would risk serious injury or worse. They were only sparring, there was no need to take such a risk. At least, not for Ladan.

He took the hit to the kidney and went down clutching his side.

'That's enough,' Alangba said, stepping forward to bring an end to it before No Music came at Ladan again.

No Music frowned, then made a gesture of eating porridge with a spoon. His message was clear. *Meat and drink to me.*

Alangba helped Ladan to his feet as he hissed out an exhausted breath. Their eyes met and as always, it led to mutual grins.

'I was wondering when you would show up,' Ladan said, breathing hard.

'You couldn't run long enough or fast enough to escape from me,' Alangba said. Ladan reached out and grabbed his hand. Alangba choked up as though strangled. They barely heard the door close behind them.

Someone cleared their throat instructively.

The two men turned towards the door.

Mandla stood with Telemi at his side. He looked, for once, a little dishevelled and uncomfortable. Alangba had only ever seen him utterly cool but since the Thatcher, some of that control had disappeared. Like everyone else, his soul still screamed.

'Just the two I wanted to see,' Mandla said. He gave Telemi a nod and the big man left to guard the door.

Mandla stepped forward, his raffia swishing, his staff tolling like a stone bell. He glanced directly at Alangba and his eyes seemed to flash at the sight of him. 'I am putting together a team,' he began.

Ladan set down his spear.

'Rebellion is finally brewing again in Basmine. A group who call themselves the Black Hammer Clan are fighting back.'

Alangba raised an eyebrow. 'How?'

'Bringing down statues, blocking off roads. Small things, for now, but the raging flame is born of a spark. With the right support I believe they will lay down the path for the war that comes.'

'So, this team you are putting together,' Ladan said. 'It is to support the Black Hammer Clan?'

Mandla nodded. 'We have managed to make contact with their leaders. An intelligent bunch but they do not have the experience it takes to do what they intend to do.'

'And what do they intend to do?'

Mandla smiled. 'Burn down the House of Palman.'

Alangba gave a start. 'An outright act of war?'

Mandla's smile withered to dust and his jaw tightened in a scowl. 'The Palmaine have no monopoly on acts of war.'

Alangba closed his eyes and drew in a deep breath. He swore oaths. He lived them. *Duty comes before death.*

He dropped to one knee. 'What do you need me to do, my lord?'

Mandla extended a hand to help Alangba to his feet. 'I want you to go to Basmine, Alangba, and break every chain. Remind the people what it is to have something to fight for. Remind them what it means to stand for something bigger than yourself.'

Ladan let out a small breath. 'He won't go alone.'

Mandla blinked twice. 'I do not expect him to. He would need the support of powerful shadowwielders, too. What better story to spark rebellion than the man who walks with a lion and the one who fights without a spear hand? Let the natives see what you are – what you have become. Let them remember that there is still power in the Way.'

Alangba's heart pounded. He was afraid and he could not be sure why. Ladan squeezed his hand and that seemed to ease his panic. He glanced at No Music who stood ready as the drawn-taut bowstring – the scars on his face were a life story in brief; a man born for battles.

'Who else will be on this team?'

Mandla scratched his ear. 'You'll know as soon as you accept this commission. It is a matter of the highest confidentiality.'

Alangba cast a glance at Ladan, whose jaw was tight with bristling purpose. Losing a limb was not an easy thing for even the strongest of men. Alangba had seen what the men of the coal mines had suffered after Zaminu maimed them. For some, it had been difficult to accept the impairment as something real – they existed in a state of outright denial for months and sometimes even years. For others, amputation made life itself obsolete and pointless. Alangba had seen the way Ladan trained – the man wanted to believe he was still the fighter he once had been. Wanted to feel useful and strong – needed to know that he still left a footprint in the world. *He needs this.*

Alangba's jaw tightened as he drew in a silent breath, then he dropped to one knee again and bowed his head. 'I accept. My Lord.'

13

A Chance

RUMI

Before the cockerel's first crow, Rumi was in the corridor headed for Mandla's room. He turned a corner and came face-to-face with Sameer.

Rumi raised an eyebrow. 'What are you doing here? It feels like I haven't seen your face in days. Why haven't you been in class?'

Sameer gave a start and stared for a long moment. 'I've been working on something. For Lord Mandla.'

'What?' Rumi asked.

Sameer hesitated, his eyes darting right, then left. 'It's to do with that thing I made a few months ago – the stink bomb. The one we set off in Lungelo's room.'

Rumi gasped. 'He knows we were responsible?'

Sameer grinned. 'He has always known, but don't worry, we are not going to get in trouble for it. He was glad I tested it in that way, he thinks it could be...' Sameer trailed off.

'Be what?' Rumi demanded.

Sameer dug his hands into his pocket. 'Don't mind me. What are *you* doing here?' he asked in a quicksilver change of subject.

'Tell me, Sameer,' Rumi said.

Sameer closed his eyes and lowered his chin. 'I cannot, Rumi.

Not yet. I'm not even allowed to attend mindwalking classes right now.'

Rumi gave his friend a considered look and accepted his secrecy with a long sigh. 'I am here to ask Lord Mandla a few questions.'

Sameer made a point of not asking for more information. His way of avoiding return fire with questions about his own visit.

'I see,' Sameer said.

A thought occurred to Rumi then. 'Sameer, there was something I read about, and I was wondering if you knew anything about it.'

Sameer raised an eyebrow. 'What might that be?'

'Do you know anything about... gateways to the Originate?'

'Like the one at the summit of Erin-Olu?' Sameer asked.

Rumi gave a start. 'You've heard about it?'

Sameer nodded and gave a sly smile. 'They call it the Door of Testimony. It is mentioned in half the old Mushiain books in the library. Mostly in stories about people who were lost trying to find it.'

'Does it really exist?' Rumi asked.

'I have no idea,' Sameer said, stroking his chin. 'There's a map of Erin-Olu in Mandla's room but he doesn't let anyone go near it.'

Rumi opened his mouth to speak then thought better of it.

'Mandla will never let you go looking for it,' Sameer said.

Rumi's jaw tightened. 'Why not?'

Sameer blinked, seemingly surprised by the question. 'Have you not heard about Jarishma?'

Rumi raised his chin as the memory of his near drowning in Jarishma's grove flashed across his mind. 'I have heard of him.'

'Well then, there's your answer. He will never let you go because of Jarishma.'

Rumi raised a questioning eyebrow but knew this was no time to seek a great exposition. Mandla was uncharacteristically free and that was an opportunity not to be missed. 'We have much to talk about when we next see each other, Sameer,' he said.

Sameer offered a kola nut. 'Bet on it.'

They broke kola nut, ate it in agreement and then parted ways.

Rumi continued to Mandla's door and drew in a deep breath.

Telemi answered the door before he knocked. 'Ajanla Erenteyo, how may I help you?'

Rumi cleared his throat. 'I would like to see Lord Mandla.'

Telemi frowned and opened his mouth to speak, when a deep, sonorous voice called from behind him. 'Let him come.'

Telemi made an irritated sound in his throat and muttered, 'Why do I even bother?' as he stepped aside and held the door open.

Mandla's chair was carved from a still-rooted tree, which gave it the appearance of something that had grown directly from the ground. At his side sat a golden lantern next to a thick wooden staff. His face was obscured by a thick, leather-bound book.

Rumi took a step forward and for the first time, noticed the picture on the book's thick cover. It depicted a man beneath a broken noose and a four-point star, screaming to the heavens. He gasped.

Mandla lowered the book just enough for Rumi to see his eyes. They seemed to glisten in the lantern light as he grinned. 'The Old Dog who still barks.'

Rumi bowed low and touched his toe in obeisance. 'I greet you, Lord Mandla.'

Mandla gestured to a vacant chair. 'You are wondering why I am reading the *Holy Book of Palman*, aren't you?'

Rumi gave a slow nod. 'It is a book filled with blasphemies against the gods of our ancestors.'

Mandla licked his teeth as he pressed the book slowly shut. 'It is also filled with knowledge and truth. When you eat agbalumo, you eat it whole – the bitter with the sweet; that is the beauty of life.'

'What truth is to be found in the *Book of Palman*?'

Mandla frowned. 'Where do you think their doctrine of the collective comes from? It is right here in their scripture.' Mandla cleared his throat to read, '"…it is the will of Palman for all humans to live in unity. Under the Son, there is neither rich nor poor, man nor woman, black nor white, for you are all one collective under God."'

Rumi frowned. 'Tell that to the natives who clean their temples.'

Mandla waved a finger. 'We live in a world of many colours, Ajanla. Nothing can be all bad. That is true of both the Palmaine and their religion. There are truths that run deep throughout their scripture.'

'All corrupted by one great lie. Palman is not the one true god. Their story says that Palman broke the noose of Dara and called upon fire beneath a four-point star. That all other gods were cast into the flames of hell. That is a lie.'

Mandla raised an eyebrow. 'We have the benefit of knowing that – but, of course, we have seen things that others have not.' He gestured to a painting at the far corner of the room. It depicted a bare-chested man standing with a great double-axe raised above his dog's-head helmet. A look of snarled ferocity on his face.

Xango.

Mandla's voice rose again. 'Our gods are fickle and quarrelsome, obsessed with their own infighting and conflict. They are aloof to us in ways that make it hard to muster faith. Palman places himself above them and dismisses the notion of competition. He is clear, direct, and promises a life of prosperity to all who follow his way. He doesn't ask for sacrifice, ceremony or flagellation, all he asks of his people is submission. He is a real and present god to them, and that is a truth we cannot ever deny.'

'You sound like a Palmaine priest,' Rumi said.

Mandla's jaw tightened. 'Palman's account is persuasive, but I have the benefit of knowing the superior argument. I bow to only one king. The author and the conclusion. The Dumaré-Adandan. The Dancing Lion. The destroyer of chains. Dara, the Skyfather, who first saw the world.'

Rumi shivered as Mandla spoke. He glanced up towards the painting of Xango at the corner of the room and his stomach tightened.

'May we be greater than all of our forebears,' Mandla said.

Rumi gave him a questioning look.

Mandla laughed. 'It is a goodwill prayer.'

Rumi pinched his nose as his face stiffened. 'Zarcanis told me something once – back when I had just joined the Shadow Order. She told me that the Mushiain word for human being is *yenina*.'

Mandla gave a firm nod. 'It means "the Chosen Ones".'

'She told me that any man can become a god, an agbara.'

'She spoke the truth.'

As Rumi flexed his fingers, his knuckles cracked sharply. 'How did Xango become an Agbara?'

'Perhaps he will tell you himself one day, when you read his book in the *Sakosaye*.'

Rumi thumbed at the bag beneath his eye. 'But how does it happen, Lord Mandla? How does a man become a god?'

Mandla's cheeks tightened and for a moment, Rumi thought he was going to lash out. But when he spoke, the man's voice was gentle and familiar as a village river. 'Stories, Rumi. They are what makes the temporal become eternal. For a person to ascend to the Celestial Palanquin, where only the agbara may sit, their name and story must be written in the hearts of humanity.'

'What does that mean?'

'It means that people worship you, that they praise you, that you inspire their deepest emotions – love, fear, hate, hope and pride.'

'So you have to be famous? There are many people who have become famous, but not all of them become gods. Walade the Widowmaker made grown men piss their pants when he lifted his sword – he never became an agbara. I knew a man called Tinu the Tiger who fought Bobiri until he was touching fifty and never lost a bout; they still sing his name, but he never became a god. Is there some sort of threshold or mark you have to meet? A certain number of worshippers? A distance your story has travelled?'

Mandla laughed. 'We are speaking of the affairs of eternal beings, Rumi, this is not science and arithmetic – things do not always make sense. The spiritual realm operates under different rules.'

'So you are telling me there is no way of truly knowing how a man becomes a god?'

Mandla nodded. 'We all reach for the skies but only a chosen few ever touch them. There is blood in the matter – of that we can be sure. Xango's father was Gu, the agbara of iron and war. The son became the agbara of thunder, so we see there was strength in the bloodline. Our blood contains the testimony of our ancestors. But there is no straight-line path to become an agbara — at least not that I have ever known.'

Rumi glanced up at the painting of Xango again, scratching at his chin.

Mandla's voice seemed to drop an octave. 'You must be wondering if there is some great burden on your shoulders because you carry the blood of an agbara.'

Rumi blinked. 'It has crossed my mind.'

'Follow the path that Dara has cleared for you. That is all anyone can do to live a good life. Imagine yourself as one that can become unstoppable — not in the sense of raw power or unbridled ambition, but as a wholeness of soul and mind that nothing can diminish. Follow the Way.'

Rumi lowered his voice and mimicked, 'Follow the Way.' *As though it is the damned mainland road. What does 'the Way' even really mean?*

He refrained from asking aloud.

Mandla regarded him with a sly grin and closed the *Book of Palman*. 'How is your own reading coming along?' Mandla asked.

He was referring of course to the *Sakosaye*. The living word of the Darani; almanac of the agbara.

'I read Shuni's book,' Rumi began.

Mandla nodded. 'And what did you learn from it?'

Rumi leaned forward as though speaking a secret. 'That Shirayo, daughter of Dara and the twin sister of Palman, still lives. That she carries the gift of music and has lost the power to speak and call names forth.'

Mandla nodded. 'An important story for you to understand.'

'Why do you say that?' Rumi asked.

'Because everything has both a spiritual and a temporal component, Irumide. We face a war in the temporal realm that will test us to our core, but we face something even greater in the spiritual realm.'

'The tribulation of gods?'

Mandla frowned. 'The Son of Despair and the so-called tribulation of gods is false doctrine. What we face is entirely different. A contest that began long before the world came into being.'

'Between Dara and Billisi?'

Mandla gave a nod. 'In a manner of speaking, yes. Palman stands for Billisi but the question we have to ask ourselves is – who stands for Dara?'

'It must be Shirayo. She's the only one that makes sense.'

'What did I just tell you about the spiritual realm, Irumide?'

Rumi lowered his chin. 'Things do not always make sense.'

Mandla grinned. 'Precisely. Now, that is enough about religion. I know you came here to ask other questions – I would like to hear them before our time is up.'

Rumi raised his chin, stealing another quick glance at the book. 'I have two things I wanted to talk to you about.'

'Easiest first,' Mandla said, thumbing his throat apple.

'I have a friend, a sentry, who I think would be an excellent addition to the Shadow Order. In times like these, we need all the good fighters we can get.'

Mandla raised an eyebrow. 'I presume you are talking about Nataré?'

Rumi nodded. 'Yes.'

Mandla arched his back in his chair and let out a loud breath. 'Nataré is indeed an excellent fighter, but she is not one for the Shadow Order. In every sense, she is the essence of a sentry. She watches. She waits. She knows the forest as well as anyone. We lose more than we gain in admitting her to the Shadow Order. There are many who can wield a sword and swing it well, but how many can make out figures in the full dark? How many sleep light as a feather without a full night's rest? We need people like Nataré watching our backs. I fear also that her shadow, if we can unlock it, may be too dark for her to control. I know she wants a glorious redemption but it won't be through the Order.'

Rumi frowned. Mandla was right. Nataré had a watchfulness that few could match and as a tracker was unrivalled amongst the sentry. She would never be as great a shadowwielder as she was a sentry.

He cleared his throat. 'I only ask that you consider it, Lord Mandla – it is what she wants and as you know more than I, sometimes it is better to let people decide for themselves what is best for themselves.'

Mandla's eyes widened and he blinked twice in consideration, then he drew in a breath and let it out in a short blast. 'She brought a forbidden charm within our walls. Sentries above all should know the danger in that. She will *never* be a part of the Shadow Order.'

'Everyone makes bad decisions, Lord Mandla.'

'And every decision has a consequence.'

'Lord Mandla—'

'That is my final answer, Ajanla.'

Rumi took a moment, then lifted his gaze. 'I understand. May I ask my second question – it is to do with something I read in the *Sakosaye*.'

Mandla leaned forward. 'Go on.'

'The *Book of Aja* says that there is a gateway at the summit of Erin-Olu that leads directly to the Originate.'

Mandla sat perfectly still, offering no confirmation or denial. 'I'm listening.'

'Well,' Rumi said, scratching his cheek. 'I want to know if it is true. If such a gateway truly exists.'

Mandla rolled his shoulders and let out a sharp exasperated breath. 'The Door of Testimony. Jarishma has spent half his life searching for it.'

'So it *does* exist?' Rumi asked.

'Nothing written in the *Sakosaye* is untrue. If Aja's word speaks to its existence, then I believe that at one time it certainly existed. As to when and how, I cannot say for sure.'

Rumi narrowed his eyes. 'So, let us assume it does exist – would it be possible to pull someone from the Originate into the Lower World?'

Mandla closed his eyes for a long moment before he spoke. 'Irumide, I understand that you grieve your mother's loss but there is no good sense in risking your life to try to call her back from the Originate.'

Rumi's mouth was agape. 'My mother?'

Mandla narrowed his eyes in confusion before he realised what he had said. 'Of course,' he said flatly. 'You were thinking about your brother.'

'You mean to tell me there is a chance to call my mother back too?'

Mandla pinched the bridge of his nose. 'Rumi, we have many challenges to face right now. This isn't the time to lose focus.'

'So, there is a chance then,' Rumi said.

Mandla's voice cut through the air like a blade. 'Leave now.'

When Mandla was angry, he didn't raise his voice; he lowered it. Now his voice was almost a growl. It was only the second time Rumi had felt genuine ire come from Mandla. It was like being burned for the very first time. The age-old instinct of forgotten beatings told him to get gone before Mandla's fury rose to a crescendo. He bowed low and backtracked from the room. 'Thank you, Lord Mandla.'

He gave no answer as Rumi left. There was no debating it – if there was a chance to get his family back Rumi would take it. Nothing else mattered.

14

The Darkman Rises

RUMI

Zarcanis raised her safespear high and looked down at Rumi with a note of disappointment. She had beaten night and day out of him, but stood with a face completely bereft of any hint of triumph. 'You're distracted,' she said. 'What is it?'

Rumi sat up and stretched out a hand. 'Nothing.'

She pulled him up and let out an exasperated sigh. 'Don't make a song and stanza about it. Just tell me what it is and we can see how to help you.'

Rumi scratched at his cheek. 'Some of the Suli have started rumours about me.'

Zarcanis angled her chin up. 'Like what?'

'That I didn't really face the Priest of Vultures. That I didn't beat Yomiku, either. They are saying I am just Mandla's paper champion. That I don't deserve to be in the Shadow Order.'

Zarcanis narrowed her eyes. 'Some people have to pull a man down to feel tall. Their opinions shouldn't matter. But you knew that already – I insult you every day and you have finally learned to let it wash over you. What is *really* bothering you?'

Rumi closed his eyes and drew in a breath. Zarcanis was inevitable. She could read emotions the way most could read storybooks.

'I read something...' Rumi said. 'About a gateway at the summit of Erin-Olu.'

Zarcanis nodded slowly. 'The Door of Testimony.'

Rumi snorted. 'So, everyone in the Eredo has heard about this but me?'

'So it would seem. There are babies who are bored sick of that rumour.'

'It's just a rumour?'

Zarcanis shrugged. 'Jarishma left to find it and hasn't come back since. There must be something he has seen that's keeping him there. He would have returned otherwise. We all thought he was dead until you turned up with his blessing.'

'So, you think it exists?'

'If I was a betting woman, yes. Just damned hard to get to.'

Rumi lowered his head, unconsciously gathering his right hand into a fist.

Zarcanis frowned. 'Oh no, you've got that look again.'

'What look?'

'The precious little hero-boy look you got when you were trying to get revenge on your mother's killer.' She pinched the bridge of her nose. 'You're thinking of going, aren't you?'

'Wouldn't you?' Rumi asked.

She narrowed her eyes. 'Probably.'

Rumi was surprised by her answer. He had been near certain she would ridicule him for wanting to go.

'Erin-Olu is an old place with ancient magic. The higher you climb, the less likely it is that you ever return. Only go if you can come to terms with never seeing my face again,' Zarcanis said with the hint of a smile.

Rumi grinned. 'Now you're just goading me to go.'

They both laughed. At a gesture, Rumi followed her towards

the botanical ward. It had become almost a custom for them after sparring.

Zarcanis held the door open for him. 'You pretend you want a solution but what you really want is sympathy,' she said. 'If you are looking for my encouragement, Rumi, you won't get it. Erin-Olu has been death to far more experienced explorers than you.'

She drew in a heavy breath. 'But I won't stop you from going, either. You are at your best when you are driven by something and have a goal that focuses all your restless energy. I have no use for you if you are going to spend our sessions daydreaming about the Door of Testimony, so perhaps you *should* go.'

'Tell me one thing,' Rumi said. 'If the Door of Testimony does exist, do you think that I can make it there?'

She gave Rumi a long, appraising look, then lowered her chin. 'I didn't think you could beat Yomiku, but you did. I didn't think you could defeat the Priest of Vultures, but you did. I'm done doubting you, Rumi. Your story is one of endless surprises.'

Rumi thought he saw the whisper of a smile on her lips when, suddenly, Uroma and half a dozen botanicals walked in. They were carrying the mangled body of a man whose clothes were soaked through with blood. The man was a Truetree by the looks of it.

'Who is that?' Rumi asked, watching them cart the shadow-wielder away.

Zarcanis quirked up an eyebrow. 'That is Latun. One of the Truetrees who went to get Oké water from the summit of Erin-Olu.'

'Doesn't look like a successful trip.'

Abruptly, an almighty cry of alarm rang out from one of the other wards. Rumi glanced over his shoulder just as Zarcanis slipped into *panther stalks the rabbit*.

He followed her, his senses pulsing with the awareness of a shadow unleashed. It was the trembling, merciless power of a shadowwielder with the strength to bring down buildings.

Zarcanis sniffed at the air and went still.

Rumi glanced at her. 'What is it?'

She straightened. 'That shadow is *familiar*.'

She turned sharply left and pushed a door open. For a moment, they both stood agape. Griff, Rumi's father, stood with arms aloft and bandages falling from his naked form. Oozing from his skin was an outrageous eruption of blistering shadow. Enough to kill with a blow. The air was thick with it and Griff's eyes had gone ink-black. He looked, in a word, triumphant. Utterly so. *This is why he was once so feared, why they called him the darkman.*

Two helpless botanicals stood with hands raised to protect themselves.

'He's burning too much shadow,' Rumi said, raising a hand to cover his eyes.

Zarcanis didn't answer. Instead, she closed the distance between them in a single stride and touched Griff's face. 'Put that thing away, you're scaring people.'

Her voice, quiet as a whisper, seemed to draw all the shadow away and Griff's eyes went wide with new awareness.

Smiling, he whispered low. 'Zaiyana.'

She frowned. 'Don't.'

Griff's smile disappeared and his shadow dissolved into a shiny pool of blackness before returning to its typical shape. He bent forward and exhaled as though for the first time ever, then dropped to a knee. Only then did Rumi notice the scars across his body – thick lines of sealed skin that were dark as oil. Rumi let out a silent gasp. *They sealed his wounds with shadow.*

This man had dined with death, cheek to cheek. Yet here he

was, alive and breathing, due to an almost unimaginable use of shadow.

Rumi was stunned but Zarcanis did not look even a little surprised.

'How do you feel?' she asked, almost casually.

Griff rolled his shoulders and grunted. 'Worse than I ever have but I'll be back with time.'

Zarcanis turned to the two botanicals. 'Get him some Oké water.'

The botanicals glanced at each other nervously, but didn't move.

Zarcanis's eyes darkened with shadow. 'Now,' she said.

The botanicals took off running.

Griff coughed. 'Don't be so hard on them.'

Zarcanis blinked and gave Griff a sharp look. 'They know their work but sometimes need to be pushed.'

Griff glanced at Rumi. 'I am guessing we won the battle?'

Rumi drew in breath. 'We did,' he said, without a note of triumph.

Zarcanis narrowed her eyes. 'Rumi killed the Priest of Vultures.'

Griff's eyes widened as he regarded Rumi. 'How?

Rumi answered honestly. 'I don't completely understand it myself. I attacked his shadowmind with everything I had. I felt... agbara power, but only for a moment.'

Zarcanis blinked. 'You broke him from the inside.'

'Incredible,' Griff said. 'That must have been some emotion.'

Rumi gave a slow nod. 'It was.'

The corner of Griff's mouth tightened slightly as he shifted his leg. 'I'm...' He hesitated. 'I'm so proud of you.' He bit his tongue.

Rumi knew he wanted to call him 'son' but wasn't sure if he had earned the privilege yet. The truth was that he had not – but not all that is given is earned. Rumi cleared his throat. 'Thank you, Father.'

As he said it, it was as though a weight had been lifted from his chest and he was finally able to breathe in clean air.

Griff winced as though struck, straightening to his full height. He looked at Rumi and though he didn't smile, he radiated a warmth that could not go unnoticed. 'Right then,' he said, sniffing as he dabbed the corner of his eye. 'I had better find some clothes.'

Zarcanis didn't move. 'I knew that love was what was strongest in you when I heard you play your drums,' she said to Rumi. 'You will always be at your best when you choose love over fear. When you risk the nettle to touch the flower. There is a song within you playing all the time and you will always be better when you listen before you scream. I suppose that song is why you want to go after the Door of Testimony.'

Griff gave a start. 'What?'

'I only asked if it exists,' Rumi said.

'Does he know about Jarishma?' Griff asked.

Zarcanis shook her head. 'I was trying to tell him.'

'What about Jarishma?' Rumi asked.

Griff drew in breath. 'Jarishma was once an elite member of the Shadow Order. He could do things with the shadow that most of us could only dream of. We all looked up to him – Mandla most of all.'

Zarcanis looked away, as though not wanting to hear the next part.

'He had a daughter named Molewa, barely thirteen years old.'

Rumi lowered his chin, guessing where the story would lead. 'She died?' he whispered.

Griff gave a solemn nod. 'She and some friends somehow found their way into the armoury and thought to take a few turns swinging the weapons in there.' Griff let out a breath. 'Molewa picked up the late King Olu's spear. A weapon touched with deep juju. The weapons of the old Kasinabe kings have an *isakaba* charm over them; if anyone not of the blood touches the weapon of a king, they would have a sudden urge to impale themselves.'

Zarcanis heaved in a breath. 'The Eredo trembled to its foundation when Jarishma saw her body.'

'He was never the same,' Griff said. 'Mandla begged him to stay, but he couldn't be reasoned with. He left to find the Door of Testimony to bring Molewa back. And he hasn't returned since.'

Rumi closed his eyes as his mind brought to memory the man he had met in the Nyme forest, with eyes tattooed on his chest. It was only because of Jarishma's blessing that Rumi had ever been let into the Shadow Order.

Griff seemed to read his mind. 'If Jarishma could not find the Door of Testimony, then I doubt anyone can.'

Rumi narrowed his eyes and tapped his foot impatiently. 'Doubts are made to be overcome.'

Griff tilted his neck until it clicked on each side. 'Rumi you are a Suli and only barely so. You know very little about the shadow. Hardly anything about the deep juju that runs in darkness. You could kill yourself just by eating the wrong fruit in the forest. Besides, everyone knows there is something dark in Erin-Olu.'

'Something like what?' Rumi asked.

Griff glanced at Zarcanis then back at Rumi. 'Some say it is a god. Some say it is some kind of spirit. Some even say it is Ojuju Calabar, the Yellow Masquerade.'

Rumi barked a laugh. 'You actually had me worried for a moment there. The Yellow Masquerade? Ojuju Calabar? What next will you tell me? Watch out for the iroko man?'

Griff's expression didn't change. 'Ojuju Calabar is not just a scary story Rumi.'

'Says who?' Rumi asked. 'Have you seen him?'

Griff frowned.

'How about you, Zarcanis? Have you seen the Fearsome Yellow Masquerade?'

Zarcanis rolled her eyes. 'Sometimes your skull seems such an empty place. We are trying to tell you to forget it, Rumi. What part of "move on" don't you get?'

Rumi narrowed his eyes. 'If you had ever loved someone – truly loved them – perhaps you would understand.'

'Is it really about love, Rumi? Is it? Or is it about your guilt?'

Rumi was about to fire off his retort when Griff let out a raspy cough, spattering blood. Then, abruptly, he choked. Zarcanis moved with startling speed. In a blink, she was at his side. She tucked a hand under his arm and steadied him. 'Where are those damned botanicals?'

'We're here.'

The two botanicals returned with what must have been less than half a cup of Oké water. Griff drank it slowly and drew in a deep breath.

'He needs more,' Zarcanis said.

'That's all we can give for now,' one of the botanicals replied. 'There are many people still wounded here and our supply of Oké water is nearly tapped out.'

'What about Latan and the Truetrees who went to get some?' Zarcanis asked.

'Latan was the only one who returned. They were ... unsuccessful.'

A thought struck Rumi then, and he almost jumped as it hit him.

The darkman gritted his teeth and straightened. 'I'm fine,' he said, brushing himself down.

Zarcanis's face was a picture of concern. For one of the first times Rumi had ever seen, she looked gentle as she helped the darkman to full height again.

'I'm fine,' Griff said again, more to himself than to anyone else.

He was anything but fine. How could he be? Most would have died from the wounds that had left broad scars across his body. He needed Oké water and lots of it.

Rumi met Zarcanis's eye, lowering his voice so only she could hear him. 'The darkman is going to need Oké water. It is at the summit of Erin-Olu, too. Not far from where the Door of Testimony is supposed to be.'

Zarcanis frowned. 'It's a suicide mission.'

Rumi raised his chin. 'No one will want to go up there. Not when they see what happened to Latan. Without Oké water the darkman will die. Someone needs to go up there – someone who will stop at nothing to get to the summit. Someone full of surprises.'

She gave him a long, contemplative look, then shook her head slowly. 'Lord Mandla will never *let* you go.'

Rumi wasn't entirely sure, but he thought as she spoke, she had placed particular emphasis on the word 'let'.

'I'll need a map,' Rumi said.

They locked eyes and she nodded once. 'I long for the day you get tired of chasing death.'

That night, when others were fast asleep, Rumi read from Kuda Kamo's *Letters From the Fires of Hell*.

'On the long road to Hell, there are many signs to turn back but people choose to stay the course. For even in Hell, there is solace in the fraternity of the fallen,' Rumi whispered. He sat up slightly and glanced over his shoulder – the last Suli had finally fallen asleep. Slamming the book shut, Rumi called his shadow. The power embraced him like a spurned lover at reconciliation. His hands trembled as he firmed his grip on it.

He had pushed himself to his limits before and found new ones. He had dedicated himself to his craft as the lioness to the hunt. That time had come again – the time to drop everything in pursuit of a higher office. Somewhere in Erin-Olu lay a gateway to his brother Morire, and if he had to face a nightmare to find it, he would. Nothing would sit or stand in his way. He swore on his mother's soul. On her mother's soul. On everything.

He closed his eyes, gathering shadow as he drew in a preparatory breath. 'Whatever it takes,' he whispered to himself.

15

Balance

RENIKE

Renike set her foot back and bent her knees to find her balance. *Kiwinje* was a game they had played often in preparation to become Seedlings. It was simple – two people stood across from one another on a thin bench, armed with straw clubs; the winner was the first to knock the other from the bench.

Renike liked kiwinje because there were so many ways to win. You did not have to be the strongest or the fastest to defeat a more athletic opponent. There was space for timing and precision and intellect. All the things that Renike felt were her own strengths.

Zarcanis had drilled so much into her. How to shift the forms to serve herself. 'To turn curses into gifts.' She held her straw club away from her side, allowing her to swing at the perfect angle of her shoulder – just as the Viper had taught her.

Her opponent was a boy called Jaja. One of the more experienced Seedlings, with four lines of shadow rank to match N'Goné. You could see from the thick ridges of muscle along his arm that he was dedicated to the craft. He bowed low with hands clasped in a show of respectful greeting. Renike clasped her hands and responded in kind.

Chief Gaitan, who served as umpire, stepped back from the

bench as the two raised their straw clubs. He cleared his throat and spoke loud. 'Engage.'

Jaja took a tentative step forward, with his club pulled back over his shoulder. That made Renike inwardly proud. He did not underestimate her – as so many others did. She took her own step forward, careful to maintain her balance.

Jaja darted forward with a gust of speed and swiped at her foreleg. She shuffled back out of range, her foot kissing the edge of the bench. *Balance is everything.* Jaja's eyes widened with her so close to the brink. He heaved in a breath and rushed in to finish the work.

Renike grinned, knowing by instinct exactly what to do. She leaned forward heavily on her lead leg, offering him an irresistible target. He took the bait and she sold him a feint to bamboozle the agbara. As he swung, she leaped forward in a dancer's bound, clearing his shoulder as he smashed thin air. She whirled with the club, almost delicately, striking his back as he was overextended forward. Momentum was his sworn enemy and he stumbled forward, trying to stop himself toppling over.

'Well fought,' Renike said, as she swung with all her strength.

Jaja went over the edge, falling face-first into the soft cushions around the bench.

'Winner!' Gaitan cried. 'Rain again.'

He raised her hand and she grinned as she stepped down from the bench, elated.

'Who would like to go up against her next?' Gaitan asked.

No one answered right away. Renike had proven herself to be proficient at kiwinje and some of the best shadowwielders were not prepared to risk losing to her in front of the entire class. She was confident she could beat most of them, but the one person she did not want to step forward was Kharmine.

Kharmine was a tall, gangly, fair-skinned man with hair cut

short enough to see a stitched-up scar that ran from the top of his skull down to his collarbone. He was softborn too, though no one treated him as though he was anything soft. In her time in the Shadow Order, Renike had never once heard his voice. He was avoided in the fighting pit because he fought with angry intensity and when he punched, it was with concussive force. He had never lost – not once. Not even come close to losing. He wasn't the most elegant shadowdancer but it was clear he carried something spiteful inside him.

'Anyone?' Gaitan asked again.

Kharmine shrugged and stepped forward. Without speaking, his point was clear – if no one else will, I'll do it.

Gaitan frowned. 'Ah.'

Kharmine bared his teeth and bent forward in a stretch. Renike hated the fact that his smile made her slightly afraid. She had been trained by Zarcanis – she would not be anyone's easy prey.

'Let's go,' she said, gesturing at him with her chin.

Kharmine grinned at her confidence as he hefted his straw club and followed her onto the bench.

Gaitan raised a hand. 'Ready?'

They both nodded.

'Raise your clubs.'

They obeyed.

Gaitan dropped his hand. 'Engage.'

What happened next was so sudden that Renike had trouble putting the pieces of it together. One moment, she stood with her club held in a cross-guard stance; in the next she was staring up at the ceiling. When Kharmine struck with the straw club, it hit like a tree trunk. It wasn't just that he was fast, but his power was staggering for a man of his age.

She let out a breath, gathering her bearings. Kharmine

extended a hand to help her up. She accepted it, staring at him as she did.

He gave her a respectful nod and walked away.

Gaitan patted Renike on the back. 'Good effort.'

It didn't feel like a good effort at all.

The class continued, but Renike's gaze would repeatedly wander back to Kharmine. He seemed almost bored all the time – only half listening. Yet there was something alert and watchful about him. It was as though his learning was of a different kind to everyone else.

Abruptly, he turned towards her and met her gaze, his eyes dark and endless. There was no running from it – Kharmine terrified her. He didn't look away, his expression a dire threat. Though she was afraid, she was also Odu and it would not do her father's pride to look away. So, she hardened her stare, raised her chin and matched him hate for hate. He held her gaze for a long moment, then smiled and looked away.

'What was that about?' N'Goné murmured from beside her.

Renike leaned back and let out a breath. 'The future. He wants to know if I'm the sort of flower that breaks in the strong wind.'

N'Goné laughed. 'What was it you said to Zarcanis again – You're not a flower at all. You're an iroko tree.'

16

The Head of the Snake

LETHI

Lethi leaned back in his chair and glanced up at the portrait above his office door. It depicted Meladron, the first archangel of Palman, holding a stone tablet in one hand and a shining sceptre in the other. Meladron was known as the scribe of God who recorded the rights and wrongs of all people. Though he was not mentioned in the *Holy Book of Palman*, several Palmanic texts had made mention of him – Meladron, the keeper of the watch. The great archangel who sees all. Handwritten in cursive below the picture were the words, 'Beware the rage of angels'.

Naming his Temple Knights the Meladroni was something only a man like Zaminu would do. Zaminu was born on the continent to travelling missionaries. After returning to Palmaine with his parents, he had come back to the continent in his adulthood as a philanthropist, eager to spread the benefits of the Palman religion. That had been his first disguise. Before long he'd had the patronage of both the crown and the four-point star to bring the four kingdoms under Palmaine rule. Lethi had read Zaminu's book, *The Mandate of the Light*, twice. The old governor-general saw himself as a soldier-priest. He was a master of mixing the spiritual with the temporal to bind people to his cause. Failing to meet your quotas was not simply an act of laziness or inefficiency; Zaminu called it an act of disobedience to God. He portrayed his atrocities as a thing of glory, for he acted under the mandate of the light; the everlasting aegis of spiritual justice.

Lethi frowned as he glanced up at the painting. The archangel Meladron seemed totally at peace. Lethi was the opposite.

The half-full decanter of wine on Lethi's desk had kept his mood level in the hours he had spent alone. He poured out another measure and threw it back with a single gulp. Setting his glass down, he let out a long, exhausted breath, then hiccupped as the door swung open and slapped against the wall.

Azamon stepped inside. His shirtsleeves were speckled with what looked like blood and his collar was rumpled at the neckline.

'We've found him,' Azamon announced, slamming the door shut behind him.

Lethi reached for his glass again. 'Found who?'

'The leader of the Black Hammer Clan. The one we captured just gave him up. Told us his location and everything.'

Lethi poured more wine and took another long gulp. 'How do you know his information is reliable?'

Azamon gave a dismissive sneer. 'He wouldn't lie to me.'

Lethi glanced at the stained shirtsleeves. 'Do you have any other information that corroborates what he has told you?'

'Oh, don't you worry about that. The bastard's babbling was corroboration enough, trust me.'

Lethi didn't trust him. In fact, what he felt for the man was as far from trust as east was from west, but he could ill afford to make an enemy of Zaminu's son. Illegitimate or not, it was plain that Zaminu placed some faith in the man. Lethi drew in a breath and poured out the last of his wine.

'Where is he? The leader?' he asked.

'In the south,' Azamon said. 'A village called Oké-Dar. One of those one-whore slums where they still hang tree-charms on their doors. We won't face much opposition when we go in.'

Lethi raised an eyebrow. 'There's only one road fit for carriages that far south. It's a few hours from the Citadel as well.'

Azamon made a dismissive gesture with his hand. 'Don't tell me you're scared of a few bush natives?'

Lethi scratched his nose, offering no immediate response to what he knew was an attempt to bait him. 'A little caution always helps.'

'Didn't you say you wanted to sever the head of the snake? This is our chance. We have the snake in our sights. If we ride fast we can be in Oké-Dar tonight,' Azamon said.

'A snake is a poisonous creature. Cunning and elusive. You have to be careful before you strike. Certain.'

'This is no time for your Guyarican shilly-shallying. Not with a war coming,' Azamon hissed. 'Our mission is to destroy the Black Hammer Clan once and for all. They pose no threat to us – we ride on them tonight with enough force and we'll have the Black Hammer Clan dead within a week.'

'Tonight?' Lethi asked, confused.

Azamon nodded. 'Tonight. The carriages will be ready in an hour and we're riding south – you can stay here if you wish.' He turned towards the door, muttering as he left, 'And they said you were a soldier.' He slammed the door shut.

Lethi let out another exasperated breath. The man was a fool to be sure, but there was some truth in what he said. Zaminu wanted the Black Hammer Clan gone fast. The bishop did too. They would probably both side with Azamon on this. It was also true that there was little chance of the Black Hammer Clan posing much of a threat to a heavy, well-trained and armed battalion of the consular guard. If Azamon rode south alone and succeeded, it would be the end of Lethi's expedition in Basmine and a huge blow to his attempts to rise in rank.

He rose to his feet, grabbing the edge of the desk to steady himself. He had drunk a little too much wine. Shaking his head clear, he pulled on his jacket and spun around the room. *Where did I leave that damned rifle?*

Less than an hour later, Lethi stepped outside. There were four carriages ready to depart. Each carriage could take about ten people and the two waiting were chock-full of consular guard. A further twenty or so men were on horseback, dressed in full battle uniform. They were chatty and boisterous with the promise of violence. Here was their chance to unleash their anger on some unsuspecting natives and they were giddy with it.

Lethi's fire team of Dareem, Banasco, Attem and Roadie were in the third carriage. He returned their salute through the window as he strode past. Azamon sat alone in the bishop's carriage. Lethi joined him and they set off south.

To his credit, Azamon did not share the cocksure cheer of the consular guard. He seemed focused and pensive, deeply set on his desire to root out the Black Hammer Clan.

Lethi studied the man. Perhaps there was more to it than that. A desperation to impress his father. To prove that he was more than just half an Alharan.

Lethi sat still, his chin angled to glance out the window as they slipped onto the mainland road. 'Did you grow up in Basmine?' he asked.

Azamon moved with the slowness of a statue just now brought to life. 'I did,' he said. 'I wanted to visit Palmaine but...' He hesitated. 'It wasn't possible.'

Lethi looked at his face and knew almost immediately. Saw it plain as mud on a tablecloth. Azamon was no fool, he knew the risk even in this. It was like looking at an old portrait of his own pain. The unspoken ache of men not beloved by their fathers.

The pain of knowing you were a little bit unwanted. Lethi didn't need to hear Azamon say another word to know what drove him. They were different men – if Lethi was the straight and narrow, Azamon was the wide and twisting – but in this pain, they were closer than kin. He could read it in his set jaw and thrown-back shoulders. The man was so desperate to impress that he would take any risk – the Black Hammer Clan must have seemed like the wall blocking his path to joy, and at the same time a route to success.

'Do you have any brothers and sisters?' Lethi asked.

Azamon's face hardened. 'Not from the same mother, no. My half-siblings are in Palmaine, they've never been here.'

Lethi winced. Zaminu had probably never told his other children he had a son in Basmine. Lethi knew how, to the Palmaine, this could be a different world. One where rules were not real rules and wives were not real wives. The things Palmaine did in Basmine were not things they would have the temerity to do anywhere else.

The carriage swayed roughly and Lethi was reminded just how wine-drunk he was. Narrowing his eyes, he gave Azamon a searching look. 'It must have been difficult. Growing up here. Away from half your family.'

Azamon blinked. 'I had my mother. She did her best.'

'How does she feel about—'

'No,' Azamon hissed, raising a hand. 'I would like to focus on the night ahead, if you don't mind.'

Lethi nodded. 'Of course.'

Azamon glanced down at his weapon. 'Governor-General Zaminu gave us one instruction tonight, don't waste bullets – like the old days.'

Lethi narrowed his eyes. He had heard of this policy before, back when Zaminu was squashing rebellions.

Under Zaminu's command, to prove that no bullets had been wasted, a Palmaine soldier of the consular guard was required to present the severed hand of each rebel killed. As a result, cartloads of severed hands came back after each fight against the rebels. It was said that soldiers who had bad aim would take to cutting off the hands of the living to present as justification for their misfiring. For some reason, Zaminu went crazy about lopping off hands after that – every indiscretion was reason enough for maiming. Disobedience, inefficiency, indecency.

The carriage had gone silent and they rode without another word for the span of several hours. At last, in the small hours of the morning, they turned off the mainland road and came to a stop just shy of the Oké-Dar gates.

Azamon dismounted and moved directly to address the gathered consular guard. There must have been almost forty of them – all armed with intent to kill. They had brought along a brass cylindrical cannon with a ring at the cascabel to aid accuracy and manage recoil. Azamon had not come for stealth. He had come to make a statement.

Lethi took the opportunity to speak with his own team. He met Attem's eye and gestured towards the slum. 'What do you think?'

Attem sniffed at the air. 'Too quiet. They are watchful. Waiting.'

Lethi gave a solemn nod. 'So, an ambush then?'

Attem shrugged. 'No, I don't think so. Something else.'

'Do you want a first look?'

Attem considered the question for a long moment, then nodded. 'Yes.'

Lethi turned to where Azamon was addressing some of the consular guard. A few had left to surround the place, but over a dozen had remained with their rifles at the ready. As Lethi strode up to them he heard the words, 'show no mercy'.

He waited for Azamon to finish, then gestured for his attention.

'What is it?' he said, striding up to Lethi.

'Let my man go in there first – have a look around, just to make sure there is no ambush.'

Azamon glanced over his shoulder. 'Which one?'

'The native,' Lethi said.

Azamon snorted. 'No chance.'

'He can see things that we won't. He knows them better than we do.'

Azamon shook his head. 'We go in once. Hard and fast. Turn the place upside down. Burn it if we have to. We'll find them.'

Lethi opened his mouth to argue, then decided against it. This was Azamon's moment – his chance to prove himself. He would do anything to have it.

Lethi frowned and lowered his head. 'If you insist.'

Azamon nodded to himself, satisfied with this small triumph. He turned towards the consular guard and raised his voice. 'We have them surrounded. Storm the place and kill anyone who offers armed opposition. The leader of the Black Hammer Clan is in there and I expect to ride back to the Citadel with his head.'

The consular gave a muted cheer as they moved into formation. Lethi slowly shook his head. Most of the consular had faced street brigands and drunks as their greatest peril. They had no true knowledge of what it meant to meet armed opposition – men and women who were ready to die for what they believed in. Natives or no, if they thought this was a time to smile then they were in for a rude shock.

Azamon gave the signal and they marched towards the gate.

They moved in perfect rank, almost perfectly synchronised as they strode forward. Lethi and his team were an utter mess by comparison, but battles weren't won by the prettiest marchers.

A few paces from the gate, the town watchman appeared. He walked as though just awoken from sleep, his entire body swaying as he raised his spear to halt them.

'Stop,' he called out.

Azamon gave a bored yawn. 'Open the gate. We come under the authority of the Eye of the Light.'

The watchman didn't seem to flinch at that. 'That is no authority here.' He hoisted his spear. 'Go in peace.'

Azamon frowned and reached into a jacket. He produced a brilliant four-point star emblem and raised it high. 'Open the gates... now.'

The watchman scoffed at the symbol and cleared his throat. 'My Lord, this is Oké-Dar, I cannot—'

A gunshot rang off and the watchman's stomach exploded. The spear fell from his hand as he stumbled forward clutching his split gut.

'Demons,' the watchman screamed.

Demons. It was what they called them in Guyarica, what they would call them here. Lethi lowered his head and raised his rifle. *Demons it is then.*

Azamon seemed to grin at being called a demon. 'At the count of three,' he said, raising his hand.

Lethi reached for his rifle and found his shoulder disappointingly empty. He had left it in the carriage.

'One,' Azamon said.

Lethi took off at a run to retrieve his rifle.

'Two,' came the shout, just as Lethi reached the carriage door.

'Three!'

The sound of the cannon filled the air and there was a

wailing, ugly crash of such reverberant noise that it took Lethi a moment to realise where he was.

A loud cry of alarm rang out as the first line of consular burst through the gates. A gunshot signalled the likely demise of another native. All at once, chaos had come.

Lethi snatched up his rifle and scampered back out. He had lost his team, but this was no time for coordination. As soon as the cannon fired, the outcomes had changed.

'Long live the king!' someone shouted, and the clap of gunfire followed the salute.

Lethi sprinted towards the fighting, his eyes straining to catch any movement in the night. The mind played games at the highest moments. Every sound seemed sinister, every movement seemed with motive to murder. Lethi was terrified and focused all at once.

Screams ripped the air ahead. Lethi knew what a massacre looked and sounded like, and this had the makings of one. The screams were of that pitch. The gunshots came at that frequency.

Fire-red light flared. A house had been set alight, illuminating the night sky. The consular were wasting no time doing their worst.

A screaming man ran towards Lethi with a spear raised high. A gunshot cracked and the man's head was half blown off.

Another building went up in flames. Whoever was doing the burning was making quick work of it.

Ahead, Azamon stood behind a half dozen consular guard who were breaking down the doors to a squat drinking parlour. The doors must have been barred across the middle for they repelled every effort to force entry. Scrawled in the wood above the door were the words 'Mama Ayeesha'.

'Take it off at the hinges,' Azamon said, when he saw the door wouldn't budge.

The consular obliged and almost immediately managed to break the door open.

'Move,' Azamon snarled, pointing into the drinking parlour. His men obeyed. Each one of them was consumed by the gnarled hate that came only in the teeth of full violence. Lethi had seen this place before. The place where dignity died. When life and death hung in the balance and the anchors of decency had given way to pure feral instinct.

They spilled into the room like hyena, jittery at every sign of life. A man cowered under a faraway table, pleading mercy. He got none. They shot through his upraised hand and the shrapnel ripped his skull.

There was something strange about it all. *Where are all the people? There should be more people than this.*

Azamon didn't seem to care. He moved to the head of the host, shoving past the bar counter into the kitchen.

The kitchen was empty, save for the still simmering pan of beancakes that had burned black in the fire. All the smells of a forgotten supper were there. Thyme, chicken broth and crushed tomato.

'Over there,' Azamon said, pointing.

An iron door with thick bars of metal across it loomed ominously at the far end of the room. A few of the consular shot at it – but there was no use. It wouldn't come down from gunfire.

'Bring in the cannon,' Azamon commanded and two consular left to retrieve it. Moments later they dragged it into the kitchen. Cut from perfect brass, the nostril was still snorting smoke. Lethi backed away, putting fingers in his ears as Azamon counted down the cannoneer. The blast was louder than he could have prepared for. His ears rang as though full of birdsong as he gathered his wits and glanced ahead. The door was gone. The doorway too. All that was left was a gaping hole.

Azamon shouted something, but Lethi could barely hear it above the ringing in his ears. It must have been something along the lines of 'charge' or 'forward', for the consular streamed through the gap with weapons raised.

Lethi followed them inside and found himself in a darkened corridor with paintings and sculptures along the wall. They depicted figures and scenes from what must have been old Darosan mythos. *This is it. The pit of the snake.*

His hearing was coming back as he pressed through. He came across what he thought was a barber's chair with locks of hair strewn along the floor and imagined that just moments before, people were going about their business as usual. *They must have taken cover when they heard the gunshots.*

Their group came at last to what had the look of a wine cellar, with hundreds of amphorae stacked tight against the wall. Azamon broke one, to make sure it was wine – it was some kind of spirit. Home-brewed gin or something of the sort. He turned his attention to a barrel at the far end of the room and tugged it open by the ring-pull. One look inside set him to smiling.

'This is it,' he said, stepping aside. 'A tunnel.'

Lethi's mouth drooped. *Yes, this is it. The snake pit.*

A tunnel disguised by a wine barrel was the work of the highest subterfuge. Whoever was down there had no intention of ever being found.

'Are we going in?' one of the consular asked.

Azamon gave him a disgusted look, which was all the answer he was ever likely to receive. The consular winced and immediately clambered into the barrel.

Lethi watched them crawl, one after the other, into the tunnel on all fours.

Azamon waited until all the consular were inside, then gave Lethi a mocking smile. 'I told you we would find them.'

Lethi nodded. 'You did.'

'Time to sever the head of the snake,' Azamon said, before he disappeared into the tunnel.

Lethi let out a long breath and placed his knee atop the barrel preparing to climb inside but was struck by a hint of something in the air. The amphora that Azamon had cracked open was still leaking out onto the floor.

He sniffed at the air and froze. The gin was very potent.

He drew in breath just as a shadow fell across his face. The blow came from his blind side, knocking him off his feet. Stars bubbled in his vision as the wine roiled in his stomach. He could feel the blood roll down his cheek as he tried to gather his bearings.

A thick, heavyset woman stood above him with a large black hammer in her hands. She was bare to the waist and seemed to walk with a stutter in her step. Her face, though half shrouded in shadow, was murderous.

Lethi glanced at the hammer, held comfortably in her hands and feared in that moment she would smash his skull to powder. Instead, she grabbed him by the lapel and stared right into his eyes.

Men moved behind her in the shadows, pouring the contents of the amphora down the tunnel. Lethi's eyes widened as he realised what they were going to do.

'Who are you?' Lethi breathed, staring up into the woman's face.

She grinned. 'I suppose I'm the head of the snake.' She turned to a tall, thick-necked man beside the barrel and nodded.

He struck a match to flame and threw it down the tunnel.

17

Soothe the Shadow

RUMI

Rumi rolled the pounded yam smooth in the palm of his hand and formed a little pocket for the vegetable soup with his thumb. He scooped up a sufficient dollop of spinach and meat then brushed it with tomato stew. *Heaven is a place on earth.*

The dining hall was alive with the bustle of the dinner hour and the clatter of plates and cups was heavy in the air. His mind was on the Door of Testimony – Zarcanis had reluctantly arranged for the map to be placed in the care of Latan – the lone surviving Truetree who had tried and failed to reach the summit. When Rumi was ready, he needed only to visit Latan in the botanical ward to collect it. His task now was to find a way out of the Thatcher and past the wall-gate.

He licked his teeth and glanced down at the tomato stew. There was only one person who could help with that, but for the moment his focus was the pounded yam.

'You're eating like a proper Odu man now,' Sameer said, with a laugh.

Rumi glanced up. 'What's that supposed to mean?'

Ahwazi laughed. 'You were a little too fond of your calabash shards when you first got here, now you know the real technique.'

Rumi swallowed another mound of pounded yam.

Miselda appeared at the corner of his vision. She moved with her hands swaying, in a way that was almost impossible to miss. In everything, her face was almost completely expressionless. It was as though someone had stolen the part of her mind that told her face when to show joy, or sadness or intrigue.

She turned sharply towards him and caught his glance. He buckled under the pressure of a threateningly blank canvas.

'What the sheg are you looking at?' she said, loud enough for the people between them to hear.

Rumi narrowed his eyes but gave no answer. It was the first time he had seen any hint of emotion in her.

She gave him a withering scowl and turned on her heel. 'I thought so,' she hissed.

'What is that girl's problem?' Rumi said, watching her walk away.

Sameer raised an eyebrow. 'Miselda?'

Rumi nodded.

Sameer and Ahwazi exchanged glances then burst into simultaneous laughter.

'What is it?' Rumi asked, confused.

'You broke her sister's leg at the Ghedo,' Sameer said.

Rumi's eyes widened. 'Labalaba? We were in a competitive fight.'

'She thinks you were a bit smug about it,' Ahwazi said.

'Smug?'

'You did smile a bit, when she limped away,' Sameer said.

Rumi blinked. ''Cos she was so sure she would put me on my arse. She was cocky.'

Ahwazi laughed. 'So you *were* a little smug.'

'Maybe a little.'

'We start general sparring tomorrow,' Sameer said. 'All

shadowwielders in the Order fighting against one another. Miselda will be wanting a piece of you.'

Rumi shrugged. 'She can join the line. I've heard half the Suli want to make a name beating Ajanla.'

Sameer narrowed his eyes. 'We won't let them.'

'I'll do my best,' Rumi said.

'Swear it on your blood,' Sameer said. 'No one beats us in there unless it's by incapacitation.'

Rumi gave Sameer a long look, then touched his chest and nodded. 'I swear it on my blood.'

Ahwazi touched his chest. 'I swear it on my blood.'

Sameer gave a satisfied nod and poked Rumi's collar. 'If it comes to a fight between you and Miselda, watch her feet.'

Rumi nodded. So much about shadowdancing was about pattern recognition. Things happened so quickly in the fighting circle that there was scarcely enough time to think. It was why you had to run through the forms over and over again so you knew what would come and when it would come. If a person stood with *shepherd holds the crook*, there were only so many angles you could take a hit from. If they stood with *eagle stands amongst the cockerels* you knew to expect a surprise. It all had to become pure instinct. Though he was not a great fighter, when it came to pattern recognition there was no one better than Sameer. He treated every fight like a game of seraiye, thinking several steps ahead. He knew every single one of the forms and all their variations. He could tell by the way someone walked into the fighting circle what form they would start with. He knew every single Suli's strong and weak side. That was how he survived in the Order – by knowing what was coming before it came.

★

Sameer pushed his plate forward and leaned back in his chair. 'Well, that's me done. Do either of you wish to join me for some gin and seraiye at the dorms?'

Rumi shook his head. 'Sorry, I can't.'

Sameer blinked. 'Where is it that you always go after dinner?'

Rumi hesitated.

Ahwazi smiled. 'For a smart man who has binoculars for spectacles, you do miss a lot, Sameer.'

Sameer blinked in confusion. 'What have I missed?'

Rumi retained his silence, the whisper of a smile twisting at the corner of his mouth.

Ahwazi sighed. 'He goes to see that sentry girl up in the Thatcher. Spends hours sometimes. Always comes back with a fat smile on his face.'

Rumi's silence was as good as a confirmation.

Sameer slapped his forehead. 'How did I miss that?'

'You're too busy on your top-secret project with Lord Mandla,' Ahwazi said. 'Everyone has secrets in the softborn clan but me.'

'We just don't care about your secrets, Ahwazi.'

Ahwazi touched his chest with a look of wounded pride. 'Ouch.'

Rumi rose to his feet. 'I'll see you both later.'

Ahwazi slapped the table. 'And off he goes again.'

'Gin and seraiye tomorrow?' Rumi offered.

Sameer rolled his shoulders. 'Fine,' he said. 'But we work the forms in the morning.'

Rumi slapped his chest and pointed to the ceiling. 'Count on it.'

Rumi made his way up to the Thatcher, where Nataré was waiting by the door. Her lips curled into a smile when their eyes met. It was a smile that Rumi had learned to brace himself against – because it made his heart pulse every time. She had the making and the breaking of him in the centre of her hand, like he was an ant on her palm. To speak the truth to her was to walk onto a battlefield with no armour. With a word she could ruin his day, or she could make it. But he had learned that the secret of their connection was their unspoken truce – to the world they could be fierce but when they were alone, they would only be gentle with one another. It was madness, no doubt and yet nothing in his life seemed more essential than the moments he spent in her presence.

'Ajanla Erenteyo, so we meet again.'

Rumi walked right up to her. 'So it seems.' He extended an elbow and she curled an arm around it. His heart leaped as her skin brushed against his.

'My friends have finally figured out where I come every evening,' he said.

Nataré smiled. 'Took them long enough.'

'What do the other sentries think you get up to?'

Her smile receded. 'I don't have very many friends in the sentry guard anymore. Not since the Thatcher.'

Rumi lowered his chin. 'I'm sorry, I didn't—'

'It's fine,' Nataré insisted. 'I know you didn't.'

'You don't have to be a sentry, you know,' Rumi said. 'There are so many other things in the Eredo you could do.'

She frowned. 'Like work in the kitchens? Or sew kaftans for the Order?'

'You could be a botanical, or a scribe, or a hundred things.'

She shook her head slowly. 'I brought the Priest of Vultures to our gates. I am the reason so many people are dead. You think I want to spend the rest of my life hiding from that reality?'

'Don't do that to yourself,' Rumi said. 'The Priest of Vultures wanted his name back and he wanted *me* dead. He would have gone to any length to achieve that. Eventually, he would have reached our gates – with or without you. You made a horrible mistake, but you cannot blame yourself for everything that happened here. You have to move past your mistake, Nataré.'

'So, it's that easy for you? To just move on? Forget everything? All the bodies that we found? When I close my eyes, I can still hear the buzzing flies and mosquitoes.'

A long pause. Rumi's arm tingled. He would not let pain be the breaking of the peace they had built.

'It isn't easy,' Rumi said. 'But we can't let the past define the rest of our lives. I've made mistakes that cost me more dearly than I could ever imagine. I share the blame for all my deepest losses. I lost my mother and brother for decisions that I made. But in the Order, I've come to learn that I am more than my mistakes. More than all my shame.' He touched her cheek. 'And so are you. You are so much more than anything you've ever done. Your greatest, brightest days are still ahead of you.'

Another long pause ensued as her eyes softened. 'That's one thing I've always admired about you, Rumi. No matter how many people insist that you hate yourself, you only ever come up with love.'

Rumi leaned forward and narrowed his eyes. 'That's because I am famously loveable.'

They both laughed and Rumi's entire body shivered with relief. Peace was restored, their secret place untouched.

They trod thereafter as though on an old, rope-sewn bridge. Avoiding all the places where a fall into conflict seemed possible. They talked for hours about things that didn't matter and things that mattered a lot. It was heaven while it lasted but soon the time came to part ways and Rumi couldn't shake the feeling that Nataré carried a weighty burden and that she would never be able to set it down until she felt she had punished herself enough.

He had been in that prison before – unable to forgive yourself and seeing suffering as the only road to redemption. It only ended one way.

He cleared his throat, knowing that he had a deeper commission to ask of her. She looked at him and he refused to meet her gaze.

One glance was all she needed to know that something was on his mind. In so many ways, she had mastered him. As she had the forest. She knew, by the whistle of the wind, what was to come.

'What's wrong?' she asked.

Rumi drew in the breath of a soldier preparing for war and let it out slowly through his nose. 'I need your help, Nataré.'

The lean muscle at her thigh flexed as she straightened. 'Anything.'

Rumi met her gaze. 'I need to find a way to get to the Nyme.'

She blinked at him, her face still expressionless in the dark.

'Only you know the forest and can get me past the gate,' Rumi said.

She narrowed her eyes. 'Rumi, the Nyme is not the sort of place you just *decide* to visit. Even the sentries are only allowed to go in groups of five. You know how dangerous it is.'

Rumi studied her face. There was no hiding – he had to tell it all. 'What I am looking for is at the summit of Erin-Olu.'

'They are sending warriors to get the Oké water. Shadow-wielders with experience.'

'They sent them already. They failed. We do not stand a chance in this war without Oké water.'

'And you think you'll succeed?'

'I do.'

Nataré blinked. 'Have you gone completely mad, Irumide?'

The sound of his full name on her lips was a beautiful rebuke. Rumi could almost smile, though this was serious business. He drew in breath. 'I know what I am asking you. You don't have to say yes. I'll understand. But this is something I need to do.'

He stepped onto the bough of a tree and studied it for a moment. She touched his shoulder.

'How could I possibly say no when you told me you need me? You didn't come here to ask me, Rumi – you knew I would say yes. You came here to compel me.'

'Nataré—'

She raised a hand. 'Don't treat me like a child; we both know what this is. You were there when I needed you. I will be there when you need me. I can get you through the gate. I can lead you through the Nyme. There is just one thing I need to know.'

Rumi lowered his gaze and met her stare. 'Go on.'

'What could possibly be so important that you would risk going back there? And don't tell me it's just about Oké water.'

A tremor shot through Rumi's jaw. Her expression was one of genuine concern – she thought, as she had every right to, that he was a man on the edge of madness. 'I heard about something called the Door of Testimony. If we can get to it, I might be able to save my brother and bring my mother back to life. I need Oké water from the source of Erin-Olu too, to help my father. The Nyme holds a chance of saving my family – all of it, in a way I've never known,' he said. 'If we can get to the summit of Erin-Olu then I have a chance.'

She stared at him for a moment and drew in a breath. 'I'll need one week. I will have to find a way through the wall outside our patrol routes – one that I can assume responsibility for.'

It was longer than he had hoped but he had no other option. 'Thank you.'

She shook her head. 'Save it for when I get you through.'

He grinned. 'Oh, I know you'll get me through. You're the knife-edge.'

He leaned forward for a kiss but stopped short as he felt a sharp pull in the bond. Hagen's emotion hit him, clear as a struck drum. *Fear. Trepidation. Sadness.*

Rumi called his shadow instantly.

'What is it?' Nataré asked.

Rumi narrowed his eyes. 'Trouble.'

Without another word, he took off running.

The days of loss were over – no one had any right to make his lionhound feel fear. No one. He would kill for Hagen without the whisper of a question. The bond flashed stronger in his mind. *Fear. Concern. Helplessness.*

Rumi quickened to a full sprint. The bond grew thick enough to taste and he came at last to a large, bent-double tree. Now it was the smell that arrested him – thick and unmistakable in the air. *Agbo.*

'Hagen?'

Rumi heart shifted as he stepped past the shadow of the tree. Miselda lay with legs askew, milk-white agbo drooling from her mouth and nose. Her eyes had the glazed-over, porcelain cast of a play doll. Hagen loomed over her, panting hard, trying to wake her up. Kaat too was there, lapping at the downed shadowwielder. The fear Hagen had felt was not for himself.

Rumi cleared his throat. 'What are you doing?'

Miselda gave a delayed start and sat halfway up to get a good look at him. Instead of words, a long glottal groan slithered from her mouth.

Rumi shook his head with disappointment. *How could a shadowwielder be a lickhead?*

As the sharp pounding in his chest dulled to quiver, he was starting to think. Three options came immediately to his mind. He could leave her there and pretend it never happened. He could take her directly to Mandla and be sure she would be brought up for conduct unbecoming. Or he could take her somewhere else – a place she could recover before she was inevitably found.

The first option seemed irresponsible; the second, unduly cruel. He glanced down at her and furrowed his brow, then he let out a deep sigh as he pulled her to her feet.

He draped her arm around his shoulder and pulled her to her feet. 'Let's go.' Hagen followed beside them and his emotion shifted to hope, relief and pride.

About halfway across the Thatcher, Miselda stopped, pushed him aside and vomited. Rumi gave her a wide berth as she spilled her stomach. Never could he have imagined that the self-assured shadowwielder he knew from class could make such an unseemly spectacle.

She gave a ragged cough, wiped her mouth clean and straightened. She glanced over her shoulder and her pupils widened as though seeing him for the first time. 'You,' she said.

Rumi gave her a confused look. 'First "him", now "you"… I suppose eventually you will call me by my name.'

She pointed an accusatory finger at him, but then buckled and stumbled forward. Rumi caught her in his arms and draped her arm over his shoulder again. 'You're in no shape to insult me right now.'

'Give me an hour,' she said.

Footsteps tapped nearby and Nataré appeared behind him. She took one look at them and frowned.

'Who's that?' she asked.

'She's a shadowwielder. A Suli. I need to get her back inside.'

Nataré hesitated for a small moment, then took up her other shoulder. Together, they ushered Miselda to the Thatcher door, where Hagen flashed encouragement, hope and satisfaction as his goodbye. Rumi gave back irritation and reluctance. Hagen seemed amused by that.

'I'll see you soon,' he said to Nataré

'And I'll have a way ready in a week.'

They parted ways and Rumi continued inside.

The walk to the botanical ward was a long one but no one bothered him while he held the shadow. It wasn't unusual for shadowwielders to get into a fight and need the attention of a botanical. They entered the waiting room and Rumi set Miselda down against a wooden bench. 'Wait here,' he cautioned as he turned towards the large wooden desk ahead.

She gave a phlegmy grunt in response. The agbo drool had run clear but her eyes still had the glazed-over appearance of a lickhead.

Rumi asked the nearest attendant for Uroma.

The botanical appeared a few moments later and her eyes bulged when she noticed Miselda.

Rumi gave her a pleading look. 'She needs help.'

'I can see that,' Uroma said, pulling Miselda up and directing her to a private room.

Rumi followed them inside.

Uroma called her shadow and placed a hand on Miselda's forehead. 'You know what she was doing?'

Rumi nodded. 'Agbo.'

'Were you doing it too?'

Rumi shook his head. 'No, never. I don't know why any shadowwielder would.'

Uroma glanced over her shoulder at him. 'You've never heard of shadowsoothing?'

Rumi blinked. 'Never.'

Uroma let out an exasperated breath. 'Leave her with me. I'll make sure she gets back to her hostel safely. Don't worry, I won't tell anyone. But if I see her here again, I will have to.'

Rumi nodded. 'Thank you.'

He turned to leave but Uroma gave him a sharp look. 'Is she your sister or something?'

Rumi shook his head.

'Girlfriend?'

'No.'

'A friend, then?'

Rumi drew in breath. 'She's a Suli. That's enough for me.'

Uroma's nostrils flared as she formed a thin line with her lips and gave a soft nod. 'All right then.'

18

A Poke in the Eye

LETHI

It reminded Lethi of the old farm fair. When he was a child, all of Barnham Wood would run down to the village green on the first day of summer where the farm fair lay stretched out before them like some grand bazaar with tents and canopies arranged in huddles across the grass. The great attraction of the fair was the pig. Brined and roasted whole on an oscillating spit. The smell of it was something Lethi would never forget. It reminded him of home. He was a long way from home now, but that smell was still there — except this time it wasn't a pig on the spit, it was the men and women of the consular guard.

They screamed from inside the burning tunnel, like lost souls in the underworld pleading for their forgiveness.

The thick woman sat cross-legged on the floor, utterly calm, listening as though to the twittering of birds at her window. There would be no forgiveness now. Four men stood around her, clustered like guards to protect their precious queen.

This was her — the head of the snake, the tip of the spear.

There must have been at least ten men burning in the tunnel and amongst them was Azamon, the head of the Meladroni. It made no difference who was who now, Lethi couldn't tell one scream from the next. They were gone and soon he would be too.

Oké-Dar was loud. Not with the noise of battle, but with the fervent passion of music. Through the dark window, Lethi saw shadows move as faceless voices sang loud native songs of triumph. The Black Hammer Clan had set a trap for fools and Azamon had walked into it with a smile. 'It is too quiet,' Attem had said. It wasn't quiet now.

A shard of light illuminated the slumped corpse of a fallen consular. The spear protruding from his chest leaned in the wind like a coloniser's flag.

Lethi wondered then where Attem and the rest of his men were. Had they made it out alive? Was it even possible to make it out alive from this hell of a slum?

He glanced down at the shackles on his wrists. He'd be dead soon, he knew. How soon was the great question. *What's taking them so long?*

At last, the screaming in the tunnel stopped. The heavy woman, satisfied they all were dead, rose to her feet. She walked with a discernible limp and stared out through the small window. 'I think our work is finished here.' She turned her gaze on Lethi.

'You must be the one from Guyarica,' the woman said, narrowing her eyes.

Lethi gave no answer.

The woman grinned. 'Yes, Marlé told me about you.' She stroked his chin. 'You still haven't shaved.'

Lethi's entire body tensed at that but still he offered no response.

She drew in a long breath. 'Put him in the hold.'

Some of her men bristled uncomfortably at that. Plainly they wanted Lethi dead.

They snatched Lethi up by the collar and dragged him to his feet. The woman halted them and ripped the gorget patch from his jacket.

'We are coming for you,' she said. 'You flew too close to the sun. You came across a people with too much pride and dignity to make settlements under the shadow of your boots. We are the people of Xango, Gu and Kamanu – our song grows louder in the storm. The consular killed thirty of our people today. Most of them unarmed. But we killed twenty-eight of them in return. I count this round for my people. You kill ten of us, we kill one of you and count it as victory. We will outlast you because we fight for something you will never understand. For a story you never were told. Furae Oloola, Lieutenant. Tomorrow begins today.'

Lethi gave her a long, appraising look then curled his lips into a smile. 'Good luck with that.'

He was dragged from the room and tossed into a dark cellar. The side of his head still throbbed with pain, his wrists were red and raw, and he had a cut that needed stitching, but he was still alive, and so long as there was life, there was hope.

When he woke on the fourth day, Lethi had lost all hope. He spent each day with darkness and silence as his only companions. The low growl of his stomach and the insistent scratching of rats against the cellar cobblestones were the closest thing to conversation he'd had in days. He scratched a single mark across the cobblestone, next to three lines already there. If not for those four scratchings, he would have lost all sense of time. Whether it had been hours, days or weeks; he could not truly tell. The only thing he had to mark the time were the four lines counting off his sleeps.

The cellar was little more than a crate. If he stretched his arms out sidewise, he could touch two walls. The only light came from the flickering lantern that shone through the gap beneath the door. The closest thing that came to joy was the brief moment of brightness when one of the Black Hammer Clan brought his food for the day.

His wrists were chained together, the door was barred, and the corridors were patrolled. There could be no physical escape from Oké-Dar. Only the final, eternal escape of the dearly departed.

His mind flashed to Marlé. Her skin. Her touch. Her kiss. Her betrayal. *How long had she known I would end up here?* He buried the questions away. This was no time to bear more than his mind could carry. He had only one goal ahead of him now – survive.

About an hour after waking, the jangling of keys made him straighten. The door slid open. A tall woman stood before him. Above her collarbone was the darkened shape of a hammer pressed in ink – the emblem of the Black Hammer Clan.

A slight breeze ruffled her kaftan, which was of dark navy and extended all the way to her ankles. Lethi shuddered as she entered, afflicted by the sudden scent of something that smelled like month-rotten eggs. She looked at him as one would a sworn enemy. Everything smacked of an unspoken disdain.

'Eat up,' she said in rough Common Tongue.

Only then did Lethi notice the tray of food in her hand. That was what was giving off that awful smell. Lethi reached forward hungrily as she handed it over. He set it down as she stepped out of the cellar and folded her hands.

He sniffed it and scowled as the door slammed shut. He couldn't be sure exactly what the food was. The thick folds of brown meat could have come from the rats that scratched against the cobblestone and the sickly yellow oatmeal looked more like something you threw up rather than took in. But this was no time to be picky. *Just survive.*

He ate with his fingers, with no regard for anything above

his survival. He crunched something metallic and spat it out licking his lip, where a small cut had opened up. It shimmered in the dark, slightly bigger than a coin – Azamon's golden medallion. He let out an exasperated breath, licked the bowl clean and slumped back against the cellar wall. *Survive.*

Moments later, the door slid open again. The woman had returned with a look angrier than the first time. She shuffled awkwardly into the room and went down on one knee. The figure standing behind her appeared. Spindly legs of lean muscle. A face dark as the starless light.

'Attem,' Lethi breathed, staring up in disbelief.

Attem's expression was grim. 'Let's go, now.'

He kept his spear levelled against the woman as he dragged Lethi to his feet and made her unlock his chains. They backed out from the cellar and slammed the door shut, double-locking it with the thick bars of brass.

'Follow me,' Attem whispered.

Lethi nodded as he crouched close. They crept down the corridor with the quiet of ants. A shadow ahead fell across the corridor. Attem froze, put a hand across Lethi's chest.

One of the Black Hammer Clan stepped into the lantern light. Before he knew what they were about, Attem had a spear pressed against the man's throat.

'Make a noise and you die.'

The man barely hesitated.

'Escape! The omaku has—'

Attem punctured his throat before the sentence was finished but the damage was done.

'Run!' Attem hissed as they turned back on themselves.

Lethi could barely move, on account of having spent days in a cramped room, crouched down and bent over. Even so, he mustered the strength to run as Attem crashed through a window.

Lethi groaned as he tried to follow after him. Attem helped to pull him through and before long, they were outside the building. Far ahead, Lethi spotted the broken town gates.

Footsteps clattered behind them but they had a chance now and Lethi wasn't going to let it go.

'Run!' Attem repeated.

Lethi obeyed. Gritting his teeth, he gave everything to eke out a desperate sprint. Heart pounding, body aching, he ran. Shutting his mind to everything but the rise and fall of his footsteps. *Just survive.*

Attem was in incredible condition. He moved with the graceful stride of a gazelle, never slowing his pace, turning sharp as a hunting knife. It was the struggle of Lethi's life just to keep within shouting distance. After what felt like a hellish eternity, the sounds of pursuit faded behind them and Attem slowed his pace. They came together again beneath a bent-over tree. Two miles of running barely seemed to have drawn sweat from Attem, while Lethi was blowing like a beached fish. It took a full three minutes to halfway catch his breath.

'What happened to the rest?' Lethi managed.

Attem's expression was steady. 'Dareem is dead. I saw his corpse.'

Lethi frowned. 'Banasco and Roadie?'

Attem shrugged. 'They escaped.'

Lethi winced. *Dareem.* A talented soldier at the best of times, albeit one who cut corners a little too often. Death was too final a punishment for any of his transgressions. Lethi straightened and gave Attem an appraising look. 'Why did you come back for me?'

Attem narrowed his eyes and looked away. 'I don't know,' he said honestly. 'It felt like the right thing to do.'

That hit Lethi like an unseen slap. A splash of startling honesty that left him a little dazed. Attem — a man whom he had never treated as anything more than a tool — had saved his life, 'because it felt right'. Banasco and Roadie had run and yet here stood the furthest from his kin — risking his life to get him out.

Lethi touched the four-point star pendant, drew in a deep breath and let it out with a slow wheeze. He straightened and turned to the mainland road. 'For the Son sees our hearts and brings peace to those who resist evil.'

19

Where Gods are Buried

RUMI

The grand assembly hall was teeming with shadowwielders. It was a sight to behold – Seedlings, Sulis and Truetrees, gathered together as one. Rumi's heart was thumping in his chest. He could feel the heat of stares at the back of his neck. The scent of roasting plantain in the air was thick enough to bite. People had gathered around the edges of the theatre to sell food and drink. Others had come clearly with the intent to gamble and wager.

Ahwazi gulped down half a bottle of tigernut milk and let out a loud, satisfied 'aaah'. 'Today is the day, Ajanla,' he said with a smile.

Sameer stood just behind, his kaftan extended only to the knee, baring his stick-thin legs. His expression was one of deep focus. He wasn't built to be a fighter in the physical sense but he made up for it in all the other ways a man could fight.

Some shadowwielders worked through the forms, practising ahead of what was certain to be a challenging day – others kept their calm, preferring not to give their prospective opponents any advantage.

A woman dressed in a deep-orange, loose-fitting kaftan brushed her shoulder against Rumi's ear. He glanced up at her, a little surprised by the deliberate shove.

'Watch yourself,' she hissed.

Rumi met her gaze.

'Miselda,' he breathed. 'I thought you might still be in the botanical ward. You know, recovering.'

Her frown deepened. 'You'll be there yourself soon. I've heard you can barely handle a lick of shadow.'

Rumi arched an eyebrow. 'You really want to talk about what we can handle?'

She narrowed her eyes to dangerous slits and stepped close, lowering her voice. 'Don't, for one moment, think I owe you anything.'

Rumi matched her gaze, hate for hate. 'Don't worry – I wasn't expecting a thank you.'

They held their stares for a long moment, then she hissed and moved on. Rumi watched her leave, a little confused by the encounter.

He turned to Sameer. 'What is shadowsoothing?'

Sameer's eyes darkened as he jolted from his inward silence and grabbed Rumi by the scruff of his kaftan.

'Don't tell me you're thinking of trying it!' he said. 'Surely you are not *that* foolish.'

Rumi shook his head. 'No, not me.'

Sameer let out a relieved breath. 'Calling the shadow and embracing dark emotions can take its toll on the mind. Agbo has been known to provide relief from that pressure. Just a few licks of agbo and you can embrace unbelievable volumes of shadow.'

Rumi nodded. 'It doesn't sound *that* foolish, the way you have explained it.'

Sameer spread his arms in a stretch. 'Aside from the fact that agbo is terribly addictive and bad for your health, mixing it with the shadow has been known to have far deeper effects.'

'Such as?' Rumi asked, leaning in.

'Shadowsoothing robs you of your emotion slowly. Depletes your sense of feeling until there is nothing left. No joy, no fear, no hate. Just... nothing.'

Ahwazi finished the rest of his tigernut milk and leaned forward. 'No one survives long when the emotion is gone. When there's nothing to feel... there's nothing to live for.'

Rumi formed a thin line with his lips. Losing all emotion seemed too high a price to pay for a prize too low. What in all the world could make Miselda take that risk?

He glanced over at her and caught her eye as she scanned the crowd. Now he saw her expression for what it was. Not hate but indifference. She didn't care about him. Didn't care about anything.

'Ajanla Erenteyo,' came a voice, breaking Rumi from his thoughts.

He glanced over his shoulder and saw a large Kasinabe with marks of shadow rank across his arm. In his left hand he held a silver flute. Thin as a knife but more capable of stunning a man.

Rumi smiled. 'Stake.'

The big Kasinabe returned the grin. 'We are still waiting on you and your drums. You promised you would join us soon.'

Rumi let out an acknowledging breath. 'It's been a little difficult for me.'

Stake blinked and nodded. 'The music helps. It really does.'

Rumi nodded, knowing this to be deeply true. 'I'll come around soon.'

Stake shook his head. 'Not soon. Tomorrow.'

'Tomorrow then,' Rumi agreed.

A bell rang and a shiver of murmurs shot through the gathered crowd. It was time to spar.

Stake's eyes narrowed to slits as he touched his elbow, limbering up. 'Have a good session, Ajanla.'

Rumi nodded. 'You too, Stake.'

Rumi rejoined Sameer and Ahwazi, who were standing beside the other Sulis.

Sulis were still the largest group in the Shadow Order. When Rumi had first arrived, there had been six hundred Suli – three hundred men and three hundred women. The number was closer to three hundred and forty now, with a slight edge in favour of the men. It was expected that each Suli would spar at least three times with a counterpart of equivalent shadow rank.

The crowd parted ahead, as Chief Gaitan bolstered through.

'Suli, to me,' he called out, beckoning them forward.

He led them out from the assembly hall down a rock tunnel with a low ceiling. They arrived at the top of a wide flight of stone stairs.

Rumi turned to Sameer who, perhaps more than anyone, knew his way around the Eredo. 'Where are we going?'

Sameer gave him a sharp look. 'The catacombs.'

'Where people are buried?'

'Where gods are buried.'

Gaitan's voice echoed about the walls from far ahead. 'We have changed the rules for general sparring,' Gaitan announced. 'We wanted to emulate the truth of combat where there is no such thing as a fair fight. You will be divided into two teams and set across each side of the catacombs. One team will be given blue cowries, the other team will be given red ones. Each cowrie is worth one point. The goal is for one team to accumulate more cowries than the other. How you do that is entirely your choice.'

'Who will act as umpire?' someone asked.

Gaitan's reply made the Sulis quieten. 'There is no umpire. You fight until surrender. If someone pleads for surrender, you take their cowries and let them leave the catacombs.'

Rumi turned sharply towards Sameer. Ahwazi was looking at him too.

'Don't worry about me,' Sameer hissed. 'I'll be fine.'

'We stick together,' Ahwazi said, with a tone that offered no invitation to argument.

The narrow entrance passageway opened into a series of tunnels that extended into a network that spanned the entire subterrain of the Eredo. Here and there were spiralling staircases of stone and hollowed out caves that were strewn with centuries-old rubble. Gaitan led them deeper still; past caves marked with stone inscriptions and pillars of limestone that looked as though they had seen the beginning of the world.

At last, they came to a chamber large enough to host a banquet. There were at least six tunnels that branched out from the chamber, with grated gates of iron that had been unlocked and pulled open. At the centre of the chamber were two almighty heaps of safespears. One heap marked with red, the other marked with blue.

Gaitan began the work of separating the group into teams. He picked Suli one after the other, and it was as though he had made a deliberate effort to pick out the very best and most skilled Suli for the red team. He sized each Suli up and examined their shadow rank before taking the best away. Miselda, Dasuki and one they called Deadpike were all amongst the red.

Rumi, Sameer and Ahwazi were left on the blue team with a squadron of all the other less than stellar fighters. They had been set up to lose. Sparring fodder.

'Red team, you come with me. Blue, you stay here. The bout begins at the sound of the horn.'

He led the red team from the chamber through the centremost tunnel, leaving the rest to consider their inevitable fate.

They looked about themselves, sizing one another up. The Kasinabe were never a people to accept defeat but the disparity between the two groups was stark. Gaitan had set them up as underdogs and set the alpha wolfs to the hunt.

Rumi could feel the gazes settle on him. Most had seen him spar at the Ghedo. Others had heard what he did at the Thatcher. Though he had just eight lines of shadow rank, he was perhaps the only one who had any real reputation as a fighter amongst them.

Someone in the group said the obvious. 'They've set us up to fail.'

The declaration sent a shiver of murmurs through the crowd; mostly in agreement.

Even so, the unspoken question lingered in the air – *who will lead us?*

A slender Suli stood under the cover of shadow, leaning against his safespear. He stepped into the light and raised his hand high, letting his sleeve fall to the elbow to expose a forearm marked with at least thirteen lines of shadow rank – perhaps the most amongst their group. 'Have no fear, brethren,' he said, pointing at Rumi. 'We have the *Old Dog* on our side.'

His words were invested with such mockery that a dozen or so Suli sniggered and laughed.

Rumi's jaw throbbed as he gathered himself and rolled his shoulder.

'He rides the unbridled Shinala,' Chief Lungelo had once said of Rumi. A sentiment that spoke to his seeming lack of control at times of the highest consequence. Rumi's control slipped away as he surrendered to his affronted pride. Pride of the martial eagle – a weapon, if you knew how to use it. They would see it now.

'Did you count them?' Rumi asked the slender Suli.

'What?' the Suli replied.

'Did you count our opponents?' Rumi said.

The Suli's eyes narrowed to slits of ire as his grip tightened on his safespear. 'What is the point?'

Rumi tilted his neck until it gave a loud, popping click. He stepped forward with shoulders hunched. He saw now that he was taller and broader at the shoulder. He could smell the hesitation mingling with the Suli's confidence.

He spoke slow. 'If you had counted you would have seen that they number one hundred and fifty on the other team. We outnumber them by at least forty.' Rumi stepped even closer to him. 'I am no easy meat. Especially with the strength of numbers behind me.'

The murmurs quietened a little.

He raised his hand to his chest as though swearing an oath. 'I fight with the legacy of my mother, Adunola. My father, Griff, who they call the darkman. My brother, Morire, who faced worse odds than this every day of his life.' Rumi drew in breath. 'I will make *hell* for our opponents today.'

His words seemed to echo off the cavern walls.

The slender Sulis seemed to shrivel at that, slouching till his gaze fell away and he bowed like a beaten dog. In that small moment, Rumi saw him for what he was – *afraid*.

The other Suli stood a little straighter now. Clutched their safespears a little tighter. The flicker of belief had been scratched alight. Rumi's jaw tightened as his mind scrambled for what to say next. He had their attention and even their belief now, but he was no good at knowing where to direct it.

Sameer blew out a loud breath and stepped forward. 'Thank you, Ajanla,' he said with half a smile. 'We needed that.'

In that moment of uncertainty, the Suli found his voice again and glanced up. 'Another softborn? Is this a softborn seminar?'

Sameer didn't flinch. 'Shut up, you, or I'll get Ajanla to pummel you to dust.'

There was open laughter at that one.

'Proper sheggin' scoundrel,' Sameer muttered as he turned to address the rest of the Suli. He raised his voice with all the practised eloquence of a veteran politician and it carried through the chamber. 'Most of you don't know who I am. Those who do probably think I am not fit to be in the Order. I am weak, I am small, I am softborn. I am many things that you despise.'

Rumi blinked, studying the crowd – allowing his shadow to recede as Sameer shifted forward.

'I know these catacombs better than anyone in the entire Eredo,' Sameer said.

A few laughed at that. Disbelieving.

Sameer's expression didn't change. He called his shadow, and scattered wisps of black formed around his body. One gesture and the shadow formed a long tunnel. 'I can map this place out from memory,' he said, running a finger over the tunnel of shadow. 'I call this the godwalk,' he said, pointing to the centremost tunnel. His shadow extended to form the image of another tunnel. 'It runs underground through the very centre of the Eredo.' He waved his hand and another tunnel appeared. Then another. Slowly he built an interconnected network. 'The way the catacombs are built, there are only three ways to get across. The godwalk is the fastest way but also the most obvious. It's no secret the red team have the better fighters – but I suspect we have them bested for brains, discounting that prick, of course,' he said, pointing at the Suli.

More laughter.

Sameer made his shadow flare and raised his voice. 'Today you let the softborn lead. None know better than us what it means to beat the odds. Believe in my strategy and we will win today.'

A thick-headed Suli with a scar across his face stepped forward. He gave Sameer a long, appraising look then lowered his head. 'And if you don't win?'

'Well, then you can always blame the softborn. We're used to it.'

20

Blood in the Catacombs

RUMI

'Here they come,' Ahwazi whispered.

You didn't need his warning to know it. You could hear the footsteps on stone. They were moving with the frantic eagerness of wolves falling on a herd of sheep. They saw no real opposition in their opponents – only glory and validation. They must have known, as Gaitan led them to the other side of the catacombs, that they were by far the more experienced team. There was hardly one among them who had fewer than twelve lines of shadow rank. They must have seen it as a test – the best fighters against the rest. Winning in such matters could not be by small margins. They wanted to give out a decisive beating.

Rumi could hear it as they whizzed past in the neighbouring tunnel. They were sprinting. Their confidence was absolutely supreme – victory, as they saw it, was certain. Sameer had been right; their opponents would have a blisteringly simple plan – 'they will try to run through us as quickly as possible. They will underestimate us and therein lies our route to victory.'

'How long do you think we have?' Ahwazi asked.

'Ten minutes at the most, I'd say,' Rumi said.

Less than a third of their team had stayed behind – lambs to the slaughter as far as the plan was concerned. Against those in red, there could be no great stand – Rumi and Ahwazi had to get around their opponents and fast. Sameer had given them a layout of the catacombs. Just a few metres ahead, the tunnel they were in was supposed to fork into three.

It was a daring plan. They just needed those left behind to hold on long enough.

The neighbouring tunnel went quiet and Rumi let out a held breath.

'Let's go!' he hissed.

They took off running down the tunnel with their safespears raised. Sameer had insisted that they resist calling their shadows until the very last moment. Ahead the tunnel forked into three, just as Sameer had promised. They followed his instructions and split into two.

'With me,' Rumi called, moving to the front of his group. They followed him with no reserve of commitment. Say what you may about the Kasinabe but when it came to a fight, they gave it their all. Ahwazi led the rest down the second tunnel.

They began to hear the clamour of a fight ahead. Rumi's jaw tightened as he resisted the urge to call his shadow.

'Not yet,' he urged, reading the minds of those who followed behind him. They held their nerve. Not one shadow had yet been called.

The fighting grew louder and from the noise it was going worse than expected. Sameer was a brave fighter and a smart one, not a good one.

Rumi saw the glint of lantern light ahead in the tunnel and narrowed his eyes. 'Get ready,' he called out as they closed in.

They huddled closer, heads bowed low with spears pointed forward as the lantern light grew bolder.

Rumi closed his eyes as they spilled out of the tunnel. 'Now,' he snarled.

They called their shadows and smashed into the rear of the team in red. Rumi had only once held more shadow. He felt almost infinite with the amount pulsing through him.

'Bring hell on them!' Rumi shouted.

A Suli with a red spear whirled and brought his spear up to strike at Rumi. He lunged forward but Rumi knew the form too well. *Fox enters the henhouse* was no danger to a ready *shepherd holds the crook*. He moved his safespear in a sideways motion and knocked the Suli's spear harmlessly wide. With a swift movement, he brought the back-end of his safespear up and smashed the Suli's kneecap. *No umpire.*

The Suli jerked forward with a yelp of pain. In some other life, Rumi might have felt the call to give mercy but no such call came today. He raised his safespear and struck the Suli down with a blow to the collarbone. The Suli raised a trembling hand. 'I surrender.'

Rumi snatched the cowrie from him and pocketed it.

He caught movement at the edge of his vision and swerved left as a safespear came at his face. The breeze shifted as the safespear missed its mark; Rumi struck out a powerful counter – catching the enemy Suli at the armpit.

He narrowed his eyes, pitiless as he spun his safespear and struck the Suli at the top of his skull. The blow caught him flush and he went down with hands and legs spread star-like as he hit the ground. The Suli spasmed and twitched on the floor, eyes completely closed.

It was incapacitation, Rumi decided as he snatched his cowrie.

The red team had realised what was happening now and were slowly turning to face their real threat. The attack had had the desired effect and thrown them into complete disarray. Only brazen overconfidence had allowed them to believe they were facing the full complement of Suli. Just a brief moment of introspection would have revealed it was a trap. But even the most intelligent fighters had a habit of going bone daft at the height of battle. It was why every group of fighters needed a voice in the darkness. A master of the vision. A leader.

'Squeeze!' Sameer shouted.

Rumi glanced ahead and saw him in the thick of the melee. He had survived. That gave Rumi pride as he pressed forward.

'Squeeze the life out of them!' he snarled as he came at them with shadow everywhere.

Ahwazi's team spilled out from the other tunnel and pressed forward, their fear entirely abandoned.

Another Suli twisted around, shouting obscenities with his safespear raised high. Rumi lashed out in the shadow and struck him so hard on the cheek that he saw the teeth fly as he spat blood.

'I will show you a paper champion,' Rumi snarled.

All thoughts of a plan, of tactics, of contingency vanished as Rumi drank in the shadow. Fear was gone, anxiety had fled, only the hottest emotions flashed through his mind – *shame, fury, vengefulness*. He pulled at his lust for vengeance and his shadow swelled. It was revelling in this, the highest moment. Under this romantic camouflage of training, he would make a name they wouldn't soon forget. *Not now, not ever.*

Emotion swelled as he lunged into *raging rhinocerous* and threw himself into the swell of bodies. He was something more than just a Suli in that moment. He was Ajanla, the Old Dog, and he howled.

The crowd parted for half a moment and a figure appeared ahead, shrouded in thick shadow. Rumi gave a start, the swell of the fighter's high receding for just a moment.

It was Miselda. Her shadow was as dark and thick as a forest night, her spear seemed stupidly long, and she loomed large amidst the other Suli. Rumi could see the effect of her shadow-soothing now – she looked utterly destructive, her shadow at its height. Her dark safespear gleamed as though doused in silver.

Their eyes met and she grinned. It was the first time that Rumi noticed that she had two gold teeth for canines. Rumi took a step back, cautious as her chin shifted up and she turned towards him. Though there were people between them, he knew they were going to dance.

Anxiety returned. He had never seen her fight before but knew the lines of shadow rank that ran to her elbow were not obtained by chance. She was formidable, and had been shadowsoothing too.

Rumi swallowed and raised his chin. He had made Sameer a promise. Sworn it on his blood. 'No one beats us in there unless it's by incapacitation.'

He rolled his shoulders, breath coming in short, sharp gasps as she approached. Sudden as the night wind, she broke into a run and came at him with spear shifted upward for a rising blow. He shifted a step left, with his safespear poised to parry but instead of lunging, she stopped short and brought the haft of her safespear dragging across the gravelly floor, spraying up flecks of stone at him.

'What the sheg?' he murmured as he raised a hand to protect his eyes.

Her safespear shot out as he stepped back and only the baked-in instinct of practice past reminded him to duck as her weapon hissed overhead.

He breathed out a sigh, even as he hopped out of range. It was a feint for the ages. A masterwork in subterfuge and brutality. Half a moment of sluggishness and she could have punctured his throat. She didn't just look the part – she was it. Forget the war in months to come, she was battle-ready now.

Rumi shifted into *eagle stands among the cockerels* but she was already thrusting forward with *raging rhinoceros*. A thought occurred to Rumi as he darted back, shifting his hands at speed to parry each blow. *Where have I seen that sequence before?*

It hit him like a name remembered. *Her sister did the same thing at the Ghedo.* Though this was at least twice as fast with four times the murderous intent. Rumi knew then that the gleam on her safespear was definitely blood.

That was why Sameer had told me to watch her feet.

'You're better than I expected,' she said as she slunk back into *leopard watches the fire*, circling him.

Rumi wouldn't let the words shift his focus. She was as deadly as a snake and needed only a moment. He watched her feet, trying to bring to memory his fight with her sister.

One of the Sulis on her team tried to come to her support and she struck him down with a hammer blow. 'Leave us,' she snarled, and the others gave them a wide berth.

Only then did Rumi notice that the fighting around them had quietened. His team had the dominance in numbers and had encircled the red team completely. In every way that mattered they were poised to win the day. But sometimes, people needed more than that. Stories. *'Tis the story doth animate the gods.*

That was why they were here. Why they watched. Ajanla against Miselda.

Rumi gritted his teeth and closed his eyes, searching for the emotion that never failed him when called upon. The image of his mother flashed through his mind. Her words came with it. 'One way or another, I will make a story.' Pain hammered him with the force of a veteran blacksmith. He embraced it, letting the shadow use the emotion to lend him power. *It still hurts.* Shame came next – at the way he had pissed himself when the Priest of Vultures snatched him up by the neck. He accepted it and the shadow swelled thicker. *I was a coward*. Love bound it all and he remembered his mother's dying voice as he came back to life. 'Whatever it takes.' *I miss her so much.*

His eyes snapped open and Miselda seemed smaller in his sight. She had more than twice his lines in shadow rank but would find it a challenge to match his emotion.

'Let's go.'

She came at him with blistering speed, her safespear so fast it blurred.

Rumi snaked under it, shifting his own spear sidewards as he darted past.

She hurdled the attempt and rolled up to her feet, catlike in the ease of it. They broke apart, circling each other again. Rumi's heart was thumping now. He watched her with the coiled-tight focus of an archer with bow stretched taut.

She set her feet wide and the reminiscence melded instantly with his instinct. It was that same stance again. The one her sister had.

This time when she charged he feinted to parry. She shifted her spear to slip under his guard and he lunged forward. Her eyes widened with surprise for only a moment before his knee hit her stomach. She doubled over, spitting blood and he brought his fists double-handed against her back. She hit the floor hard. He raised his safespear high and thought to demand her surrender but knew it would not come. He could feel the heat of her pride. Wounded as she was, she would die before giving up in front of all these people. His choice was simple — beat her unconscious or let her come at him again.

He narrowed his eyes as she coughed out blood and curled up to one knee, preparing to stand.

'Finish her!' someone shouted.

Rumi recognised the voice. It was the slender Suli who had

taunted him before the fight. The sound of it hit his ear as though from a struck bell and he knew instantly what to do. *The third way.*

Rumi dropped to a knee and reached into his pocket as she struggled to stand. Their eyes met and her jaw tightened as she braced herself for his attack. Instead, he pulled his cowrie out and presented it to her. Head bowed, spear spurned.

She glanced at the cowrie as though it was poisonous.

'Brave Suli, it was an honour,' Rumi said.

He raised his gaze to meet hers again and saw that her face was completely expressionless. Her pupils flared with suppressed fury and she backhanded the cowrie from his grasp.

Struggling to her feet, she spat at the ground and hobbled away from the catacombs. The rest of the fighters watched her leave and broke from the suspended silence. The red team threw down their spears and gave up their cowries. Rumi had given Miselda a surrender she didn't deserve. Even if the red team managed to overcome the numerical advantage, he had tainted their effort. There was no honour in it for them and so they surrendered.

Rumi closed his eyes, breathing hard. Someone gripped his hand.

He glanced up. It was Ahwazi.

'Ajanla Mbo! Ajanla Mbo!'

The others in blue took up the chant. 'Ajanla Mbo!'

Rumi let the shadow slip from him as he slumped onto Ahwazi's shoulder and he was carried out from the catacombs as a champion once again.

21

The Council of War

FALINA

Queen Falina took her seat at the head of the war council. There were nine others seated around the table. They all looked to her – for direction, for inspiration, for leadership.

She swallowed and closed her eyes for a moment. The beaded crown was uncomfortably heavy on her head as she tried to maintain her straight-backed posture. They all sat in silence – waiting. For a moment, her eyes met Alangba's and she was certain for that instant that he could see past the veil to her face. She wanted to ask for his help; his guidance. But she was a queen now and that meant she had to act as one.

She stole a glance at Maka Naki, who stood just behind her. He offered her a gentle smile and it was just the morsel of encouragement she needed. He was unbearably handsome but there was something subtle about him too. Something smooth as spider silk that had changed her entire impression of who he was. She smiled back but knew he couldn't see it from behind the veil.

She drew in a heavy breath and opened her eyes. 'How are our preparations?'

Mandla spoke first. 'We have recruited heavily in the Shadow Order, Your Majesty. We expect that within a month we should have doubled the fighting capacity of our shadowwielders.'

Queen Falina nodded. 'All of the requisite standard?' she asked.

Mandla narrowed his eyes. 'Requisite for this very moment, yes.'

Her eyebrows rose. 'Very well. And what do you think of the standard, Zarcanis?'

The red-haired woman raised her gaze, her expression grim and expressionless. 'It has dropped, but I trust the trainers to raise again with time. Some yam takes longer to boil.'

Falina looked to Gaitan. 'I was led to believe that there were traitors in our midst. Weeds among the wheat who let Zaminu go. Have they been rooted out?'

Gaitan lowered his gaze. 'Our investigation continues, my Queen.'

Falina turned back to Mandla. 'And our efforts in Basmine?'

Mandla gestured to Alangba. 'I have put together a team, led by Alangba, to rouse the sleeping spirit of rebellion in Basmine. There are those there who will be glad to ally with our cause.'

'How many fighting men do we have as things stand?' she asked.

Chief Gaitan cleared his throat. 'Around one thousand, Your Majesty.'

Falina blinked. 'And how many do the Palmaine have at the ready?'

Gaitan lowered his gaze.

'How many?'

Gaitan cleared his throat. 'At least twelve thousand,' he said. 'And they have guns, too.'

Falina frowned. 'So, we have no chance as things stand?'

Gaitan shook his head. 'Dara the Skyfather and Dumaré-Adandan leave nothing to chance, but it would appear that we are overmatched, Your Majesty.'

Falina let out a mildly exasperated sigh. 'How do we close the gap? I will not send an army to Basmine to wage a war that we cannot win. My father did that before – I won't make the same mistake.'

Gaitan opened his mouth then closed it again. Falina was sure he meant to speak a word in protest but what grounds could he possibly have? She had lost more from that decision than perhaps anyone else at the table – she had a right to call it a bad one.

She goaded him. 'You disagree?'

Gaitan drew in a breath and let it out slowly through his nose. 'It was a different time, Your Majesty. We had lost so much. Perhaps in different circumstances cooler heads may have prevailed but our heads had been set on fire.'

Falina's hard frown softened and she drew in a deep breath of her own. It was true. Her father had been a shaken man when he rode into that battle. Too shaken to be still. She lifted the crown from her head and set it on the table. She saw the faces of the others clearly. They saw hers. Tears had rolled down her cheeks, certainly trailing lines from her eyepaint. She raised her chin. 'I need to know that there is a way we can win. I need to believe in this.'

'What if we begin with a smaller part of Basmine – the southlands – and then take more territory incrementally?' Gaitan offered.

Falina shook her head. 'We will never have a better chance than we do now. Once we strike, the Palmaine will know the strength of our forces and have the resources to call ten thousand reinforcements. They will encircle us and strangle us out of the southlands. Besides, the natives from other tribes will see it as a territorial dispute, not an existential one. We need to take all of Basmine or none at all.'

There was silence around the table. Gaitan lowered his gaze and closed his eyes. Mandla looked to the heavens and whispered in prayer. The other chiefs refused to meet her stare. Only Zarcanis and Alangba looked her way.

'Four thousand good people,' Alangba said. 'I believe we can find four thousand good people in Basmine that still believe we should be free. Who will fight for that right and fight well. I have found hundreds all over the world. I found you, my Queen. There are other fires that still smoulder. We need only to look in the dark.'

Zarcanis nodded. 'The Odu will join you, perhaps even some amongst the Saharene.'

'The Kuba must join us also,' Falina said. 'We cannot stand at the head of an army of just three tribes. All four must act as one. A thousand Kuba, at least. A house divided will not stand for long.'

Alangba glanced at Zarcanis with a rueful look, then nodded. 'May the Agbara make it so, Your Majesty.'

Falina narrowed her eyes. 'We need something we can offer them. Something that the Palmaine cannot.' She pinched the bridge of her nose and glanced down at the crown in front of her as a thought struck her.

Mandla must have had the power to read minds for he immediately shook his head. 'No.'

'Not forever,' Falina explained. 'Only for a time. All four kingdoms will take their turn to be king. Ten years, perhaps.'

'It cannot be,' Mandla said. 'Each tribe will seek only their own interest for their time as king. The nation would be unstable.'

'It is no different to what it was in the Kasinabe kingdom,' Falina said. 'When my father wore the beaded crown, there were complaints he favoured his kin over the other noble families. Before the Almarak family had the throne, it was the Oranya, and the people everywhere groaned when an Oranya was named market chief. Before the Oranya were the Wolodu, who lasted only three years after they seized rice fields from the Ajiboye family. Even within our tribes we find ways to divide ourselves. Softborn and Kasinabe. Old blood and new. Darker skin and lighter skin. Short hair and long. I have even heard it said that those who write with their left hands are closer to God than others.'

Mandla straightened and gave Falina another long look. 'Wisdom. I see it true. Wisdom is your footstool, Your Majesty.'

Falina blinked at that. Then she cleared her throat. 'We will always find a way to see the differences between ourselves. But we will be the first to abandon suspicion in favour of trust. We cannot become prisoners of the same story of despair. If Basmine is to be a true kingdom, then love must come before domination.' She slapped the crown across the table. 'It is only a symbol. Only something I wear by accident of birth. Leadership – true leadership – is about service. About sacrifice.' She glanced up at Alangba. 'About love. Duty comes before death. If I am to lead Basmine then my allegiance is to *all* its people. Not just the Kasinabe.'

A stunned silence snatched control of the room. They stared at her, struck by the passion with which she had spoken and the implications of her words.

Chief Karile backed away from the table and for a moment, Falina thought she would storm off in protest. Then she bowed low to *foribale*, pressing her forehead to the ground in the highest possible salute.

'Ka-Biyesi O. All hail the Golden Eagle. May she live forever.'

Gaitan rose from the table and bowed to *foribale*. 'Ka-Biyesi O.'

Zarcanis did the same, then Alangba, then the First Ranger and all the other chiefs.

Mandla was the last to rise and in his eyes was the shocked awe of a man who had discovered an elephant in his bedchamber. He took Falina by the hand and kissed her fingers, then he bowed low until he was pressed against the floor like the others. '*Ajanaku*. Blessed of the blood. Music beyond our hearing. You *are* your father's daughter, and victory is Dara's promise for you. Ka-Biyesi.'

Falina stared down at the crown which sat at the centre of the table. There was no running from it now – she was here. So much of her life, she had told herself to keep her head down. Now another voice had screamed from the void. The voice of her father. Of her beloved sister. Of the Almarak and all the precious people whose lives she had the potential to change.

Raise your head high.

She took the crown with both hands, raised it high and crowned herself again. 'I know of only one successful rebellion against the Palmaine.'

'The Blatini war,' Gaitan offered.

She nodded. 'Exactly. The benefit the people of Blatin had was threefold. First of all, the Palmaine crown was nearly bankrupt after its successful campaign in Basmine. Secondly, there was infighting amongst the Palmaine noble families which eroded the stability of the established social order, and third, they had the willing support of other nations who despised Palmaine domination. We will need these three factors to also fall in our favour if we are to stand a chance.'

Mandla nodded. 'We will send envoys to other countries who would gladly come to our aid if they believe it will hurt Palmaine.'

'We will have to disrupt Basmine's trade. Hamper their

exports to Palmaine if we can. Strike them where they care,' Falina added.

'Let it be so, Your Highness.'

'On the matter of the Palmaine social order, we need to find a way to break them down.'

Mandla smiled. 'Oh, I have a plan for that also.'

Falina nodded. 'Then we have a great deal of work to do. Palmaine is strong but not invincible. We defied death before, now we must defy defeat.'

Gaitan grinned and puffed out his chest. 'Defiance is what we do.'

22

Enliven the Flame

ALANGBA

Alangba sat submerged in the bathing tub staring up at the ceiling mural as he worked soap into his beard until it formed a foamy lather. The soap smelled wonderful; a rich, citrus and honey scent. He wished he could bathe with a soap like it every day, to smell so fresh, but this would be his last luxury for a while. In a few hours, he would be on a journey again, where things like sweet-smelling soap were closer to a dream than a desire. *Duty comes before death.*

The soft swish of the door made him glance over his shoulder. Four men in dark robes filed in with ornamental spears. They formed an honour guard at the entrance and Queen Falina stepped easily through.

Alangba half rose from the tub before remembering that he was naked as his bornday. Stopping himself, he bowed at the waist to preserve his modesty.

'Your Highness, sorry, I had not expected you.'

Falina raised a pacifying hand. 'Please, Alangba, you had no way of knowing I was coming. I wanted to see you before you left, at a time when we might be able to speak privately.'

She nodded to her guards and they all left the room.

Alangba sank back into the tub and glanced up at the queen.

'I see you, Omoba,' he said, with half a smile.

She smiled back as she slid the beaded tiara from her forehead, slipped off her shoes and strode to sit on the wooden stool beside the bathing chamber.

'I wanted to let you know that you were right,' she said.

Alangba narrowed his eyes. 'Which time?' he said with a grin.

She smiled. 'I've never met anyone quite so silently smug as you.'

Alangba combed through his beard, rinsing it. 'And I have never met someone quite so loudly stubborn. It is why I always knew you would be the perfect queen.'

She blinked and straightened in her chair. 'How could someone like you ever believe in someone like me? I am not strong, I have no battle experience, I have never led a single person in my life. Why do you believe in me?'

Alangba held her gaze. 'The first time we ever met, you said something that has stayed with me. Something I kept coming back to on our long journey here.'

She raised an eyebrow. 'What did I say?'

He gave a wry smile. 'When we told you we were taking you to Basmine, you said, "I will not go quietly". Such a simple thing but it meant so much to hear you say it. All our greatest leaders, all our most inspiring warriors share one essential trait: they speak. To speak is to live. It is to inspire change. You promised me then, in your stubborn way, that you would always speak your mind, you would always tell it how you see it. For so long in this country we have let lies live. Today in the council, you proved me right again. You spoke when others were silent. That is who you are – the shout in the eerie silence that enlivens the flame. You were a captive of the Palmaine for over a decade and you never lost your fire. Never lost your voice. Who else could lead a nation that no one speaks up for but the one who will not go quietly?'

Queen Falina formed a thin line with her lips and nodded as though to herself, then closed her eyes and covered her face. Alangba could see she wanted to cry but was wrestling with the indignity of it.

With her face covered, he rose from the bathing tub and strode over to the door, ensuring it was firmly shut, then he slipped into a bathing robe. 'There is no shame here – especially not for a queen.'

She let out a soft sob and shook as she let the tears fall. For a long moment, there was silence as they let the tears have their way. Then Falina straightened and it was like seeing a veteran soldier lift her sword again. The look in her eyes, the set of her jaw. His chest rose with pride.

'You really will be a great queen,' he said.

She looked at him and raised her chin. 'Promise me you will return safely.'

Alangba's smile was gentle. 'I will do my best.'

'I command it as your queen,' she said. 'Duty comes before death. So do your duty and don't die.'

Alangba laughed. 'I will be leaving one of my team behind, to look after you.'

Her eyebrows shot up. 'Maka Naki?'

Alangba nodded once and then he offered her a full-toothed smile. 'I see you, Omoba.'

An hour later, Alangba walked into the Shadow Order. As Third Ranger he had the freedom of the Eredo but even so he felt like a trespasser. There was a time he would have given anything to be a shadowwielder but he had learned with experience that it was just as much a curse as it was a blessing. He had heard Ladan talk in his dreams. To confront that emotion and anguish time after time took its toll on a person.

He stepped up to a Suli dormitory and studied the names written beside the door. *Ajanla Erenteyo.* He stepped inside.

He found Rumi at the corner of the room, sat beside a small-boned Kuba man and a muscle-bound albino. When their eyes met, Rumi rose to his feet and Alangba saw that so much of the boy had changed. He stood with arms spread apart and a hand just to the side, about an inch out of striking range – a fighter in every habit. His eyes seemed to have lost that glaze of boyish innocence that Alangba had seen on the day he first found him with Renike. If you let it, life would have its way with you; even so, it was a thing of sorrow that this was who Rumi had to become to stand his ground in the world. Hardship makes a man better than ease does. Trouble was, the hardship sometimes made a man too hard and they could never find ways to be soft again. Alangba's inward hope was that Rumi would keep some of that softness he had seen in the forest.

'Alangba,' Rumi said, extending a hand.

Alangba brushed his hand aside and pulled the boy into an embrace. He whispered low. 'Don't be that way with me, Irumide, we have seen too much together.'

Rumi was tense for a moment of surprise, then he relaxed and squeezed the back of Alangba's kaftan. They held that embrace for a moment then broke apart slowly. His friends, to their credit, saw that this was a private moment; the Kuba boy tapped the big fellow on the elbow and they moved on to some other business. It was good Rumi had friends like that – smart and sensitive. That gave Alangba hope.

He touched Rumi's shoulder. 'I'll be leaving before the morning and I wanted to say goodbye.'

Rumi's jaw moved but his eyes stayed level. 'How long will you be gone for?'

Alangba hesitated, then said, 'I don't know.'

Rumi nodded. 'Thank you for coming to say goodbye. You honour me.'

Alangba squeezed Rumi's shoulder. 'The honour has always been mine, Irumide. War is coming and the truth is we might never see one another ever again. You are going on to do great things – I can see it in you.'

Rumi gave a small smile. 'Thank you.'

Alangba shook his head. 'I did not say it to compliment you. I say it so you can understand what lies ahead. You know my words.'

'Duty comes before death.'

Alangba nodded. 'They do not have to be yours, but when the storms which lie ahead hit you with everything they've got, you'd best have an anchor that keeps your feet planted. Something you can hold on to when you do not know which way to turn.'

Rumi pinched his bottom lip and twisted it. 'How did you find your own words?'

Alangba drew in a heavy breath. 'I was... a dishonourable man once. I still am, underneath it all. I need "duty" because without it, I am nothing. I didn't find my words, they found me.'

Rumi grimaced. 'I too am a dishonourable man—'

'No, you are not,' Alangba snapped. 'And you need to stop telling yourself that you are. The way you love, the way you feel, the music you play. I wish I had that like you do. I had to teach myself to love, but it flows out of you. You are not a dishonourable man, you are a kind one.'

'I had a good teacher,' Rumi said, closing his eyes. 'The best teacher. My mother.'

Alangba nodded. 'What were your mother's words, then? What did *she* always tell you?'

Rumi squinted for a moment, then raised his chin. 'Put love first.'

Alangba beat his chest twice and pointed to the ceiling. 'There are your words, Ajanla! You will be a dangerous man one day. A dominant one. But remember what your mother told you. Put love first. There is no greater power than to turn an enemy into a friend.'

A glint of emotion touched Rumi's face and Alangba thought, just for a moment, he saw that boy he had found in the Nyme again. One who was facing up to a world where the ones he had loved above all else were lost forever. Rumi grabbed Alangba by the collar and pulled him into a hug. 'Go well, Alangba. We will meet again – I am certain of it.'

Alangba rested his chin on Rumi's shoulder. May it be so. By Dara, may it be so.'

23

Servant of Light

LETHI

It was the first caravan to stop for them. Two had hastened past as soon as they noticed Attem and only by hiding him in the shrubs were they able to get the third to slow down. They drew close to the halted caravan when Lethi noticed a mark on the side of it.

Attem froze.

The sign depicted two crossed-over pick-axes – the symbol of the Palmaine Mining Company; the mining outfit financed by the Royal Bank of Palmaine.

Governor-General Zaminu had run the Palmaine Mining Company until his atrocities with its workers had garnered the attention of a writer named Axel Al-Morel whose subsequent report on the company had led to Zaminu's withdrawal as governor. Lethi had seen the severed hands himself, piled up like cuts of meat outside the mines. The king had long known of Zaminu's work but Al-Morel's report left a stain on the Palmaine claim to be an ennobling force in Basmine.

Attem sniffed at the air as they got closer to the caravan, noticing the heaped bulk of coal in the wagon behind the caravan. Lethi had seen that look on the tracker before and it always preceded his spear getting bloody.

He took Attem by the wrist. 'Don't lose your head. It's just a caravan.'

Attem glared at the wrist and let out a slow breath. 'Of course,' he said, nodding.

The wheelman looked up as they came around, beaming when he saw Lethi in uniform. When he noticed the tall, dark, native behind Lethi, the smile faded.

Lethi raised his hands as though in surrender. 'My name is Lieutenant Lethi Altayir of Barnham Wood. I am a soldier in the Palmaine army. My...' He hesitated as he cast Attem a glance. '...servant and I were attacked. We need to return to the House of Palman. We have no money on our person, but rest assured that you would be handsomely compensated, should you be so kind as to help us.'

The wheelman looked from Lethi to Attem, to Attem's bloody spear.

Lethi smiled and leaned forward. 'We had to do our best to defend ourselves.'

He gestured to Attem, who lowered his spear and flashed a horribly unconvincing smile.

The wheelman raised the reins and drew in breath, plainly about to drive off. 'I don't think—'

'Wait!' Lethi urged, desperately, but the wheelman was already turning away. 'Wait!' he said again, this time he raised Azamon's medallion high so the wheelman saw it clearly.

The caravan stopped as the wheelman sat, transfixed for a moment by the shimmering gold ornament.

'The Meladroni,' the wheelman breathed.

Lethi stepped towards him, knowing now that he had restored some authority. He fixed him with the same stare he had just received from the jailer who served him food. 'That's right, and we need to be taken to the House of Palman... now.'

The wheelman swallowed. 'Of... of... of course, my lord. Please climb in. I will have you there before you know it.'

Lethi let out a silent sigh and climbed aboard. Attem followed with a load more suspicion. They took off at a boisterous pace and Lethi finally allowed himself to fall into a blissful, desperate sleep.

He awoke to the sound of water rushing through the fountain at the House of Palman. Attem sat motionless at the corner of the caravan. It was something Lethi had noticed about the man more than once – when he wanted to, he could be perfectly still.

'We are here,' Lethi said, to get his attention.

Attem moved so suddenly that Lethi gave a start. They climbed down from the caravan and told the wheelman to await payment for his fare.

The wheelman roundly refused. 'I walk in the Light. I need no payment from the Meladroni.'

Lethi shrugged. 'If you insist.'

They were barely through the doors when Zaminu appeared, storming down the corridor. He was dressed in the full uniform of a governor-general with the ceremonial sabre in his right hand.

'Where is Azamon?' he asked.

Lethi cleared his throat and stared up at the once-governor-general. Zaminu's look was one of the long-truant student who knew his day of punishment was at hand.

'He was killed, my lord,' Lethi said.

Zaminu took a startled step back as though struck. For a moment the corridor was suspended in silence. His breathing came in sharp gasps as he leaned against the wall, gathering himself.

'My Lord—'

Zaminu let out a shuddering sob and whispered a single word. 'No.'

Lethi's stomach tightened in a knot as Zaminu kept repeating that word.

'No... No.' He thumped the wall with the side of his fist. 'No!' he snarled.

The man had totally fallen apart and it took him several long moments to remaster himself. After a prolonged silence he straightened and managed three words.

'Who killed him?'

Lethi blinked and cleared his throat. 'The Black Hammer Clan.'

Zaminu's jaw tightened as he looked away. 'Follow me,' he said.

Lethi obeyed, trailing Zaminu down the corridor until at last they turned into a small room with short wooden doors. It was dark inside until Zaminu lit the hanging lantern and a small circle of light illuminated the twin chairs at the centre of the room. He lit another lantern and the room grew brighter still. The far wall was a panel of wood, with figures from the Palman holy book carved into it. Lethi saw the Son and the broken noose beneath a four-point star. He saw a man with a vulture perched on his shoulder and a woman with two cats at each side. Another figure carved into the wood clutched his stomach as though in the throes of bellowing laughter.

Zaminu slumped into one of the chairs as though exhausted. 'I always said the boy was half-witted. But what is one to expect of a mixed-blood child? He will be missed.'

The words were spoken with a thoughtless, unaffected distance. One would think Zaminu had lost a favourite plant and not a son. But Lethi had seen the truth of it in the corridor when the man had first learned Azamon was dead – pain had been the first feeling, but now he was distancing himself from that pain.

Zaminu drew in breath. 'I expect he charged in there like a baboon.'

Lethi gave a start, speaking before he could think. 'He was brave, my lord. He died serving the light. No one could have seen that ambush coming.'

Zaminu snorted. 'You are quick to lies, Lethi. Leave my son's wounded pride alone – it won't leave a scar now.'

Lethi looked away to hide his scowl and drew in a breath.

'Do you know why they chose me to rule this land, Lieutenant?'

Lethi shook his head. 'I do not, my lord.'

Zaminu glanced at the painting on the wall. 'Because I understand the natives deeply. Better even than most of them understand themselves. Deep down at the centre of their bones, the natives understand that they are an underclass that deserve to be controlled. Chaos needs order – they crave our domination.'

Lethi gave a start as the erstwhile governor-general pulled open a drawer and retrieved a pair of cream riding gloves along with a golden kola nut.

Zaminu pulled the gloves over his fingers. 'It is our duty as Palmaine to live up to their expectations. To give them the illusion of consequence they need and lead them by the hand. That is our greatest burden. To control all populations in a way that they can respect. Firmly and purposefully. That is why we are here, Lieutenant, to serve and to save. To bring light to darkness.' Zaminu touched his chin. 'Will you serve in my son's stead, Lieutenant? Will you lead the Meladroni?'

Lethi blinked. He knew immediately that this was not a commission he could refuse. No one could rightly refuse the call of the Light. He drew in a breath and met Zaminu's gaze. 'Yes, my lord.'

Zaminu's lips curled into a knife-cut smile as he pushed the golden kola nut forwards. 'Seal it with a promise.'

Lethi glanced down at the kola nut, confused. 'Excuse me, my lord?'

Zaminu raised an eyebrow. 'Don't tell me you have never heard of the custom? The natives believe that to seal a promise by breaking kola nut is a solemn oath.'

Lethi stiffened. 'I am familiar with the custom.'

'Do you know where it comes from, Lieutenant?'

Lethi shook his head. 'No.'

'It is said that when Xango, the Darani god of thunder, sought to wage war on the Kingdom of Niben, the King of Niben appeared to him in a dream and offered him kola nut to settle their differences. Xango agreed in the dream and broke kola nut with the king though he had no intention to honour that promise in the waking world. When he awoke from his sleep, he could still taste the bitterness of the kola nut but marched out to war all the same. As his armies battled the Kingdom of Niben, he realised that every time he struck a soldier of Niben down, one of his own would fall dead. When his brother and friend, Kokou, fell dying, Xango realised that something was amiss. He called back his armies, but even as he retreated, his men continued to die. So Xango sought out Balaye, agbara of healing, in prayer, hoping to bring an end to his tribulation. When Balaye heard what Xango had done, he rebuked him ten times, for he had committed a deep abomination. When kola nut is broken, to act against another is to act against oneself. Xango, seeing the error of his ways, pleaded for forgiveness but the agbara shunned him – for he had broken a golden rule by attacking the Kingdom of Niben. He was tormented by screams as his men continued to die. He made parlay with the King of Niben and pleaded for mercy and only then did the dying stop. They broke kola nut again and now even evil men know that when kola nut is broken – it is an unforgivable abomination to act against it.'

A knock sounded at the door and both Lethi and Zaminu turned towards it.

'Come in,' Zaminu ordered.

A Kuba man slipped inside. He wore the uniform of a governor-general but the slump-backed, head-hanging posture of a man who knew his best days were behind him. Blaise Paru, the acting Governor-General of Basmine. He moved like a dog that knew it was going to be kicked at any moment. You didn't need to see the strings to know he was a puppet – one wave from Zaminu and the man would dance.

Zaminu scratched his collarbone and adjusted his kaftan. 'Blaise, I want a clear message sent to the Black Hammer Clan.'

The Kuba man straightened, his eyes narrowing with attention. 'Of course, my lord.'

Zaminu let out a breath. 'The punishment for conniving with the Black Hammer Clan is death. Any village where a member of the Black Hammer Clan is found will be burned to the ground.'

Blaise Paru hesitated for a moment, before giving a slow nod. 'I will move it with the council, my lord.'

'There is no need to get it through the damned council!' Zaminu snapped. 'I have made provision for such things.' He pointed at the shelf. 'Bring me *Hansah's Laws*, volume eleven.'

Paru turned to the books, trailing a finger along the shelf until he picked out a thick tome and pulled it free.

'Page four hundred and twelve or thirteen,' Zaminu said.

Paru raised an eyebrow as he flicked through the pages. He stopped at a page and glanced up. 'The Collective Responsibility and Punishment Ordinance?'

Zaminu nodded and cleared his throat. 'The existence of an armed insurrection would justify the use of any degree of force necessary to meet and cope with the insurrection. Any district believed to harbour militant forces may be summarily punished collectively.'

Paru narrowed his eyes. 'That's what it says.'

'I know that's what it says, you fool – I wrote it,' Zaminu snapped. 'Put things in place. I need a township burned before the week is up.'

The puppet's head gave another perfect bop. 'Yes, my lord.'

He gave Zaminu a questioning look as though to say, 'Please, may I leave now?'

Zaminu gave him a dismissive wave and the man smiled, nodded and left the room.

Zaminu turned his gaze back on Lethi. 'I want Oké-Dar burned to the ground. You can let the women and children live if you wish, but all the men must die.'

Lethi swallowed but let no emotion touch his face. He touched his pendant and glanced up at the ceiling. A mural spread across it depicted Archangel Meladron with the tablet in his hand, his eyes watchful.

'One hundred consular will escort you,' Zaminu said. 'I want you to send a strong message. Let the blood flow. Heap the bodies up. Burn everything but the Palman temple.'

Lethi grimaced. 'Understood.'

Zaminu gave him an appraising look. 'Why do you have that look on your face? I know you have a soft place for the natives, but we must be stern at times like this. We must remember our commission. They ...' He hesitated and Lethi saw that pain again.

He drew in breath. 'They killed my son – a servant of the light, and for that there must be heavy recompense.'

Lethi bit his tongue, neglecting to mention that just last week Azamon had thrown a man's son into an oven.

'Darkness flees in the presence of light. Destruction is another form of creation. We are a refining fire and we must never be afraid to burn away impurities in this land. It is our duty.'

Lethi gave a silent nod. His jaw was stiff.

Zaminu gestured to the wooden carvings along the far wall. 'Come with me.'

Only then did Lethi see the wall for what it was. Not a wall at all – a partition. Zaminu slipped a hand into a handle at the centre of the wood and slid the door aside.

Lethi let out an awed breath as he stepped in after Zaminu. It was a large room with a great bathing chamber at its centre. The ceiling mural depicted the Son sat cross-legged against a pure blue sky, smiling down at the world of humanity. Incense burned from thick candles, bathing the room in a dim, yellow glow.

Zaminu took his shoes off and rolled his trouser legs up to the knee. Then he stepped into the bathing chamber. 'Come,' he summoned.

Lethi followed his lead, ripping his boots off before stepping into the bathing chamber. Zaminu stood at the centre of the pool, up to the waist in water.

Lethi drew in breath as the water rose to his midriff. Something about the incense had an intoxicating effect and he could feel himself drifting between sleep and wakefulness.

'My Lord,' he muttered, feeling faint, as the mist rose from the still-steaming water.

At the corner of his vision, he noticed Zaminu draw his ceremonial sword from its sheath and raise it high. For a moment,

Lethi's stomach lurched. He raised a belated hand to block the blow but knew it was far too late.

The blade fell and touched his shoulder, but no pain followed. Lethi glanced up in relief.

'I name you First of the Meladroni. The Night and the Knight. Servant of Light.'

Lethi bowed his head and closed his eyes and whispered a prayer. The water seemed to grow hot as Zaminu spoke words of consecration.

Sensing a third person in the room, Lethi glanced up. Zaminu stood with arms raised in triumph. Something felt utterly wrong. It was as though, for a moment, a dark, thick cloud of blackness had fanned out above Zaminu's head. Dark as bitter storm cloud, thick as a forest fog. He blinked once and it seemed to dissipate into nothingness again.

Lethi heaved out a breath, his heart thumping and looked again to the ceiling mural. The Son stared down at him with eyes red with rage. Lethi let out a silent sob. *For the Son sees our hearts and brings peace to those who resist evil.*

Zaminu's voice broke through the fog. 'Arise again, Lethi. Servant of Light.'

Interlude

AGBAKO

Agbako stared down at the ingredients spread out before him. Eggplant, groundnut, amaranth and ugwu arranged in lines like a platoon of willing soldiers. Next to that he had two human hearts, one brain, one pound of fresh flesh and a gourd of just-drained blood. The cookpot was at the perfect heat and his cutlasses were lined up in order of size.

'Should I make a stew or cook it all dry?' he wondered aloud.

Stew would take too long, he decided. He set to work, letting his mind wander as the staccato sound of the severing knife beat in tandem with his thudding heart. Here, more than anywhere else, was his safe place. His sanctuary. His peace.

As the flesh started to simmer, he sniffed at the air, drawing in the aroma. He could almost laugh. The all-too-familiar smell reminded him of when he first began the work. When he first took the step to becoming a witch doctor. It felt like millennia ago now. All bright-eyed and innocent, taking an hour to lop off a hand. *How things have changed.*

There, in that enveloping silence, it was as though he could understand everything. He could tell by the steam when the pot was ready. Know by the colour of the okra how it would taste with the flesh. He looked to the moon and felt like he knew it to its smallest crumb. Understood the earth down to its yolk. He smiled as he tossed hand-washed grains of rice into the now-simmering pot.

Sweat touched his brow. His stomach seemed to curl against itself, ravenous in its want. Cooking of this kind was not about sustenance or appetite – it was about power. In some small way, everything was about power if you saw it true. Agbako had decided long ago that he would never be powerless again. He had started that walk. Now he had travelled too far in the darkness to turn back. Light would be blinding now.

But power of this kind was corrupted. As poisonous as it was enriching. He would never sire children. Never have a partner to call his own. All he would ever have now, was power. He put his chin over the pot and drew in the aroma. His insides came alive and he grinned. *Power has its benefits.*

He caught the faintest hint of a strange scent and sniffed at the air. His eyes went wide as he stretched out a hand. A blade, black as ink, materialised in his palm and he turned slowly to face this unwelcome visitor.

His heart jolted at the sight of her. Though Agbako had long ago lost interest in the indulgences of the flesh, this was a truly stunning person. Her skin seemed to command the moonlight to deliver its greatest gleam. She walked as though every step was a prelude to attack. She smiled at him, meeting his gaze, and he saw her eyes were not like those of a human. They were the eyes of a cat. Pupils vertical and irises yellow. Though she appeared as a young woman, there was something in her eyes that was ancient and knowing. *Not a human then – a spirit.*

'What are you cooking?' she asked.

Agbako stood in front of the pot, gesturing with his blade. 'Who are you?'

She glanced down at the blade and smirked. 'Put it away if you are not going to use it.'

Agbako gave her a long, calculating look, then tossed his blade harmlessly to the side. She smiled and he saw that her teeth were sharp as those of any wolf or hyena.

She arched, catlike, in a deep stretch, and Agbako could only stand transfixed. Her attractiveness was withering his wits to mush. Every moment passed slow, for he sensed the hour of his death had come. He would face it bravely. He had power.

'Some call me Pretty Yelloweye. You might have heard of me.'

Agbako's breath caught as his mouth went suddenly dry. Pretty Yelloweye. Queen of Cats. The one who killed Gu and tore him to pieces. He took a stuttering step back as he glanced subtly at his blade again. There was no use reaching for it – he was no true opposition to her.

'Relax,' she purred, touching his chest.

Agbako glanced at her hand and cleared his throat. 'What do you want from me, *godhunter*?'

She grinned and her eyes sparkled with the animal intensity of a lioness. 'Is that what you call us? Godhunters?'

'It is your work, is it not? To hunt gods?'

'Gods is too strong a word for what they are. They are merely jumped-up spirits bloated on human praise and sacrifice. We sanctify the world in removing their stain.'

Agbako's face was blank. 'So what do you want from me?'

Pretty Yelloweye made a show of looking him up and down. 'I need your help.'

Agbako blinked, his surprise so sharp that he hiccupped. '*My* help?'

Yelloweye gave a single nod. 'Why do you seem surprised?'

Agbako cleared his throat. 'I would not have imagined that an immortal godhunter could ever have need of a wretch like me.'

'The godhunters are not immortal – the Priest of Vultures proved that already; but we are desperately hard to kill. Truth be told, it is quite liberating to know you can die. You grow lazy when nothing is ever truly urgent.' She rolled a thumb over his chest and down till she touched his navel. 'Passion, desire, lust, it all fades when you have lived every fantasy ten thousand times. But there is something about mortality that makes everything so ... exciting.'

She wet her lips and something in the timbre of her voice set Agbako alight with animal want. He needed her like he needed his next breath. Sudden as the summer storm, he was overrun with the feral need to kiss her lips; pull her close. His jaw tightened as it took every fibre of iron will to stop himself from falling prostrate and begging for her kiss.

She held his gaze for a long moment, and then her face split in a dangerous grin. 'You are strong-willed. I like that. I need a strong-willed man for the task that lies ahead. Someone who knows the Nyme forest well. Who can reach the summit of Erin-Olu.'

Her hold over him loosened and the oppressive pressure of her allure relieved him. He let out an exultant breath. She was ten times as dangerous as she was pretty – he knew that from only a piece of the stories. She had killed more gods than he had fingers to count.

'This is a time for urgency, Agbako. The fate of the world will be decided in the days to come. The attention of immortals is awakened and you stand at the heart of it. I need you to help me find something.'

Agbako grunted. He knew what she had come to ask. A question so many had asked before.

'I do not know where the Door of Testimony is,' he answered, with a note of irritation. 'If I did there would be no need for all this,' he said, gesturing to the cookpot. Only then did he notice that the flesh had started to char. He scowled as he sniffed at the air. He liked to eat his flesh rare.

The godhunter shot him a dangerous look and his heart jolted again.

'I did not come for the Door of Testimony,' she hissed. 'Do I look like I need a door to enter the spirit realm?' She gestured to herself. 'If I need to touch the spirit realm I need only click my fingers or take one long breath.'

Agbako glanced up at her. 'Then what did you come for?'

She narrowed her eyes and, in that moment, they were closer to the red of fire than the yellow of the sunset. She glanced up and met his gaze. In all eyes there was some flicker of innocence. Some promise of love. But when he looked into her eyes, Agbako saw nothing at all but hate.

She spoke softly. Almost as though to herself, but Agbako heard her words. Heard what she needed his help to find.

'The Son of Despair.'

Lightning flashed and thunder groaned above. For one, blink-long moment, Pretty Yelloweye gave a nervous look to the skies as though worried a bolt would hit her directly. Then she remastered herself, cracked her knuckles and stretched out a kola nut. 'So, here is my offer.'

24

When the Music Plays Again

RUMI

Rumi spread his palm across the drum hide. It had been about a month since he had played. In years past that would have seemed an eternity but times had changed and music had found stiff competition in his life.

'You look nervous, Ajanla,' came a voice from behind him.

Rumi arched his back in a deep stretch, then he turned to Stake. 'I haven't played in a while.'

Stake smiled. 'Music is a forgiving mistress. She will let you come back, with time.'

The big Kasinabe raised his Florinian flute as a warrior might his sword and pressed it to his lips. The first note hit hard as an axe blow. A tremor of awakening stirred Rumi entirely to life.

There were five players in the room. Rumi knew their skill well. Wilfried, who played the kora, was the first to answer the call. Zokora, who was merciless on the oud, lowered his head and started to work. Damayo, whose voice was satin lined with silk, set her hands to the harp, cleared her throat and joined the noise. All four looked at Rumi, challenging him, eyes bright with expectation.

He pulled his drums close and started to play. The first song was familiar to all. A simple gateway to the complexity that lay ahead.

Better the pestle than the yam
Better to die than meet the Great White Ram

They played through and Stake turned the song to 'Queen Moreem', a less familiar but gentle song, which told the story of the warrior queen who sacrificed her son to save her people.

Stake's voice rose above the music. 'All right, enough games. It is time to play.'

He launched into 'Akiti the Hunter' and Rumi set his jaw. Lowering his head, he pounded his drum in time with the beat. The song was not built for a drum – its two lines of song danced together but were separated by pitch. Rumi gave no surrender. Pulling his drums closer, he began to beat at two simultaneous levels.

Stake quirked an eyebrow and glanced at him as the song reached its chorus. Rumi licked the edge of his mouth, as a smile curled about his lips. He rose to three levels with a grunt of effort. The air seemed to buckle and bow. He saw the notes before they came as his hands melded into effortless song. Stake had been right; music was a forgiving mistress and had returned without a fight. She had run to him as a mother to her lost child. His vision blurred as the tears came – sudden as ever. 'Akiti the Hunter' was Morire's favourite song. The one his brother always wanted them to play.

He could remember Morire's smile. His laughter. The way his eyes went wide before he ate. *He can't be gone forever.*

Rumi delved deeper into the music – surrendering himself. He heard the other players fall away as they gave him the space to vent in song. He built more levels of music. Beat the drums with eyes closed, his stomach clenched as he tapped into something that came from a place to which there was no true direction. As the bird to its flight. As a leopard to its first hunt. This was entirely what he was built for – to play.

He held the song for one peerless chorus then, wincing, he brought it all to an end and heaved out a breath.

Stake stood with arms folded and eyes wide. 'I had almost forgotten how good you are.'

Zokora nodded. 'I have never heard someone play the drums the way you do. Never. It is like it isn't an instrument at all with you. Something more. Now I understand why Mandla wanted you here.'

Rumi's eyebrows rose. 'What?'

Zokora gave a confused look. 'Oh, I am sorry,' he said. 'I thought you already knew.'

'Knew what?' Rumi snapped.

Stake cleared his throat, raising his hands as though to soothe Rumi. 'Mandla wants us to write a new song. Something that will travel. He said it would be wise for us to involve you.'

Zokora nodded. 'Something to rival even "Furae Oloola".'

'The whole Eredo preparing for war and he wants us to write a song,' Rumi said.

'Songs last longer than kingdoms do, Ajanla.'

Rumi blinked. 'I am no songwriter. I can play the music, but I have never been able to write the songs. I am no good with words.'

Stake smiled. 'Don't you worry. With the way you play – we'll find the words.'

Damayo spoke with her feather-soft timbre. 'You just keep giving us the music. We'll take care of the rest.'

The door flew open and Sameer burst inside, his eyes wide with panic, his forehead beaded with sweat. 'Ajanla, come quick. It's the darkman.'

Panic surged as Rumi called his shadow. He followed Sameer down the corridor until they arrived at last at the botanical ward.

Griff was surrounded by botanicals who were all holding their shadows. Rumi glanced through the gap amongst them.

Griff lay quivering in the bed. The wound across his side was thick and purply with spores of pus riding across the side of his chest.

'He will live,' came a familiar voice.

Rumi glanced up at Uroma, who wore a silk veil over her head and shoulders. 'What happened?'

Uroma narrowed her eyes. 'We told him not to call his shadow but he did. All our bindings burst. The shadow is too much power for his body to take right now. We could have done more for him with water from the source of Erin-Olu, but without it we have to be more careful. His body will need time to heal.'

Rumi bit down on his bottom lip. 'What happens if he calls his shadow again?'

Uroma looked away. 'We might not get to him in time.'

Rumi winced.

'We'll have someone with him through the night,' Uroma said. 'To make sure he doesn't accidentally call his shadow in his sleep. That happens sometimes with experienced shadow-wielders.'

Rumi glanced down at Griff, who was still convulsing. 'How long before he's able to call his shadow again?'

Uroma closed her eyes. 'With Dara's favour, maybe a few years.'

Rumi lowered his head and whispered a curse. No shadow-wielder could resist the urge to call the shadow that long.

'Is there nothing more we can do?' he asked.

Uroma rolled her shoulders. 'No.'

Rumi's jaw clenched. 'What about if we had Oké water from the source of Erin-Olu?'

Uroma gave him a thoughtful glance. 'Then there would be more we can do.'

Rumi closed his eyes. 'Understood.'

'You should go back to your room,' Uroma said as she turned back to Griff. 'There is nothing you can do for him now. We'll help him as much as we can.'

The look in her eyes was solemn. Rumi didn't need to hear her say it — he knew what they all were thinking because he was thinking it too. *The darkman isn't long for this world.*

A violent tremor wracked Griff's body and all the botanicals jerked in response. In that small moment, Rumi's mind was made up. He closed his eyes and whispered words he hoped his father would hear. 'I'll be back for you.'

He left his father's room and stepped into another. Inside lay Latan, the Truetree who had attempted to reach the summit and failed. Losing all his companions along the way.

Rumi walked right up to his bedside and looked into his eyes. 'It is time, Shadowwielder.'

Latan sat up halfway and gave Rumi a long look. 'So, you're the one with a death wish.'

'Quite the opposite.'

Latan smiled. 'Zarcanis told me you were crazy, but I suppose nothing unimaginable has ever been achieved by entirely sane people.' He pulled a rolled-up parchment from under his pillow and gave it to Rumi. 'They say you killed one of the Priests of the Son.'

Rumi reached under his kaftan and tucked it under his waist band. 'I did.'

'Pray that whatever god helped you then, helps you now,' Latan said.

'Tell me, Shadowwielder, what is out there?' Rumi asked.

Latan frowned. 'Erin-Olu is a place of total wildness. But

wildness is a form of freedom. Everything there, from the smallest ant to the largest elephant, wants to kill you for threatening that freedom. We are trespassers there – it is not our place. I watched my brothers and sisters die trying to do what you now attempt, if I have any advice, it is this – don't go. There is too much to lose.'

'And if I decide to go anyway?'

'Then make peace with your enemies, petition your gods and if you see yellow trees – run.'

25

Into the Nyme

RUMI

Rumi tapped Sameer on the elbow. The skinny Kuba stirred and groaned something in his sleep.

Rumi let out a soft sigh. 'Sameer,' he whispered.

His eyes snapped open as it took him a moment to gather himself. 'I was dreaming about Chief Karile,' he hissed in frustration.

Rumi raised an eyebrow, confused. 'Really?'

Sameer sat up. 'She's so knowledgeable – I find it very alluring.'

Rumi shook his head. 'You are a strange man, Sameer.'

Sameer made a dismissive gesture with his hand. 'Why did you wake me up?'

'Yeah, why did you wake us up?'

The second voice had come so suddenly from behind him that Rumi nearly jumped out of his skin.

'Don't sneak up on me like that,' Rumi snapped.

Ahwazi rolled his head in a single circle. 'How was I to know you were so jumpy?'

Sameer touched each man on the shoulder. 'Why did you wake us up, Rumi?'

Rumi cleared his throat and straightened. 'I am going into the Nyme.'

Sameer narrowed his eyes. 'What?'

'I am going after the Door of Testimony. To bring my family back and get Oké water from the summit.'

Sameer pulled his bedcovers back up. 'Wake me up when you are ready to behave.'

Rumi's face hardened. 'I mean it, Sameer.'

'You can't possibly mean it. We are preparing for a war and every soldier counts. Especially the shadowwielders. You know hardly anything about the Nyme and how to get to its summit.'

Rumi nodded. 'That's why I need someone who is excellent with a map,' he said with a grin. He produced the rolled-up parchment.

'I am no good with a map,' Ahwazi said.

Sameer blinked at the parchment. 'What is this?'

'It's a map.'

'Just never got the hang of them,' Ahwazi said.

Sameer unfurled the parchment and stared at it. 'Even with a map, we stand very little chance of making it to the summit.'

'I like that you said, "we". We've faced little chances before,' Rumi said. 'Many times, in your case.'

'Flattering me won't work, Ajanla.'

'But I know what will,' Rumi said, leaning close.

'What?' Ahwazi asked.

Rumi let out a breath. 'You won't let me go alone.'

'Are you sure about that?'

Rumi nodded. 'I am.'

'Why?'

'Because I would *never* let you go alone. Even if it was to the hellmouth.'

Sameer closed his eyes and looked away as though stung. 'Blackmail.'

'Absolutely.'

Ahwazi gave a low groan. 'But it's working.'

Sameer sat up and fixed Ahwazi with a defeated look. 'Softborn clan is forever. You two would be useless in the Nyme without me.'

'Who said I was going?' Ahwazi croaked.

Rumi laughed. 'Oh please, Ahwazi. You were ready to go the moment you woke up.'

Ahwazi grinned. 'I suppose you're right – you two would get killed without me watching out for you.'

'When do we leave?'

'Same time tomorrow night,' Rumi said.

'How do we find a way out?'

'I'm working on that,' Rumi said.

Sameer nodded. 'I'll bring some supplies,' he said, reaching beneath his bed for where he kept bottles of gin.

Ahwazi arched his back in a stretch. 'I'll find a way to get our weapons out.'

'We'll need someone who knows the forest,' Sameer said.

'That's taken care of.'

Sameer gave him a searching look. 'You'll be putting her in real danger. Is she ready for that? After everything that happened in the Thatcher?'

Rumi's stomach stirred at that. It was the question lodged at the edge of his mind that he had refused to answer. One he pretended did not exist. Now that Sameer had spoken it out loud, every pretence was broken.

'She's ready,' he said. 'She is a fighter.'

Sameer gave him a long look before pulling his bedcovers aside and rising to his feet. 'This will be the most dangerous thing I have ever done.'

Rumi drew in breath. 'There is a township near my old

village called Oké-Dar. If you want to test how easy your pocket is to pick, all you need to do is walk through any road in Oké-Dar and count your losses afterwards. It is the sort of densely cramped place where the whole township knows who snores, and death visits more often than fathers do.'

'We have those at the peninsula too,' Sameer said.

Rumi nodded. 'There was this lady in Oké-Dar, they called her Mama Akara. Word was she had the best beancakes in all the world. She set up stall in the middle of Oké-Dar and people from as far as the Citadel would travel all the way down just to taste them. Longest queue you've ever seen. She made enough money to buy the whole township and yet she never moved her stall. Wealthy Citadel folk saw the potential of her business and offered to take her to the Citadel but she refused. To go to Oké-Dar, even on the best of days, was always a risk. It was a seedy place. But Mama Akara said the same thing until she died – "Some things are worth the risk".'

Sameer raised an eyebrow. 'And you think *this* is worth the risk.'

Rumi considered Yami and heard Morire's explosive laughter in his mind. 'Yes, I do,' he confirmed. 'We save the Eredo with Oké water.'

Sameer gave a slow nod. 'I guess we'd better get ready then.'

The next day was spent making every preparation. Packing supplies, charting the path. For their escape to be successful they needed to leave without a trace. Anything less than a day's head-start and the sentries would track them down before they made any progress.

As Rumi stepped out onto the Thatcher, the thought came again of telling those closest to him. Renike, Ladan and Alangba. But he knew Ladan and Alangba would not approve – they were too loyal to themselves and Mandla. Renike would insist on coming with them, but she was too young and new in the shadow. It had to be just the four of them.

He strode towards the slouched over tree where Nataré sat along a thick bough. Her scent carried on the wind and hit him like the first gulp of white malt whiskey. He straightened, his eyes enlivened by her presence.

Rumi decided it was best to get straight to the point. 'We have to leave tonight.'

Nataré gave him a look which he could only read as disappointment, then she curled her lips and let out a sigh. When she spoke, her voice was soft as cotton without a hint of fear. 'I knew you wouldn't wait a week.'

'We don't have a choice.'

'We always have a choice,' she said, rising to her feet. 'And I guess yours is made. I was expecting it. Three hours past midnight, be at the Thatcher door.'

'We'll be there.'

Rumi felt a pang of guilt as they parted ways. He was asking them all to risk their lives for the mere chance to save his family. A chance that was far from certain. It was far too much to ask of anyone. *I should go alone.*

But they would never let him go alone and he needed them. He had given them the chance to say no – even if he had known they would never take it. He was doing this for Yami and Morire – he owed them more than all of the world combined.

A pulse flashed through the bond and he stretched out his arms. Hagen lunged into view, alive with excitement. Rumi lowered to his haunches and stroked behind his ear. 'Are you ready for the Nyme, Hagen?'

Confusion, anxiety and readiness travelled across the bond. Hagen was readiest of all.

★

Night fell like a stumbler in the dark. They stole into the Thatcher with all the stealth of thieves. Nataré was at the door – waiting, just as they had agreed. Hagen was crouched beside her, his aura as calm as Rumi had ever seen it. It was cold at this hour of night.

'Let's go,' Nataré said.

Her words produced a visible cloud of mist amidst the chill night air.

She led the way, moving about the shadows and snaking a path through the shrubbery and trees. After close to an hour they came at last to a quiet part of the Thatcher where the wall-gate was yet to be reinforced by steel.

Nataré went suddenly still.

'What is it?' Sameer asked.

At the corner of Rumi's vision, something moved. An animal, perhaps – startled into the underbrush. He glanced over his shoulder. There was nothing.

He was halfway turned when he heard a sound. He stiffened.

The sound came again; unmistakeable. A twig breaking underfoot. That was when panic fell. *Someone is coming.*

It was the fullness of dark. They could barely tell the trees from the bushes and rocks. Everything was a vague abstraction of black.

'What is it?' Sameer asked again, his voice thick with nervous impatience.

Nataré reached for her sword just as a figure lurched into view. The speed of what came next was so startling and sudden that Rumi wondered if his eyes had deceived him.

Miselda stood with her hand wrapped around Sameer's wrist. Nataré had her sword out, pointed at the intruder. Ahwazi had called his shadow.

'What are you all doing?' Miselda hissed. She was teeming with shadow, just as she had been in the catacombs. If things came to violence, blood would spill on each side.

Rumi summoned his calm. 'I should ask you the same question, Miselda,' he said, stepping between them. 'I know what you do out here.'

She ignored him and glanced at the wall-gate. Then she noticed the thick burlap sacks they each had strapped to their backs. Then she saw the curled-up map Sameer was holding. Then she grinned. 'You're trying to leave the Eredo.'

Rumi frowned, offering no confirmation or denial.

'Where are you going?' Miselda asked.

No one spoke.

She wet her lips. 'You are going to have to kill me if you don't tell me. The minute you leave, I will tell Mandla and everyone that cares that you softborn are conniving with our enemies. They will hunt you down like dogs and drag you back before the cockerel's crow.'

Rumi narrowed his eyes. 'Sheggin' lickhead. I should have told Mandla about you while I had the chance.'

She grinned and her two gold canines glistened in the moonlight. 'But you didn't. So, either you tell me what in the hell you are doing, or I tell Mandla my own version of events. Who knows what I will say once I've had a lick.'

Nataré's sword was still raised and Rumi saw then her willingness to do what needed doing. He needed only to ask. Only gesture.

He stepped into the breach between them with hands raised in peace. 'We are going into the Nyme. To Erin-Olu.'

She raised her chin. 'Why?'

'For Oké water from its summit,' Rumi said.

Her eyes widened as she gave him a look of new appraisal. 'Are you unwell?'

Rumi shook his head. 'My father is.'

Miselda gave a start and scratched at the side of her head. A long moment of silence passed before she spoke again. 'Take me with you.'

'Absolutely not,' Rumi snapped.

'Ajanla—' Sameer pleaded.

'She's a liability, Ailera.'

Sameer blinked and nodded. 'Better a liability we can control,' he whispered.

Rumi frowned. Sameer was right. If they left her there, she would destroy their plans. Anything short of killing her would lead their adventure to utter failure and no one but Nataré had the stomach for killing her.

'Fine,' Rumi hissed. 'You come with us.'

Miselda gave an accepting nod and they passed under the breach in the wall.

Ahwazi made a low sound in his throat. 'I guess it is into the Nyme we go.'

26

Levels

RUMI

In the forest, Rumi learned that there were levels of darkness. Rumi knew all too well the near-full dark of unlit corridors and fire-doused bedchambers, but this was a new darkness. Everything around him was totally black. He could not see his own hand. He could not tell the difference between his eyes closed and open.

The sounds of night were there too. A mosquito hissed its ultimatum at his ear. Ghost frogs croaked their rebuke for this unwarranted trespass. Unseen crickets let it be known this was their hometown. You didn't need a map to know it – they were in the Nyme.

They formed a chain with their hands. Nataré led from the front. Somehow, she knew her way about the darkness. Rumi had stumbled half a hundred times but she hadn't lost her footing once. She moved as though she had a lantern held high. *How many times has she done this?*

A half-heard sound made Hagen lower into a hunched crouch. Through the bond, Rumi felt his anger, readiness and fear.

Nataré came to a stop and held out a hand.

'Is something wrong?' he asked.

She gave no direct answer. 'Hold on,' she whispered.

They obeyed. Moments later came the sound of something grunting, snorting and scurrying like a demonic pig. It passed ahead of them, scratching earth aside as though in pursuit of its night prey. The thump of Rumi's heart was like a punch from inside.

'What was that?' Ahwazi whispered.

'A pig,' Nataré said.

'It didn't look like a pig,' Ahwazi said.

Nataré's voice was cold flint. 'Trust me, better for your mind you think it was a pig.'

The questions stopped after that.

They were barely an hour into the journey and regret had come to rest on Rumi like a cloud overhead. The Nyme was the furthest thing from safe. They were still close enough to return and pretend that none of this had happened. The Eredo and relative safety were still within their reach.

Nataré seemed to pause then, as though she had read his mind and thought to give him time to make a decision.

'Do we keep going?' she asked.

Rumi couldn't see her face, but he could imagine it. Everything blank but her eyes that were full of expression. Eyes that seemed to imprison the light and cast it back with new freedom.

He gritted his teeth and straightened. 'We keep going.'

Nataré let out a quiet breath. 'All right.'

After a half hour of trekking they came at last to something close to a path. Cuts of moonlight shone through the canopy of trees above. Some courage was restored when they could see themselves.

'Do we make camp soon?' Ahwazi asked.

Nataré glanced up at a nearby tree. 'Tomorrow they will send sentries after us and when they find our trail they will chase us down. They won't follow us into Erin-Olu, though – no one will. It is only a few hours away but there are dangers along the way that could make our journey a very short one.'

'So we don't stop until we get to Erin-Olu,' Rumi said. 'We take no chances.'

Ahwazi didn't like it, but he offered no protest. This was a time to set their hands to work and they all understood that. Tired, hungry and lost in the darkness, they gritted their teeth and kept going.

Rumi's mouth ran dry but it was too early to drink from his waterskin. Miselda hissed out a wordless grumble behind him but even she showed her resilience and kept going. As to why she had insisted on coming with them at all, he had no answer – but so much about that strange woman was a mystery.

They kept the silence as they walked. The pace Nataré set was murderous, but no one outwardly complained.

In darkness such as this, every sound took on a sinister edge. A snapping of wood could be a bush baby or a forest spirit. A whistle of wind could be a witch doctor in wait. Rumi's heart thumped with every step. Fear was pressing hard, but it had not mastered him. He kept a loose grip on his halberd, ready as the forest-jack, but knew that in times like this, being too swift to swing could lead to a bloody accident.

'Easy,' Nataré urged. 'Nothing to kill yet.'

Hagen forged ahead, sniffing at the ground as they walked. Through the bond, Rumi could feel his fear. He too knew that this was a forsaken place.

They kept walking until the darkness ebbed and Hagen came to Rumi's side, plainly more relaxed in the light.

Miselda snorted and spat. 'What is it between you and that dog?'

Rumi glanced over his shoulder at her. 'This isn't the time for it, Miselda.'

She laughed. 'You brought us to the bloody Nyme. We could be dead any moment – the time for everything is now.'

'No one forced you to come with us,' Ahwazi said.

'I have my own reasons,' she said. 'Don't worry, I won't do anything to stop us from getting to the summit. We need that water.'

Rumi blinked. So that was why she was there. Perhaps she had some friend or relative ailing in the botanical ward. Someone who needed the purifying water from the source of Erin-Olu.

'I'm bonded to it,' Rumi said.

Wrinkles formed at her brow as she regarded him. 'And we will tell old stories again,' she whispered.

'What?' Rumi asked, confused.

'It is from Kuda Kamo's book,' Sameer explained. '"Things thought forgotten will name themselves true and we will tell old stories again."'

Rumi gave a confused look. 'Right.'

They passed a large iroko and Rumi squinted as a clearing appeared ahead.

'We are close,' Nataré said.

The sky had brightened overhead as the sun prepared for its grand arrival. Rumi was mere steps from utter collapse. They had been walking at an unforgiving speed through the night. Not once had Nataré slowed down or stopped for anyone. Rumi suspected she was trying to prove a point. Each of them had taken turns to lag behind, but never too much and always catching up.

Rumi stopped for a moment and doubled over with his hands pressed to his knees. Sweat touched his eyes, blurring his vision as he took a minute to catch his breath. Something moved in front of him. He reached instantly for his halberd but stopped short as he realised what it was.

A pink and yellow butterfly. Beautiful and graceful, small but approachable – it seemed a memento from a lost time, where beauty could be just that. Looking up, Rumi noticed a darkening – as though the light of the sun was a candle beginning to whimper and die.

'There it is,' Sameer said.

The cool brush of river mist touched Rumi's cheek as he turned. A scene from a storybook lay ahead. There it was – Erin-Olu. It was a terrifying, mystical, dangerous place, but above all else it was beautiful. Seven distinct cascades along the western slopes of a massive waterfall. The trees loomed high above the waterfall such that it always seemed to be a place stuck in the moment between day and night.

Thick gushes of water spilled over moss-covered rocks, spattering foam and mist. Butterflies of every colour flitted about. Frogs croaked their joy. Monkeys laughed. Birds sang. If it were a painting it would be the perfect depiction of Dara's hand in the world of man. But this was no painting, and Rumi knew all too well how Erin-Olu's beauty had a sinister undertaste. All its allure changed nothing about its true nature. This was a place where more people died than lived. Poisoned honey.

'Dara, Father of All, I will fear no evil for I walk in the refuge of your shadow,' Nataré muttered.

Rumi stepped close to her and took her hand. 'We breathe out all our cares and breathe in your strength. May we walk under the shadow, where death wins no victory.'

Sameer stood stupefied. He had unfurled the map in one hand but hadn't managed to tear his gaze from the waterfall.

'I don't know whether to run for my life or strip for a swim,' Ahwazi said.

'Neither of those would be wise,' Rumi said.

Miselda stepped forward. 'It's incredible,' she said, peering into the water.

Nataré stretched a hand across to bar her path. 'Don't get too close,' she urged, glancing suspiciously at the dark pool. 'Let's keep moving; the forest watches.'

The last time Rumi and Nataré had come to Erin-Olu, they had a Shinala to ride. On foot, they were far more vulnerable. If something decided to chase them, they had little chance of outrunning it. Even so, Rumi felt less afraid this time than the last – for he had the shadow and, with it, he would give even a god a fight to remember.

Rumi straightened as a tremor flashed through the bond. Hagen's ears shot straight up as he turned towards a tree across the pool. Four eyes twinkled back.

Rumi squeezed the back of Hagen's neck, calming him. 'Relax, they are just cats.'

Hagen flashed suspicion, alertness and irritation through the bond.

'What is it?' Nataré asked.

Rumi straightened. 'Nothing.'

There were seven levels to Erin-Olu, and each was more dangerous than the last. With a Shinala the journey could be done in a single day but on foot, Rumi thought it would take at least four.

Sameer stretched out the map and studied it. 'The map suggests we should curl around the rock path, but I can't help but think we might make quicker work if we try taking the slope on the other side.'

Nataré touched the map. 'We are at the edge of rain season – the slope is for the wild things. The rock path is the safest way. Trust your map.'

Sameer nodded and rolled the map up. 'Safety first.'

They made their way to the rock-strewn path beside the water and began the climb. Rumi's knees complained as the path steepened, clicking as he stretched to keep pace with the pack.

'We have to rest soon,' Ahwazi said.

This time they all agreed. It had been a brutal walk and the time for reprieve had come long ago. Nataré glanced off to the right and hissed out a breath.

'There,' she said, pointing to a small clearing beneath some trees. They set up camp in mere minutes. Miselda called the shadow and conjured a hammock for herself, suspended between two trees. It was an impressive feat, but Rumi's esteem for it was lessened on account of the fact that he knew her to be a shadow-soother. Perhaps he would be able to conjure a castle if he was shadowsoothing.

Sameer managed to conjure a large pillow while Ahwazi conjured a large blanket. Rumi took Nataré by the hand and conjured a bed mat for them both. Her eyes widened as she watched them work. In the Order, conjuring was common as cobwebs, but everywhere else in the Eredo, it was still a thing of marvel and mystery. Though what they had performed was a mere whisper of the story of shadowwielding, Rumi could tell that Nataré was inwardly awed.

She reached out a tentative hand and touched the bed mat the way one would touch a snake they had been told wouldn't bite. 'How does it work?' she asked.

Rumi scratched the back of his head. 'It's like drawing with your wrong hand after ink is thrown in your eyes. It is difficult at first, but eventually you see past the ink and the grip in your wrong hand grows firm and sure. I can draw a simple bed mat, others can draw...'

'A hammock,' Nataré finished.

Rumi nodded. 'Precisely. The shadow uses the strength of your most powerful emotions. When we conjure, we have to face those emotions directly.'

'The ink in the eye.'

Rumi nodded. 'The better we understand our emotions, the more the ink starts to take a different shape – no longer just a blot but more a lens. Eventually, it isn't ink at all to you – just an important part of the way you see the world.'

'That's a beautiful way of putting it, Ajanla,' Sameer said.

Miselda leaned out of her hammock and met Rumi's eye. 'It *was* a beautiful way of putting it,' she agreed. 'Except sometimes the ink is poisonous and you never, ever get used to it.'

'That too,' Sameer added.

Ahwazi cleared his throat and glanced at Sameer. 'What emotion do you use?'

'You never ask another shadowwielder that,' Miselda hissed. 'Taboo.'

'We are not just shadowwielders,' Sameer said. 'We are friends.' He glanced up at Ahwazi and grinned. 'Mostly fear. Sometimes anger.'

Ahwazi smiled and nodded. 'I use shame mostly. Sometimes envy.'

'What do you have to be envious of?' Sameer asked.

Ahwazi sighed. 'Everything, apparently.'

Sameer sucked his teeth. 'I've heard that before.'

Nataré glanced at Rumi, who had gone silent at this part of the conversation. He could feel her eyes on him but neglected to meet them. Sameer and Ahwazi were looking at him too.

'Fine,' Miselda snapped. 'If sharing our greatest weakness is what we're doing then I might as well join in.'

She slipped out from her hammock and slapped a kola nut down at the centre of their makeshift camp.

'What's this for?' Ahwazi asked.

'If we are going to be friends then we might as well know each other's real names.'

Ahwazi gave her a confused look. 'I said *we* were friends,' he said, gesturing to Rumi and Sameer. 'We already know each other's names, you're not—'

Sameer snatched the kola nut up and broke it. 'Sameer,' he announced.

Ahwazi studied him for a moment, then took the kola nut and broke off another part. 'Ahwazi.'

Rumi reluctantly came next. 'Irumide,' he said, meeting her eye.

Nataré neglected the offer. 'Keeps me awake,' she said.

It was true that kola nut had that effect but that was not the reason for her refusal. She never told anyone her true name.

Miselda took the kola nut back and broke it once again, biting till she winced from the bitter juice. She set her jaw strong and threw her shoulders back. 'My name is Muriel,' she announced.

There was a long, indeterminate moment of total silence.

Then Ahwazi exploded with laughter. 'Muriel,' he hissed, almost choking to death. 'Are you one hundred years old? What sort of name is Muriel?'

In a blink, her blade was at his throat and her stance had shifted into *spider waits in web.*

Ahwazi swallowed. 'I think I'll stick to Miselda,' he wheezed.

She gave him a long, level look and then she too burst into laughter.

Ahwazi rubbed his throat as he narrowed his eyes. 'Not funny.'

Sameer touched his shoulder. 'Miselda is fine for me too.'

They all agreed on that.

Ahwazi blinked. 'So, what emotion do you use? Fear?'

Miselda laughed. 'The world has done its worst to me – it cannot threaten me anymore.'

'Anger then?' Sameer offered.

She shook her head. 'Not really.'

'What then? Regret?' Ahwazi asked.

It was Nataré who spoke the answer. 'Shame.'

Miselda gave a solemn nod.

'What is the difference between regret and shame?' Rumi asked.

Miselda met his gaze. 'You feel regret for something you have done but feel shame for something you have become.'

A moment of contemplative silence had its way after that and it was Nataré who first had the sense to break it up. 'Now that we're all a merry band, rest your legs. Sleep if you can. We should start moving again at full morning. The first level is the safest of them all, but even here we must be cautious.'

Her eyes were hard and level. It was as though she was fighting an inward battle and was on the brink of a horrible defeat. 'I'm going to take a look around,' she announced.

As she stepped out of the clearing, Rumi moved to walk beside her.

'Where are you two going?' Miselda called out.

Rumi didn't answer. He caught up with Nataré and she glanced at him, smiled then touched his hand. He squeezed her palm and spoke the words he knew she spoke to herself when she was afraid. 'You are the knife edge.'

She took in a deep, solemn breath as though his words were rain after a desperate drought. Then she nodded to herself.

Something about the way she quirked her lips made his stomach lurch. He could not help but consider those lips. How soft they were to kiss. What a delight it would be to press his lips on hers, and brush down her neckline. He let his eyes wander to her neck. Smooth and supple as a potter's masterwork. His eyes wandered lower as heat rose in his chest. She caught his glance and narrowed her eyes. Then, quite suddenly, she pushed him gently aside.

He stiffened. 'What is it?'

She squinted, sniffed at the air, then drew her sword. 'I think you had better call your shadow.'

27

Call Your Shadow

RENIKE

Renike stared up at Zarcanis through half-closed eyes. The copper-salt taste of blood in her mouth was now a near constant feature of their sessions.

The Viper's expression was one of utter disappointment.

'You are distracted, Rain. Your mind isn't here,' Zarcanis snapped.

Renike sat up and let out a tired breath. She didn't have it in her to get up, so she just sat there. She wanted to apologise but Zarcanis hated apologies.

'We are training for war, Rain. Real war. I am not losing you in a fight. Not losing any of my trainees in a fight. I need you all the way here. You can't half-arse this.'

'I am trying,' Renike breathed.

Zarcanis met her gaze. 'It's because of Rumi, isn't it?'

Renike looked away. Of course it was. How could she concentrate on anything when she knew that Rumi had run away to the Nyme? It wasn't just that the Nyme was dangerous. Not even just that he had gone. The deepest sting was the knowing that he had not told her about it. Not spoken a word. Not given the whisper of a clue.

'Are you in love with him?' Zarcanis asked.

The words hit her ears wrong. She had asked herself that

very question so many times. What she felt for Rumi was deep, strong and real, but it wasn't love. Not romantic love anyway. She loved Rumi as one would a deep friend. A dear brother. But nothing more than that.

'I love Rumi,' Renike breathed. 'Of course I do, but not like that. He is my first and dearest friend. He took care of me when most others wouldn't. I spent entire seasons on his shoulders. He is the closest thing I have to family here.'

Zarcanis studied her. 'You are hurt that he didn't tell you he was leaving?'

Renike blinked, then nodded. 'Yes.'

Zarcanis arched her back in a feline stretch and let out a breath. 'He did it to protect you.'

'I know,' Renike hissed.

'Then stop being a child about it. Commit to this, completely, and the reward is knowing that you will never, ever be left behind again. Your friend Rumi is a hard one to kill. He'll be back. But if you want to help him – this is where you do it.' She gestured to the fighting pit. 'Stretch off and gather your breath. We go again in five minutes.'

'Have they sent anyone after him now?' Renike asked.

'Mandla considered it,' Zarcanis said, 'but we cannot afford to risk any more shadowwielders on a journey into the Nyme. They stand a slim chance of catching them after a full night's head start. If Rumi returns, it will be under his own will.'

'You mean *when* Rumi returns,' Renike said.

Zarcanis made a weighing up gesture with her hands as though to say *could go either way*. 'I won't coddle you, Rain. You know that. I am here to make a soldier of you and that is exactly what I am going to do.'

Renike drew in a breath. 'Sometimes I wonder if bad things happen to me because I don't have enough faith. I wonder if

I just don't believe in Dara enough and that's why He's never saved me.'

Zarcanis gave her a curious look. 'Faith and doubt – the Great Oppositions, none is good without the other. Faith is what it is. There is no virtue in it. I prefer a healthy dose of doubt, personally. Sometimes doubt breeds curiosity and ingenuity. It leads us to great discovery. But unshakeable faith…' She shook her head. 'It leads to foolery, hard-heartedness and false piety. Now, I know plenty of bone-daft zealots who bless Dara every time they pass wind but believe me when I say they die in war same as the non-believers. I've stuck swords in both priests and sinners and can confirm they die much the same. But you' – she pinched her forehead – 'you faced down an Obair and won. With no shadow, no sword. If that isn't a sign Dara is on your side, then I don't know what is.'

Renike blinked back a tear as she regarded Zarcanis. She wanted to hug her but knew Zarcanis would likely cuff her if she tried.

'Thank you, Zarcanis,' she said instead.

The Viper shrugged. 'Don't let your guard down with me, Rain, I won't take it easy.'

'I won't,' Renike said.

Zarcanis gave a nod and turned to N'Goné. 'Nagode, you're up.'

N'Goné grunted and stepped forward. She helped Renike to her feet, bent forward into a stretch and bounced into the fighting pit.

Zarcanis had her back to them. She glanced over her shoulder and said, 'Call your shadow.'

N'Goné obeyed and her shadow poured out like steam from a kettle spout. N'Goné had already managed to garner four lines of shadow rank. Far more than any of the other new Seedlings.

Her shadow was, from the look of it, the closest Renike had seen in serenity to that of the Viper. Flat and sinuous as a velvet coat, moving only as N'Goné did.

Zarcanis called her own shadow as N'Goné pulled a flower from her pocket. That small flower was her secret weapon. Chief Gaitan had taught them that nostalgia was a powerful emotion, which, when channelled in the shadow, unlocked incredible power. N'Goné had since made it a habit to keep a steady collection of red hibiscus flowers. When she was in the captivity of witch doctors, the scent of red hibiscus had always been thick in the air – the jujumen used it for their rituals. The scent of the flower gave N'Goné a powerful blast of nostalgia and other locked-tight emotions were set free.

She sniffed at the flower and her shadow bulged and expanded, casting half the fighting circle into darkness.

Zarcanis was unperturbed. N'Goné was already in the stance of *shepherd holds the crook*, but Zarcanis was taking her time.

At last the Viper called her shadow and stepped into the fighting pit. N'Goné raised her safespear, wasting no time to advance. Zarcanis danced out of range.

'You are strong, Nagode,' Zarcanis said, 'but you are also impatient. It makes you far too easy to predict. Give me subtlety.'

N'Goné checked her run and pulled her safespear back.

'Show me something,' Zarcanis whispered. 'Prove you are something more than just an angry victim.'

N'Goné sprang forward with her safespear raised and Zarcanis again slipped out of range.

'You are too predictable,' Zarcanis said. 'I need variance. I need creativity. Don't think about how you are going to hit me. I want you to know that you are going to do it.'

N'Goné snarled as she let off an absolutely incredible flurry of beautiful violence. She threw out her left hand then lashed out with the spear in her right. Zarcanis barely managed to sidestep before N'Goné brought the safespear back in a wide arc. It brushed off the Viper's shoulder as N'Goné stepped into the strike. Four, five, six hits came in the space of time that most would manage just one. Zarcanis was equal to it; moving with such perfect balance that nothing struck true.

'Better,' Zarcanis said. 'Much better.'

Now Zarcanis came back at her. Moving, as always, at an entirely different level of speed. If N'Goné was the rushing water, Zarcanis was the morning light – everywhere all at once. She moved in and out of N'Goné's guard, touching her gently just to let her know she was there.

N'Goné lashed out with an overhand blow, in a mixture of frustration and fury.

Zarcanis grinned. 'You are breathing hard now. Good. Save your energy for when I really come at you,' she said.

N'Goné's frown lasted only the fraction of a second, before she lunged again. She swung her safespear but Zarcanis leaned out of range. The backswing was double-quick but Zarcanis saw it coming too. She took one immaculate step past N'Goné's guard and dealt the girl a vicious blow to the kidney. The punch produced the dull sound of a rice sack hitting the floor.

N'Goné doubled over and coughed, spattering blood. Zarcanis, who had raised her safespear to strike again, went still at the sight. Her eyes widened as she put a hand on the small of N'Goné's back. 'Breathe, don't try to fight it. Cooperate with your pain. Let it have its way.'

N'Goné's face hardened as she heaved in a ragged breath.

'Easy,' Zarcanis breathed as she helped N'Goné to straighten. Gone was the combat intensity of the Viper, now Zarcanis was all concern and affection. 'That's enough for today. I'll get a botanical,' Zarcanis said.

N'Goné nodded as she released the shadow.

Without Oké water from the source of Erin-Olu, shadow-wielders had to be more careful when sparring with their trainees. Gone were the days of beating them half to death in the knowledge they would recover completely within minutes of gulping down a cup of water from the source. There were still other herbal remedies that could quicken recovery but nothing had the restorative power of water from the source.

Zarcanis reappeared with a botanical and the two led N'Goné out to the ward. It was a precautionary step, Renike knew. N'Goné was not one to be held down for long. Despite this, she couldn't quite bite down her concern. She followed them out to the botanical ward, where N'Goné was given herbal tea with crushed bitter leaf and a bucket to spit the blood out.

They sat together – all three – in the ward, ensconced in a companionable silence. Zarcanis was the first to speak after what felt like a small forever.

'Are you sure you want to do this, Rain?'

Renike blinked and glanced up at the older woman. 'I am.'

Zarcanis scratched the back of her neck. 'Why?'

'Because I am tired of being overlooked. Tired of being told to run and hide when danger comes. Every native under the sun knows that danger will come our way eventually. When next it comes, I want to number amongst those who stand, not those who run.'

Zarcanis shook her head. 'So, pride, then?'

'Not pride,' Renike said. 'Dignity. There is a difference. Pride is a feeling we keep for ourselves. Dignity is a feeling that nourishes others. When N'Goné, Toshane and I faced an Obair in the corridor, I felt liberation beyond anything I can easily explain. With the shadow, I stand not only for myself but for

Rumi, for N'Goné and Toshane. For you. For everyone I love. Everything I believe.'

'A noble "why" but I think there is more, Renike. I think it's deeper than that.'

'What could possibly be deeper than that?'

Zarcanis shrugged. 'That's what we are here to find out. You Seedlings always think you are here to become something. The truth is you are here to see the truth of what you already are.'

N'Goné drained the rest of her tea and set her teacup down. She gave Zarcanis a questioning look.

Zarcanis laughed. 'Oh, I already know why *you* are here, Nagode. I know what you are down to your bones.'

N'Goné lowered her gaze and looked away with the shame-faced stare of a pick-pocket caught about the wrist.

Renike gave them both a look. 'Why is she here?'

Zarcanis rose to her feet. 'I won't do your work for you. Learning what makes a person act is the key to knowing what they are going to do. Master that and you are a true shadow-wielder. Every overreaction to a minor annoyance is the shadow shouting. You need to learn to hear that expression. What is N'Goné's shadow shouting?'

Renike looked to N'Goné but her friend avoided her gaze and contorted herself into a tight-backed pose that said the words N'Goné didn't have the voice to say. *Leave me alone.*

28

Oké-dar is on Fire

LETHI

Lethi stared up at the painting of Meladron. He who sees all sin. What would the archangel's report be after tonight?

He straightened to his full height and smiled at the painting. *Hell can wait.*

He lifted his rifle, rolled his shoulders and tilted his neck until it made a soft click. He had worked out a plan with Attem, one he knew his men would find hard to accept.

The one weakness of the Palmaine was their arrogance. It meant that sometimes they underestimated their opposition and refused to do things that would hasten their success. The natives understood this; in Guyarica, one village had left a marshy swamp at the rear wholly unguarded because they believed that no Palmaine force could stomach the indignity of crawling through mud to fight them. They had been right, until Lethi came along. Tonight, they would throw their arrogance away once more.

A knock rattled the door.

'Who is it?' Lethi called, already knowing the answer.

'Roadie, sir.'

Lethi sucked in a sharp breath as he pulled the door open. Roadie's dark silhouette filled the doorway. They were of a height but where Lethi had muscle, Roadie had the thinnest sheet of flesh. A man so skinny it looked like he could break a bone getting out of bed. From the look of him, one would never know what violence he was capable of. His hair was uncombed above a face cut from hard lines and sharp sinew. The Northern Palmaine were a mountain people and they were infamously pale, but Roadie was so bone-white that at a distance one would think he were a corpse returned to life. In a beauty contest of pack animals, Roadie would be an underdog. He was ugly as blasphemy and his smile only made it worse.

Roadie gave Lethi an appraising look before leaning forward in a subtle bow. 'We are all waiting for you, sir.'

Lethi coughed on a snatched breath, straightening to full height. 'All right, let's go.'

They stepped out together. Banasco was waiting right by the door — no doubt he had been the one to send Roadie. Making a show of hurrying the commander.

Banasco had been made second-in-command after the embarrassment at Oké-Dar and since then, the man had made no secret of his desire to take Lethi's position. Though he looked the part of a soldier, Banasco would be a frontrunner at any idiot competition; yet these were the sort of men who had come to dominate the Palmaine forces. Men whose greatest asset was their ancestry.

'Are we finally ready ... sir?' Banasco asked.

The 'sir' was pointedly belated. Spoken as though it was an act of charity.

Lethi completely ignored him. Didn't even give him a look.

Outside, a small battalion of fighters were waiting. From the volume of their songs, it was plain they knew what they had come to do. Burn a village to the ground. Make a statement. Things sounded nice and easy when spoken in haste but how many of these soldiers really had the stomach to burn people inside their homes? To keep going when they had the smell of burning flesh thick in their noses? Lethi guessed not many.

In his mind, Lethi saw a young boy with wide, lifeless eyes and blood oozing from the hole in his head. He forced the image from his mind. More than perhaps any other night, tonight he needed a clear head.

He spotted Attem, at the far corner of the room – leaning against his spear, his shoulders perfectly still. He gave him a soft nod of acknowledgement and the native soldier nodded back.

'Having second thoughts, sir?' Banasco enquired.

Without thinking, Lethi swivelled and cuffed him hard on the cheek. Because it had come so suddenly, Banasco yelped. He touched his cheek as though expecting the slap to have drawn blood. Lethi was too careful for that; he knew it was a crime punishable by flogging to spill blood on holy ground. The slap would leave a bruise and nothing more.

Banasco lifted his glare up to Lethi. The other soldiers were laughing.

Lethi's expression was blank, but inside he was fuming. That Banasco, who had left him to die in Oké-Dar, had the temerity to speak in the way he did was an insult he could not bear.

'You're not coming,' Lethi hissed.

Banasco's lip quivered with fury as he searched for the words to speak. 'You ... you can't do that.'

'Yes, I can.'

Banasco's nostrils flared. All pretence of politeness faded away as he squared up to Lethi. 'You cannot send me away. There is nothing you can do to stop me from coming. I am an officer of the Light.'

Lethi raised an eyebrow. 'You are a deserter. You ran from this village before. I don't trust you.'

Banasco moved to hit Lethi, but Lethi had seen it coming.

He darted left out of the way and countered with a right cross that made Banasco double over.

Lethi frowned as the man straightened to his feet. This had gone too far. *I shouldn't have done that.*

Banasco came at him like a furious wave, his eyes wide with hate. 'You Zarot-loving shit.'

Lethi kicked Banasco's ankle, buckling him, then dealt a powerful uppercut to his chest. Before he could fall, Lethi caught him, cradling him like a lover and lowered him gently to the ground.

As Banasco gasped for air, Lethi stood over him. 'You are done.'

He tried to sit up and Lethi gave him an open-hand slap. He gestured to the closest guard. 'Take him away, have him stripped, flogged and chained. I will deal with him when I return.' He glanced up and summoned Attem. 'You are second-in-command now.'

Attem jerked back as though a swarm of bees had cut across his path.

Lethi knew why. For a native to be a part of their force at all was audacious. To make him its de facto commander was an abomination to most. But Lethi had no time to put men like Banasco in charge. Such men would only be led like the pig, to wallow in their own pomposity. He gestured to the guards who had restrained Banasco. 'Give him Banasco's quarters.'

The men seemed to go still at that, waiting for Lethi to rescind what he had said. But no such reversal came. Attem was the best leader he had and so he would lead.

The men turned woodenly away, dragging Banasco along.

Attem stepped up to him and spoke low. 'You cannot be serious.'

Lethi quirked up an eyebrow. 'I absolutely am.'

'You want to incite them to mutiny?'

'If they are not disciplined enough to stand behind you, then mutiny is unavoidable. The Palmaine are many things, Attem, but they are not undisciplined. They will grumble and they will complain inwardly – but they will comply.'

Attem shook his head. 'Until they slit our throats while we sleep and claim it was the work of natives.'

'You know the plan. Are you going to lead or not?' Lethi said. 'Say the word and you're back to the lowest rank.'

Attem drew in breath and closed his eyes, then he turned towards the other soldiers. 'Oké-Dar is a vigilant town. They watch their west gate well and are guarded by two parallel walls on the east. Load up our grappling hooks. Tonight, will not be easy.'

Lethi felt a smidge of inward pride at that, smiling as Attem moved to the centre of the room. 'Move out.'

★ ★ ★

It was near night by the time they finally arrived at Oké-Dar. Attem had been right: the east wall had been left largely unmanned. They didn't have the manpower to watch both sides and so they hoped the walls would do the work that they couldn't. Getting over the first wall was the hard part.

It was far too high to scale and had spikes scattered across the top. But Attem knew a way under. The native led the men to a girded sewage pit, which was directly connected to the latrine inside the first wall. They stared at him for a long moment.

'You cannot be serious,' someone muttered.

Attem ignored him and led by example. He tore off his overcoat and descended into the sewage pit. The others hesitated before another finally had the courage to follow and then they were streaming in, one after the other. Lethi went in last. The smell was unbearable, but the pit was roomier than one would expect. He emerged from the latrine largely unscathed from the crawl.

The second wall was far from impregnable. At Attem's signal, men launched the grappling hooks and the assault began. The first line of attack scaled the wall and threw rope ladders back over it. Then the men peeled into the village, close to silent in the dead of night.

Lethi was the last to climb over. It was almost eerie how quiet it was in this part of the township. A part of him was struck by the sudden fear that this was another ambush – planned to perfection. But there were no signs of it. The natives were not expecting them because none with good sense would have believed that Palmaine soldiers would emerge from a latrine.

He beckoned Attem close as the men formed rank. 'Find the leaders, bring them to me alive.'

Attem gave a soft nod and turned to face the township. 'Understood.'

The slender native beckoned six forward, amongst them Roadie and another maniac they called Sharp Sharp. He led them towards the drinking parlour where they knew there to be an underground lair. Lethi did not think they would still be there after his escape but whoever searched the place had to be careful.

He organised the soldiers into teams of five and gave them instructions on what to destroy. He made a competition of it, for he knew that to be a surefire way to make soldiers do their jobs effectively. 'Whoever burns the most houses gets one hundred cowries.'

They took off into the night and Lethi stood back to watch. There are some things you need a scalpel for, for others you need a stone maul. This was a moment for the maul. They had to make a performance of violence that would utterly demoralise their enemy. Nights like this were for the soulless.

He pulled out his pipe and sucked in a deep drag. A building at the far end of the township had already gone up in flames. Two more went up at the same time, just a moment after. In little more than minutes, the moonlight darkness was bathed in fire-red. 'Everything burns,' Zaminu had said. 'I want the place extinct before sunrise.'

Lethi blew out a small cloud of smoke, coughing silently as he prayed. 'For the Son sees our hearts and brings peace to those who resist evil.'

Another building went up in flames and a child screamed. He dragged deep on his pipe.

A boy ran out, his clothes half scorched to rags. One of the Meladroni chased after him. As the child made to sprint past Lethi, he stuck out a leg. The boy tripped and went down hard. The Meladroni caught up with him and snatched him by the collar. 'You are going to die for that one, boy,' the Meladroni hissed at the child. The boy howled as he was dragged away. Begging, pleading, screaming for his mother.

Lethi looked away and put another light to the pipe. *He brings peace to those who resist evil.*

The ground bucked and trembled underneath him as the township burned. Lethi watched it all. Saw every single building go down. *Did it really have to be this way?*

Perhaps, someday, he would find a way to answer yes.

Three figures approached from the midst of the inferno. Lethi squinted as they made their way towards him. Attem, Roadie and Sharp Sharp.

Lethi put out his pipe as they came fully into the light. 'Did you find them?'

'We did,' Attem said.

Lethi frowned. 'I told you to bring them to me alive.'

Attem looked to Roadie.

The pale man tilted his head. 'They escaped,' he said. 'We had them almost surrounded but they had unexpected help.'

Lethi narrowed his eyes. 'What sort of help?'

The three men looked at each other. No one seemed willing to speak.

'What sort of help?' Lethi asked again, with a note of irritation.

Attem cleared his throat. 'They had strange help. One man who runs with a lion. Another with only one hand who fights in a cloud of blackness. They killed ten men in the time it takes to kill one. I have never seen such speed.'

Roadie gave a rueful shake of his head. 'Neither have I.'

Sharp Sharp agreed. 'The way they moved. They were like spirits.'

'Spirits,' Lethi spat. 'You expect me to believe that *spirits* stopped you doing what we came to do.'

Attem shrugged. 'It is the truth.'

Lethi let out a long sigh. 'Show me to the bodies.'

29

Until We Reach the Summit

RUMI

Rumi squinted into the darkness with his halberd raised and ready. Two figures appeared under cover of shadow.

They moved into the moonlight and Rumi caught a clearer glimpse. They were witch doctors, plain and true. Their black, broad-brimmed hats cast their faces in shadow, but their eyes seemed to shine in the dark. They wore necklaces linked with bones and dead fruit, and they were bare to the waist. They sat astride horses that had exposed bone and rotting flesh where their coats ought to have been. It was, by any sane measure, an utterly terrifying spectacle. Rumi's grip tightened around his halberd as he awaited the moment to call his shadow.

The first witch doctor raised his chin as he pulled his hat back. He had a mirthless grin with gaps between every tooth. 'Are you lost?' he asked.

Nataré raised her sword high. 'I promise you violence.'

The second witch doctor laughed aloud. His ramshackle cackle reverberated through the forest. What did it say that this man had no fear of making noise in the Nyme?

A third voice rang through the night, deep as the pits of hell. 'But I told you this before, I have made peace with my violence.'

The newcomer stepped into the light. A giant of a man, with a protuberant stomach to rival any village drunk's. From the second of the thick copper chains around his neck hung a live tortoise wriggling its limbs over his belly.

'Agbako,' Nataré breathed.

Agbako, the witch doctor, bowed. 'We need not make this ugly.'

'It will be hideous,' Nataré hissed.

Agbako raised an eyebrow. 'Does she speak for you?'

Rumi raised his halberd. 'We speak with one voice.'

'A loud one,' said Sameer from behind.

The rest had come to join them. Rumi closed his eyes as he finally called his shadow. The wind for a moment was rainwater cold and the power filled him to the spout.

Agbako gave a nod of understanding. 'So, you know the shadow.'

Rumi nodded. 'Well.'

The two witch doctors on horseback seemed to stutter slightly, for the first time realising the truth of their opposition.

Agbako gestured to the two witch doctors to stand back. 'We did not come here to fight you. We are here to offer collaboration. Humans need to stick together in this place.'

Nataré didn't lower her sword. Rumi didn't release the shadow. The two witch doctors, seeing no truce on offer, raised their hands as grey-white swords materialised in their palms. Rumi narrowed his eyes as he prepared for a fight. On horses, they had the advantage, but they were up against shadowwielders, who knew how to defend themselves.

Just then, a flash of black shot out from behind him. One of the horses screeched as a spear of pure shadow lodged itself into its mangled side. The witch doctor clutched the reins as the horse kicked up violently. Another spear of shadow shot out, taking the horse in the throat. It toppled back, nearly landing on the witch doctor as it fell.

Miselda stepped forward. 'What are we waiting for?' she snarled.

'No!' Agbako boomed. 'Everyone calm down. We need not kill one another now.'

The fallen witch doctor snarled and hissed in complaint. Agbako muttered something that made him go still. Then the giant witch doctor raised his hands. The trees bucked and bent and the forest grew misty cold. The spray of moonlight was blotted out as Agbako chanted in deep Mushiain. Rumi felt an intense fog of corruption as the witch doctor's power began to strangle the air. His eyes were the reddening black of burning coal and the tortoise on his necklace seemed to glisten in the darkness. There was power there; real power.

'If we *must* fight, then I promise you a bloody one,' Agbako said. 'There will be screaming on your side, I am sure. Perhaps there will be screaming on ours also. You must know I am not squeamish about blood. I will give you one final offer. Lay down your swords. You will never succeed in reaching the summit without our help. Lay down your swords and we will work together to reach the summit; I swear it on my blood.'

Miselda spat. 'I don't trust him.'

Rumi glanced over his shoulder at Sameer.

'Neither do I,' Sameer said, still holding the shadow.

'We go as you go,' Ahwazi added.

Nataré raised her sword high. 'Just say the word.'

Rumi narrowed his eyes. Agbako was right. A fight now would not end until all on one side were dead. Even if they won, at what cost would victory come? He could lose Sameer, Ahwazi, Nataré. Any or all of them. No one could trust a witch doctor's word but to fight one was a far more vicious gamble. He had brought them here, he had to put them first. *Put love first. There is no greater power than to turn an enemy into a friend.*

Rumi searched the bond and found Hagen just behind in the

bushes – crouched down and ready. He knew the lionhound only needed one lunge and he could take down the biggest witch doctor, rip his throat out before he knew what the whole business was about. Hagen signalled his emotion. *Ready. Willing.*

Rumi closed his eyes and let out a breath. 'Everyone lower your weapons.'

'Ajanla...' Miselda hissed.

'Lower your weapons,' Rumi said again.

There must have been something final in his voice, for they listened the second time. The trees straightened again and moonlight returned, illuminating the scene.

Rumi summoned Hagen and the lionhound crept out from behind Agbako. The big witch doctor let out a sharp laugh.

'You had a surprise waiting for me,' Agbako said.

Rumi gave a small nod.

The witch doctor made a gesture with his hands and two full-grown lions stepped out from behind Miselda and Ahwazi. 'It would have been a festival of surprises,' Agbako said.

Rumi narrowed his eyes. The two lions would have taken Miselda and Ahwazi completely by surprise.

'I believe we want the same thing – you and I,' Agbako said. 'You want to reach the summit, and so do we.'

'Why?'

'For all the same reasons that you do – there is great power there,' Agbako said, meeting Rumi's gaze. 'We are better as friends than we are as enemies. We know this terrain well and have shared interests.'

No greater power than to turn an enemy into a friend.

Rumi held out a kola nut. 'No more surprises. We fight together until we reach the summit.'

Agbako took it and broke it in agreement. 'Until we reach the summit. You can rest tonight and when you wake, we go.'

30

Sovereign

SHOTUGA

Shotuga smiled as he entered the room, smoothing over the right side of his pink *agbada*. From behind his dark-lensed glasses he took his time looking over the people at the table in front of him. Olae glared at him with eyes that could pierce flesh. Kunde's stare was something entirely different, an apologetic one. Zahim looked bored.

They had all once been his music instructors but now everything had changed.

'I was sad to read this,' Zahim said, looking up from the short letter with the broken blue seal. 'You will certainly be missed; you are a terrific player.'

Kunde nodded in approving support. Olae just stared daggers at him. The stupid woman was still so mad for the lost Zarot drummer boy. *She should show more respect now.*

Shotuga drew in breath and gave the smile he had seen his father use on lesser nobles. 'I will miss the Golden Room terribly, but the call to be Secretary of the Governor-General ... well ... no good citizen can resist that call.'

'You will serve Basmine well,' Kunde said.

Olae hissed audibly.

'Is there a problem, Olae?' Shotuga said.

'Mistress Olae, always Mistress Olae, boy. I have books older than you,' she said.

Zahim stirred. 'Olae—'

'Have we fallen so low, Zahim? Have we? A young man goes missing the day he embarrasses this *pony* and we act like all is well.'

'I answered all the questions from the consular, *Olae*, and was found innocent of any accusation. I still hope he is found.'

'We all hope he is found,' Zahim said.

Olae looked away.

'I do not take kindly to your accusations, and I will be sure to make my displeasures known to Governor-General Blaise Paru.'

'Piss on your displeasure.'

'Olae! Enough!' Zahim said.

She rose to her feet and walked out of the room. Her eyes were solemn as a promise as she strode past.

'I ... I apologise for that Sho— High Secretary Shotuga. Our doors will always be open to you, and we wish you the best in your service,' Zahim said.

'Thank you,' Shotuga said, shifting the folds in his agbada.

'My regards to your father,' Zahim said with a bow.

Shotuga left the room with a smile on his face. He was finally becoming the man he was born to be. He didn't stop grinning until he was seated in the back of his carriage and even then, he smiled inwardly.

The Golden Room was connected to the House of Palman by a single private road. The two buildings shared the same foundation. They rode for only a short while before they arrived at the entrance to the House of Palman.

Shotuga's smile returned as he stepped down.

Men saluted as he passed, women curtsied. He took the private walkway towards his father's office and arrived in the small anteroom. There were a handful of visitors waiting, all with sacks full of cowries. That had been the way of it for near a month. His father had masterminded the inauguration of the first native governor-general and for that he had earned a rich reward. To think that Basmine now rested in his family's hands made him buoyant.

Most of the visitors were of the grey-haired, bent-backed variety. Idle veterans looking for a chance to curry favour with the hand of power. There was one man, however, who looked half the age of all the rest. He stood out not only for his age, but also for the fact that he looked, quite plainly, to be a Zarot. He wore a black velvet agbada with golden damask pressed along the side. Woven here and there into the fabric was a circular design that made it look like leopard spots. The effect was quite striking. About his neck was a red coral beaded necklace and on his hand were three gleaming gold rings.

Were it any other time in his life, Shotuga would have wanted to know who the strange Odu man was, but those days were gone. He was always the most important man in the room now. The future of Basmine.

He neglected to greet any of the visitors and turned to climb the short flight of stairs that led to his father's office. He came to a door guarded by two armed men in uniform. When Shotuga tried to walk past them, they formed a cross with the noses of their guns to block his path.

Shotuga raised an eyebrow. 'Do you know who I am?'

'His Lordship is not to be disturbed,' said the one on the right.

'I am his son,' Shotuga snapped.

The guards did not move.

'Tell him it is me,' Shotuga said.

'We were given strict instructions; he is not to be disturbed,' the guard said.

Shotuga's scowl deepened as he inspected their guns. They would not harm him. He studied their faces. *They wouldn't.*

Better not to take the risk. He shifted the folds of his agbada and stepped back from the door to wait. The guards seemed to relax as he did so, returning their guns to their sides as the silence resumed.

After about half an hour, the door finally opened and none other than the governor-general, Blaise Paru emerged.

'Governor-General Paru,' Shotuga said, kneeling. 'I did not know you were here.'

The governor-general put a hand on Shotuga's shoulder and smiled.

'Let us keep it that way, Shubi.'

'Shotuga,' he corrected.

The governor-general nodded and smiled then he turned towards the stairs. Shotuga's father emerged next, arm-in-arm with a tall and skinny Palmaine man. Shotuga's eyes bulged as he realised who it was. Dressed in a red djellaba with twin chains of gold around his neck and burgundy cap over his shaved head. *The Bishop of Basmine.*

Shotuga dropped closer to the floor and bowed prostrate before them. 'I greet you, Your Eminence.'

He glanced up at the bishop, who had bloodshot eyes and a bent nose. They stared at one another for a long moment before the bishop pulled his cowl up.

'Your son?' the bishop said, looking down at Shotuga.

'Yes,' said Shotuga's father.

'Does he walk in the light?'

The bishop's eyes traced Shotuga's face.

'Yes, my lord,' Shotuga's father said.

'Good,' the bishop said.

Shotuga's father bowed low.

The bishop nodded and the two guards followed to escort him out. Shotuga turned to his father.

'I am sorry to disturb you, Father, I did not know—'

Splat. A ring-fingered slap knocked all the hearing out of Shotuga's right ear before he could finish his sentence. He groaned, rubbing his cheek as the pain flashed across his face. He would wear a palmprint on his cheek for the rest of the day.

'Don't you ever, in your life, wait outside my room like a bloody thief!'

'Yes, Father... I am sorry, Father,' Shotuga said, rubbing his cheek.

'If I see anything beyond the back of your head in a bow for the next week, I will have you flogged in the open courtyard.'

'Yes, Father,' Shotuga said, with his nose touching the ground.

His father's feet came closer.

'Tomorrow, you will go to the retired Governor-General Zaminu's office, tell him that the bishop and I have spoken and now speak with one voice.'

Shotuga wanted to lift his nose from the ground, but he dared not. 'Yes, Father.'

His father made a dismissing gesture. 'Get away from my office.'

Shotuga rose to his feet, feeling shame colour his ears as he turned to leave and started down the stairs The visitors in the anteroom were mostly gone, save for the young one, who wore the leopard print agbada.

Their eyes met and the Odu man rose to his feet.

'Astonishing agbada, Your Excellency,' he said, with a delicate bow.

Shotuga raised an eyebrow, observing the man. 'Do I know you?'

The man straightened and smiled. 'Sadly for me, you do not, but I have always wanted to make your acquaintance.' He held out a hand.

Shotuga glanced down at the offered handshake then gave the man a long look. He was plainly a man of means, despite his Zarot background and was – he had to admit – almost frighteningly handsome. He accepted the handshake. 'Your name?'

'My name is Kola Coldwater. I'm a member of the Citadel Legislative Council.'

Shotuga gave him another look, not loosening the grip of his handshake. 'Representing what district?'

'Alara,' the man announced.

Shotuga dropped his hand like it was leprous. 'Sorry, I have never heard of it.'

He tried to move past but the Coldwater fellow followed him.

'It's in the south,' Coldwater explained.

Shotuga gave a nod. 'I see.'

He shuffled to get away, but the tall Zarot was persistent.

'I brought you a gift,' he said, producing a small gold box.

Shotuga glanced down at the box and took it. It contained a golden Selistre pick, edged with what looked like crushed ivory. An exquisite gift to any true player.

'Thank you,' Shotuga said honestly.

Coldwater nodded. 'I heard you played the Selistre and thought you would like it.'

'It is remarkable,' Shotuga said, running his thumb over the riddled edge.

Coldwater seemed genuinely pleased. 'Everyone else is gifting your father, but I can read the wind. I know people say that you are just your father's fingerboy but I've seen enough of you to know this isn't true.'

Shotuga stopped and raised an eyebrow. 'Who said I am just my father's fingerboy?'

Coldwater gave an almost bashful smile. 'Don't mind what the people on the council say. They are all liars and cheats. It's a pit of snakes.'

Shotuga let out a breath and rolled his shoulders. 'So I have heard.'

Coldwater grinned. 'Snakes can hiss, but they all know that soon, men like you will lead this nation. They just aren't ready to accept it yet.'

Shotuga gave a nod. 'Absolutely.'

The man had spoken the truth, but Shotuga could not be entirely sure that he wasn't just buttering his bread. Flattery and sycophancy were the meat and drink of the council, and he had settled in his mind not to play that game with them.

The man seemed to read his mind. 'I am not trying to flatter you,' he said, 'but when you are a Zarot like me, you have to think ten steps ahead. I know where the future of the realm lies, and I want to be part of it. I know the South and I know my place. You will need allies on the council – from *all* tribes. I just want you to know I am here and that I was the one person glad to hear that your Lord Father finally did the wise thing in making you High Secretary.'

Shotuga narrowed his eyes. Though rumours of his appointment were rife, the Zarot spoke as though he knew it for certain. *What else does he know?*

'Representative for Alara, you said?'

Coldwater nodded. 'That's right.'

Shotuga nodded and drew in a breath. 'Well, I suppose we will meet at the council soon.'

Coldwater nodded. 'Indeed.'

'Thank you for the gift,' Shotuga said.

Coldwater grinned deeply. 'Any time.'

31

The Second Level

RUMI

The darkness seemed to thicken at the second level. From up above in the trees came the noise of a different kingdom. Home to a nation of birds, monkeys and other things that jump, fly and climb. The air was spiked with the spray of mist and with every step forward, Rumi had the unshakeable feeling that he was being observed. His hand never wandered far from his halberd and his heart never slowed to resting pace. The forest was alive, but so was he.

Agbako pointed to a clearing a few paces ahead. 'We camp there for the night.'

Rumi and his travelling companions agreed and quite quickly they set up camp for the night.

They struck up a fire and shrouded it in shadow to stop the light from drawing predators to their camp.

Left with few alternatives, they scraped flesh from the ghoulish dead horse and roasted it above the fire. Agbako took his horsemeat so rare it was practically raw, but the rest had it charred to a crisp on account of the fact the creature had clearly been corrupted by a witch doctor's blasphemies. The final result was far from tasty but no one complained save for Sameer, who made a bone dry joke as he chewed. 'I suppose you should never look a gift horse in the mouth.'

Rumi and Nataré were set to take the first watch when Agbako cleared his throat. 'I won't have you two guarding us together.'

Rumi shot him a sharp look. 'What?'

'You nearly missed us coming because you wanted to kiss,' Agbako said.

Sameer gasped.

'But we didn't miss you coming,' Nataré snapped.

'Nearly did,' Agbako muttered. 'I'm just saying that guarding the camp in the Nyme needs focus and you two steal it from each other. We'd take watch ourselves but you probably don't trust us enough to do that yet.'

Rumi lowered his chin as he glanced around the fire. He could read it plain on the others' faces, they agreed with the big witch doctor.

'Fine,' Nataré hissed. 'I'll take the first watch with someone else then.'

Ahwazi rose to his feet. 'I'll come.'

Nataré nodded and the pair moved to take the first watch. The rest of them settled around the fire. The two witch doctors who had come with Agbako were yet to offer their names, so Miselda had taken to calling them Horse and No-Horse. No-Horse twitched every time she called him that because she had been the one to kill his steed. Rumi could tell that if care was not taken, his animosity would run over.

The sudden prickly heat from his cowrie necklace made him pause. A sliver of silverlight sparkled at the corner of his vision and Rumi glanced halfway over his shoulder. A little winged woman, no bigger than a forearm, watched them from beside a tree. Her night-dark skin seemed to glisten and shine in the darkness with ethereal sheen. Her hair was tied in a braid that fell past her shoulders.

'A Blackfae,' Rumi said with a smile.

Agbako straightened and scowled, turning in the same direction. 'You see one of the Blackfae?'

Rumi nodded. 'Don't you?'

Agbako shook his head. 'They don't reveal themselves to everyone. Most never see them without a ghost stone.'

Rumi's eyes widened as he recalled the last time he had come to Erin-Olu and had been given a ghost stone. It made all spirit creatures visible. Perhaps now they were surrounded by Blackfae who had simply chosen not to reveal themselves.

He narrowed his eyes as he stared at the Blackfae. *Why is she showing herself?*

Rumi went still as the Blackfae flitted close. For a moment he was sure she was going to attack, then she moved to his ear, leaning over to whisper.

'Sora o, awon toni ikulapo wa nile. Pe ara.'

Her breath was like ice-water. He turned to face her but she was gone. He gasped silently as the words impressed themselves on his mind. *Sora o, awon toni ikulapo wa nile. Pe ara.*

Agbako noticed his expression. 'What happened?'

Rumi closed his eyes and let out a breath. 'It spoke to me.'

Agbako edged closer. 'What did it say?'

'I don't know what it means. It was deep Mushiain.'

'Tell me,' Agbako urged, his eyes suddenly hungry.

Just as Rumi opened his mouth to speak, a long dormant remnant of market instinct told him to lie. It was something ravenous in Agbako's eyes. Like a silk trader asking for the price of damask. You never gave him the true price.

'I don't remember,' Rumi said. 'I don't know what the words meant.'

Agbako gave him a long look, his eyes narrowed with

intensity. He seemed to make his mind up about the matter and hissed. 'What a waste.'

Rumi tried to piece the words together in his mind. He knew *sora o* was a warning to beware. He knew also that *ikulapo* meant death in their pocket. *Who or what was she warning me about? Who has death in their pocket?*

Speculation chewed at his mind. He was so lost in thought that he didn't see the kola nut coming until it struck the side of his head. He gave a start.

Miselda was staring at him, with an apologetic look on her face. 'Sorry, I didn't realise you weren't looking. I didn't mean for it to hit you.'

Rumi grimaced. 'What is it?'

'She was asking you a question,' Sameer clarified.

Rumi met her gaze.

She blinked and straightened. 'What is it like, in Basmine?'

Rumi gave a start. It hadn't occurred to him that Miselda had never seen Basmine. This journey, he reasoned, was likely the furthest she had ever been from the Eredo. The softborn knew Basmine but Kasinabe like Miselda had spent their entire lives shielded from it. She had never seen the lantern lights that hung from the Citadel streets. Never seen a Palman temple. Never been called a Zarot or ridden a caravan.

'What?' she asked.

He'd been quiet too long.

'Basmine is... difficult to describe.'

'Try,' Miselda said.

Rumi tongued at a piece of horsemeat stuck between his teeth, then he cleared his throat and raised his chin. 'Basmine is a difficult place. Having self-respect is seen as an act of rebellion. You are asked to become an accomplice of your own terrors every day and when you don't, they isolate you.'

Miselda yawned. 'Doesn't sound as if it's worth going to war for.'

Rumi thumbed his eyelids. 'Basmine is not worth fighting for, but its people – all those old Seedlings and Suli and Truetrees and sentries and Chainbreakers – are. They are worth being reminded what we were and what we could still become.'

Miselda arched her back in a stretch. 'Oh, we'll give them a reminder. Don't you worry.'

Sameer laughed.

Miselda turned to Agbako and waved a hand to get his attention. 'Got any agbo?'

Agbako gave a confused look, then shook his head. 'No.'

She rolled her eyes. 'What sort of witch doctor doesn't have agbo? I would have thought you'd have a bountiful supply. How else could you stomach this place all the time?'

Rumi gave Miselda a studying look and lowered his voice. 'I have a question of my own for you.'

She blinked and sighed. 'Go on.'

'Why do you shadowsoothe? I've seen your footwork, watched the way you fight. You would be a great fighter without all that extra power. Why take the risk?'

She let out a quiet breath and rolled over to her side. 'I don't do it for the power. I couldn't care less about all of that.'

'Then why do it at all? You are harming yourself.'

She laughed. 'I thought you would understand that better, Ajanla. I heard you lost your family.'

'I did.'

'Then you must know that sometimes the inward pains are far more terrifying than the outward ones. Have you ever tried agbo before?'

'Never.'

'Then you cannot speak on it. Without agbo, I'd already be dead.'

Rumi narrowed his eyes as he licked the corner of his mouth. How could he forget? The times not long ago when death would have been to him like a loosening of the noose. Perhaps he too would have found solace in agbo had his mind still been aflame. He looked at her with new eyes.

'There are other ways to fight it, you know.'

She turned to look at him, her expression one of utter boredom. 'Let me guess, I have to "embrace the pain". Or, no, "make a friend of the stone in the shoe".'

'No, that's not—'

You think agbo corrupts the mind, but it is quite the opposite. It liberates the mind. It helps you to see the truth of life.'

'Which is?'

'Life is a joke and death is the punchline. None of this is truly that serious or important. I've heard it all. I know I'm broken, and I don't need to hear about all the ways to fix it. They don't work for me. When I get a lick, I feel... free. Unafraid. Light. Nothing else in the world gives me that feeling. It is an intense pleasure that you cannot speak on, until you have tried it.'

'Maybe it's because—'

'I don't want to hear it,' she snapped, cutting him off. 'You have your ways. Leave me to mine.'

Rumi tongued the horsemeat between his teeth and it finally came blessedly free. 'Fine,' he said.

Silence returned after that, and it was a quiet wrought with unspoken frustration. The witch doctors sat eerily still, making no effort to relieve the tension.

This was a fragile peace, and Rumi knew they would not make it to the summit whole without something more binding than their destination.

Sameer, always seeming two steps ahead, rose to his feet. Reaching into his pocket he produced a kola nut, which he slapped down on the floor. 'There's only one way this is going to work. We don't leave one another to our ways here. That's not what we do. We've shared our stories with each other. If you're going to come with us, then you share yours too.'

'And if I don't?'

'Then one of these nights you will wake up and find that we have left without you. We are in this all the way, or not at all. So, whatever it is that is bothering you, wherever it is your pain lies – you share it tonight. The lone sufferer dies quietly, but in the softborn clan, we suffer as a collective.'

At that, Agbako nodded to his companions and they all backtracked into the shadows, still listening from the darkness.

Miselda stared down at the kola nut and, for a moment, Rumi was sure that he glimpsed relief in her eyes. Then she broke it with an irritated snap of her wrist. 'Softborn clan is such a stupid name,' she muttered.

Sameer's retort was stick-whip quick. 'Your name is Muriel, dear. Muriel.'

'Fair play,' Miselda muttered as she chewed the nut. When she was done, she let out a long breath, staring at the trees above as though hoping they had the answers she did not. 'I never met my father. He died before I was born. My mother met another man – a sentry. They got married and my sister was born soon after. Everything was all right until my stepfather died.'

Rumi leaned ever so slightly forward as he listened.

'My mother used to cry when she thought we were asleep. Not loudly. Cried like a kicked dog that doesn't want anyone to know it's been kicked. We tried our best to be there for her, but what could we do beyond tell her that we loved her? Soon enough she started on the palm wine. She would sit beside the door of our room and wouldn't come back in until she had drained at least two skins of it. Her speech got slurred and stayed that way. Even when she was sober, she looked drunk. She stopped working and that was when she finally found agbo.'

Sameer let out a shallow breath.

Miselda kept going. 'When she first started on the agbo, her condition actually improved. For the first time in months she made beancakes for breakfast. It was like seeing a candle flicker just before it goes out. A small flash of what she used to be. It didn't last. Within a week she was getting licked to start the day. When she came down from the high, she would say terrible things. She'd say my sister and I were bad omens. Claimed that she lost a husband each time she became pregnant because we were cursed. She would braid my hair too tight, no matter how much I screamed and complained. She would beat my sister almost bloody whenever she didn't sweep the parlour correctly. She called us names no mother should ever call their child.'

'Did you ever talk to anyone? There are people in the botanical ward that are supposed to deal with this precise sort of thing.'

Miselda shook her head. 'That wasn't our way. My sister and I knew she wasn't well. We could handle it. She would have been even worse off without us. There were good times too, don't get me wrong. Sometimes she would make fried plantain with ewa agoyin beans and cut little bits of meat into it. It wasn't all bad.' She gathered her breath and let it out slowly. 'Then one day...' She hesitated again.

Rumi was still. He knew precisely what sort of pause this was. Everything before was a preamble to this, her descent into hell. He could see it in her eyes, read it in the set of her lips, the stiffening in her shoulders. There could be no rushing. They had to be patient.

Sameer could sense this too, for he was quiet and patient as the half-full moon.

'One day she took a knife to Labalaba. Accused her of trying to poison her eggs.' Miselda drew in breath. 'I broke her wrist and one of her legs. It was the only thing I could do to stop her.' She closed her eyes as she spoke the rest of it. 'We had to take her to the botanical ward. Just a few mouthfuls of Oké water from the summit and she would have been all right but before we left, she snatched the knife from the counter when my sister and I weren't paying attention. She... she cut herself deep. By the time we made it to the botanical ward, she was...' She let out a choked sob. 'She was gone.'

Rumi closed his eyes and lowered his head. For a long moment, there was nothing to be said. Then he closed the distance between them and took her by the hand. 'I am sorry that happened to you.'

Sameer appeared at the other side. 'May your mother find the peace in the Higher World that was unavailable on ours.'

Agbako's voice rumbled low from the shadows. 'You did the best you could in the worst of circumstances.'

Miselda sniffed hard and let out a shuddering breath. 'Thank you.'

Rumi squeezed her shoulder. 'It's hard to share at first, but easier once you have let it out.'

She gave a rueful nod as the tears fell. 'Softborn clan. What a ridiculous name.'

Rumi laughed, seeing the joke for what it was. A bluff. An act of misdirection. Sincerity was a difficult thing to sustain and in moments like this – moments of shocking clarity – it was natural to dilute the tension with humour. Normal to reach back for the mask. She needed the joke, that little dishonesty, to bear the armourless vulnerability of the naked truth. What she had done, in telling them her story and showing them how much it hurt, was an act of valour and bravery. More impressive than anything she had shown in the shadow. It wasn't all, but it was a beginning. They say the monkey's dance starts with a clap and Rumi saw it true – something had changed in their group.

'So why did you come with us?' Sameer asked. 'I am sure we have all been thinking it.'

Miselda thumbed her eyelids as she let out a breath. 'I was told that bathing in water from the source would cure any ailment, take away any kind of pain.' She pointed to her temple. 'When you told me you were going to the source, I figured it would be worth a try. Maybe if the source can take away pain of the body, it can also take away pain of the mind. I don't want to use agbo, but I don't stand a chance against it right now.'

Sameer gave her a considered look then lowered his head. 'I hope for your sake that Oké water helps.'

They shared more stories after that, and when Ahwazi and Nataré returned, the stories continued. They remarked upon the fact that most people in the Order had difficult stories and Sameer explained that it was the intensity of emotion that made shadowwielders what they were. It was late into the night when they finally slept. A wall had been scaled and there would be no going back without betrayal. Miselda was an inductee into the softborn clan, as Nataré had been, and they would fight for each other, at least for now, until they reached the summit.

With a quiet moment alone, Rumi saw a chance to ask Sameer a question that had been heavy on his mind.

'You speak Mushiain, don't you Sameer?'

Sameer made a gesture with hands that meant 'a little'.

Rumi lowered his voice to a whisper. 'What does "Sora o, awon toni ikulapo wa nile. Pe ara" mean?'

Sameer scratched his chin and glanced up at the sky. 'It means something along the lines of "Be careful, those who carry death in their pocket are around. Call thunder".'

Rumi stirred. That was the part he didn't totally understand. Ara meant thunder. *Be careful, those who carry death in their pocket are around. Call thunder.*

32

Break the Hammer

LETHI

Lethi straightened as a knock sounded at his office door.

He cleared his throat. 'Come in.'

Attem and Roadie stepped inside together. The native had been wise in keeping the Palmaine Northman at his side. It dulled the cutting edge to him being second-in-command. The rest would find it easier to accept him if they thought he shared his post with an unmistakably Palmaine man.

They both bowed and Lethi gestured to the vacant chairs for them to sit.

Attem spoke first. 'They hid their trail well, considering they travelled with a lion, but we managed to find some sign of them a few miles from Oké-Dar.'

Roadie grinned. 'The harmattan night must have been too cold for them. They built a fire.'

Lethi retrieved a map from his topmost drawer and spread it across the table. 'Show me where you found their trail.'

Attem studied the map for a long moment, then pointed to a tuft of barren land that had once been part of the Odu kingdom.

'Any villages there?' Lethi asked.

Attem gave a non-committal shrug. 'If you can call them villages. Clusters of mudbrick houses, not more than twenty or thirty in any one place. The southlands are full of those. Oké-Dar, Alara and Kokomaiko are the largest but there are many others.'

Lethi raised an eyebrow. 'And they could be in any one of those villages.'

Attem nodded. 'Yes.'

'So, we search them one by one, as we did in Guyarica.'

Attem stroked his chin. 'It would be a risk. People in the villages communicate with drums. If we appear in one small community the drums will begin to sound from everywhere and all the southern villages will know we have arrived within minutes. The Black Hammer Clan will have time enough to get gone if we don't find them immediately.'

'So how do we get to them?' Roadie asked.

'We need something that brings all the South together at once, where we can spring an attack on them,' Lethi said.

Attem made a grating sound in his throat. 'Yes,' he hissed. 'That's right.'

'Festival day,' Lethi said, decisively. 'We strike at them on festival day.'

'What is festival day?' Roadie asked.

Attem scratched his neck. 'In the past, festival day was held to escort the soul of a departed king into the Higher World and would take place whenever a monarch died. Eventually it became a way to honour a visiting king or chief. Now that all the kings and chiefs are dead, the people are always looking for excuses to announce a festival day.'

'So, we will give them an excuse on a day of our choosing,' Lethi said. 'Something for which they will have no choice but to call a festival day.'

Attem shook his head. 'It is a risk.'

'All of this is a risk, Attem,' Lethi said.

'What are you thinking?' Roadie asked.

Lethi drew in breath. 'We get the governor-general to make an official visit here.' He pointed to a village on the map marked 'Alara'. 'It is the largest of the southern villages. If we are lucky, the Black Hammer Clan will find the opportunity irresistible and try to attack, but we will be ready for them.'

'It is against native custom to shed blood on a festival day,' Attem said.

Lethi grinned. 'Even better.'

'It's ambitious,' Roadie mused.

'Messy,' Attem complained.

'It's the only way I can see,' Lethi said. He glanced up at Attem. 'Unless you have a better idea?'

Attem seemed to wrestle with his thoughts but relented when he saw he had been grappled fast. 'No,' he breathed. 'Festival day it is.'

'Good,' Lethi said, gathering his things. 'Begin to put our plan together. I have a meeting to attend.'

He slipped out from the office and into the corridor. The angels in the mural above seemed to glare at him as he walked deeper into the inner temple. He took a final right turn and came at last to a door guarded by an old, scholarly man in maroon priestly robes. The man was thin to the verge of skinny with haunting eyes that looked like they were carved deep into his old folds of skin.

On each side of the door there were twin seraphic statues of angels with long, curved sabres. Written in old Palmanic along the curved arch of the doors were the words 'Halleni de Halle'. It meant the Holiest of Holies. This was a sacred room – though the entire House of Palman was regarded as holy ground, this was God's special preserve, the likes of which only the highest officers of the empire and temple were permitted to enter.

Lethi tried to move past and the old man made a disgusted noise as he shoved him back.

'No halflings,' the old man snarled. 'This is the Holiest of Holies.'

Lethi angled his chin and pulled a clasp on his jacket, letting it fall aside to reveal the shining four-point star pinned to his breast. 'Do I look like a halfling?' Lethi asked.

The old man squinted as he looked Lethi up and down. When he noticed the badge, his eyes widened enough to pop out. 'Double thousand apologies, my lord, I ... I did not look at you properly. For a moment there you looked ...'

He neglected to finish the sentence.

Lethi snatched the man about the priestly collar and pulled him close. He spoke low, hot fury reverberating at the centre of his voice. 'Never make that mistake again.'

The look in the elderly man's eyes was one of pure fear. His head went limp as he whispered a response. 'Please forgive me, my lord.'

Lethi let him go and the man fell in a heap. Not bothering to help him up, he strode into the Holiest of Holies.

Inside the inner sanctuary, the bishop of Basmine stood with his back to Lethi, his gaze arched towards the altar, behind which a stained-glass window depicted the Priests of the Son. Again, there were six of them, instead of five.

Lethi glanced around the rest of the room. It was illuminated by candlelight and the thuribles hissed with sweet-smelling incense.

He took a step towards the bishop and the man quite suddenly spoke.

'I will not fail again,' he hissed.

It took Lethi a moment to realise the bishop wasn't talking

to him. He was addressing the stained-glass impression of the woman with the yellow eyes.

'They cannot prevail. The House of Palman has never been stronger. Five hundred men fall prostrate at the sound of my voice,' he said.

The bishop went quiet for a moment, listening as though garnering a response from the painted glass. Lethi didn't know whether to make his presence known or run for his life. He opened his mouth to speak twice but closed it each time as the bishop continued to rant at the window.

'The elephant pays no mind to the affairs of gathering mosquitoes. We will overcome them.'

A moment passed and the bishop jerked back as though someone had screamed at him. A cold breeze prickled the back of Lethi's neck and he once again had the urge to leave. He took a slow step backward to leave the room.

The bishop spoke again, pleading and hysterical now. 'Forgive me, Your Holiness, I stand only to serve. We will break the hammer and defend the Temple. You have my word.'

Lethi backtracked silently towards the door as the bishop's voice rose.

'And the Son shall give you, the first priests, dominion over all others and they shall writhe at the sound of your voices.'

A loose tile shifted beneath Lethi's foot and he slipped, clattering into a hanging thurible as he did so. The bishop jerked his head at the sudden explosion of sound.

'You,' he hissed.

All the candles went out at once and a strange silence fell upon the room.

In the darkness, Lethi heard the bishop's voice. 'Were you trying to sneak up on me, soldier? Are you an agent of the darkness?'

Lethi heaved in a staggered breath, his heart suddenly pounding in his chest. 'Never, Your Eminence,' he pleaded. 'I was told you sent for me.'

The bishop lit a candle and a small circle of flame spotlit his face. He held Lethi's gaze for a long moment, then he slowly looked away. 'I *did* send for you.'

The relief as the bishop's eyes slid from his skin was almost metaphysical.

The bishop stepped up to the front of the altar and took the goblet of consecration. 'You have failed for too long in breaking the Black Hammer Clan, Lieutenant. My patience is waning.'

'We will have them imminently, Your Eminence.'

'How imminently?' the bishop asked.

'With your support, we need only a fortnight. We will crush the Black Hammer Clan once and for all.'

'What manner of support do you need?'

'We wish to hold a festival in the south and we will need the participation of the governor-general.'

The bishop narrowed his eyes with disgust. 'A pagan celebration.'

Lethi raised his chin and pointed to the fifth commandment, reading aloud. 'Above all, for the greater good all things are permissible.'

The bishop held his gaze for a long moment, seeming to weigh up his words as though working though a bout of arithmetic. Then he gave a satisfied nod and let out a breath. 'For the greater good.'

33

The Third Level

RUMI

The heat was merciless as they made their way up the steep edges of the second level. It was a curious heat, for though they were shaded by the trees, the sun managed to send its vengeance alongside the humidity. They had not been walking for long but exhaustion was close at hand. Even so, their troop was a happy one – thus far there had been no dangerous encounters with the creatures who dominated Erin-Olu, and Rumi saw that as Dara's own blessing. Truth be told, Erin-Olu was proving to be rather tame.

No sooner had they crossed the threshold to the third level than mockery was made of his blessings. A lone hooded man stood under cover of shadow ahead. Rumi's cowrie necklace flashed kettle-hot. Nataré reached slowly for her bow as they approached him. The man turned and pushed his hood back.

Rumi lurched.

It wasn't a man, not by any stretch of the imagination. It had teeth the colour of polished steel that were long as a middle finger. Its tufted ears were pointed and curved. Its eyes were deep blood-red and its tongue was forked.

'What the sheg is that?' Miselda snarled, seizing the shadow.

'Obayifo,' Agbako hissed.

Rumi gripped his halberd as the creature skittered into the bush. Never in life had he seen anything so quick. It moved so fast it seemed to blur in the darkness. In a blink, it appeared in a tree directly above them, hanging bat-wise, hissing with blood-hate. The words of the Blackfae resounded in his mind. *Sora o, awon toni ikulapo wa nile. Pe ara.*

Miselda hurled a spear of shadow at the creature, but it darted out of range.

'Kill it,' Miselda snarled.

They set to doing just that. Nataré landed the first blow as her loosed arrow struck the creature directly at the throat apple. It seemed to have no effect. Without a moment of concern, the creature broke the arrow at the stem with the careless indifference of the hunter to a mosquito bite. Rumi hefted his halberd and took a swipe but the Obayifo was unperturbed. It was plain that it regarded them as cornered prey.

As it jumped left, Sameer let out a string of shadow that tripped the creature up. It rolled once and sprang back up to its feet in a seamless motion that would make a fair-dancer blush.

The witch doctor they called 'No-Horse', raised his grey-white sword and muttered an incantation as he lunged towards the creature. It ran up a tree and doubled-back on No-Horse, snatching his shoulder as it somersaulted over him.

No-Horse whirled with the sword but the creature was too fast. Grinning, the Obayifo caught the witch doctor about the chin and twisted sharply. The sound of his neck snapping was like a kola nut being cracked. The witch doctor fell lifeless from the Obayifo's hands as it hissed, triumphant.

Horse screamed and charged at it from atop its steed. The creature whirled as it darted out of range and turned its glare upon Nataré and Rumi. Rumi put everything into his swing, the creature ducked, snatching him at the neck and throwing him casually across the forest. He hit a tree hard and slid down the bark. Pain shot up his back as he stumbled to his feet. The Obayifo was already moving.

Agbako stepped forward and raised the tortoise on his necklace. The Obayifo gave a feral scream as it lunged at him. The two got into a rolling tangle the likes of which Rumi had never seen before, exchanging dominance a dozen times as they circled across the forest floor. At last, Agbako got the upper hand. What followed was a display of brutality to rival all the world's worst blood-violence.

First Agbako smashed the creature's skull in with the hard shell of the tortoise; then he snapped its neck with a sharp jerk of the wrist. Incredibly, the Obayifo still wriggled and writhed in Agbako's grip. The big witch doctor snatched the arrow from its throat apple and punctured each eye. Ahwazi turned away in disgust as blood fountained.

Sameer muttered a prayer. 'Dara, born once and once again. Hide me in your shadow.'

Agbako continued to rip the creature apart, limb by limb, snarling his curses all the while. The sounds were akin to those of a busy slaughterhouse. Ripping and tearing and butchering meat. As hard as it was to watch, Rumi found it impossible to tear his eyes away. They simply stared in stunned silence.

'Sheggin'... die...' Agbako hissed, through short breaths.

The work was finally done and Agbako loomed breathless over the bloody corpse. No one dared to speak. If there had been doubts about his dangerousness before, they were long gone now. The witch doctor had a beast inside and it was just as wild as anything in the forest.

The silence continued for a moment longer before Agbako heaved out a breath and rose to his feet. 'Be careful. This is the third level. No more playing around now.'

Rumi's heart pounded. All else before had been the shadow of the nightmare, now came the beating heart of it. *We are out of our depth.*

He could see it in the faces of his companions too. This was no storybook adventure. No hero's journey. Nataré raised an eyebrow and made a questioning gesture with her chin. Rumi instinctively knew what it meant; something along the lines of 'Do you still want to keep going?'

He wet his bottom lip and gritted his teeth. Fear was there, no doubt, but surrender was not near him. Yami would have faced far worse for his sake. She had walked with death to see him live. He would die before turning back but that was his decision, not theirs.

He cleared his throat. 'There is a path just behind us that leads back towards the Eredo. If anyone wants to leave now, I will not try to stop you. This is no journey for the half-minded.'

Sameer swallowed and turned to face Rumi. He held his gaze for what seemed a long moment but was likely only a second. 'I go where you go, Ajanla.'

Ahwazi tapped his chest. 'Same here.'

Nataré tapped her own chest. 'Always.'

They all turned to Miselda.

She looked back at them, one after the other, then let out an exasperated breath. 'I suppose I have to stay now, don't I? After the whole kola nut thing? It would be rude to leave.'

Agbako chuckled. 'So, we continue. Good. Keep your wits about you. The Obayifo rarely hunt alone and there's worse that will catch the scent of you.'

Sameer drew in a rough breath as he stared down at the bloody mess. 'The Obayifo. Bloodsucking nightwalkers. I'll have something for them next time.'

The big witch doctor looked over the creature's corpse and

picked organs from the carcass, stuffing them in his stack with all the nonchalance of a farmer's mistress plucking potatoes. That, more than anything, sealed it for Rumi. They were in deep shege now.

They passed a cursory glance over No-Horse's body and came to silent agreement that this was no time to bury him. Horse stayed the longest by his comrade's body, but his goodbye was cut short when Agbako nudged the corpse into the stream and they watched as the current carried him away.

'May the salt of the ocean wash him clean and its waves carry him home,' Sameer said.

Agbako barked with laughter. 'There isn't enough saltwater in all the world to wash him clean. We are witch doctors, he's definitely off to hell.'

A sobering comment, Rumi thought, but not far from his own mind. Witch doctors had forsworn the old gods and the new, and their salvation was far beyond the petition of prayers.

'Let's go,' Rumi said, moving to stand beside Nataré. He held out a hand and she took it — there was no place for modesty here. He needed her.

Nataré's face hardened as she touched his shoulder with hers.

Sameer glanced at the map and gestured to Agbako. The witch doctor nodded and stepped to the front of their group. The passage from Kuda Kamo's book crossed Rumi's mind. *On the long road to Hell, there are many signs to turn back but people choose to stay the course. For even in Hell, there is solace in the fraternity of the fallen*

They walked with weapons at the ready. More than once, rustling movements in the bushes made them fall into fighting stance but no confrontation came. Soon enough they got into a good walking rhythm and the fear receded just a touch. As they approached the fourth level, Agbako brought their trek to a halt.

'Night falls soon,' he explained, 'and I would rather we pass the night here than halfway between the third and fourth level. It seems to be calm here.'

There was, of course, no protest. On matters of the safety of Erin-Olu, they deferred to the bottomless experience of the man who lived there.

They set up camp and took up what had now become a uniform sleeping arrangement. Miselda made her shadowstrewn hanging hammock, while the rest took up bed mats. Horse took the first watch alone with his horse and the forest grew suspiciously quiet.

Sameer let out a breath as he laid his head to rest. 'I have a question, Agbako?'

The big witch doctor inclined his head. 'Go on.'

Sameer's breath smoked in the air and he spoke. 'What is the most dangerous thing in Erin-Olu?'

Agbako gave a low grunt and drew in an audible breath. 'Difficult to say. I haven't seen all the Erin-Olu has to offer. I have never been beyond the fourth level without a ghost stone.'

'Then what is the most dangerous thing you have seen?' Sameer asked.

He sucked his teeth. 'I have seen a full-grown kongamoto. Beak like a boat, breathing fire in the skies.'

'We saw a kongamoto too, once,' Sameer said. 'Terrifying creatures.'

Agbako nodded. 'Indeed, though I have never been truly afraid of them. They are not violent creatures, except if you encroach upon their territory or attack their young. Mostly they are not looking for human flesh.' He scratched his neck. 'But the Ojuju, *that* worries me.'

Sameer sat up. Rumi did too. Even Ahwazi raised an eyebrow.

'The Ojuju is not real,' Sameer insisted. 'The Yellow Masquerade does not exist.'

Agbako shook his head. 'Not real in the way you understand, perhaps, but there are many ways to be real in this world and the next.'

'Have you seen it before?'

Agbako sucked his teeth and spat. 'Only the signs; trees gone rancid yellow. Water running blood-red. A flock of dead birds arranged in a circle.'

'Those could be caused by other things,' Sameer protested.

Agbako shrugged. 'Perhaps.'

Rumi wanted to believe that Agbako was teasing them, but his expression was one of dead seriousness. Even in stories, when Ojuju Calabar appeared, you knew it would end in blood. They called Ojuju the Yellow Masquerade. A forest-dwelling spirit that mothers used to scare errant children as a very last resort. As a child, there were three words that would always make Rumi fall in line – 'Ojuju is coming'. The sheer thought of the Yellow Masquerade was a thing of fear.

'There is no such thing as Ojuju,' Rumi said decisively. But there in Erin-Olu – where there were Blackfae and kongamoto and Obayifo – he could not be sure.

34

The Hammer and the Scalpel

ALANGBA

The cuts of pepper in the soup made Alangba's eyes water. It had been a long time since he'd tasted Odu pepper soup.

Mama Ayeesha, one of the leaders of the Black Hammer Clan, gave him a wry smile. 'Need some water?' she asked.

Alangba stole a breath and nodded. 'It has been a while.'

Ayeesha gestured with her hands and one of the men behind her produced a coconut shard full to the spout with water.

Alangba sipped slowly between small breaths. Through the window he saw an armed woman stride by on patrol, a rifle slung over her shoulder. Further on, near the centre of their township, a lone sculptor was chiselling away at a large slab of stone. The top half of the statue was nearly complete — it depicted a bare-chested woman with five scars across her forearm with a halberd held high. Her face was deeply familiar, but Alangba did not know why.

Across the room, standing under the shadow of the wall, was Ladan. He loomed like a beautiful spectre. Alangba could not see his expression from this far away but surmised that he too had seen the way the Black Hammer Clan were set up.

'Where are we?' Alangba asked.

Ayeesha's eyes flitted towards the window. 'A town called Ajego. Not very far from Alara. It used to be a farming town, which suits us perfectly. We are surrounded by rice fields and there's a watchtower at the centre of the town that gives us a good enough view to spot any surprises.'

Ladan stepped into the light. 'Quite the operation.'

Mama Ayeesha glanced over her shoulder at him. 'We do what we can.'

'How many soldiers do you have?' Alangba asked.

She scratched her nose. 'Just over two thousand. Though some are not very well trained or armed. We have operated underground for over a year now and our network has expanded as far as the Citadel.'

Alangba nodded. 'Impressive.'

She finished the last of her soup and set the bowl aside. 'It isn't nearly enough. The Palmaine have at least twelve thousand armed soldiers at the ready and if we don't strike soon, their king will win their wars elsewhere and be able to send reinforcements. I hope you bring news of a ten-thousand-strong army coming.'

Alangba shook his head. 'Not more than two thousand are well-trained. We are recruiting every day, but we will not come close to ten thousand when the time arrives.'

She did not seem surprised.

Alangba pointed at the statue outside, still being worked on by the sculptor. 'Who is that supposed to be?'

Mama Ayeesha gave the sort of private smile that was more for a time long gone than for the here and now. 'A dear, *dear* friend,' she said. 'An incredible woman. Her name was Adunola.'

Alangba's eyes widened as he immediately recalled the name. 'Rumi's mother?'

Mama Ayeesha blinked and gave him a second look. 'Yes.'

'I saw him, just before we left the Eredo. He spoke very highly of his mother.'

Ayeesha nodded. 'And how are my children, Rumi and Renike?'

Alangba took a long gulp of water. 'They fare exceedingly well. Alara did incredible work in raising them.'

Mama Ayeesha's cheeks swelled as she gave her most earnest smile. '*Ajanaku ki iya kokoro. Eni erin-in bi erin njo.*'

Alangba smiled and nodded. '*Be-eni.*'

Her Odu words meant the elephant does not beget an ant. The child of an elephant is also an elephant.

Ladan touched his chest and pointed to the sky; a gesture of agreement.

She cleared her throat and closed her eyes. 'Adunola, his mother, was …' She trailed off, unable to finish her sentence. 'May their parents' sins be forgiven and may they rest evermore in Dara's bosom.'

'May it be so,' Alangba said.

Mama Ayeesha narrowed her eyes and gestured towards the guard behind her, who quietly closed the door.

'We have something planned for tonight.'

Alangba inclined his head. 'I'm listening.'

Ayeesha cleared her throat. 'The Citadel Legislative Council is meeting. The bishop of Basmine will be there, along with the acting governor-general and representatives from all the Palmaine and native noble families and business interests.'

'You mean to attack them?'

Ayeesha rolled her eyes. 'I am many things, Alangba, but I am not a fool. Give us some credit. Just because we call ourselves the Black Hammer, does not mean our only tool is blunt force. We know when to work the hammer and we know when to work the scalpel.' She made a summoning gesture to one of their guards and the door was pulled open. 'What we plan calls for the subtlety of the serpent.'

The man who entered was dressed in a tailored waistcoat and breeches of sober black velvet. His dark hair was softened and parted left of centre in old Palmaine style and his neck was covered in a deep burgundy cravat. He was wickedly handsome and though he had a relaxed, elegant bearing, he radiated power and capability. From one lobe hung an earring fashioned in the image of a blazing sun.

Ayeesha grinned. 'Meet Kola Coldwater, the newest representative for Alara on the Citadel Legislative Council.'

The man's bow was an act of perfect Palmaine choreography. Bending at the waist, weaker foot inched back just enough. 'A pleasure to meet you, Alangba.'

Alangba gave him an appraising look. Though the man had the sun-darkened skin of a native, there was something utterly foreign about him. In his eyes, in the way that he stood.

'Who are you really?' Alangba asked.

Kola Coldwater's lips curled into a smile. 'My true name is Kang Damascus. I am the second son of Sir Kojo Damascus.'

Alangba raised an eyebrow. 'You mean *that* Kojo?'

Kola nodded. 'Kojo the Betrayer, yes. Leader of the amotekun. The freedom fighter who became a Palmaine stooge and Warden of the South.'

Ayeesha raised a mollifying hand. 'Kang and his brother are loyal to the cause. They gave us all their inherited lands, helped us gain a foothold in the Citadel.'

'Our father might have been a traitor, but for a hundred years before, our family fought for the Odu people. I am here to redeem my bloodline.'

'Tonight, Kola Coldwater is going to be making a petition for independence before the Citadel Legislative Council.'

Alangba raised an eyebrow.

'The Palmaine will never accept it,' Ladan said.

Alangba shook his head. 'They don't need to.'

Kola Coldwater grinned. 'Exactly. All we need to do is sow the seed. Lay it down for a vote.'

Alangba nodded his understanding. 'The native nobles will see an opportunity.'

Kola nodded. 'The Palmaine will resist it too strongly.'

Ladan grinned as he caught on. 'Infighting.'

'Precisely,' Ayeesha said. 'We need to give the native noble families a reason to act against the Palmaine.'

'Divide and conquer, using the Palmaine tricks against them,' Ladan said. 'I love it.'

'We will follow up the petition with public protests, sit-ins and stand-offs. We will set the nation on fire again, put the "demon" in demonstration,' Kola said. 'I would estimate that nearly a third of the Palmaine's armed forces are retainers of the native noble families. If we can bring them to our side, then we have a significant advantage.'

'What would that do to our chances?' Alangba asked.

'We would still be outnumbered, even with the native families on our side, but it would give us a fighting chance,' Ayeesha said. Then she pointed to Ladan. 'And if half your Eredo soldiers fight like him, then I'd say it would be a hell of a fight.'

Ladan raised his chin as his shadow poured out from the corner of his eyes. 'You will need eyes on you, when you go to the Citadel. Protection to and fro. The Palmaine are a cunning people.'

Kola Coldwater nodded. 'I have a bodyguard who—'

'Real protection,' Ladan said, cutting him off.

Alangba rose to his feet. 'Ladan and I will accompany you to the meeting.'

Kola Coldwater glanced at Ayeesha, who gave him an accepting nod. 'Very well,' he said. He gave them each a look up and down, taking in their blood- and mud-tracked robes. 'We will need to get you both... a change of clothes.'

Ladan gave the grin of a man who knew he had a winning hand of cards. 'This is going to be interesting.'

35

Weed Amongst the Wheat

FALINA

The queen threw back a glass of dark liquor and winced at the wood-washed aftertaste. A crystal decanter lay drained to the dregs beside her as she let out a deep sigh. Maka Naki tried to retain his soldierly posture, but a whisper of concern twisted the corner of his mouth.

'What is it, Maka Naki? Speak your mind.'

The warrior straightened to his full height as he angled his frame towards her. He was sinfully handsome at the worst of times, but when he pulled in all his masculinity – it was a truly potent force.

He bowed. 'My Queen, forgive me, it's just that...'

'Spit it out,' Falina said.

He chewed at the corner of his mouth. 'I am worried about you.'

Falina raised an eyebrow. 'It is your job to worry about me, Maka Naki.' She gestured to the vacant chair beside her and he took up a seat.

His scent was rained-on wood, amber and honey-apple. She should have been used to it by now, but it still struck her each time.

'You have been drinking more than usual,' Maka Naki said.

'I can hear you pacing around in your room whenever I stand guard outside the door. You aren't sleeping enough.'

'How could I possibly sleep when the fate of so many people rests on the decisions I make? I have no experience in this. I am no queen, Maka Naki.'

Maka Naki's face hardened. 'If there has ever been any true queen in the world, it is Falina Almarak. The Golden Eagle. I would give my life for that truth because I believe in it. You have everything you need to be a great leader.'

'Because my father was a great leader?' Falina asked.

'Because you embody everything that makes the Kasinabe what they are. You are resilient. Years in captivity and you retained all your royalty. No matter how much you try to reject it – you care about people. Despite your lack of experience you have united a nation and inspired them to dream again. We have had many kings and queens who did not deserve to wear the crown but sometimes the gods' favour shines on us.'

A soft quiver of surprise turned in Falina's stomach as he spoke. 'You flatter me.'

He turned his gaze on her again, his eyes sharp and hard as a boning knife. 'I do not, my Queen. You are the one to lead us, but you cannot win the game the way others did. Play your own way.'

Falina opened her mouth to speak when someone knocked at the door. Her heart leaped as she gathered herself, cleared her throat and raised her chin. 'You may enter.'

A woman stepped inside holding another crystal decanter. She couldn't be more than thirty but you could see the lines of hard experience in her face. 'My Queen,' she said, bowing prostrate till both knees touched the ground.

Falina urged her forward. The woman smiled as she stepped up to the table and poured out another measure of liquor.

Falina could almost taste the woman's nervousness – it still struck her just how reverent some of the people of the Eredo were when they met her.

'Thank you,' Falina said, raising the glass.

The woman didn't answer. Her eyes seemed trained on the glass. Falina hesitated and lowered the drink.

Maka Naki gave her a worried look. 'Are you all right, my Queen?'

Perhaps it was in the blood, perhaps it was instinct. Maybe it was pure luck or some incredible combination of all three. Falina leaned back, just as the woman beside her lashed out with a blade.

Maka Naki moved fast, gripping the woman's wrist, twisting it back until it made a loud snap and wrenching the knife free. The woman screamed in pain, then ranted like a person possessed by spirits. 'Long live the king! Blessed are the children of Palman. A peculiar treasure unto the Son above all people. May they rule over us forever. May we learn to appreciate the prosperity they have given us. There is only one God and his name is Palman.'

Maka Naki pressed his knee to the back of her neck. 'Who sent you?'

She closed her eyes and screamed. 'Palman reigns! He will reign forever and always!'

Falina's heart was pounding as she heaved in a breath. 'An assassin.'

'Weeds amongst the wheat,' Maka Naki said. 'We are lucky she was poorly trained. A more subtle practitioner would have slit your throat.'

The woman continued to scream. 'Palman reigns!'

Footsteps in the corridor followed as a knock sounded at the door. 'My Queen?' someone shouted.

'Chainbreaker?' Maka Naki shouted back.

'Sixth ranger. The rangers stand,' the voice answered.

'The queen has been attacked,' Maka Naki said. 'Only bring Chainbreakers in with you.'

Two rangers stalked into the room like wolves on the hunt. They bound the assassin at her wrists, knees and feet.

'Secure the door,' Maka Naki ordered. 'Send for a mindwalker.'

A third ranger stepped inside with his sword drawn and stood beside the closed door.

Falina touched her neck. 'How is this possible? How could she get so close?'

Maka Naki stared down at the would-be assassin. 'We'll know soon enough.'

Another knock sounded at the door and a Chainbreaker poked his head into the room. 'The mindwalker has arrived.'

Maka Naki nodded as a woman stepped into the room.

'My Queen,' she said, bowing as she entered.

It was Chief Karile. Though she was plainly dressed, her stately countenance was the tell-tale sign of one accustomed to command. Her gaze shifted to the assassin and she narrowed her eyes as she stepped close. Wisps of shadow steamed from her pores as her eyes went black as coal. She seized the assassin by the unbroken wrist and spoke low. 'Show me.'

The assassin moaned and writhed as Chief Karile walked through her mind.

'No!' the assassin screamed. 'No!'

Karile bared her teeth and her shadow flared, casting the room halfway in darkness.

'Show me,' she hissed.

The assassin went limp and quiet as Karile leaned close to

read the contents of her mind. After a long moment, she let her wrist go and stepped back.

'What did you see?'

Karile narrowed her eyes and raised her chin, her jaw pulsing as though she were chewing rocks. Her voice was hoarse. 'There is a traitor in the Shadow Order.'

36

Mindwalking and Pain

RENIKE

'Instinct, anticipation, timing and precision,' Gaitan said. 'All these are your allies in a fight. Do not neglect them. There is another unspoken ally that those of great skill may use in a fight. Does anyone know what that is?'

'Strength,' someone offered.

Gaitan nodded. 'Strength is certainly of benefit to a fighter, but not what I am talking about now.'

'Speed,' someone else shouted out.

'Not what I am talking about either.'

A third voice struck a discordant note among the rest. 'Mindwalking,' Ngoné said.

Gaitan turned to look at her, his eyes narrow with concentration. 'Yesssss,' he hissed.

Renike raised an eyebrow. 'Is it possible to mindwalk *while* fighting another?'

'With proper training, yes,' Gaitan said. 'Usually we do not teach Seedlings this because it puts a great deal of stress on the mind – but these are different times. There is a place in the walk of the shadowwielder when you can become completely at one with the shadow. Seeing everything all at once. Mind, thought, intention, action. If you come to that place, you will be able to mindwalk even in the heat of a fight and see everything your opponent does before they do it, before they even conceive it. Every move you make will be perfect.'

Renike's eyes bulged. *Perfect.* If there was one way to describe Zarcanis the Viper in a fight, that was it. She was perfect in all the ways it was possible to be so. Never a foot out of place, never a blow short of the mark. Even when she got hit or lost in an exchange it was an act of charity. Renike knew that if Zarcanis never wanted to get hit, it would be so. *Is she mindwalking while she fights?*

Gaitan cleared his throat. 'Kiwinje teaches us about the importance of balance, not just in footing and stance, but in defence and attack, in moving forward and holding back. Body and mind. Every victory starts here,' he said, pointing at his temple. 'Not here,' he said, pointing to his bicep. It was a remark Gaitan was always repeating. He wanted them to be thinking fighters who prioritised strategy over strength in all things. 'If you learn to mindwalk in combination with your attacks, you add a new dimension to the work. You may think I am trying to teach you but what I am really doing is trying to give you a lifeline. The time comes soon when these words might save your life in a battle to the death. After class, for those with the desire to learn more, I will be holding a session for advanced mindwalking. Come at your own discretion, for it will be painful on both body and mind.'

Renike glanced at N'Goné who gave her a silent nod. Nothing more needed to be said. They were going.

When class came to an end, N'Goné and Renike waited in their seats for Gaitan's lesson. They were not alone. Not a single person left the room. Gone were the days when people were casual about their training. War was coming and no one was taking shortcuts.

Gaitan cleared his throat, impressed. 'I see we have a committed cohort.' He raised a hand and a wisp of shadow curled in front of him. He furrowed his brow and the shadow became a perfect circle. 'Can anyone tell me what emotion I am using?'

There was silence for a moment, then N'Goné cleared her throat.

'Gratitude,' she said.

He glanced up at her and nodded. The circle turned into a flat plate. 'What about now?'

N'Goné waited for a moment then answered again. 'Anticipation.'

He blinked as the circle became a big-bowled goblet. 'Now?'

'Admiration.'

It became a helmet. 'Now?'

She hesitated. 'Surprise.'

'Now?'

'Admiration ... awe.'

Gaitan let out his breath and his shadow winked away. 'Incredible,' he said, glancing up at her. 'How do you read emotion so well?'

N'Goné shrugged. 'Luck.'

It was far from luck. N'Goné had spent time in the captivity of witch doctors. She had gone weeks without speaking a word, months without hearing any language she could understand. Reading body language had become an essential part of her survival. Knowing when to brace for a punch could be the difference between a bruise and a tooth missing. When you live in a place where your death is only a minor inconvenience, you learn to watch for any small sign of danger. N'Goné had learned to read emotions the hard way. She could tell by the size of the space between your eyes if you were tired or hungry. Could see by the tightness of your fist if you were angry or afraid. She had tried more than once to teach Renike the signs but most were far beyond her learning.

Gaitan gave her an appraising look. 'You have a powerful gift. It will aid you as you mindwalk. Understanding a person's emotions is halfway to total understanding. If you work hard, the minds of all people will be your parlour. You will come and go through the hearts and minds as others go through gardens and gates.'

Gaitan put them through an intensive mindwalking exercise that required them to face off against one another and predict their opponent's form before they took it. It meant you had to mindwalk and shadowdance with only the smallest interval for thought. Predictably, N'Goné was the best at it. She could see what form her opponent took before they even set their feet and could counter just as quickly. Gaitan watched them all with silent intensity.

When a person walked your mind there was sometimes a strange feeling when they left. It was as though someone was pulling at your skin – but from the inside. It took some getting used to.

'Renike,' Gaitan urged, 'now you face off against Kharmine.'

A shudder of panic ran through to Renike's wrist.

Kharmine grinned when he learned he would be paired up against her, showing a double line of stark-white teeth.

Renike's expression didn't change. She strode across to the fighting pit without a word. *Life is for the living, not the dead.*

They took up their safespears and waited for Gaitan's cue.

'Engage!'

Kharmine walked across the fighting pit as an egret treads the water. His eyes were fixed on Renike with an intensity that in any other context would have seemed adoring. He tapped his safespear across his shoulder twice – a gesture of respect that Renike had not seen coming. She held her safespear across her body in *shepherd holds the crook*, preparing to counter his inevitable attack.

'Take it easy,' Gaitan warned. 'Remember we do not have much Oké water left. Gentle contact only.'

Renike nodded her understanding and Kharmine did the same but the look on his face hinted at a dark seriousness.

'Walk the mind,' Gaitan urged. 'See the strike before it comes.'

Renike made a sharp attempt to enter Kharmine's mind and was struck by a vision of such uncompromising horror that it shattered her concentration completely. Before she knew what was happening, Kharmine had stepped into *eagle stands amongst the cockerels* with his safespear jutting into her sternum. The power was unreal and her breath left her as she hit the ground.

'Stop!' Gaitan called out, putting an instant end to the fight.

Renike stared up, her vision still blurry from the sudden turn of events. She had seen — she was certain — a demon in Kharmine's mind. Red-faced, bird-beak nosed, with eyes that had seen the fires of the hellmouth.

Kharmine offered a hand to help her to her feet, but she refused it. *Why did he have a demon in his mind? Perhaps it was some sort of mind defence. An apparition to startle her — knowing she would intrude.*

Gaitan took one look at Renike and his face fell. 'That's enough for today.'

After a good two hours of work, the class had come to an end.

As they packed their belongings to leave, N'Goné stepped close. 'What happened to you in the fighting pit? You seemed dazed for a moment there.'

Just as Renike opened her mouth to answer, Gaitan appeared.

His voice typically filled the room but now when he spoke it was in hushed tones. 'I would like to speak with you two.'

Renike glanced up at him as N'Goné gave an insouciant shrug and nod.

When the others were gone, he straightened and cleared his throat. 'The Eredo owes you both a great deal. Had you failed to secure the door, many more lives would have been lost. You answered even when nothing was asked of you.'

Renike met his gaze, her stomach tight with the knowledge that something important was coming.

'Now we *do* have something to ask of you,' Gaitan said. 'Something important.'

Renike raised her chin. 'Anything,' she said.

Gaitan furrowed his brow. 'There is a traitor in the Shadow Order. Learning our ways, revealing our secrets and plotting to kill.'

Renike gritted her teeth. 'Not possible.'

'Perhaps in the past, but these days we have been forced to bring so many into the order that we cannot be sure. Someone tried to kill the queen. We suspect that another will try to kill again. It is more than likely that the traitor is a Seedling and it is for that reason we need your help.'

'Just one traitor?' Renike asked.

'As far as we know,' Gaitan said. 'Could be more, but I would say that is unlikely. We will carry out our own investigation, but we need more eyes and ears in the Seedling dormitories. The traitor is not likely to expect us to send Seedlings.'

'Or softborn,' Renike added.

Gaitan narrowed his eyes. 'The Voltaine knife still cuts through.'

'And will you also have other eyes and ears watching us?' N'Goné asked.

Gaitan gave half a nod and produced a thick satchel. 'Naturally. No one can be entirely above suspicion.' He pulled a thick cobalt collar out and held it high. 'This is an Odeshi. Also known as the quartercuff. It diminishes a shadowwielder's power to a quarter of what it is meant to be.'

Renike gave a shrewd nod. The Odeshi was a well-known instrument on account of the fact that Zarcanis famously wore one all the time – even when sparring.

Gaitan reached into the satchel again and produced a small golden bracelet. 'This is a dreamwalker. It allows you to pierce through the dreamscape and venture into a shadowwielder's dreams undetected. You will be able to investigate all their tendencies and predispositions without any obvious signs of mindwalking.'

N'Goné stared at the bracelet with more interest than Renike had ever seen her have in anything.

'Last of all is this,' he said, producing an iron whistle. 'If you blow this whistle, the chiefs will immediately know exactly where you are. Use it if you have found the traitor or find yourself in imminent danger – we'll come right to you.'

Renike inspected the whistle and placed it back into the satchel. 'Who else knows about this secret mission of ours?'

Gaitan scratched at his throat. 'That is no concern of yours. Do not speak of it to anyone else and only use the dreamwalker when no one is around. This is important – we have to find the traitor before they destroy everything we have built.'

37

No Man Can Kill a True Ghost

RUMI

Rumi coughed as he startled himself awake. A figure loomed above him.

'What the sheg?'

The man wore a wide-brimmed top hat, a black tailcoat that extended to his calves, dark-lensed glasses and cotton plugs in his wide nostrils. His face was painted in the imitation of a skull. The shovel slung across his shoulder glistened in the moonlight and the fat cigar in his mouth brought out his pearly white teeth.

'Twice in a lifetime, you're a lucky boy,' he said, as he blew a cloud of cigar smoke in Rumi's face.

'Saturday,' Rumi breathed.

Saturday, the agbara of death, tipped his hat and gave a mocking bow. 'In the flesh.'

'Am I dead?'

Saturday shook his head. 'That question is layered, in a philosophical sense. In some small way, we are all dead. When you have seen as much as I have, you start to see birth as the beginning of a slow death.'

Rumi pinched himself. 'But I am not dying now?'

Saturday sniffed. 'No, not now.'

'Then why are you here?'

He touched his chest. 'Ouch, can't the old gravedigger visit an old friend?'

Rumi gave him a doubtful look and Saturday laughed.

'Fine, I am here on other business,' he said, pointing to Rumi's burlap sack of belongings. 'You get to read my book now.'

Rumi blinked. 'I didn't know the new agbara had books in the *Sakosaye*.'

'It is the living story. One day, perhaps you will have a story to add to the book.'

He stamped out glistening ashes from his cigar and adjusted his top hat. Rumi noticed a night-dark flute peeking over the top of his jacket pocket.

'What's that?' he asked, pointing.

Saturday tucked it away. 'You think you are the only one with a knack for music? I am known to draw quite the crowd with this one,' he said, tapping the pocket pridefully. 'A three-of-a-kind instrument.'

Rumi gave him a confused look.

'You'll understand that one later,' Saturday said with a smile, as smoke teemed from the crevices in his top hat.

'How fares my mother?' Rumi asked. 'Will I see her in the Originate?'

Saturday angled his chin and sighed. 'Love dies hard.'

'Saturday, please, I—'

'All the best, Irumide. I suspect, sadly, that the next time we meet, you actually will be dead.'

Rumi gave him a rueful smile. 'May that be a very long time from now.'

Saturday grinned. 'You wish.'

The smoke engulfed him and within moments, he was gone. The patch of grass he was standing on had gone a dead, putrid brown, and the scent of cigar smoke was still thick in the air.

Rumi reached into his burlap sack and pulled the *Sakosaye* out. He found the page marked 'Baron Saturday' and began to read.

People often ask how I became the new agbara of death. To answer that, we must understand this – death knows no master. The agbara of the wind commands the wind. The agbara of thunder calls upon the thunder. The agbara of the wilderness commands all wild things. But the agbara of death is a servant. He is commanded by death, not the other way around. Death is a power that none but Dara has dominion over. *Iku tobi loba*. Death is a mighty king. A king that has servants amongst all the peoples of the world. Before me, there was another who served death for the Darani – Oya, the Mother of Nine, wife of Xango. She was the first leader of the *egun* – the eternal army of the dead. She carried the shovel before I did and served long. They call Oya the Mother of Nine because she had nine pregnancies and each one ended in a stillbirth. She knew death too well. Had seen the bone and marrow of it. Tasted the bitter bile one too many times. After her ninth stillbirth, she revolted against death, chastised it and threw down her shovel and sickle. So death spurned the Darani and treated them according to his whims such that none could gain admittance to the Higher World which is also known as the Originate. For their souls were not buried by an agbara of death. Our fortunes began to fail as all our spirits and ancestors were locked out of the Originate from where they could work in our favour.

I was born so that the Darani may die well again and be readmitted to the Originate.

Dara has always smiled upon me. I was born on a Saturday, in the howling cold and the bucketing rain. My mother gave me no name, as she thought I was not long for the world, for I was weak and sickly. But Dara smiled upon me, and I lived despite it all. My mother, it turned out, was the one not long for the world – she died before I had learned to speak. I was alone with her corpse for three days, but Dara smiled upon me and I was found by a Darani priest.

He was no normal priest, for he was touched of Dara and knew things no man ought to know. The priest looked in my eyes and saw that I had seen the face of death and he wept with sorrow and took me as his own. And he called me Saturday, for he had found me on the sixth day and I became his apprentice. He taught me how to honour the dead and perform their last rites. He taught me the seven secret words that allow a person's soul to be accepted in the Originate even without an agbara of death. I learned that death was not of decay and blackness but also of rest and new beginnings. But the priest too was not long for this world, and because he had told me the seven secret words, death made claim on him. Once again, I was alone; but Dara smiled upon me.

At ten, I was sold to the captain of a ship called the Guyarica Packet who dealt in slaves and tobacco. Before I turned eleven, I was the third mate onboard the ship. Whenever someone died, I was the one who made sure the last rites were performed in the Darani way such that they would gain passage to the Originate. In nineteen years on that ship, I saw more death than any veteran executioner. I learned every way it was possible to die. From sickness, from slaughter, from suicide, from accident and from arrangement. I could tell by the smell how a person died. I could judge by the warmth of the neck what time, to the hour, their soul had left them. Despite my circumstance, Dara smiled upon me, and I was revered by slave and master alike.

When I turned thirty, I had earned enough to buy my freedom, for I had found great favour with the captain. But the captain's heart was hardened against me and on the eve of my freedom, he refused to honour our agreement, insisting he was owed ten more years of labour. Though my fury was great and my heart was full of rage, Dara smiled upon me. There was a revolt the next day and the captain was cast into the sea. And I was honoured among the enslaved people for I had served them long and dutifully.

When the ship next berthed in Guyarica, I was free. I searched for my people and found them gathered beneath an iroko tree, just as the stories promised. And I lived among them for a score in years, doing what I had always done: burying the dead and speaking the words such that they might find smooth passage to the Higher World. And Dara smiled upon me. My story travelled far and wide and I became known as the Priest of Death, for I believed that all people should die with nobility and be accepted into the Originate. People knew me both by name and appearance, and wherever I went I found favour, for the goodness of my work was widely known.

At my final hour, death itself approached me weeping and offered its petition; an eternal truce with the Darani, that I might serve death and gain eternal life. And I laughed, because Dara had smiled upon me again – even in the eyes of death. And I raised the shovel high in acceptance, for there is no greater commission than to give a person dignity in death. Life is nothing without death. And I became a new agbara, born in the hearts of the enslaved. And I was given charge over the *egun* – the army of the dead who had once served Oya and who walked between worlds. And I grew in power and in name. I have walked with death, these two score years, serving as both harbinger and guardian, guiding souls to the Originate. I have kept the seven words that grant a soul passage to the Originate. No man can kill a true ghost.

Rumi heaved in a breath as he closed the book, his body stiff with concentration. *What lives the agbara have lived.* He returned the *Sakosaye* to his burlap sack, his mind still alive with the meaning of Saturday's story. Oya had been the first agbara of death and saw nine children die. The egun were under Saturday's command. The Darani had lost favour when their ancestors were locked out of the Originate and there were seven words that granted one passage into it. *No man can kill a true ghost.*

Rumi surveyed the camp. Ahwazi, Miselda and Sameer were fast asleep. The other bed mats were empty. Agbako and Horse were likely on watch duty, but there was nothing to account for Nataré's absence.

Silently, Rumi rose to his feet. He brushed himself down and left the camp. He hadn't wandered far when he heard water splashing faintly. His jaw tightened as he stepped past a cluster of trees, halfway to calling his shadow as the sound of the water grew louder. He emerged from the trees at a clearing illuminated by the near-full moon.

The breath caught in his throat as he saw her. The cords of muscle across her bare back were like the work of patient sculptors. Her arm flexed as she reached back to wring water from her hair. He stood frozen, suspended by the unexpected intimacy of the moment. Unable to look away.

She must have sensed his eyes on her for she glanced over her shoulder and met his gaze directly. Her stare went from dark and intense to relieved and inviting in the time it took to blink three times. Still, Rumi could not look away, his heart pounding in his chest with more fury than he had ever beat his drums.

Nataré's grin was a wicked vow, and in that moment he was drawn to her in a way he had never been drawn to anything in his life. The pull of her was frighteningly strong.

She beckoned him close with her gaze and he slowly reached for the collar of his kaftan as he stepped towards her. Dressed only in moonlight, she turned to face him. He kicked off one boot after another as he pulled his kaftan over his head. Just as he was about to step into the water something made him stop.

Someone had a firm grip on his shoulder.

'Irumide, stop,' came a voice from behind.

Woodenly, he turned to see who had spoken his name. He blinked twice. 'Nataré?'

This second Nataré gave him a pleading look. 'It isn't who you think it is,' she hissed, wrapping her hands around his elbow and pulling him away from the water.

He looked again at the Nataré in the water. Her perfect form glistened in the moonlight.

'Come,' said the Nataré in the water. It was faint, but there was something urgent and desperate in her voice. Something strange. The pull of her receded as he gave her a second look. He blinked. The face had changed slightly. Those were not Nataré's eyes. Not quite the ink-black hair that Nataré had.

'It's a mami water,' said the real Nataré beside him.

Rumi let out a shuddering breath as he saw it true. She was right. Not Nataré but a water spirit.

Sensing that her trap had failed, the mami water's eyes darkened as she spoke with a voice now thick with hate. 'Olodo,' she hissed, and she dipped beneath the water. It meant fool in Mushiain.

Nataré let out a breath. 'Dara, Father of All. Thank you.'

Only then did Rumi realise that he was near naked and that Nataré had her hands wrapped around his chest. She seemed to break from the trance at the same moment and stepped back, her eyes narrowing with muted embarrassment.

'I thought it was...' He didn't finish his sentence.

Her eyes widened and he saw that she knew what he was going to say.

Her eyebrows rose. 'You find me *that* desirable?'

He held her gaze for a long moment. His heart thudded with reproach but now was the time for truth. 'Of course I do. Honestly, I would do anything for you, Nataré. It has always been that way.'

She shook her head. 'I am so broken, Rumi, so badly broken. In ways you don't even understand.'

Rumi recalled Karile's words of long ago. 'I know what it means to be broken. Believe me. But sometimes broken things are more beautiful and true than whole ones.'

She looked at him for a long moment. 'Do you know when I started loving you?'

Rumi blinked. 'When I fought by your side in the Battle at the Thatcher?'

She laughed. 'Dara Almighty, of course not,' she met his eyes. 'It was the first time we came to this forest. Before you ever joined the Shadow Order. When you leaned into me while we were riding the Shinala. You were afraid.'

'And what was so special about that?'

Her eyes narrowed. 'We build trust when we show where we are weak. Not when we show where we are strong.'

Rumi leaned forward. 'Well, I am weak here for you,' he pointed to his chest, 'and here,' he pointed to his right knee. 'Nataré.'

Her name – on his lips, in his mind, in his ear – was the true gateway to a higher world.

She looked at him, not saying a word. She puckered her lips

and angled her face towards his. A call as familiar to him as his own voice. A challenge and a command.

He couldn't stop himself, he wanted her more than he wanted air in his lungs. He took her in his arms and pulled her close. She looked at him for one silent moment as he leaned forward and kissed her. Her lips had more restorative power than all the water in Erin-Olu. One kiss and he was full of new life, his whole body on fire with attention.

He threw everything into the kiss and Nataré met him with the same force. They toppled over a bush, a branch ripping at her ash-grey shirt. It didn't matter. His hand glided over her body with holy reverence, learning every curve and crevice. She made a soft sound in her throat that came from a pure, untamed place. He pulled at the buttons of her shirt as she slipped a hand into his waistband.

They were in perhaps the most dangerous place in the world but in that moment, nothing else mattered. She locked her fingers in his hair and pulled him gently to the ground. They made love over and over, until every droplet of sweat was wrenched out of their bodies.

38

Native Hands

LETHI

It was one of those blistering hot days. If Lethi had left a slab of meat outside, it would have been cooked to a crisp. Yet somehow, by some marvel of Palmaine design, the audience chamber of the House of Palman was cool.

The men and women of the Citadel Legislative Council sat on either side of the small wooden lectern at the centre of the hall. Chairs were steeped along the perfect bowl structure. Every eye was on the central lectern. Seated along the tiered rows were the people who ran Basmine. Some were rich as any duke with lands and business interests spanning huge swathes of land, others owned nothing more than a chicken coop in some one-whore town. What they truly had in common was a collective commitment to greed.

Lethi sat far away from the proceedings; he was there as an observer, not as a participant. His plans to arrange a festival day were going smoothly and soon he would be free to find some rest.

The governor-general, Blaise Paru, stepped up to the lectern. Though Lethi knew him to be a puppet of Zaminu and the bishop, the man made a good show of having his own backbone. He walked with a born-to-rule bearing and wore robes that had all the finery of the office of the governor-general. His dark agbada was of sanyan damask, with imprints of the sigil of the Palmaine king stitched into the fabric.

The congregated audience rose in a gesture of respect as the governor-general reached the lectern and set down a heavy book.

'Ladies and Gentlemen, I now call this meeting to order. Please be seated.'

He thumped a wooden gavel on the small, rounded block and they all took their seats.

Blaise Paru opened the book cleared his throat. 'Let us begin with the matter of the grievance of one Deleke Wizi against the consulate.'

The doors were opened and a Kuba man dressed in simple, homespun ankara with a blue fila cap stepped into the hall. He stopped before the lectern and pulled off his fila cap to reveal a balding scalp. He glanced up at the lectern and Lethi recognised him immediately.

It was the baker whose son Azamon had thrown into the oven.

Lethi's stomach churned as he glanced down at the man. His face was gaunt with dark patches about his eyes and his expression carried the shamefaced humility of a man who had no expectation of fair treatment. He pressed the hat to his chest as he looked up to the governor-general.

'Deleke Wizi?'

The baker nodded. 'Yes, my lord.'

'What is your grievance?'

The baker closed his eyes and swallowed. 'My son was thrown into an oven by an officer of the Meladroni.'

There were a few murmurs of concern but nothing close to outright outrage. Plainly the matter of a child being thrown into an oven was nothing to get excited about.

The governor-general glanced down at the man as though expecting more, then he heaved in a breath and said, 'I am afraid that is a matter for the commission of justice, not the legislature.'

He was right, Lethi was sure, but the response seemed terribly insensitive.

The baker raised his chin. 'I made an application to the commission of justice and they did nothing. The commissioner himself told me to "go to the governor-general for all I care".'

Blaise Paru glanced towards the consular guard with a raised eyebrow and they moved slowly towards the man. 'I am sorry for your experience, Mister Wizi, but there are indiscretions in times like this when darkness connives with light. You are welcome to make an appeal and my office will ensure it is heard.'

A consular guard put a hand on the man's shoulder but he shrugged it off. 'You are a native son, a Kuba man like me,' the baker said, pointing at Paru. 'You let them get away with anything on your land. Let them degrade your people. You are no better than a lapdog. Kairu!'

Now the crowd came alive and there were murmurs of outrage and amusement. The consular guard seized the man.

The baker pointed at a uniformed Palmaine man. 'For so long you have lied to yourselves that you are better than us, and you still believe it no matter how low you sink. Your religion means nothing and all your laws are a farce. You promise justice! You promise fairness! But you are the enemy of justice! You are liars, thieves and rapists.'

'Mister Wizi,' the governor-general hissed.

That seemed to ignite the baker. He turned on the governor-general and made a god-honest attempt to break from the hold of the consular, jabbing a finger at him as though it were a spear. 'You shut up! Kairu! Kairu!'

Lethi was not fluent in the Kuba language but everyone knew the word 'kairu' meant dog. He had called the governor-general a dog in the centre of the council chamber. *Foolish.* The man would likely be killed for that, and then who would defend what was left of his family?

The man kicked and cursed as he was dragged from the chamber, saying every treasonous thing there was to say about the Palmaine and the governor-general. Lethi noticed that people had stopped gasping in outrage – they were listening.

It took a moment to restore some piece of decorum. There was hot gossip and scandal on offer and Lethi had learned that the council was the most thriving market in Basmine for both.

The governor-general had almost pummelled his gavel to splinters by the time he managed to get a word in. The men and women of the council, enlivened by the outrage on offer, took their time to get quiet again.

The Blaise Paru let out an exasperated breath. His agbada, which had just moments ago looked the epitome of pristine, now looked broken and dishevelled at the shoulders. The disgrace of being called a dog in open council was carved into the crevices of his face. He was a touch away from incandescence and only the veneer of propriety kept him from shedding his agbada and cursing like a beer parlour drunkard. Just a push and he would fall over the edge.

'To the next matter of business,' the governor-general said, turning the page of his book. His eyes narrowed as he read it out. 'A petition presented by Kola Coldwater of the Alara legislative district.'

The doors opened and three men stepped inside. The man at the head of their procession had the walk of the noble born. If you had said he was a battle-tested soldier or a famous warrior, Lethi would have believed it. He was powerfully built and walked with quiet authority. His dark tailcoat extended to his calves, over a chalk-white shirt and burgundy cravat. Though he was dressed like a Palmaine man, he had the night-dark skin of an Odu. Lethi leaned forward to get a closer look as the man stepped up to the lectern. This must be Kola Coldwater. There was something faintly familiar about the man, but Lethi couldn't be sure what it was.

The two men just behind made Lethi straighten with attention. It was something about the slow, deliberate way they moved. Those, he knew, were the movements of veteran killers. Plain as the sun in a cloudless sky. They were dressed in ash-grey hooded kaftans draped blanket-wise over themselves, obscuring their features. *Where is my rifle?*

A part of him wanted to shout in alarm but he knew the men had to have been disarmed before entering the room. There could be no reason to fear. Even so, he kept an eye on them.

Coldwater stepped up to the lectern and spoke in a voice that dominated the room. 'Thank you to His Excellency, the governor-general; His Holy Eminence, the venerable Bishop of Basmine; His Excellency, the former Governor-General Zaminu Elha Shangria; and to the honourable councillors here present. All protocols observed. My name is Kola Coldwater, I represent the legislative district of Alara, and my petition today is for the independence of Basmine as a new republic.'

There was a moment of stunned silence that seemed to last unnaturally long. Then, seemingly all at once, the crowd exploded. Someone in the crowd muttered the word 'treason' rather loudly, which made Kola Coldwater roll his eyes as he cleared his throat to speak.

Lethi leaned further forward. *This just keeps getting better and better.*

'If I may,' Coldwater began.

Something powerful and resonant in his voice somehow squashed the room to silence. The muttering stopped and all eyes were trained on the man.

'No,' came the voice of the governor-general. 'We will have no talk of independence here. Not today.'

Coldwater narrowed his eyes dangerously and the governor-general's mouth drooped slightly.

'You would deny me, a native son of this land, my immortal right to speak before a council of my peers as is enshrined in the law that grants you every power you have in this land?'

The governor-general glared at him. 'This is not the proper forum. Sensitive matters such as this should be communicated in writing.'

Coldwater touched his throat and spoke as though in recital. 'Rule number one of the constitution of this august council: every member of the legislative council shall be entitled to speak on any matter concerning the body politic, once having raised petition through the proper channels. Without the rule of law, we are nothing, governor-general – every person of character knows that. This is my first and most important right as a councillor – you wish to deny me even that?'

The governor-general's stare was murderous. Coldwater had put him in an impossible position. Every part of Palmaine culture and custom emphasised the importance of rules. The sanctity of law. For a position as officious and symbolic as the governor-general it was something of a stain to be seen as one who did not obey the laid down law. Especially one that was imposed on lawmakers.

'Let him speak,' someone near the front cried out.

The governor-general glanced up at the ceiling mural, as though his answers lay there. Then he let out a sigh and lowered his chin. 'I will permit your petition in this instance. You have three minutes. The floor is yours.'

Coldwater grinned deeply. 'Our gracious governor-general Kairu,' he said.

There was a sputter of laughter from someone in the crowd.

Coldwater winced, seeming to just then realise his mistake. 'Paru, of course I meant Paru.'

If he had meant it, it was subtly done.

The governor-general's stare could cut through granite. 'Go... on,' he hissed.

Coldwater turned to the thickest part of the gathered audience. 'It is with humility and joy that I stand before this great caucus. This powerful audience comprises eminent men and women, of Odu, Saharene, Kuba and Palmaine extraction – amongst them of course, the very first indigenous governor-general of our blessed nation. We have grown in the years since the four nations began our existence as one. Our birth was bloody but somehow, we found a way to make peace.' He locked eyes with a hard-faced Odu woman. 'But it was a painful peace. We suffered blows and insults morning, noon and evening because we are natives. We have been beaten to our knees and told to pray in that position.' He raised his voice. 'The time for change has come. We have paid our dues and learned our lessons. Enough is enough. There was a time when this council was dominated by a minority of Palmaine custodians. That is no longer the case, I see all the colours of Darosa when I look at the faces gathered here. We have proved that we are up to the task of good governance and the world is beginning to believe what we have always known; that the black man and indeed the black woman – contrary to what some may believe – can govern their own affairs.'

There was a low groan of agreement. Gentle but resonant.

'When I became a member of this council, I swore an oath to be faithful and bear true allegiance to "the Crown". A crown that never rested on any native head. A crown that knows nothing of the texture of native hair. Why is my allegiance to *that* crown? It is contaminated. That oath makes me a traitor. Today I ask that we swear a new oath. Affirm a new allegiance. To the precious people of a new republic. To the Kuba, Saharene and Odu.'

There was a shout of 'hear, hear' from someone at the back of the hall.

Coldwater didn't let up. 'We thank the Palmaine for all they have done in this land – you have been gracious, garrulous and ghastly in equal measure, but it is high time the Citadel is put in native hands. We can take it from here. The age of the political bondage of the native is over. All people are equal – this is my great belief. I nail it to the wall, I shout it from the roof, scream it from the gallows. Under no circumstances will I swallow the lie that the native man is inferior to the Palmaine. If you are liberated from that lie, then join me in liberating our people from it, too. I move for a vote one month from now on the independence of Basmine.'

The council erupted in shouts of agreement and cries of abuse. Urgent calls for caution and inflamed bellows of treason. Chaos reigned, and amidst it all Coldwater was the only calm person in the room.

The governor-general pounded his gavel. 'Order. Order. Order!'

It was total disorder.

A Kuba councillor from Wittadere, the most prosperous native district in the country, shouted over the din. 'What government do you propose to rule in the new republic?'

'This is no forum for discussions on this matter!' the governor-general snapped.

Coldwater ignored him. 'A government premised on adult suffrage and the mandate of the people. Let native hands till this land.'

The words sent a shiver up Lethi's spine. He could see the same effect amongst the crowd. *Let native hands till this land.* Sometimes a simple phrase could be more dangerous to an empire than an army of ten thousand.

Lethi spotted a Kuba lordling rubbing his thighs with glee – they knew that once the Palmaine left, the Kuba stood to benefit the most. A new elite in waiting.

The Palmaine were outnumbered on the council now, and those who remained had grown indolent and lazy.

The governor-general pounded his gavel like a man possessed but his authority had shrivelled rotten for the day. He needed Zaminu present, or the bishop of Basmine to stand alongside him. Someone who commanded fear and respect. Paru had neither now, and alone at the lectern he looked terribly frail.

A white-haired Palmaine man, dressed in the uniform of a decorated officer, rose to his feet. 'Arrest him!' he snarled, jabbing an accusatory finger at Coldwater.

Coldwater rolled his shoulders and the two hooded men straightened beside him. Not a single consular moved. Didn't even pretend to. Lethi swallowed. Like the first thread pulled from a quilt, this had the beginnings of a great unravelling.

The governor-general seemed to have seen it too, for he slowly dropped his gavel. He glanced up at the audience who were chattering away with no heed to his call for silence, then he looked down at Coldwater who stood, with shoulders back and chin raised – imperious in opposition.

'Session adjourned,' the governor-general breathed, abandoning all hope of recovery. The shouting rose to a crescendo. Coldwater, sensing the moment, nodded to his two hooded companions and all three slipped silently from the room. Lethi pushed his way down the stairs, desperate to follow after them but there were too many people in his way. By the time he arrived in the corridor, they were gone.

Someone in the crowd repeated Coldwater's chilling words. 'Let native hands till this land.'

Two sides were beginning to emerge and at the centre of it all was a powerless governor-general. *Everything changes now.*

39

The Fourth Level

RUMI

Joy, in certain special circumstances, is both an act of bravery and rebellion. It is a triumph over fear, hopelessness and despair. As Rumi stared into Nataré's eyes, nothing in the world could frighten him. Hope was in his heart and the pride of the martial eagle lifted him higher. If Ojuju the Yellow Masquerade himself had arrived, he would fight him and win. At least, that was how he felt in that small moment when he looked into those eyes and knew that they were as one.

Nataré blinked and held his gaze.

He stared back at her, brushing vines of hair from her face.

She let out a breath and pulled his hand away. His forearm tightened as he sensed her withdrawing from him.

Rumi exhaled as well, feeling the moment slip from his fingers.

'We should go,' she said. 'Before everyone else wakes up.'

He closed his eyes for what felt like a long moment, then he nodded his acceptance. 'All right.'

She rose to her feet. The dried sweat left patches of dark along her back and he felt another enervating jolt as he sat upright. She had him in every way there was to be had. There were words — many of them — that he wanted to say, questions even that he wanted to ask; but he couldn't trust his instincts in this matter. This was a delicate moment — just as one wrong ingredient spoils the broth, so too one wrong word would ruin the memory forever. He took no chances and chose silence.

They dressed quickly and made a quiet return to the camp. The rest were still asleep. *Or pretending to be.* Agbako and Horse were yet to return from the watch. It seemed for the moment, that no one had noticed their disappearance.

In no time at all, the sun had begun its slow rise to the skies and the others were stirring awake again for their climb to the fourth level.

Miselda took a look at Nataré's braid and grinned. 'Rough night?'

Nataré gave her an inexpressive look. 'Rather gentle, actually.'

Miselda's smile broadened. 'Glad to hear it.'

Agbako and Horse returned and then began the trek to the fourth level. As they climbed the stone-ridged side of the waterfall, the chorus of ghost frogs grew loud and incessant. Rumi could recall his encounter with them at the fourth level and how close they had brought him to death. There were hidden ponds in the ground and he would not be fooled by one again.

'Watch your step,' Rumi said, studying the ground. 'The ground here is deceitful.'

To demonstrate, he picked a small rock up and tossed it into a pool that had the appearance of a patch of wet grass.

Miselda jerked back in surprise. 'Shege.'

Rumi nodded. 'One false step and the ghost frogs will drink you dry.'

Agbako looked over each shoulder then held out a hand. 'Something is coming. Quick. Move.'

Sensing the urgency in his tone, they ducked behind trees and into bushes. It was all too slow and too late. Rumi's cowrie necklace flared with heat as a low branch struck the back of his head. Chaos commenced as three winged Obayifo darted into view. The first of them snatched Sameer off his feet and hoisted him high into the air.

Nataré loosed three arrows in quick succession, but had to duck away herself as the second Obayifo lunged at her. Rumi had the halberd in his hand and was already streaming shadow, but it was a poor weapon in a defence against flying Obayifo. They were too fast; too agile.

Agbako chanted as he raised his tortoise shell high. Miselda launched a thick spear of pure shadow and it struck one of the creatures under its wing.

'Sameer,' Ahwazi shouted, but he was long gone with the third Obayifo.

'Get behind the trees,' Rumi shouted. 'Attack them from behind the trees.'

They obeyed and loosed arrows and hurled spears of shadow at the remaining Obayifo. Agbako and Horse chanted curses and hurled charms at the monsters, causing them to slow and circle the gathered group. A bolt of shadow struck one of the Obayifo hard across the wing and it slowed its speed. Screeching, the creature swivelled in the air and flew off. The last Obayifo gave them a long, rueful look then followed its companion.

'Where is Sameer?' Ahwazi called.

'He's here,' came a deep, sonorous voice that seemed to sound from inside their skulls.

Something crashed into a tree just ahead and fell dead to the ground. It was an Obayifo with a spear of pure shadow, thick as a closed fist, lodged deep in its head. What struck him most about the disgusting display was the angle of the spear; it seemed to have been hurled from above the creature, rather than from beneath it. He glanced up into the sky and saw a figure coming slowly down.

'Sheg me,' Miselda breathed. 'I have seen it all.'

It was Jarishma, suspended in the air like an angel of the dark. Protruding from each deltoid were wings of pure shadow.

'Dara, father above, protect me from the powers beyond my knowing,' Ahwazi muttered.

Jarishma had Sameer in his arms, carrying him as one would a just-born babe. He grinned for just a moment, then swooped down. They stood back from him; mouths drooped in true awe. *Wings of shadow.* The shadowwielders knew what an awesome feat of strength in the shadow and ingenuity it was, but even those who could not touch the shadow could see this was something truly magical.

He landed with all the gentle aplomb of a thrown-down feather and set Sameer gently on his feet. The wings dissipated into mist as he looked over them one after another.

'You should have told me you were coming,' Jarishma said with a smile. 'I would have made up the table for six.'

Agbako grinned. 'It's never too late to add a few seats.'

Moments later, they were all seated inside Jarishma's grove. The sun was high in a clear sky. Gentle waves of heat produced a warm and temperate air. Jarishma had set a luncheon over the stumps of severed trees. It was painfully strange to be having a picnic in the middle of the bush of ghosts, but Jarishma was a painfully strange man. It was plain he had set strong wards of magic around his dwelling place, for creatures seemed to curve their paths to avoid it.

'That is the last time an Obayifo gets the better of me,' Sameer hissed.

'It caught you by surprise,' Ahwazi said. 'You'll have the last laugh.'

Sameer was nodding his affirmation when Miselda hissed out

a stream of curses and jumped back as she seized the shadow. Rumi sprang forward, calling his own.

A black and orange lizard, large as a human child, hung upside down from a thick iroko. As Miselda conjured a spear of shadow it raised two hands in a placating gesture.

'Don't,' Jarishma said.

Miselda launched the spear anyway. Jarishma moved at unreal speed, conjuring a shield to protect the creature in the time it takes to blink. 'He works for me,' Jarishma said as Miselda's spear dribbled harmlessly down his shield. 'His name's Timayne. He's a kobold.'

The creature flipped out from the tree and landed in a bow. Though his head was that of a lizard, his body was somewhat human-like with arms that bent at the elbow and ended in talon-like claws.

'You know what to do, Timayne,' Jarishma said.

Timayne nodded and scurried across the garden to a pale copper bucket from where he retrieved a dozen or so calabash shards and arranged them over the slumped tree that had been carved into a table.

'How do you do that?' Sameer asked.

Jarishma grinned. 'Mindwalking. With a little time and practice – you can train animals to understand you. You can do even more if you really get into it.'

Sameer narrowed his eyes contemplatively. 'I see.'

Rumi wet his lips as he glanced over the table, loaded with an array of dishes. Stewed beans, twice-washed rice and a boar roasted whole.

'What is that?' Miselda asked, pointing at the boar.

Only then did Rumi realise that it wasn't quite a boar. It was too big and muscular, with tusks too long and flesh too thick.

'Ghostboar,' Jarishma explained. 'The best pork you have ever tasted.' He whittled off a cut of crispy flesh and presented it on a plate of shadow. 'Try it.'

Miselda glanced down at the meat, blinked, then threw it down in one bite. She squirmed a little, then nodded with more than a hint of delight. 'Dara above, that is incredible,' she said, pulling a knife out to taste more.

Jarishma smiled. 'I told you. It was made with loving hands.'

Timayne bowed.

Rumi squirmed a little, glancing at the kobold's talons.

Lunch began in earnest. Miselda had been right, the ghostboar was sensational. The stewed beans, too. Every now and then, he would steal a glance at Nataré and when their eyes met, it was like they were speaking that secret language again. The one that only they seemed to understand. The bow of her lips, the white of her teeth; everything about her was cause for excitement.

'Rumi?' Sameer asked.

Rumi gave a start, realising only then that everyone at the table was staring at him. He cleared his throat. 'I am sorry, I wasn't listening.'

Sameer glanced at Nataré with the hint of a smile. 'Jarishma asked us why we are here? What we are looking for.'

Rumi drew in breath. 'We are going to the source of Erin-Olu.'

'To draw Oké water, for the Eredo?'

Rumi nodded. 'Yes.'

Jarishma narrowed his eyes. 'They would never send Suli for such a task. Only veteran shadowwielders have been this high before.' He locked eyes with Rumi. 'You are here without permission.'

Rumi offered no answer but Jarishma did not require one. He knew.

'What *else* are you here for, Irumide?'

Rumi winced at the mention of his full name. He could feel Miselda staring at him. She was the only one who didn't know the true object of their expedition.

Jarishma nodded to himself. 'Of course, I should have known.'

'Does it exist?' Rumi asked.

Miselda dropped her calabash shard. 'Does what exist?'

Jarishma closed his eyes and let out a long breath.

Miselda thumped the table. 'Can someone please explain what is going on?'

Rumi set down his calabash shard. 'I wasn't completely honest with you at the walls of the Eredo.'

Miselda frowned. 'So much for softborn clan. I thought we suffered as a collective?'

'I was going to tell you ... eventually.'

'So, tell me now,' she said, her voice hard as stone.

Rumi met her gaze. 'We are going for the Door of Testimony.'

Agbako wolfed down a behemoth strip of roast ghostboar and elbowed Horse. 'And *we* are supposed to be the crazy ones.'

Miselda's jaw tightened as some faint realisation seemed to come upon her. She turned to Jarishma. 'Is it true what they say about the Door of Testimony? That you can call names back from death there?'

Jarishma gave her an impassive glance. 'It is true they say that, but who can know if it is true what they say?'

'You've been looking for it for years,' Rumi said. 'How close have you come?'

Jarishma's eyes darkened. 'Close,' he said. 'More than once.'

'What stopped you from finding it?'

He lowered his gaze and closed his eyes. 'There is something at the sixth level. Something that guards the way to the seventh. I have not found a way past it yet.'

'Something like what?' Rumi asked.

'I will not speak of it,' Jarishma said. 'There are some names that you do not speak in Erin-Olu.'

Rumi studied the man and saw his temple pulse. He knew what that look meant – Jarishma was bringing difficult things to memory; reliving his failures.

Ahwazi chewed a strip of ghostboar. 'Like what? Oju—'

Jarishma slapped his palm against Ahwazi's mouth so hard he nearly choked. 'We do not speak that name here. Ever. Don't tempt fate in the bush of ghosts, boy.' The crease at his forehead thickened.

Ahwazi took the reprimand well; rather than protest, he washed down his ghostboar with a gulp of water and said, 'noted'.

Rumi stiffened. 'You will have support getting to the seventh level this time. You won't go alone.'

Jarishma sputtered a laugh. 'Four Suli, two witch doctors and a sentry who works the bow?'

'I am good with the sword, too,' Nataré said. 'Nasty with the spear.'

'And Sameer here is perhaps the most talented conjurer the Eredo has seen in a generation,' Ahwazi offered.

'Rumi killed the Priest of Vultures,' Sameer offered.

That made Jarishma straighten. 'Is that true?'

Rumi gave a slow nod. 'I had help, but it is true.'

Miselda cleared her throat. 'I guess I am going to have to speak up for myself since no one else is singing my praises.'

'I'll sing your praises,' Nataré offered.

Miselda grinned. 'Finally.'

'Miselda is fast, sees threats quickly and strikes with shocking accuracy. I don't know much about the shadow, but she calls her own more quickly than anyone else and has easy command of it.'

Miselda smiled at her. 'Thank you.'

Jarishma scratched the back of his neck and turned back to Rumi. 'Tell me this, have you learned your true name yet?'

Rumi nodded. 'I have.'

Jarishma narrowed his eyes. 'It is a big name, is it not?'

Rumi hesitated and then allowed a slow nod. 'Some might say.'

Jarishma gave him an appraising look. 'You have the blood of an agbara running through your veins don't you?'

Rumi gave no direct answer, which in a sense was answer enough.

Jarishma nodded to himself. 'Do you know what gives the shadow its power?'

Rumi nodded. 'Strong emotion. The ones you have neglected to explore and allowed to grow in the darkness.'

'Correct,' Jarishma said. 'Now tell me, what gives the agbara their power?'

Rumi raised an eyebrow. 'Dara?'

Jarishma scoffed. 'Think again.'

Rumi scratched his forehead and narrowed his eyes as the truth of it came easily to him. 'The emotions of others.'

Jarishma grinned. 'Precisely. Their love. Their devotion. Their fear. Their hope. Human emotion is the lifeblood of the agbara. It is why the agbara are eternally concerned with the affairs of men. They need us just as we do them. They crave our love, our adoration, worship and sacrifice. If you have the blood of the agbara, then there is a chance you too can draw power from the emotion of others. Maybe it wasn't just your own deep emotion that filled you when you defeated the Priest of Vultures. There were others that were afraid, desperate to see you win, and you pulled from that too.'

The words rendered Rumi speechless. He recalled to mind his moments of highest power in the shadow – they were all times of great collective emotion. The Ghedo. The Arakoro. The Catacombs. The Thatcher.

Jarishma gave Rumi a long look and rolled his shoulders. 'I want you to know that you barely stand a chance,' he said, almost casually. 'The odds are that you will all die in this forest and never know a new voice. If you decide to keep going, your story could end here and there will be no funeral.'

Rumi shrugged. 'That's typically the way of it.'

Jarishma gave a small laugh and then grinned. He turned to Timayne, whose eyes were wide and watery as he listened. 'Gather my things, Timayne – I am going for the door again.'

40
Demons

ALANGBA

Alangba leaned back in his chair as he watched the two boys stalk about the fighting circle. Ladan was instructing them in the Odu martial art of Bobiri.

The taller of the two boys had a quiet confidence, but to his credit, it had not ventured into arrogance. In the Bobiri circle, arrogance was a dangerous thing to carry. A slight opponent could be more dominating in a grapple than a heavyset one, with clever ways to make you bleed with elbows and knees. Every opponent demanded respect.

The taller boy sprang forwards with arms outstretched. He wrapped his opponent in a tight clutch as they scrambled for supremacy in the grapple.

'Have you ever wondered why our young take so easily to fighting?' came a voice from behind him.

Alangba glanced over his shoulder. Mama Ayeesha stood with hands clasped, her eyes fixed on the fight.

'Because they know they will have to fight much more than others in life,' Alangba offered.

Ayeesha frowned and offered him an elbow. 'Walk with me.'

Alangba curled his arm around hers and they walked in a wide circle.

'I understand that Kola Coldwater's appearance at the council was even more successful than expected,' she said.

Alangba nodded. 'The seeds are in the soil. May Dara bless us with rain. I noticed Zaminu was not at the meeting – why do you think that is?'

She shrugged. 'Perhaps he is attending to some other business.'

'What could be more important?'

Ayeesha stopped and frowned. 'I don't know.' She walked on for a moment and cleared her throat. 'There is something I wanted to ask of you.'

Alangba scratched his throat. 'What might that be?'

'There is an armoured carriage that will be making its way down the mainland road to the Citadel tonight. Inside it we expect there are precious stones worth a fortune.'

Alangba raised an eyebrow. 'Stealing?'

She shook her head. 'You cannot steal your own birthright. This is reclamation. The stones were taken from our soil. Mined by native hands.'

Alangba smiled. 'Is that what you tell yourself?'

'It is what I believe,' she answered without a hint of uncertainty. 'We are foolish if we believe Palmaine benevolence will bring the end of our oppression.'

'So, we take their trinkets tonight, and what next?'

'It is not about the stones; it is about the story. We are trying to wake a sleeping giant – it will not be done by silence. Strip the carriage of its cargo. Make a show of it. Let the natives see our defiance. Blacken the Eye of the Light.'

Alangba nodded his understanding. 'We do have some experience in blackening eyes. How many guards do you expect on the carriage?'

She formed a thin line with her lips and made a weighing

gesture with her hand. 'At least five. They will be armed with guns.'

'Naturally,' Alangba said.

'How many men will you need?'

Alangba glanced past her and stared at Ladan, still teaching the boys at the edge of the fighting circle.

'Just one,' Alangba said.

Ayeesha's brow rose. 'What?'

He met her gaze. 'You said it is about the story, right? Besides, we are short on true fighting men. We should not put more lives at risk than needed.'

'And you think you can handle five armed men, just you and Ladan? I would agree Ladan is capable of handling two, perhaps even three men, but you think you can face two alone?'

Alangba reached into the bond and Ijere, his full-grown lion partner, stepped up beside him. Ayeesha let out a shuddering breath, leaning on her walking cane at the sight. It was a credit to her that she didn't scream.

The lion gave her a long look, then glanced up to the skies to let out a full-throated roar. She shook a little on his arm.

'I never walk alone,' Alangba said.

Ayeesha looked from the lion back to Alangba. Her face was stitched from both courage and fear. She knew, of course, what Alangba knew – every bad-minded bandit in the South was capable of waylaying an armoured carriage on the mainland road. It didn't send a true message. Inspired no one. Told no story. But when two men overwhelm a band of five or six with the aid of a lion – that was the sort of story that would travel.

Ayeesha let out a deep breath and adjusted the knot of her skirt wrapper. 'Dara guide you.'

Alangba nodded. 'And may His ways be yours.'

She touched his shoulder and smiled, then, like the great

market women of old, her jaw tightened as she turned on her heel to leave.

Alangba watched her go. She was a true Odu woman. Durable as the iroko, strong as the southern breeze. What she had built was a miracle, but they needed so much more.

Alangba tilted his neck until he heard that exultant cracking, then he turned towards Ladan. Their eyes met from across the fighting pit.

They came together at the mid-point of the intervening distance and Alangba spoke low. 'We have work tonight.'

Ladan lowered his chin. 'What sort of work?'

Alangba's eyes narrowed to slits. 'Hard work.'

Ladan sighed and rested an elbow on Alangba's shoulder. He glanced over at the fighting pit as the smaller boy bowled over his opponent.

'It's like you always say. Duty comes before death.'

When night fell, Ladan and Alangba left the camp, leaving No Music to guard it. The part of the mainland road they had chosen for their ambush was half an hour away on foot. Isolated but not remote.

From their burlap sacks, they retrieved shovels, with which they dug a small divot into the stone carriageway. Just enough to slow the passing carriages down a little.

With the digging done, Ladan wiped sweat from his brow and glanced up the mainland road. 'How will we know which carriage it is?'

'The symbol marked on its side. The Palmaine Mining Company.'

Ladan nodded. 'So, what do we do now?'

Alangba stared down the road. 'We wait.'

★

Alangba and Ladan spent their wait crouched down in the bushes.

Four caravans passed without incident. One laden with sacks of rice and three others loaded with livestock. The price of everything went up with every mile travelled towards the Citadel. It meant that all of Basmine, in one way or another, served the centre. Alangba could still recall the faces of the people of the council – utterly disconnected from the truth of the nation.

'There,' Ladan whispered.

Alangba looked up. A bulky carriage was making its lumbering way up the road. It had steel-plated protective sides with thin firing slits for windows. Marked on the side of the carriage was the symbol of two crossed-over pick-axes. *The Palmaine Mining Company.*

Alangba drew in a breath. 'Here we go,' he whispered.

Ladan straightened.

The carriage wheelman had a silver whistle hanging from a rope chain and wore a royal blue uniform with the sigil of the Palmaine king. The carriage was markedly slow, on account of the weight of steel plates on the protective sides.

Alangba could tell that Ladan was ready to go, but timing was everything on nights like this. He squeezed Ladan's shoulder. 'Not yet.'

The wheelman spotted the divots and raised his whistle halfway to his lips. Then decided that the caravan could ride over it and lowered the whistle again.

'Not yet,' Alangba said.

Ladan silently called his shadow, his stare level and his eyes still.

The caravan hit the divot and tilted dangerously forward. The wheelman drew hard on the reins, urging the horses forward.

They snorted with effort and strained to pull the carriage across.

Alangba slowly let go of Ladan's shoulder. 'Now.'

A dart of perfect shadow – thin as a pointing finger, sharp as a hunting knife – perforated the wheelman's neck. The man could only manage a gasp before a gush of blood spurted from his neck and he slumped forward in his seat.

The horses shrieked as the wheelman fell, trampling him as they lost all composure. Alangba moved without thinking, climbing onto the roof of the carriage in five, fleet-footed steps.

The door of the carriage was thrown open as a soldier appeared with rifle raised. Alangba cleaved his skull in two from above and the soldier fell down dead. Without hesitation he leaped from the roof as a gunshot rang out from the firing slits.

He darted into the bushes as two soldiers came barrelling out from the second carriage door. They were firing as they came out and a bullet struck a tree not three paces from where Alangba stood. *Where is La—*

The answer came before he could finish the thought. A blur of shadow preceded a projectile spatter of blood as Ladan cleaved through a soldier's chest as though it were a loaf of fresh bread. His compatriot whirled, still firing, but Ladan was too close. He pushed the gun muzzle down as he elbowed the man, then he snatched the rifle from him and broke his nose with the buttstock.

'Lock it down,' the soldier screamed but Ladan was teeming with shadow. In this form he was closer to a god than a man. He ripped the steel plate from its hinges and turned it over to block the door, lodging it tight so that it shielded him from the barrage of gunfire from the soldiers inside.

A soldier leaped from the second door and fired into the

night. A bullet grazed Alangba's knuckle as he leaped out of easy range.

'Die!' the man snarled, firing madly into the bushes. A second bullet scuffed the cloth at Alangba's shoulder, narrowly missing his neck.

Alangba gritted his teeth as he reached into the bond. A knot tightened in his stomach as Ijere pounced on the man from behind. A single gunshot cracked in the air as the lion ripped his throat out.

The downed soldier, broken-nosed, lay beside Ladan, watching it all with a look of utter disbelief.

'Demons,' he breathed, as he glanced at the entrails of his severed comrade. 'Demons.' All the fight left him and he stared up at the sky. He clasped his hands, closed his eyes and prayed. 'Wherefore is light given to him that is in misery, and life unto the dead in spirit. Palman the Son, Ever-victorious god above all, give me this final triumph. Give me the treasure of death.'

Ladan glanced down at the man, his eyes pitying as he raised his sword high. 'Don't worry; you don't need to call your god for that.'

The man's eyes widened with fear as he saw the hour of his death had come.

Ladan closed his eyes. 'May your sins be forgiven and may you pass safely into the evermore.'

He brought the sword down on the soldier, killing him.

Alangba noticed the nose of a rifle slip silently through the firing slit at the front of the carriage. A soldier was aiming for an unsuspecting mark. Alangba moved swiftly and yanked the door open. He caught the man unawares, pulled him into a headlock and dragged him out through the door, stabbing all the way.

The stiff staccato of the blade biting flesh pulsed in his ears as he watched the life leave the soldier's eyes. The man reached out desperately to Alangba, as a child would to his mother, breathing frantically as he gripped at the last vestiges of life.

Alangba muttered a prayer as the man died. 'May you find rest in the next world that was unavailable in this one.' He took the man by the chin and slit his throat, ending it.

The carriage was quiet now.

Ladan stood panting silently at the other side of it. There was one soldier left inside but the man had elected not to shoot yet. He knew he was outnumbered and alone.

In no urgent hurry, Alangba and Ladan took a moment to arrange all the corpses in the Darani way, that they may be accepted by Baron Saturday and ushered into the evermore. They were only soldiers after all — doing their duty, they deserved to die well.

Alangba gathered his breath, then knocked on the carriage door and cleared his throat. 'Surrender the stones and leave with your life.'

There was quiet again for a long moment, then the soldier threw a steel chest out from the other side of the carriage. Alangba snapped it open and jerked back at the startling brightness of precious stones. Though he was no prospector, Alangba could tell with a glance that this was treasure enough to feed five villages for a year of total drought.

He closed the chest slowly and straightened, raising his voice again. 'If we come in there and find that you have more than this, we *will* kill you. This is your last warning.'

There was another interval of silence, then another steel chest was thrown out.

'That's the last of it,' the soldier screamed. 'I swear it. Don't kill me.'

Alangba shook his head. Even in the eye of death, people still found space for greed. Ladan gave Alangba a warning look as the sound of horse hooves pounded in the near distance.

Alanga yanked the door open and met the soldier's eye. The man had the rifle pointed straight at Alangba, but he knew there would be no gunfire. Fear had mastered him and to kill was to die. He spoke low, making sure the soldier heard every word. 'Tell your employers what you saw tonight. No longer will you steal from our land without resistance. There is a penalty for all your thefts.' He leaned forward and whispered: 'The Black Hammer lives.'

41

The Shadowmen

LETHI

Blaise Paru threw a ceramic vase across the room and it exploded against the wall. Entrails of the potted plant left a muddy smear on the embossed wallpaper as it slid down to the floor. As a show of fury, Lethi gave this outburst a solid eight out of ten marks.

'What do you mean another carriage was attacked? We doubled the guards with every pickup,' the governor-general snarled.

The man before him shuffled nervously in his seat. 'We cannot man the entire mainland road, Your Lordship. The bandits are better organised than we have ever seen them. They don't attack every carriage. They are strategic. The guards are getting…'

The governor-general glanced up. 'The guards are getting what?'

The man swallowed. 'Afraid, sir. They say one of the bandits walks with a lion. Another one of them has a cloud of shadow following him and can lift a carriage off the ground with one hand.'

Lethi glanced up at that. It was the same report that Attem had given when the Black Hammer Clan escaped from Oké-Dar. 'Strange help,' Attem had called it. He had spoken of a man who ran with a lion and another with only one hand who fought in a cloud of blackness. He leaned forward.

'What else did they say about the bandits?' Lethi asked.

The governor-general gave him a disgusted look. 'I don't care about the foolish bandit scare stories.'

Lethi ignored the governor-general and gave the seated man an imploring look. 'What else did they say?'

The man looked at Lethi and seemed to find some calm. 'The number of bandits changes but some things are consistent about the attacks. For one, the lion is always there. It springs up on people when least expected, especially when you challenge their leader.'

'Their leader?' Lethi asked.

The man nodded. 'The one who runs with the lion, that is their leader.'

'What about the one who fights in a cloud of shadow?'

'He's the most dangerous. They say he moves faster than the wind.'

Lethi's eyes narrowed to slits. 'Is there anything else peculiar about the attacks?'

The man lowered his chin and seemed to think for a moment, then he licked his teeth and glanced up. 'They always leave survivors. Every single time. They tell the survivors to tell the others of what happened.'

Lethi drew in breath, his eyes widening. 'They are trying to spark something,' he whispered, almost to himself.

'What?' the governor-general hissed.

Lethi glanced at him. 'Stories, Your Lordship. They are trying to inspire people with the stories of their exploits. Myths are an essential part of any rebellion. Humans live by beliefs. If they can make the people believe in rebellion, then they can bring it into being.'

Just then, the door behind them flew open. A breeze whistled as Zaminu stepped inside. His face was dour as a stormcloud and his eyes were narrowed to slits.

'Paru,' Zaminu hissed.

He had spoken the name as though it was a stain on his uniform.

Governor-General Blaise Paru straightened. 'Your Lordship.'

'What is this I hear about raids on the mainland road?'

'We are dealing with it, my lord,' Paru insisted.

'Three shipments in a week?' Zaminu said. 'You have a pathetic way of dealing with it.' He turned to Lethi. 'What say you, Lieutenant?'

Lethi met his gaze. 'We've heard strange reports about the raids.'

Paru shot Lethi a warning look.

Zaminu leaned forward. 'What sort of reports?'

Lethi drew in a breath, avoiding Paru's glare. 'That there is a man amongst them who runs with a lion and another who fights in a cloud of shadow.'

Zaminu's eyes widened as his jaw flexed. He worked his mouth as though chewing and drew in air from his nose. 'They are here,' he whispered, almost to himself.

Lethi raised an eyebrow. 'Sir?'

Zaminu nodded to himself and rolled his shoulders. 'Come with me,' he said, looking at Lethi. Governor-General Paru moved to follow and Zaminu shot him a disgusted look. 'Not you.'

Lethi followed Zaminu through the corridor to the bishop's sacristy. Priestly robes hung from wooden hooks along the wall and paintings depicted the saints of scripture performing great wonders. The bishop was sat behind a large ornamented credenza, reading from the holy book. Behind him, something stood covered in a dark sheet that made Lethi's stomach tighten.

The bishop glanced up as they stepped inside and gave Zaminu a questioning look.

'The man who kidnapped me has returned to Basmine. The one they call Alangba.'

The bishop closed the book. 'How do you know?'

'They say one of the bandits on the mainland road runs with a lion. It is him.'

The bishop straightened in his seat. 'And does he have a shadowman with him?'

Zaminu nodded. 'At least one.'

The bishop rose to his feet. 'Then it is time.'

'Yes,' Zaminu said.

Lethi gave Zaminu a confused look but the former governor-general offered no explanation.

The bishop unclicked the silver latches on each end of the credenza and the top of the cabinet slowly creaked open. He pulled a lid back and three trays inside fanned out, displaying a full gamut of strange instruments. There were at least four blades of differing size and shape, glass vials of what looked like blood, a hammer, a chisel and six ceramic bowls.

Lethi glanced up at Zaminu. 'Your Lordship?'

Zaminu met his gaze. 'Have you ever heard of the mudskin shadowmen?'

Lethi blinked. 'No.'

Zaminu stepped towards the door and doubled the lock. He turned to Lethi and cleared his throat. 'When Palman missionaries first came to this land, they travelled as far as the God-Eye mountains to spread the faith. The greatest of the missionaries was a man called Brother Tahinta-Rae. He spent years on this commission, going further east than anyone had thought sane. Decades later, when he returned to Palmaine and told the king about all his exploits, he spoke of ferocious men and women who fought in clouds of shadow. He called them mudskin shadowmen. Some laughed at him, others thought he was mad. We treated the reports as superstition. Brother Tahinta-Rae had lived for a long time amongst the natives and would not have been the first to find his wits contaminated by their banality. He died alone in Palmaine and his journal was the first Palmaine report of the shadowmen. A few years later, we arrived on these shores with soldiers to finish God's work. As our campaign raged on, we heard more reports of these shadowmen in the east. Still, it was treated as nothing more than a rumour.' Zaminu lowered his chin. 'I wouldn't have believed it was true, until I saw them myself. My army was ambushed in the desert by King Olu of Kasabia. They slaughtered my men. Shadowmen, plain and true. I saw it with my own eyes.'

Lethi blinked. Men saw all sorts of things in the desert. After marching for days with nothing but sand and dust on each side, hallucination was not uncommon.

Zaminu continued. 'No one believed what I saw, not even the king. I started to look into the shadowmen. I found nothing at all until I met the bishop; back then he was still a High Priest.'

The bishop nodded and smiled.

'The bishop had read Brother Tahinta-Rae's journal too and had seen similarities between his work and the words of a particular verse in scripture.'

The bishop spoke aloud. 'Beware of those who fight with the shadow of Leshbon, for they are the children of darkness.'

Zaminu gritted his teeth. 'We found out that Leshbon was a place, named after the native pagan god of warfare.'

'When I was named bishop of Basmine, I named Zaminu

the natural choice as governor-general. The king agreed and we finally had the resources to find Leshbon.'

'Did you find it?'

Zaminu nodded. 'Yes, we did.'

'And what did you discover?'

'Nothing at first, just a thick bush with barbarous people and no signs of civilisation. But there was something unnatural in the air, an almost choking sense of a deeper presence. So, we started to dig and only then did we realise what it was.'

Lethi's eyebrows rose, now intrigued. 'What?'

Zaminu grinned. 'An ancient burial ground said to be where a pagan god was buried. We found books, symbols, icons and pictures in his tomb. That was our first big breakthrough. The bishop and I have spent years since then – piecing things together, digging further into the shadowmen and the deepest secrets of the occult.'

Lethi swallowed, looking down at the vials of blood. 'And what have you found?'

Zaminu glanced at the bishop, then back at Lethi. 'Answers.'

The bishop sniffed and rolled his shoulder.

'The shadowmen are still out there,' Zaminu explained. 'Dozens, maybe even hundreds of them, and I have seen first-hand evidence of what they are capable of. If the shadowmen are unleashed on the world, there is no telling what damage they can cause.'

The bishop squeezed a knuckle. 'But we will not let them,' he said softly. 'We have spies in their midst. Shadows amongst the shadowmen who stand for the light. Finally, our spies have given us an understanding of the root of their power. We have everything we need to make our own shadowmen.'

Zaminu met Lethi's stare. 'The trouble is, it doesn't seem

to work with pure Palmaine blood. We need someone with a touch of native blood.'

Lethi blinked and swallowed. 'A native who we can trust with such power, I do not—'

'Stop pretending,' Zaminu said, cutting him off. 'I know what you are.'

Lethi looked away. 'I am not sure what you mean, my lord.'

Zaminu seized him by the wrist. 'I knew your father well. A lusty fellow if I ever saw one. You look just like us but I know a half-blood when I see it. Your mother is not from Barnham Wood. She was from right here, in Basmine. Probably a whore.'

Lethi's glare hardened as he snatched his hand free. 'I'm afraid you are mistaken, my lord.'

Zaminu didn't stop. 'Your father took you back to Palmaine with him because you looked the part of an Altayir. He left your younger brother here – a little too dark, that one was. He died, by the way. I know you hoped to find him here.'

'You have the wrong man,' Lethi breathed, barely convincing himself.

'Don't sink to lies now, Lethi,' Zaminu said. 'The light has brought you here for this ordained moment. Accept your role in the battle for the light.'

The bishop pulled a dark sheet away to reveal an ironwire birdcage. A small bird flittered against the bars with its wings and feet clipped. The bishop unlocked the cage gate and pulled the bird out. 'You, Lieutenant, will lead our very own regiment of shadowmen.'

Zaminu touched his shoulder. 'This will not be pleasant.'

42

Abobaku

RUMI

Day had slipped into night as they settled around the fire in Jarishma's grove. In the morning, they would leave for the fifth level, where Jarishma had warned that the forest completely changed. The way he told it, the fourth level was the last bastion of sanity in Erin-Olu. To cross into the fifth level was to enter the land of utter madness; the true bush of ghosts.

Miselda was restless. Rumi could see the soft signs of her withdrawal from agbo. She scratched her thighs incessantly and bit her lip whenever there was silence.

'What are those?' she asked, pointing at the collection of trinkets that Jarishma was loading into his travel pack.

'Charms,' Jarishma said, without looking up to her.

She shifted towards him slightly. 'What sort of charms?'

Jarishma gave her a brief look, then pointed at a small sack of powder. 'This is *awure*, it brings good favour.' He pointed at a stark-white stone then gestured to Rumi and Nataré. 'Your friends are familiar with this one. It is called *aferi*, the ghost stone. It is a vanishing charm.'

Nataré frowned at the mention of it and lowered her gaze.

Jarishma moved on to the next bunch. '*Damudamu* is a confounding charm, it stupefies and fascinates enemies so they cannot act in opposition to you. It is similar to these others – *amunimuye* and *ipalodo*. Some of these were used to protect the whereabouts of the Eredo.' He pointed at a small brass trinket set beside a small, indented wooden chip. 'This is *otite*, which is a paralysing charm and *isora*, which can blunt the edge of a blade and ward off a gunshot.' He brought out a thick collar. 'And the last of these is the Odeshi. The quartercuff, which I assume you know well. It takes away three-quarters of a shadowwielder's power.'

Miselda glanced at one of the charms. 'Anything that can set my mind at ease for the night?'

Jarishma shook his head. 'I am afraid not.'

'I noticed there is one famous charm missing from your collection,' Miselda said.

Rumi raised a brow. 'Miselda...'

She ignored him and spoke the word with a sonorous hiss. '*Isakaba*.'

Jarishma's eyes darkened and for the faintest moment, Rumi thought he felt the earth tremble but then the man's jaw stiffened and he found his easy cool. He had lost his daughter to an isakaba charm – one that made anyone who touched the weapon of a warrior kill themselves with it. Miselda must have known this and yet she had taunted the jungle mage all the same – she had no fear when she picked a fight.

Sameer interjected. 'That's quite enough talk about charms, I feel. Isn't anyone else hungry?'

★ ★ ★

Cuts of roasted bush meat hung from a stick above the cookfire as the moon reached its full bloom. Rumi tossed a scrap of gristle into the fire and it hissed and sighed. Hagen sat with his head pressed to the ground and his eyes fixed on the flames.

Sameer was staring at the lionhound in a way that made Rumi wonder what he was plotting.

They sat in half a circle, save for Agbako and Horse, who sat away from the group. The big witch doctor had been quiet around Jarishma.

'Anyone have a story?' Miselda asked.

No one answered. They were all thinking about the fifth level.

Miselda threw a small pebble of shadow at Agbako and it struck him on the shoulder. 'What about you, big man?'

Agbako glanced back at her, his face expressionless in the flickering red of the fire.

She laughed. 'What drove you to be a witch doctor, anyway? At least tell us that. We've all shared our stories. About time we heard yours.'

The big witch doctor turned halfway towards her. 'It's not the sort of story you want to have close to your dreams.'

Miselda narrowed her eyes. 'Oh, I think it is.'

Agbako's brows rose as he turned fully to face her. 'If I tell it, it will only be once.'

Rumi leaned in close, his own attention now drawn in.

Miselda held out a kola nut. 'Agreed.'

Horse shook his head, warning the big witch doctor against it, but there was something decisive in his dark eyes.

Agbako stared at the kola nut for the briefest moment, then he took it and broke it in a sinuous motion.

He drew in a heavy breath and stared into the fire. 'I wasn't born as you all were. Not a market boy like Rumi or a slave like Sameer or a...' He hesitated. 'Ahwazi, what is your story?'

Ahwazi waved him away. 'Not my turn tonight, big man.'

Agbako narrowed his eyes. 'I was the son of a wealthy chieftain. Chief Areem Besola.'

Rumi raised an eyebrow. 'Of Oduland?'

He nodded. 'Yes.'

Rumi scratched his chin. 'I have heard of him. His son was Tapha Besola. Besola the Blessed. He was—'

Agbako cut him off. 'Tapha was my brother. I was the first son.'

Rumi gave him a confused look. 'I have seen paintings of Besola palace. How on earth did you go from there to here?'

Agbako's jaw tightened. 'When I turned twenty, a new king of Oduland was crowned. King Oshun. Son of the Nsala of Maroko. His wise men saw my father as his greatest competition and so I was named *abobaku* to the king.'

Rumi's eyes narrowed. 'I see.'

'What is an abobaku?' Ahwazi asked.

Sameer raised his voice. 'Abobaku is an Odu word, it means "the one who follows the king to death". It is an old traditional title. Those who are named abobaku enjoy the same luxuries of the king. Whatever the king eats; the abobaku also enjoys and if he drinks heavily, the abobaku drinks to stupor.'

'Sounds like a good life,' Ahwazi offered.

Agbako sighed. 'Quite the opposite.'

Ahwazi gave a confused look. 'Why?'

Agbako grunted. 'When the king dies, the abobaku is buried alive with him. The tradition is that he who lived with him must also die with him. It was a strategic way to secure the loyalty of other noble families and avoid succession scandals from other eligible royals.'

'So, what happened?' Miselda asked.

Agbako raised his chin. 'My father had two sons and, shrewd chieftain that he was, he figured that it would be all right to lose one, so long as he could gain the kingdom.'

'So, he had the king assassinated?' asked Sameer.

Agbako rolled his shoulders. 'You didn't hear it from me.'

'So why weren't you buried alive?'

'My brother sent me a letter to warn me on the night before the king was killed. I wasn't about to be buried alive, so I ran in the dead of the night. The next morning the king was found with his throat slit and the abobaku was gone. I was blamed for his murder and my father was killed in my stead. A few more skirmishes followed among the noble families and all the other prominent chiefs died too. That left my brother as the only surviving man with a claim to the crown.'

'Genius,' Sameer breathed.

Rumi narrowed his eyes. 'Besola the Blessed. He planned the entire thing.'

Agbako nodded. 'Every part of it. I would wager that he was the one who put my father up to killing the king in the first place. He knew how the seraiye pieces would fall and played a flawless game. Planned it all perfectly. Killed all the nobles in his way without ever lifting a sword.'

Miselda drew in breath. 'Still doesn't explain you being here with a giant tortoise on your stomach.'

Agbako glanced at the tortoise. 'When I realised what my brother had done, I ran to the only place I could, the Nyme. I knew Tapha would have his assassins looking for me, so I came to the one place they would not follow. I survived for a year in the forest before I met an old witch doctor named Ijapa. When I saw the power he had, I knew I had to become what he was. He was the one who taught me the beginnings of bloodmagic and how to garner power.' He touched the shell of the tortoise as it squirmed. 'This belonged to him.'

'You killed him, too, didn't you?' Nataré asked.

He shrugged. 'He had taught me all he could. I knew to get to the next level of power I would have to drink his blood. Witch doctors live by the order of the jungle. Even Horse knows I may have to kill him one day.'

Horse gave a rueful nod. 'Unless I kill him first.'

'And your brother?' Sameer asked.

'He was killed by the Palmaine in the end. Died in a dungeon. I hear he had a scheme to make himself Warden of the South but he was betrayed. Our score remains unsettled but I will catch him in hell.'

Rumi narrowed his eyes. 'You say you *had* to become a witch doctor. You survived in the forest for a year – which is remarkable in itself. You could have taken a different path. You could have learned other things from the witch doctor. You left blood behind and still chose a bloody path. Why?'

Agbako's eyes narrowed to slits of ire as he leaned forward. He touched the tortoise on his chest and snarled his retort. 'You think to judge me because I had the courage to recognise my own motives and admit the truth to myself?' His voice rose. 'It is true I wanted to be powerful and that I didn't care what the cost was. I killed hundreds in the pursuit of power and now I number myself among the greats. Power is the only thing that truly matters in this world – you all know it. You all want it. In different ways.' He glanced at Nataré. 'I've seen the way you watch the shadowwielders – you wish you had that power.' He pointed at Miselda. 'You had to lick agbo to get more of the shadow. So, you could feel powerful and in control.' He turned to Sameer. 'You only smile when you are the smartest one in the room.' He gestured to Ahwazi. 'You stick like okra to the one man you can always beat in a fist fight. He met Rumi's gaze, spraying flecks of spit as he came close to a shout. 'And you ... You have no authority to judge me, Ajanla, you are the essence of a hypocrite – no different to me. You brought your dearest friends here to die because you believe your story is especially important.' He rose to his feet. 'We all want power, and no one ever gets it with the intention of giving it away.

Play the saint all you want, Ajanla, but you are just one ill turn away from being just like me.'

Rumi's face was blank. He could almost hear Zarcanis's voice in his head as he closed his eyes. She knew better than anyone how to break things down to the bones.

'A bit dramatic, no?' Rumi said.

Agbako flashed his teeth and straightened to his full height.

Rumi let out a resigned breath as he glanced up at the man. 'Perhaps I am a hypocrite. Maybe I did bring my friends out here to die, but there *is* a difference between you and me, Agbako.'

'And what is that?'

'I *have* friends, and I would follow each of them into the Nyme for the precise same reasons that they followed me. I have reconciled great oppositions that you are yet to acknowledge — sacrifice and requisition. I take, but I give more. You want power because you are afraid people will harm you if you do not have it. I have been liberated from that fear, for I have known a higher power that can never be taken away from me.' He glanced at Nataré, then at Sameer and Ahwazi. 'I have love in all the places you have fear, Agbako. I want to be strong so I can protect the ones I love, not because I want to protect myself.' He closed the distance between them and met Agbako's hateful glare. 'I don't judge you. I have no interest in it — you are neither a saint nor a sinner to me, only a scared man, as we all have been. You tell yourself you have gone too far to turn back now but that isn't true. You're just too afraid to pay the price of going back. You run so hard from fear that it doesn't even need to chase you anymore. Perhaps, one day, you will find something or someone that is more important to you than you — and then you will finally feel as fearless and powerful as I do in the company of my friends.'

Agbako gave Rumi a long, studying look, then he scoffed,

spat and came within touching distance. 'I hope your platitudes protect you when next an Obayifo is screaming for your blood.'

Jarishma's voice cut like a knife. 'There are better things to fight than each other here.'

Agbako let out a breath and straightened, then turned on his heel.

Timayne the kobold crept into view holding an iron teapot up to Agbako.

They all laughed, save for Agbako whose countenance was hot enough to fry an egg. In those moments, Rumi thought he could see right through him. It was true in a way that he had once been one ill turn away from being just like Agbako. Perhaps if, while he cried over his mother's grave, he had been found by a witch doctor, he too would wear a tortoise as a necklace. But Dara be praised he had been found by Alangba, Renike and all the men who led him to the Eredo. Someone had once called it 'a great rescue' – they didn't know just how true that was. Fear had transformative power, Rumi knew, but he had come by a different kind of change.

A voice hummed at his ear. 'Did I ever mention that you are quite stately when you speak like that?'

The soft hint of Nataré's scent sent a tremor of excitement through his body. He turned to her and smiled. 'Is stately good?'

She nodded with a grin. 'Very good.' She leaned forward and whispered low. 'If you wake at night, just touch my shoulder – I'll be up.'

Heat rose in Rumi's chest. 'All right.' His favourite sort of signal.

Jarishma addressed the entire camp. 'Bargain with your gods, confess your sins, profess your love, catch a night of restful sleep. Tomorrow, we cross into the true bush of ghosts and everything changes.'

43

The Bush of Ghosts

RUMI

Before morning, Rumi found time to pray. As Zarcanis would always say, 'there is a time for community and a time for isolation. In the silence of solitude, new sounds can be heard'.

Rumi washed himself clean and found a place for silence. He spent an hour in meditation seeking the counsel of the agbara. There was no reply. There never was. They seemed to only appear to him when he hadn't asked for it.

'Guide us through the bush of ghosts. Keep us safe. Grant us favour,' he pleaded.

He was only met with more silence. The thought of losing one of his friends was a dark cloud on his countenance and nothing thus far had been able to send it away. He had finally come to a place of true understanding with Nataré – to lose her now was unthinkable. He wouldn't allow it; he wouldn't give up any one of his friends.

He finished his prayer and sat alone for a few precious moments.

Something moved behind him and he whirled instantly reaching for his weapon.

It was Timayne brandishing, as he always did, a steaming teapot.

Rumi shook his head. 'Not for me, thank you.'

Timayne narrowed his eyes and shook the teapot at him.

Rumi relented and accepted a cup of tea from the kobold. The first sip warmed his insides and did — he had to admit — have a soothing effect. 'Thank you,' he said.

The kobold blinked and scurried away.

Life had become a thing of constant surprise and now he was set to embark on a journey to a place of total wildness. He sat still in that place of contemplation for a while longer. *Is this all worth it? What if I lose someone? Even if I do find Morire and Yami, what then? What about Nataré?*

The thoughts took their turns on his mind one after another. Only a sudden flash in the bond kept him from being buried alive by the unanswered questions.

He turned as Hagen strode into view. The lionhound wore the benefits of good rest and food like a crown. He was reinvigorated and looked more at home in the wild than Rumi ever could. Lionhounds, after all, were of the wild — even more than other dogs.

'You ready?' Rumi asked.

Hagen lowered his head and gave a low growl. Through the bond he felt. *Affirmation. Readiness. Commitment.*

Rumi nodded to himself. If he was to venture into the bush of ghosts then who better to do it with than his greatest companions and a shadowwielder who had once been idolised by Mandla himself? Though he did not know what lay ahead, he knew they had a chance. *A chance I have come too far not to take.*

'It is time,' Jarishma said.

His voice tolled like a drum and everyone in the grove stirred.

Rumi turned towards Jarishma. The man had stripped himself to the waist and painted his face with blood. Emblazoned on his chest was the tattooed imprint of two watching eyes. Rumi saw now that the man, though touched with age, was all gnarled muscle and bone. *A place of total wildness.* Jarishma looked like a man of total wildness. His plaited trousers had many pockets, filled, Rumi was sure, with charms of all kinds.

Nataré came into view and flashed him a knowing nod. Her quiver was thick with fresh arrows cut from the branches of ancient trees. He looked at the others. Eight men and women who were daring death for something that might not exist.

Jarishma produced a handful of ghost stones. 'We will all need to use these when to pass through wards. Though they will make us visible to certain spirits, they will protect us from others. I think the risks are too great from here on to chance a journey without them.'

They all took a ghost stone each, though Nataré hesitated before taking her own.

'We stick together,' Jarishma said, handing them each a white kola nut. 'This will help to keep you awake. There will be no sleeping until we reach Dara's Tarry. If you find yourself getting drowsy, lick the white kola nut and it will help to restore your energy.'

Miselda licked it straight away without warning and jerked back as though struck. 'That is one serious kick.'

Jarishma frowned at her. 'I don't have time to prepare more of them. If you finish your kola nut before we leave the bush of ghosts, I won't wake you up.'

Miselda tucked the kola nut away. 'Don't worry. I'll stay awake.'

Jarishma nodded. 'Last of all, *wo-ron*. It helps you to see in the fullest dark. There are parts of the bush of ghosts where you will need it.' He handed them each a twig of dried bark. 'You chew it if the need arises.'

'I have something for you all too,' Sameer said.

He produced a dozen small shadowblack orbs.

'What are these?' Rumi asked, taking one.

'I call them light bombs. You throw them at the ground and they produce a blinding flash of light that stupefies the unsuspecting.'

Rumi examined the small orb. 'How do they work?'

'It is trapped light, sealed in shadow. Works just like the stink bomb did.'

Rumi tucked one into his pocket. 'Incredible.'

'Oh, you haven't seen anything yet. I believe we are only using a fraction of a fraction of the shadow's true potential. Metallurgy, calculus, alchemy, architecture. All these disciplines have incredible potential once we start pushing to improve them with the shadow.' He leaned closer to Rumi. 'Just to let you know, I added a little personal touch to your halberd.'

'Personal touch?' Rumi asked.

'You'll laugh when you figure it out.'

Agbako raised his eyes to the skies and started a preparatory chant in deep Mushiain, which Rumi saw no point in trying to interpret. 'Agbara gbe mi ka. Ologbo gbe mi de be.'

Jarishma glanced at Rumi as he tightened his burlap sack. 'Follow my lead. Keep up. Stay ready. I have placed markers on certain trees with the letters 'JM'. If you somehow get lost in the forest, look for a tree marked with those letters and follow the arrow carved beneath.'

They followed the jungle mage in a tight formation, hunched close together like a gaggle of soldiers fearful of ambush. They came around to the side of Erin-Olu and passed the first carved tree and an arrow pointed ahead. Rumi gasped as a stone staircase came into view behind a thick white line that seemed to have been drawn with powder.

'How is there a staircase *here*?' Rumi asked.

Jarishma laughed. 'The spirits left it as an invitation. An evil taunt. Once we cross that line, we are entering the bush of ghosts.'

Rumi swallowed and gripped his halberd. 'Dara, Father of All, protect me from the pestilence of night. May I walk ever in the refuge of your shadow.'

'It's too late for prayers now, boy,' Agbako hissed.

Rumi didn't stop, his heart pounding in his chest. 'Dara, who first saw the world, lead me in the path you have cleared. Dara, Father of All, I will fear no evil for I walk in the refuge of your shadow.'

Nataré gripped his hand. 'We breathe out all our cares and breathe in your strength. May we walk under the shadow, where death wins no victory,'

'Time for the ghost stones,' Jarishma announced.

They all put the stones in their mouths. A torrent of power shot through Rumi as he did so and hundreds of Blackfae came into view. With the ghost stone, they could see all things invisible to the naked eye.

Sameer drew in a breath. 'Dara, whose voice first called the world, speak for me as I face the eternal silence.'

Jarishma finished the prayer, 'And may your shadow be our guide.'

They crossed the line and a foul smell hit them like a hammer. Something dead, rotten and vile.

'Dara's might,' Miselda hissed. 'That smell is awful.' She wrapped a shawl around her nose and mouth.

They pressed on slowly. The forest darkened the higher they got, which struck Rumi as strange for they should have been moving closer to the light. Somehow it seemed they were moving deeper into the darkness.

The silence was true and complete. Not merely the absence of noise but something thick and palpable. True silence is louder than any sound. It is heard in the pumping of blood in your ears. In the watchful heat on the back of your neck. In the small, shrill note from the insides of your skull.

Ahwazi gave a start and cursed as something seemed to shift behind him. 'Sheg the fu—'

'Move!' Jarishma snarled knocking Ahwazi aside. Just as he did, the bark of a large red tree opened up. The broken wood split apart in the shape of fangs and the tree leaned forward in a snarling bite, just short of Ahwazi's head.

Ahwazi glanced up, his face a picture of fear as the tree snarled at him, its teeth dripping with red sap.

Miselda hurled a spear of shadow at it and the tree hissed as the spear struck true. The tree susurrated with a terrible sound. Rumi did not understand the words but knew the tone. It was a curse; a tree had just cursed them.

Ahwazi took his time getting back up, then gathered himself.

'Stay away from the red trees,' Jarishma warned. 'They can smell life and when they do, they bite.'

Ahwazi drew his sword and held it in a double-handed grip. 'I will not have my story end by being killed by a tree.'

Jarishma's head jerked at a subtle sound.

Ahead the silhouette of a large figure had appeared, shrouded in darkness.

'What's that?' Miselda whispered.

Rumi bit a piece of wo-ron to help see in the darkness.

The creature gave a low growl as it stepped forward. It was a giant, double-headed lionhound. For a moment, Rumi could only stare. Cut with planes of lean muscle, teeth longer than a Shinala's tail. A nightmare made real.

Hagen gave the low whimper of an animal cowed by fear. Instinctively, Rumi gripped Nataré's hand and whispered words of encouragement. 'You are the knife edge.'

She squeezed his hand and repeated the words to herself. 'I am the knife edge.'

Heart pounding, throat dry, Rumi glanced at Jarishma. 'What do we do?'

Jarishma spoke low. 'Do not look the doubledog in its eye. We don't pick a fight with anything that doesn't strike first. We are the trespassers here. It smells fear. Be calm and it will not trouble us.'

'Hard ask, Jarishma,' Miselda said.

'Be calm,' Jarishma warned. 'Just be calm. Hold hands if you have to, close your eyes if you must. Just be calm.'

They did as they were told and crept, quiet as nightbirds, past the large beast. Horse took an eternity to urge his horse past it but managed to force his way through quietly. The doubledog sniffed at the air as they came within range. Rumi could feel its attention on them but dared not look back. It snorted with disgust and growled low. Jarishma went still.

'Get down,' he whispered.

They all obeyed, getting low to the ground as the creature moved. Rumi shut his eyes tight and gritted his teeth. The ground seemed to shudder with every one of the creature's footsteps, but Rumi could not tell his beating heart from the sounds of the world. His leg shivered and jerked as the creature sniffed against it. The doubledog's deep panting was like something wrought in hell. A jolt of panic shot through him and his brow prickled with slowly-spreading sweat. He clenched everything. A few moments of restless silence passed and then, Dara be blessed, the creature moved on. After what felt a long time, they got back up – one after another.

Jarishma let out a breath and pushed on.

They moved with the slow circumspection of anxious travellers, avoiding red trees and stopping at every noise. The faint clatter of hooves carried on the wind and Rumi raised an eyebrow. 'Sounded like a horse.'

Jarishma shook his head. 'Heavier than that. Keep moving.'

Urged by nothing but pure will, they pressed on and gathered breath as they approached a huddle of trees.

Rumi noticed the deep silence again. No whispering wind, no singing nightbirds, no bleating cattle or scurrying wood creatures.

Silence of this order could only mean one of two things – either the forest was empty; or the forest was holding its breath.

Twack.

Rumi dodged instinctively. Something nicked the edge of his ear as it flitted past, followed by the heat of blood trickling down his chin. The sharp twang of a bowstring was embedded so deeply in his subconscious that hearing it had triggered a preternatural reaction. That little movement had almost certainly saved his life.

Nataré had other instincts. Before he could turn, she had brought down her bow and nocked a single arrow, muscles tightening at the force of the draw-weight as she pulled slowly back and loosed into the darkness. It hit something and a voice screamed. She snarled as she nocked another arrow. 'We are under attack.'

Miselda built a shield of shadow and something from the dark thudded into it. At the same time, Ahwazi built a shield on their other side, encircling them with shadow. The forest was suddenly alive with noise again. A horn rang out somewhere and creatures of night moved through the trees.

'What is it?' Sameer asked.

Jarishma narrowed his eyes. 'His name is Obun. King of the Blackfae.'

As though waiting for his cue, the Blackfae appeared, surrounding their circle of shadow in wave after sinuous wave. They were armed with blades of iron and shields of brass. Though they were no bigger than a lanky man's forearm, there were hundreds of them with more coming every moment. *We don't stand a chance.* If the Blackfae decided to attack, they would cut Rumi and his companions to pieces.

A horn blew again and the Blackfae beat their shields. 'O *Buru gan. O Buru,*' they chanted. Rumi steadied himself as the earth itself seemed to tremble.

The crowd parted and went silent as their king sauntered through. He was larger than the rest of them by at least a handspan. His arms were thick with muscle and his feet girded in gold. His dark wings were twined with starlight, his armour was of burnished brass and his horned crown curled against itself in spiralling patterns. His skin, dark as night, seemed to shine brighter the closer he got. His eyes fell on Rumi and it was like someone had punched his windpipe. Rumi saw, even in this, that to be a king meant more than to occupy an office. Here was a true king; one who had lived for millennia and still was in his prime. A man of stories who seemed more incredible in life, than he did in the imagination.

When he spoke, it was as though his voice came from another direction.

'To what do we owe this trespass, Jarishma? We have tolerated your excursions more than once before but now you have the temerity to bring strangers along with you.'

Jarishma bowed low to full obeisance, his chin and palms pressed to the ground. 'Ka-Biyesi O,' he began, greeting Obun with the proper remark. 'We come in total peace.'

Obun glanced at Ahwazi's sword and Miselda's still pointed spear of shadow. 'A strange peace you bring, Jarishma.'

Jarishma made a gesture with his hands and everyone lowered their weapons. 'We seek to reach the summit, Your Grace; we would be grateful to have your escort.'

Obun let out a sputtering laugh and all his soldiers joined him in chorus. 'Escort? Jarishma, we came here to kill you.'

Jarishma bowed low. 'I know, and under any other circumstances I would have accepted my death, but this is a different commission, one more important than any before.'

Obun's wings beat twice as he moved closer. 'Why?'

'Destiny stands with me. We make one last attempt at finding the Door of Testimony.'

A thick vein at the side of Obun's head pulsed as he narrowed his eyes. 'What makes you believe you will succeed this time?'

Jarishma pointed at Rumi. 'A year ago, I had a vision. In it I saw a dog, chased by three black shadows in a field of white sand. I saw a broken crown and a four-point star falling from the sky.'

Rumi stiffened at that. He had heard precisely the same prophecy before – from Ladan.

'Then I heard a name, spoken with the voice of thunder – *Irumitunde*. My kind has come again,' Jarishma said.

Obun closed his eyes. 'And he shall speak with the voice of thunder, breathe with the breath of fire.'

'His kind has come again,' Jarishma said. 'He is Adunola's son, and he has come to bring her back.'

Obun's eyes widened as he gave Rumi a second look.

The sound of his mother's name sent a sharp pang through Rumi's chest. He was forgetting parts of her face, desperate to see it again; to remember it in full, sparkling clarity.

'You knew my mother?' Rumi asked.

The king of the Blackfae blinked and nodded. 'She is no stranger to the forest. More than once we crossed paths.'

Jarishma cleared his throat. 'A story is brewing here, and I give you the chance to stand in it, Your Grace.'

Obun turned towards one of the Blackfae who stood beside him, a female with braided hair that fell past her shoulders. 'Is this the one you saw?' he asked, gesturing to Rumi.

She replied in Mushiain. '*Be-eni*. It was him.'

Rumi recognised the Blackfae. She was the one who had come to warn him at the second level. They had known he was coming.

'And you gave him the warning?' Obun asked.

She nodded. '*Be-eni*.'

Obun's eyes settled on Rumi. 'So, you are Adunola's son?'

Rumi rolled his shoulders and nodded. 'Yes, I am.'

Obun grunted. 'To have a famous parent is nothing special. A hundred kings and queens lived and died before me with royal blood running through their veins. Only a few are ever truly special. Tell me now, boy, why I shouldn't kill you.'

Rumi met the fae king's gaze and spoke with confidence that came from the innermost pit of his stomach. Something swelled within him and his heart pounded like the dundun drum. He was taken, as he had been too many times before, by a rage that came sudden as the clap of thunder. *He rides the unbridled Shinala*, they had said of him. He would ride it through the gates of hell now. All the held-tight feeling came rushing out in an angry gush. He raised his voice and spoke as though *he* were the one who wore the crown. '*Ajanaku ki iya kokoro. Eni erin-in bi erin njo.* I am the son of Adunola and that will always be my greatest achievement.' He thumped his chest. 'I have nothing, *nothing* to prove to you or anyone else, beyond the fact that I am still here despite a vicious campaign against me. If you think because you wear a crown that you can offer any judgement on me then you flatter yourself. I am born of flesh and blood, as all people are – I stand above no one and stand beneath no one. I will not dance for you to clap. Kill me now if that is a problem to you. My existence is my only testimony.'

One of the Blackfae snarled something in a strange language and raised his sword.

Obun lifted a hand, silencing him. 'Be still.' He moved forward and came within striking distance of Rumi, their eyes barely an arm's length apart. Rumi narrowed his eyes and held his gaze.

Obun's stare was intense for one punishing moment, then he let out a breath and smiled. 'Well, you are definitely Adunola's son. Of that, I am certain. You speak to spirits with the same authority that she did.' He turned to Jarishma. 'You have my leave to go, Jarishma. I will not offer you an escort but no harm will come to you by a Blackfae hand. We will be watching you, so tread lightly through this forest – you are trespassers, not guests.'

Obun raised a hand and his army of Blackfae departed. He gave Rumi a long, studying look. 'Go well, Priestess's Son. I hope you find what you seek. But remember in all this – we warned you.'

The horn bellowed again and Obun beat his wings. He moved at the head of the army and within moments they were all gone.

Jarishma let out a breath and gave Rumi a searching look. 'You spoke well. Dangerously, but well.'

Agbako shook his head. 'A bit of humility and perhaps he might have given us an escort.'

Rumi shook his head. 'The stories tell us Obun has been king for millennia. He has protected generation after generation of his people. He wasn't looking for my humility, he was looking for my resilience. He wanted to know if we have a chance to make it to the Door of Testimony; if he'd decided that we didn't he would have given us an honourable death. Better for all if we die by his hand than by some other monstrosity in the forest. Despite it all, the stories all say that Obun has always been a loving king.'

Sameer nodded. 'He wasn't threatening us with death, he was offering us mercy.'

44

Closer to Your Dreams

RENIKE

Renike felt the knot in her stomach tighten as she leaned forward and vomited. The golden bracelet was cold as ice around her wrist as she gasped for breath.

'What did you see?' N'Goné asked.

'Too much,' Renike said, her breath coming in short bursts as she gathered herself.

Renike had done enough mindwalking in class to familiarise herself with the strange sensation of seeing a person's waking thoughts. Dreams were another matter entirely. If the waking mind was the painting of a dog, dreams were the barking, growling reality. One was a projection and the other was the truth. It meant you would encounter all the hidden aspects of the psyche in a dream and that made a dream a dangerous place. A gentleman might let his murderous shadow rule his dreams.

They had decided, for their first venture into the dreamscape, to walk into the dreams of a Seedling known as Enari. Though she was largely unremarkable, they had decided she would be the first for three reasons. Firstly, because she had the special distinction of being a famously deep sleeper. She snored like a sea whale and sometimes had to be slapped out of her slumber when she didn't wake at the morning bell. Secondly, because the dreamwalker could not work outside a range of around ten metres and Enari's bed was comfortably close. Thirdly, they chose Enari because she had made a number of suspicious enquiries about where the trainers slept. A perfect testing ground, they had thought. The trouble was that dreams were a place for the darkest fantasies and deepest fears of those who played the part of the straight and narrow. Enari, who was by all accounts a diligent trainee, had intense feelings about her trainer Xhosa. Just a few moments in her night dreams was enough to set Renike's stomach to roiling. It was – to her dismay – pure filth.

N'Goné frowned. 'A lover's dream?'

Renike gritted her teeth so hard her jaw trembled. 'I suppose we could call it that.'

'At least we know it works,' N'Goné said.

Renike squirmed. 'Oh, it certainly works.'

'Can we strike Enari off our list of suspects then?'

Renike nodded. 'I should think so – her priorities seem to lie elsewhere.'

N'Goné managed a wry smile.

Renike straightened. 'We cannot walk through every Seedling's dreams. We do not have enough time.'

N'Goné rubbed her knuckles. 'What do you suggest?'

'It is more than likely that our traitor was not born within these walls.'

N'Goné nodded. 'So, a softborn then. There are only thirteen softborn Seedlings. That narrows it down significantly.'

Renike traced a forefinger along the side of her braid, staring up at the ceiling. 'If you were a traitor in the Shadow Order, what would you be doing right now?'

N'Goné's eyes went wide for a second before she frowned and squinted. 'Watching. Preparing.'

Renike nodded. 'Exactly. So, we prioritise the softborn Seedlings who have time we cannot account for. The ones who seem to watch others and are curious about the way our defences work. The ones we have the highest reason to suspect.'

'We single out the strange ones?'

'You don't have to put it like that,' Renike said.

'I prefer to say it plain,' N'Goné said. 'We do not have the privilege of enjoying niceties. Time is not on our side.'

Renike's shoulders drooped. 'If we weren't the ones hunting – we'd be top of the hunter's list ourselves.'

'Good thing we are the ones hunting then,' N'Goné said. She blew air through her nose and put her fists on her hips. 'I have someone in mind already.'

Renike blinked. 'Who?'

She pressed an eyelid. 'Demide turns up late for dinner every other night and always has the sleeves of his kaftan rolled up.'

Renike arched an eyebrow. 'Lamodi, too, she wakes up earlier than everyone and takes her bath before the rest of us. She never seems to spar on fighting days either. What is she doing in the early hours?'

'Maybe her dreams will tell us.'

Renike cleared her throat. 'There is an obvious name that we are not mentioning.'

N'Goné's face was expressionless. 'Go on, say it.'

Renike met N'Goné's eye as her face hardened. 'Kharmine.'

N'Goné blinked in what seemed to be surprise, then lowered her gaze to the floor.

Renike arched an eyebrow. 'Who did you think I was going to say?'

N'Goné shook her head. 'No one. It's nothing.'

Renike thought to enquire further but she knew enough about N'Goné to know that was pointless. When her friend said, 'It's nothing', getting more from her was like getting palm wine from a moss boulder.

'Kharmine, then,' Renike said. 'I think we should start with him.'

'I thought you said he had a demon in his mind?' N'Goné said.

'He did.'

'And you want to go back into his dreams?'

She nodded. 'We have to.'

'Well, we don't have to start with him.'

Renike nodded. 'We don't have time to sneak into his dormitory tonight.'

N'Goné pointed to a woman sleeping at the far end of the dormitory. 'Let's try Lamodi then.'

Lamodi's bed was on the other side of the dormitory. Not quite within easy range but close enough for the dreamwalker to make contact without anyone having to get closer. Dreamwalking was a delicate matter, but it was also extremely dangerous for two reasons. The first reason was the risk of the dreamwalker encountering the dreamer's rendition of the dreamwalker within the dream. Gaitan had warned that in such cases they had to leave the dream immediately or risk a distortion of the mind that would lock them in the dream. The second reason was the risk of the dreamer somehow noticing the intrusion of a dreamwalker. If a dreamer sensed an intruder, the mind would immediately make an effort to kill it. If a dreamwalker died in the dream, it would sever their connection with the physical world forever.

Renike and N'Goné were wary of this peril and had decided for these reasons not to prolong their time in the dreams of others. Their process was simple; while Renike wore the bracelet and walked into the dream, N'Goné would stand guard and unlock the bracelet if Renike went under for more than six minutes. Every dreamwalk was to be strictly for observation and Renike was to avoid every temptation to interfere with the dream.

'What is it like?' N'Goné asked as Renike prepared to lock the dreamwalker bracelet in place.

'It's a bit like mindwalking, except everything is a little more personal and even when it's distorted it feels more... real.'

N'Goné raised an eyebrow. 'Real?'

Renike nodded. 'Think of it like the difference between watching a person while they are awake and watching a person while they are asleep. When someone is awake, they are more alert and even when they don't notice you are there, they project a certain impression because they are conscious. But when a person is sleeping, watching them feels more intimate. You can stare. You can study every crevice. You can see the things they don't want you to see because they don't know they're being watched.'

'Until they wake up and catch you staring.'

Renike nodded. 'Exactly. Which is why she can't wake up and we can't get caught.'

'If I sense any disturbance, I am pulling you right out from the dream. One hard pinch and if that doesn't work an open palm slap.'

'That should do it.'

N'Goné rotated her wrists. 'Ready when you are.'

Renike called her shadow, drew in a deep breath and let it out slowly. 'Here I go.'

She snapped the bracelet into place and closed her eyes.

For one long eternal moment, Renike was blind and the ominous sound of a dundun drum filled her ears. It lasted only a moment.

She stumbled forward and looked around. She was at the edge of the fighting pit. Little white orbs flitted about like fireflies, but Renike knew this was not the time to touch them — they were memories, and the mind was particularly sensitive to an intruder glimpsing its memories.

A familiar voice called out from behind her.

'The shadow is only a conduit for the power that lies within your emotion,' said Gaitan.

Renike turned around.

Two creatures, teeming with shadow, were locked in a wrestling tussle. The taller of the pair was scar-faced, broad at the shoulders with half-closed eyes and a snarl in his smile. He had spiralling horns on his head and talons for nails. Between his tree-thick neck and rock-cut ankles, there was nothing but thick muscle and sinew. An incredible brute, even for a dream.

The smaller woman had straw-like hair that fell to the shoulder and a sharp, angular jaw. Her arms were paper-thin, with skin draped over the bones like a tablecloth over a feast. She looked half-dead, was about half the size of her opponent and had less than half the muscle. Renike recognised her immediately as a dream-like iteration of Lamodi. This was how Lamodi saw herself — as a frail, dying creature wrestling against an incredible enemy. A part of Renike wanted to leave — this was too intimate, too personal; but it was far too late for that.

The horned beast spoke with a voice like clotted cream. 'You are nothing, Lamodi.'

The beast wrestled her to one knee but she struggled back to her feet. The beast seemed amused by watching her squirm.

With every show of power, the beast goaded Lamodi. Stripping her of dignity. It was not the playful, good-spirited teasing one might see amongst competitors. This was spiteful. The beast wanted to humiliate Lamodi and was making a good job of it.

'Nothing,' the beast snarled.

A figure appeared in the distance, clothed in white with a golden shawl — a light seemed to shine on the figure, casting her as a cherub under a halo.

'You are something,' came the voice.

Renike squinted. It was Xhosa, Lamodi's trainer. The same woman who had trained Enari — the first dream they had walked in.

The horned beast groaned its disgust.

Lamodi glanced up at her trainer and her arms seemed to thicken with strength.

'You are bigger than this. Better,' Xhosa said.

'Shut your mouth,' the horned beast screamed.

Lamodi's face hardened as she twisted the beast's hands in her grip. She was beginning to believe.

'They are no match for you, Lamodi,' Xhosa urged. 'Not when you stand up. I have trained you these past mornings because of what you are. You are the hunter, not the prey.'

Renike blinked. So that was what Lamodi was doing in the early hours of the morning — training with Xhosa.

Lamodi's jaw flexed as Renike heard a loud clicking — she had broken the creature's hand. It raised its other, gnarled fist in response and Lamodi twisted the second arm against itself, bringing the creature to one knee.

'That is why you are in the Shadow Order, Lamodi, because you are a fighter.'

Lamodi dodged as the creature swung its other fist and caught it about the armpit. She pulled both arms back as though trying to clip the creature's wings, then put her heel to its back and pushed. The arms were ripped clean off and the creature snarled.

'You have no power over me now,' Lamodi screamed.

A downpour began in the dream. Lamodi was a shadow-wielder through and through, committed to the cause of her craft. There were no diversions to secrecy or murder — she was dreaming about overcoming her fears.

A crowd of indistinct faces cheered Lamodi on from the vaulted seats as she walked down a central aisle with Xhosa at her side. Renike followed, quiet as the night owl, careful to avoid the attention of even the faceless spectators. All it took would be for Lamodi to suspect there was an intruder in her dream and Renike would be severed from the waking world forever.

They walked through an arched door down a corridor illuminated by hanging torch lanterns. Renike watched everything with the appraising eyes of a pawnbroker. Inside the first open door was a childlike iteration of Lamodi struggling to walk. On her left side was a shadowstrewn sword and on the right a yellow-white flower — the infant Lamodi walked towards the sword. The next room showed Lamodi holding hands with a tall young man with locks that extended to his hips. They looked, to Renike's mind, completely in love — eyes shiny with want for one another. A shadow appeared and Lamodi dropped her lover's hand. Renike kept walking through the corridor. She came at last to a room where Lamodi of the present day stood, leaning with her elbow against the wall. Though she was faced away from Renike, it was plain to see that she was tired. A man materialised in front of Lamodi. Renike did not see his face immediately but when it came into view she saw he was wickedly handsome with a set to his shoulders that left no doubt that he knew the benefit of physical toil. He brushed a thick braid of hair from his face and Renike saw that his locks extended well past the waist. It was the same man from the room before — her lover, grown as she was. Lamodi straightened as she saw him and he walked right up to her, smiling.

Renike turned to leave, she had seen enough. Lamodi was

a woman who had spent her life choosing between love and destiny. She did not believe she was a traitor and seeing anything more seemed intrusive.

Renike drew in breath. She needed only to pinch herself hard enough to startle herself awake and she would leave. At the corner of her vision she caught a flash of movement that gave her just a moment's pause. She hesitated, risking a glance over her shoulder and caught a glimpse of Lamodi's side profile. The thin shadowwielder had a bloated stomach with hands placed protectively on each side. Her lover grinned and put his hand to her navel. They smiled.

She's pregnant.

A hand closed around Renike's throat. Stepping close, a figure with a scratching voice filled her ears. 'Have you never been told not to enter a person's mind uninvited?'

It was rhetorical – no doubt. The speaker was a large dog, with gnarled, dreadful antlers and teeth. It had human hands with inch long fingernails. Renike could almost taste its stale, foul breath as its cold whisper sent a shiver up her arm.

'You should never have—'

Renike kicked the creature at the kneecap, freeing herself for just a moment, then pinched herself as hard as she could manage and closed her eyes. White light, bright enough to blind, filtered through her closed eyelids in shades of orange and yellow. She sucked in a deep breath and when she let it out, she was back in the Seedling dormitory.

'Breathe,' N'Goné said. 'Breathe.'

Renike tried to do just that. She had come close as can be to being discovered in that dream. That would have been the end of their expedition.

'I'm fine,' Renike said.

She wasn't. She could still feel the heat around her neck

where the antlered dog had grabbed her. Goosebumps riddled her body and her breathing came in a series of gasps.

'What did you see?' N'Goné asked.

Renike allowed herself to catch a breath, then wrapped both hands around the back of her head. 'I don't think Lamodi is the traitor. She is a dedicated shadowwielder. She is hiding something though.'

'What?' N'Goné asked.

Renike hesitated, feeling guilty for sharing something so private, but N'Goné was one she could trust.

'She's pregnant,' Renike said.

N'Goné eyes widened. 'What?'

'That's why she's been behaving suspiciously – she doesn't want anyone to know. You know how people in the Order can be. I understand why she would want to keep that a secret.'

'Her trainers must know,' N'Goné said.

'I think they do,' Renike agreed. 'That's why Xhosa lets her off on fighting days. She is balancing shadowwielding with motherhood – that can't be easy.'

'It can't,' N'Goné agreed. 'Not Lamodi then.'

Renike shook her head. 'Not Lamodi.'

'I'll dreamwalk next,' N'Goné said, 'I can take care of Demide.'

Renike drew in breath and nodded. 'Then I will take care of the one who has a demon in his mind – Kharmine.'

45

The Shadow Answered

LETHI

Lethi lay awake, his eyes fixed on the ceiling, cursing the day he landed at the docks of Basmine. Though he was in the inner sanctum of a holy temple, Lethi had never known a more godless place.

A knock sounded at his door and he sat up with an angry jolt. It was short of dawn by at least three hours and even the morning birds hadn't dared to sing. He squirmed as the image of a bloody bird fluttered across his mind.

Another knock came. At this hour, no good intentions came with a knocked door. He snatched his rifle from the side of his mattress and called out. 'Who is it?'

A low baritone rumbled in response. 'A messenger, from His Excellency.'

Lethi winced. He wanted to pretend to still be asleep but he had showed his hand. With an exasperated breath, he gripped his rifle and pulled open the door.

A dark silhouette filled the doorway. He was freakishly tall with a face that looked as though it were chiselled in coal. He was an Odu man, that much was plain, but there was a whisper of something foreign in his eyes.

'The governor-general requires your urgent presence.'

Lethi glanced over his shoulder at the tall counting clock that stood ominously against the far wall. Just an hour past midnight.

The man leaned against the doorpost, making it clear that his commission was not merely to deliver a message. He was there to bring Lethi along.

Lethi frowned as he pulled on his jacket and buttoned it to the chest, then slung his rifle over his shoulder. The big man glanced at the weapon but said nothing as they stepped out into the corridor.

It was quiet at this hour of night and Lethi noticed for the first time just how much effort had been made to lionise the Palmaine in the ceiling mural. If Zaminu in life looked anything like his painting, men and women the world over would speak eternally of his rampant masculinity. He wondered if perhaps, one day, his own portrait would be spread across these walls. A little taller, his nose a little straighter, his arms twice as thick.

They stopped at a wooden double door and the Odu man knocked before being allowed inside where Zaminu sat behind his desk with a whittling knife in one hand and a half-carved slab of wood in the other. The half-finished carving was of a long-necked scavenger bird, with a bent-over beak and beady eyes.

He glanced up to look at them as he set the carving aside. Only then did Lethi notice the collection of carvings dotted around the leftmost side of his desk. One of a cat. Another of a jackal. In that quiet moment, Lethi thought Zaminu looked rather like a goodly carpenter – patient and diligent in his craft. But all the world knew that Zaminu was no carpenter.

He glanced down at Lethi's rifle. 'Do you mean to shoot me, Lieutenant?'

Lethi wanted, with every part of his being, to say yes; but wisdom prevailed.

'My Lord,' Lethi said with a bow. 'I brought the weapon only to be in readiness for any commission.'

Zaminu gestured to the Odu man, who closed the door behind them. 'How are you feeling, Lieutenant?'

Lethi scratched his stomach. 'A little strange.'

Zaminu nodded. 'The shadow was not made for men of our constitution but we live by the fifth law. Above all, for the greater good, all things are permissible. In times where light stands against darkness – no weapon is too low to reach for. The scriptures say none can make a clean thing from an unclean thing, but we can fight filth with filth.' He gestured to the native. 'Loba. Is the carriage ready?'

Loba nodded. 'It is, my lord.'

Lethi raised an eyebrow. 'Carriage?'

Zaminu rose to his feet. 'There is something I want to show you.'

They filed out into the night and found a grand carriage waiting near the gates to the House of Palman.

Lethi glanced at Loba as he stepped into the carriage with them. It was a great surprise to see a native sharing a carriage with the governor-general but the night seemed one of surprises.

Zaminu smiled when he noticed Lethi looking at Loba. 'A big one, isn't he? I found him in a village near the God-Eye – they were worshipping him as a god and kept him alone in a dark cave.'

Lethi glanced back at the man, trying to make out his age while wondering how it felt to be spoken about as though you were not there.

'The Son rewards mercy. I rescued him and you won't believe what I discovered.' Zaminu beckoned Loba forward. 'Show him.'

The big man whispered a word and stretched out his hands.

Tendrils of smoke billowed out from his skin, shrouding him in a cloud-like shadow. His eyes darkened until they were dark as coal.

Zaminu grinned. 'He is a shadowman. Trained in the ways of the shadow from when he was only a boy.'

Lethi looked up at the man. His face had less expression than a rock and his chin looked harder than one. One good punch from a man like that could ruin any hopes of a flattering painting.

They rode on for a good hour and Lethi surmised they had run a long way from the House of Palman.

They approached a large black gate that was pulled open without the wheelman ever having to draw rein. The gates were shut behind them so quickly that it was plain that they were expected and that this was a place to be kept secret.

Lethi studied the village as they dismounted. It was a sparse settlement but a large one, and its great centrepiece was a massive ivory-coloured bungalow. It was built from stone and unfinished wood, with a gabled roof adorned with birds of paradise across the façade – it made a powerful impression. At a glance, Lethi guessed it was large enough to accommodate a good hundred or so people.

A gaggle of chickens skirted past his foot and he noticed a young man leading a cow. He was, by his complexion, at least half-Palmaine and this struck Lethi as odd. Half-bloods like himself were rare, even in Basmine.

The young man straightened when he saw Zaminu and offered the four-fingered salute.

'Welcome, my lord,' he said, lowering his gaze.

Zaminu gave no reply as he gestured for Lethi and Loba to follow.

They walked through the village in the direction of the bungalow. Along the way they passed a man polishing a rifle who wore an apron of stained ivory. He, too, was a half-blood.

The man raised the four-fingered salute high. 'My Lord,' he greeted, as they walked past.

Two half-bloods in one village.

Lethi narrowed his eyes as though he were solving deep arithmetic. He noticed as he looked around that there were three peculiar things about the village. For one, almost all the villagers he saw were young men with the simple, straight-backed surety of those who spent a great deal of time with sword in hand. He had been around enough barracks to know that such things did not come about entirely by chance. For another, there was no village square, no market, no drinking house. The only building that seemed to have any importance at all was the large bungalow. Third, and most concerning of all, was the curious fact that every single person they had seen so far was a half-blood.

They arrived at the bungalow and a guard pulled open the door before saluting. 'You are welcome, my lord.'

Zaminu led the way inside. In the front room, they found two half-Palmaine men asleep on a bed mat. They looked to be no older than Lethi, though their arms were thick with the muscles of hard use. Lethi narrowed his eyes. *More half-bloods.*

The next room was the same. A half-blood man and woman asleep beside a third half-blood man. Lethi glanced at the governor-general and a smile quirked at the corner of Zaminu's lips.

They moved past the third room and the four people inside were all half-blood Palmaine.

Lethi's jaw drooped with horror.

Zaminu grinned. 'The idea came to me a great while ago.'

Lethi gritted his teeth as a knot curled in his stomach.

Zaminu pushed open a door and strode through. 'The best of two worlds, all made here. The power of their shadow magic allied with our superior ingenuity.'

Lethi let out a stunned breath. 'No.'

'The natives have squandered their natural resources for generations, but the Palmaine mind has always been a more fertile ground. They have spent years fighting with spears in the shadow – we will do so much more.'

'Why did you bring me here?' Lethi asked, his voice hoarse as a ghost's.

Zaminu licked the corner of his mouth. 'You look completely Palmaine. I figure you will cut an impressive figure at the head of an army of shadowmen.'

The words hit him with the impact of a stone hurled from above. *An army of shadowmen.*

Zaminu pushed through another door and they arrived at a domed room, with steeped seating around the sides, full of half-bloods. At the very centre of the room, a great, iron, tumbling spindle churned out small munitions with steady, oscillating efficiency. Such machines were not new, but this was no normal contraption. It wasn't powered by steam or coal. There was no push pedal or turning wand in sight. Half bloods stood with their reverberating shadows pressed against the wheel – making it turn.

The rolling thunder of the spindle, the dull clang of hammer on anvil, the hiss of steam, the rustle of the workers. An endless cacophony that made Lethi's ears ring as the reality of what was happening seemed to splinter his mind.

'This is just the beginning. Imagine what we will be capable of when we can put the shadow to true use across the world,'

Zaminu said. He picked up a small pellet and held it up to Lethi. 'A perfect pellet. No need for gunpowder or an iron casing. We can produce as many of these as we want with no cost.'

Lethi winced, casting a glance at the dour-faced half-bloods. *No cost at all.* He could scarcely imagine the machinations of such a tyrannical mind; Lethi himself had tasted only the smallest bite of the shadow's power and knew it was a potent weapon. With an army of trained shadowmen, Zaminu would rule the world.

'Loba, bring me the weapon,' Zaminu urged. 'I want to show the lieutenant.'

The big man stepped towards a large, padlocked chest, retrieved a small pistol and handed it to the former governor-general.

Zaminu grinned as he opened the pistol's box magazine and handed it over to Lethi.

Lethi examined the pistol, pulling back the bolt handle to see inside.

'How does it work?' Lethi asked, stumped.

Zaminu clasped his hands and smiled. 'Oh that's the best part. Call your shadow.'

Lethi glanced down at the weapon and stared. He drew in breath, gritted his teeth and whispered a word. The shadow answered.

46
A False Puppet

ALANGBA

Alangba stood in darkness as he watched the field burn. His skin was blackened with char and the far-off firelight danced in his coal-black eyes. This was the third rice farm they had destroyed in just as many days. They hadn't come expecting armed resistance, but a beer-bellied Palmaine noble had led his servants out with rifles, screaming verses from the Palmaine holy book. Unfortunately for him, No Music was all too eager to start the work of making him a martyr. Now they would have to spend at least another half hour burying the dead. Alangba would not leave them for the carrion-eaters. They had fought to defend a land they believed was theirs — there was honour in that, no matter how misguided they were.

Ladan appeared in the distance, his clothes stained with spattered blood and grey-black ash. 'That's the biggest one so far. Nearly sixteen paddies of rice.'

Alangba nodded. 'It is good.'

Ladan gave him a searching look. 'You seem quite solemn for a man who has succeeded.'

Alangba glanced at the corpses. True enough their campaign to ruffle the feathers of empire had been startlingly successful thus far, but there was no joy in it. No sense of achievement. 'What are we fighting for?'

Ladan glanced down at the stump that was once a hand. 'Our lives. Our future. Our people.'

Alangba gestured at the pile of corpses with his chin. 'And this is how we do it?'

'War is ugly, my love. You know that better than all of us.'

It was true. Alangba had seen the ugly truth of war in starker colours than this. What was different about this fight that made it so uncomfortable?

'Respect the dead,' Alangba snapped, as one of the Black Hammer Clan rolled a corpse over with his heel. The man raised his hands in apology and gently turned the body onto its side.

Alangba turned to Ladan. 'I thought we were trying to build something better. Furae Oloola. How can we claim to bring something new, when we use all the old tools and methods?'

Ladan gestured to the freshly dug graves. 'We honour and bury their dead. When did the Palmaine ever give us that courtesy?'

'They are not the standard we should look to,' Alangba snapped. 'We set our own standards and killing farm-hands cannot be it. We are better than this.'

Ladan leaned forward. 'We *are* better than this, Alangba, and the time to show it will come. Every pretty painting starts with ugly brushstrokes. You cannot bring peace without first bringing violence. You have seen Mama Ayeesha's plan. We all believe in it. One more farm and we are done with this phase of it.' He squeezed Alangba's shoulder. 'Just one more farm.'

But it was never just one more farm. Anything that started in blood, ended – every time – in blood. And yet, it was like the verse from Belize's fifth dialogue; in bloody times, there are no crimes. There was work to do and, bloody or not, someone had to do it.

Alangba winced and gave a slow nod. 'Just one more farm and then we are done.'

★

They met no resistance at the last rice field. It was nearly abandoned, save for a greying caretaker whose surrender was so fast Alangba had made them check thrice for a waiting ambush. No Music muttered curses when he realised there would be no killing, but Ladan seemed pleased to keep his blade sheathed.

Ayeesha, who rarely gave any outward signs of delight, seemed genuinely excited to be done with the destruction of these Palmaine rice fields. They too had been burning them all across Basmine. Within a week, the rice shortages would be widely known and the restlessness of the South would strangle the Citadel.

In their time spent together, Alangba had come to learn that Ayeesha was as subtle as the night spider. She played a game of high stakes seraiye. If they were to win the coming war, Alangba knew that the Palmaine would live to rue the day they underestimated the market woman who had become a finger in their eye. She had disrupted their mining operations and relieved them of an emperor's fortune in precious stones. Now she had destroyed the rice they used to keep the people fed. The price of rice would triple within a few weeks and the ripple of that would be felt everywhere. What had started as a minor civil disturbance was quickly becoming a prelude to civil war.

The Black Hammer Clan had grown like maize in the mid-season. When Alangba had first arrived they numbered two thousand; now he was sure there were at least four thousand of them, and they were better trained than ever before. Ladan had seen to it that no hour was spent idle in the town that had become their barracks. They rose early and slept late – training all the while.

'If things carry on as they are,' Ladan said, wiping sweat from his brow. 'I am beginning to think we could have a chance.'

Alangba raised his chin, his jaw tight. 'It would seem that way, but nothing is *ever* quite so straight in war.' He was under no illusions. Of all the men and women in the world, Governor-General Zaminu numbered amongst the most cunning and ruthless. He had seen every kind of battle – knew the ins and outs of war from siege to subterfuge and had learned every trick there was to learn in the process. He had not arrived at the seraiye board to show his hand but Alangba was sure that somehow, somewhere, Zaminu was planning a great surprise.

Ladan met Alangba's gaze. 'You don't think we have a chance?'

Alangba furrowed his brow. 'Chance is a frightfully indelicate word. The ant has a chance against the elephant, but it is an infinitely small one. We have made an incredible start, but the Palmaine have things we never will.'

'Ammunitions?'

Alangba nodded. 'But not just that. The strength of empire. The hearts and minds of most of the people. And the fraternity of greed that keeps this whole thing running. The people of Basmine still believe they are better off with the Palmaine than against them – we will have to prove to them that they are wrong.'

'And we will,' came a voice from behind.

Alangba glanced over his shoulder. It was Mama Ayeesha. She had lost some weight since they had first met. The chubbiness at her cheeks had receded to flat, practical toughness and she seemed taller when she straightened her back. In her left hand, she held a slender walking cane, which Alangba knew was a sheath to a long blade. She met his gaze and gave him a small grin. It was the knowing grin of a weary soldier, who sensed that victory was within reach. Before their very eyes she was transforming – no longer just a rebel, now a leader.

'Come with me,' she said, waving them forward. 'I will show you.'

She spoke with an air of command that left Alangba impressed. They straightened and followed her into a small house at the edge of the township. The sharp hint of perfume struck Alangba as he stepped inside. A table had been set out, with five people seated around it. One of the guests was a Kuba man in his middle years, dressed in far more ostentatious fashion than was available on their side of the mainland road. The seams of his tunic were bejewelled and his cuffs were twined with golden thread. Never before had Alangba seen so many sequins and so much silk in one place. It was as though he had instructed his tailor to provide a garment that screamed: 'I am very wealthy'. If so, the tailor had done his work.

Mama Ayeesha embraced the man and waved a hand of introduction to Alangba. 'This is Chief Jonay Zaza of Milverton End.'

Alangba's eyes widened. Though he had only a passable knowledge of Basmine neighbourhoods, even he had heard of Milverton End. A small seaside enclave not far from the Citadel that matched even the Paradise Isles for weather and water. It had become such a favourite of the Citadel elite that it was used as a euphemism for wealth. A poor-as-mud street boy might say 'You wait till I buy a house in Milverton End' to speak hopefully of days that would likely never come. If Jonay Zaza was the Chief of Milverton End it meant he was easily one of the richest men in the country.

Ayeesha gestured next to a Saharene man and woman who wore dashikis dyed in matching egg-yolk yellow. You could tell they were related, the way you can tell different works by the same painter. The signature was in the smiles; alike enough to be twins, possessed of the same night-dark eyes and sharp aquiline noses.

'Sakaré and her brother Bakaré Olowo,' Ayeesha said. 'Their father was once the warden of the Citadel.'

The woman grinned. 'But we were originally from the south,' she hastened to add. 'We are children of the soil.'

Alangba blinked at the shimmering gold bracelet on her wrist that glistened in the lantern light. *Children of the soil indeed.*

'They are also standing in representation for the Chief of Wittadere, who sadly couldn't be here.'

Sakaré gave a small bow. 'He sends his earnest regards.'

Ayeesha moved on. 'You've met Kola Coldwater, of course.'

Alangba nodded and met Coldwater's eye. He was dressed in a dark kaftan with no hint of frippery. 'Yes, I have.'

'Then the last introduction to make is to Shotuga Tumini. High Secretary to the Governor-General. We are honoured to have you with us.'

Shotuga was the youngest man at the table and seemingly by some distance. If Alangba had to guess, he would say the man was no older than twenty-one. His grooming was spotless. His hair was parted left of centre in perfect Palmaine style, and his agbada had an elegant, crinkled fold at the shoulders that could only be achieved with the aid of a perfectly placed iron clip. If Chief Jonay Zaza's clothes shouted that he was rich, Shotuga's simply looked you in the eye and gave you a grin that told you the precise same thing.

'Thank you all for coming,' Ayeesha said, smiling as she took up a space at the head of the table. 'These are my colleagues, Alangba and Ladan. They are the beating heart of our resistance.'

Alangba lowered his eyes as their attention settled on him. 'A pleasure to meet you all.'

Ladan met every gaze but said nothing. Alangba suppressed a shiver. On the lowest of days Ladan was possessed of the highest charm but when he was brooding, the effect was near supernatural.

They took up the only vacant seats, completing the table as wine was poured in generous proportion.

Coldwater cleared his throat. 'We are here, above all, to discuss the future,' he began. 'You have all been invited to this gathering, in the heart of the south, because you are the pillars upon which this nation stands. Forget what the Palmaine say, we know the truth of this country. It relies on the strength of the natives.'

Jonay Zaza gave a serious nod and scrubbed his chin in agreement. 'Native hands,' he said.

Coldwater smiled. 'In just a few days, the council will be voting on the proposition for independence. We are relying on your support, of course, but know that such support must be ... *incentivised*.'

Jonay Zaza grinned and clasped his hands over the table. 'I quite agree.'

Ayeesha raised her chin. 'There are seven districts that rest under the exclusive jurisdiction of the Palmaine. No longer will these districts be controlled by foreigners. Our proposition is for the foremost of these districts to go to those seated here as soon as independence is achieved.'

Zaza's eyes widened so sharply that Alangba feared they would pop out and roll over the table. You could almost see the cogs of his mind oscillating as he realised the benefits to his purse of such an arrangement.

Sakaré Olowo brushed a tress of hair aside and lowered her chin. 'Even if independence is achieved, we have no way of knowing what form it would take. If I know anything about the Palmaine, it is that they would not leave without knowing they have a person in charge that they can control. They will never let you have those districts.'

Ayeesha gave a slow nod. 'You are right,' she said, taking a sip of wine.

Coldwater placed a hand flat against the table. 'We are putting things in place to ensure that our chosen candidate is put in charge of the free Basmine. A false puppet – someone who will play the part of a puppet but, when the time comes, will sever the strings.'

Sakaré blinked and held her fingers up to the light. 'And who would that false puppet be?'

Jonay Zaza leaned dangerously forward. 'Yes,' he said, 'who will it be?'

Coldwater's face was hard and cold. 'The only man who can bring every faction of the council together.' He glanced up. 'High Secretary Shotuga Tumini.'

47

Dara's Tarry

RUMI

After half an hour they had come across no new danger. Even so, they walked with the trepidation of the besieged. Erin-Olu was as quiet as a river on a windless night. Up above, it was as though a celestial hand had pulled a lampshade over the moon, casting them into near-full darkness.

Fatigue arrived like an unwelcome guest and they all had to lick the white kola nut to keep themselves from collapsing. They crossed a tree with the letters 'JM' carved on it, indicating that they were still on the right path.

'We are almost at Dara's Tarry,' Jarishma announced. 'We can rest there for the night. Just keep going. We are almost there.'

Sameer glanced up at the trees. 'Why is it so dark here? It should be mid-morning right now.'

'There is neither day nor night as you near the summit,' Jarishma said. 'Only darkness.'

'I hate darkness,' Miselda hissed.

Jarishma smiled. 'There is a time for darkness and a time for the light. Light brings scrutiny but darkness brings introspection.'

The air cooled as they stepped into a thick fog. Rumi sucked in a breath of air – his heart pounded with a furious thump and his lungs seemed to burn in his chest.

A flurry of whispers fluttered at the edge of Rumi's hearing.

The ghost of words and curses made by no voice he had ever known.

'Does anyone else hear that?' Ahwazi asked.

There was no immediate answer.

A voice with the slithering lilt of a snake hissed in Rumi's ear. 'You brought them all here to die.'

Rumi whirled with his hand halfway to the halberd but there was no one there.

He glanced in Jarishma's direction. 'What is going on?'

'This is the bush of ghosts,' Jarishma said. 'You have to ignore the whispers. They are only the echo of spirits trying to torment the living.'

Torment was right. The whispering was incessant and vile. The spirits, if that was indeed what they were, gave voice to all Rumi's unspoken fears.

'She doesn't really love you. No one ever really has. Except perhaps your mother but then, of course...' The spirit didn't finish the sentence, instead it blurted out a skittering laugh that made the hairs on the back of Rumi's neck rise.

'Shut up, shut up, shut up!' Miselda snarled.

It wasn't just that the whispers were loud, it was that there was nothing Rumi could do about them. He couldn't hurt them back in the way they were trying to hurt him. What could he say in return to nameless, faceless whispers? He responded the only way he thought could get through to them.

'Whispering at strangers? The afterlife must be quite pathetic,' he said, with a hiss of spite.

Miselda heard it and let out a thick bellow of laughter. That set Ahwazi to laughing and soon they were all at it.

Rumi was no spirit master, but he knew the fabric of a good put-down and if the spirits could hear him, let them too be cursed and insulted.

'Is this exciting for you, spirits?' Rumi whispered back. 'Is this as good as it gets?'

The whispering grew louder, more crude and less targeted.

'Foolish boy, you will be dead soon and then you too will be nothing but a whisperer in the forest.'

Rumi grinned. He threw their curses back at them and let the incessant whispering fall to the edge of his hearing. All they could do was whisper – he had faced far worse.

Just when he was sure that the whispering had receded, the faint clatter of hooves rose behind them and he raised his halberd.

A fog descended and thickened before Rumi's eyes. He glanced around and realised that none of the others were near him. He squinted in the darkness but couldn't even make out the shapes of his compatriots.

'Ahwazi? Sameer? Miselda?'

'I'm here,' came Sameer's voice from behind.

It was impossible to make him out in the fog. Rumi's grip tightened around his halberd. 'I can't see.'

'Neither can I,' came Nataré's voice.

Rumi couldn't tell what direction her voice had come from.

'Chew the wo-ron charm,' Sameer said. 'It helps.'

The sudden pounding of hooves came again. Whatever it was – it was close.

Rumi chewed the wo-ron as he raised his halberd high. If death had arrived, he would not meet it blind.

He heard the soft hiss of a sword kissing its sheath as it was slowly pulled free. Nataré; he was sure.

A faint hint of shadow preceded the jolt of movement ahead as something hurled itself through the fog. Miselda cursed as she lashed out with the sword.

'We're under attack,' she snarled.

From what, though?

A dark silhouette cast Rumi half in shadow as a gentle breeze pushed the fog clear. The blood red eyes of an Obayifo gazed down on him as his heart dropped to his stomach. It hissed, baring its finger-long fangs. It stamped a thick hoof and extended claws like knives from its gnarled fist.

Rumi swung the halberd, hard and true. The Obayifo stepped out of range and his swing fell horribly short. Panting hard, he bent into *leopard stalks its prey* instinctively. If it had been Zarcanis he were facing, her counter would have already come and he would be on his back. But this was a creature of nightmare, who relied more on fear than it did any training. Rumi pulled deep on the shadow, pouring all his fear into it. The shadow swelled as all his emotions sharpened. His focus was on fear – fear for his friends. Fear for his life. Fear of a loud and storied failure. The shadow responded, drawing in the power of the acknowledged fear.

The Obayifo's nostrils flared as it scratched one tufted ear. Its nose, if it indeed it could be called that, was something akin to the snout of a boar. The fog dissipated and the truth of their condition was laid bare. Not just one Obayifo. Not two either. At least six full-grown Obayifo, dotted about the forest like the progeny of trees. Seven feet tall with shoulders like Shinala. They hissed their song of hate in furious chorus as Rumi raised his halberd and let out a bellow from the centre of his soul.

'No one dies quietly.'

'No one dies quietly,' Sameer repeated.

'Make it a loud one,' Ahwazi snarled.

Rumi roared as he swung for the creature's head. He connected with thin air as the creature moved with blurring speed, darting out of range. The halberd struck the bark of a tree, lodging itself deep. The creature let out a noise like a skittering laugh as Rumi tried to rip the weapon free.

Jarishma's voice rang in the darkness, thunderous loud. 'Do not forget that there are other emotions available, Irumide. Not only your own. Draw from us all if you can.'

Rumi gritted his teeth and tried to feel out the emotions of others. There was a faint trace of fear that he could sense at the edge of his consciousness but not enough to feed the shadow. He moved into *shepherd holds the crook*, backtracking as he reached out for emotion. A flood of hot anger and fearless courage hit him hard through the bond. Hagen darted into view. It was like searching for water and then stumbling upon an ocean. The emotion that Hagen felt was staggering in its intensity. The protective rage of an animal that knew only fight or flight. Rumi drank deep and the shadow swelled with power.

The Obayifo moved forward with a hand extending claw-like to scratch the underside of Rumi's chin. Rumi swung his counter – perfect in timing but just off in direction. The Obayifo smiled, believing that he had seen the opening to end him. It swung a gnarled fist and Rumi dodged – thrumming with power he brought his halberd up and caught the Obayifo in the armpit. The creature gave a surprised yelp of pain. Rumi grinned.

The Obayifo was frighteningly fast, but possessed of shadow, Rumi matched it for quickness. 'You made a mistake, Obayifo. Never should you have thought to hunt an Odu man.'

Hagen bared his teeth and howled his threat.

The Obayifo gave a guttural groan and stepped back, suddenly wary as black blood spilled down its side.

An explosion of light behind them preceded the harsh squeal of a blinded Obayifo.

'The Obayifo are creatures of the dark,' Sameer shouted. 'Show them some light.'

Another blast of light followed his voice.

Rumi took the cue and reached into his pocket. The Obayifo shifted forward with that blurring speed and brought its claw down in a murderous swipe. Rumi dived sideways, rolling across the forest floor, then threw down the small shadowblack orb. He shielded his gaze just as there was an explosion of light. The Obayifo screamed. He felt the whoosh of the creature's claw ripping past him but missed no beat. He swung his halberd with every ounce of force and shadow. The halberd clattered into the Obayifo's neck, biting through flesh, sinew and bone until there was a congratulatory ripping sound. It lashed out with a flailing hand but Rumi was all out of mercy. He chopped down on the creature's skull, feeling it break and turn to powder under the force of the blow. Fear was gone now, all that was left was the exultant rage of a man who had decided to kill. He chopped and chopped and chopped and chopped. Black blood sprayed his face as he let the fury expire.

A voice buzzed at the edge of his hearing, but Rumi kept chopping. The pumping of blood in his ears drowning everything else out to a whimper.

'Irumide!'

It was Nataré. He heaved out a breath and stared down at the ruined remains of the dead Obayifo. Hagen straightened, a bloody strip of flesh dangling from the corner of his mouth.

'We could use your help,' she snarled.

They were pressed on each side by blood-hungry Obayifo. Shaking his head clear, Rumi darted into the heart of the fighting. Jarishma streamed past him, dancing through the Obayifo with all the brutish purpose of a wolf in the hen house. The creatures fell and screamed as he swung his righteous blade.

Rumi was awestruck watching him move. Zarcanis was a more elegant fighter, but there was something horribly violent about watching Jarishma kill. He needed only one hit to do his work.

'Don't just watch,' Ahwazi hissed. 'Fight!'

Rumi blinked and ducked just as an Obayifo swung for his throat. He arched back into a somersault and returned with full vim as he drew in shadow. His halberd came down hard on the Obayifo's sternum and the creature gasped a defeated scream. Rumi wrenched the axe-head free with a gruesome spatter and spun to guard Nataré's blind side. An Obayifo lurched out from the shadows, almost taking him by surprise. He turned a little too late as the creature moved in for the kill. Rumi braced, expecting death. At the point of contact, Miselda shot out with a spear that broke the Obayifo's throat stone and skewered it to a tree.

'Watch yourself, paper champion,' she said.

As she said it, Agbako snatched an Obayifo up by the legs and threw it to the ground with such virulent force that its skull burst.

Rumi winced as he raised his halberd again, moving back-to-back with Miselda ready to take on all comers.

None came.

The forest was quiet again, save for Sameer's heavy panting and the last report of the dying Obayifo.

One of the creatures lay severed clean at the waist, clawing desperately at the earth. One look was enough to know it was Jarishma's work. Another Obayifo had been gored with a thick spear of shadow and another still was peppered with arrows. They had all done their part killing, with the aid of Sameer's light bombs.

'It is done,' Jarishma said, wiping sweat from his forehead.

Rumi let out a ragged breath and closed his eyes.

'Is everyone all right?' Miselda asked.

They all answered in the affirmative. They had all survived.

'A miracle,' Jarishma breathed.

Rumi silently counted the dead Obayifo. Eight of them lay in bloody heaps around the forest floor.

Jarishma had done the arithmetic too. He glanced at Rumi in disbelief and let out a relieved breath. 'Another attack like this and we might not be so lucky.' He turned to Sameer. 'Excellent work with the light bombs.'

Sameer narrowed his eyes. 'The Obayifo will never get the better of me again,' he said. 'Unfortunately, we used them all.'

'Worth it,' Jarishma said. 'Better we give our all in every fight if it means we save a life. Let's keep going. Creatures of the jungle will soon arrive to feed on the dead.'

The jungle mage straightened and Rumi saw that his movements were laboured. He narrowed his eyes as he noticed the silverlight gleam of something shiny at Jarishma's side. Rumi gave a start. It was blood. Jarishma was wounded and making a poor job of disguising it.

'Jarishma, are you—'

'Keep moving,' Jarishma snarled, cutting him off.

They followed him in silence past a rushing rivulet of dark green water and came at last to a tall brass gate. Though it was crackled with rust and dirt, it stood with the proud prominence of a thing that would stand forever. A wide line, etched in white, preceded the gate – no doubt set with ancient charms and wards.

'What is this place?' Rumi asked, gesturing at the gate.

Jarishma allowed a small piece of a smile. 'This is Dara's Tarry,' he replied.

They pushed through the gates and found themselves before what had once been some sort of city square. Statues of heroes past stood strong in sand-coloured stone. Ahead stood the stone carcass of a gigantic building with pillars thick as centuries-old trees. Before it lay a dry fountain with a small pool of gangrenous water. The figure at the centre of the fountain was plainly Precious Jahmine holding the hands of twin children – one in each hand.

Jarishma scratched his chin. 'It is said that when Dara first climbed this waterfall, he travelled without rest until he reached the fifth level and there he fashioned a seat and rested. So it is called Dara's Tarry, because he tarried here.'

'This is more than just a seat,' Rumi said.

'The essence of the Skyfather is a powerful thing. Men and women of ages past built a city around the seat where Dara sat to rest. It stood for hundreds of years before Erin-Olu became too wild to control. This entire place is a shrine to the Skyfather.'

'Is anyone else here?'

Jarishma shook his head. 'Unlikely. This part of Erin-Olu became uninhabitable long ago.'

They reached the dust-swept stairs of the building and stepped inside to find floors of white marble. Everywhere, the walls bore paintings and elaborate mosaics – depicting stories of people who became gods. Rumi saw Obamakin, the masked king who became the agbara Balufo of walls and gates. He saw Feray Makindé who became Gu, agbara of war and iron.

At the centre of the courtyard, which was the epicentre of the building, there was an old tree that was fashioned in the image of a chair.

Ahwazi gestured to the chair. 'You mean to tell me that Dara himself once sat in this chair?'

Jarishma nodded. 'The Dancing Lion himself. This is a sacred place. No harm will come to us while we are in Dara's Tarry. Blood cannot be shed there – not even by the spirits.'

'I am exhausted,' Miselda exclaimed. 'Could do with having a sit.'

She went to sit on Dara's chair and Jarishma raised a hand. 'I wouldn't do that if I were you.'

She hesitated and smiled. 'Just playing.'

Rumi winced and let out an exhausted sigh. 'I really am tired though.'

'It is the kola nut charm,' Jarishma explained. 'It gives you twice the power for an hour in exchange for twice the fatigue for two hours – you will tire like never before for the next two hours. Get all the rest you can now. Next comes the sixth level.'

48

By Show of Hands

ALANGBA

Alangba trailed behind Kola Coldwater as he stepped up to the dais. The room was quiet but the tension was as heavy as a boulder. It was as if the nation itself held its breath. This was a vote that some believed had the potential to change the course of Basmine.

The Governor-General Paru had no such belief. He stood at the lectern with a look of abject boredom etched across his face. He knew the unspoken truth of the entire affair – the Palmaine would not simply let Basmine go through a vote by show of hands. As far as Paru and all the Palmaine noblemen were concerned, this was no more serious than a village play.

'Ladies and Gentlemen of this august body,' Paru began, 'I am delighted to announce that I, Governor-General of Basmine, will be making an official visit to Alara – heartland of the South. This will represent the first visit of an acting governor-general in over twenty years.'

There was muted applause as the Governor-General turned to face Kola Coldwater. 'And in that vein of mutual respect and collaboration, I now invite the honourable representative of the Alara Representative district to introduce a proposition which threatens to break the beautiful friendship we have built with the Palmaine. Treat him accordingly.'

The Governor-General left the stage.

Coldwater cleared his throat and drew in a breath as he reached the lectern. He was, lest Alangba fail to admit, a perfect showman. He kept them waiting, let the tension rise to crescendo before he crushed it to pieces. Everything about his appearance and posturing dripped with sincerity. Even those with no sympathy for his cause would struggle to speak ill of him. He was a man of faultless manner and poise, and he knew better than most never to let the moment rush him.

'Ladies and gentlemen of this great council, today we are gathered here for a commission of great importance. To determine the future of this blessed land.'

Paru yawned demonstratively as he rolled his eyes.

Coldwater ignored him. 'For years Basmine has been governed by foreign powers. Guided, some might say. Exploited, others would suggest.'

There were a few sniggers of laughter at that.

Coldwater allowed a small smile. 'But today is not about the past – it is about the future. Whatever our presuppositions about what should or should not have been done with Basmine, let them fade entirely into dust. Today we speak for tomorrow. My position is simple – let native hands till this land.'

There was a spattering of gentle applause but not more than Coldwater needed. He had their attention now.

He touched his chest. 'The natives can tell if it rained from the colour of the soil. We know by the song of the fish eagle whether the river is rich or barren. We were born to this land because it sings a song we can understand. All our truths and passed-down secrets are lost when we have no voice. My opponents will tell you Basmine isn't ready. They will say that to give us independence is to ensure our collapse. In their secret places they will call us savages and ingrates. They will promise doom if we go our own way. Here is my solemn promise: if the natives rule this land, it will flourish. The native man is no less than any other man in any other land. We have no divided allegiance; we know only one homeland. We are best placed to look after our own interests. If the Palmaine refuse then this is nothing more than an armed occupation and to that I say, though we are not a threatening people, no man can live under the shadow of a boot forever – eventually he will hold a sword up and dare you to stamp. Our joy has been postponed too long. Enough is enough. We will no longer be an underclass in our own land. They say the streets of Palmaine are paved with gold and that trees grow tall as mountains, thick with fruit – if all this is true, my foreign friends, perhaps it is time you returned home. My position, I say again, is simple – the time has come. Let native hands till this land.'

The crowd erupted as Coldwater raised a closed fist and stepped down from the podium. There were cheers and jeers in equal measure – with chants of 'native hands' as the room bubbled with noise. This was only the first coat of their plan.

As Coldwater dismounted, Chief Jonay Zaza approached the dais. He was dressed in a golden kaftan with the emblem of the Palmaine king stitched into his breast pocket. His feet dragged when he walked and his stomach sashayed like a fit-to-burst balloon but there could be no doubting that he commanded respect.

He spoke in support of Kola Coldwater with only a fraction of the eloquence. Even so, it was enough to set the room aflame. The crowd had not expected Coldwater to have much support. Seeing Zaza join the cause was enough to give them licence to imagine the impossible.

Sakaré Olowo came next, dressed in a flowing boubou that

was cut from the finest silk. She too lent her voice to Coldwater and the whispers rose even more.

'Who will protect you if we leave?' someone shouted from the crowd.

Coldwater's response was fast and stinging. 'Says the wolf to the henhouse.'

The crowd shook with sputtered laughter. The tide was slowly beginning to turn.

A succession of lesser Odu and Saharene councillors spoke in favour of independence, which was entirely expected, but when the Chief of Wittadere spoke in favour of independence the battle lines were scraped into stone. Three of the five wealthiest Kuba chiefs had spoken in favour. No longer could it be characterised as a pauper's rebellion. The Odu, Saharene and Kuba had spoken in favour of independence. That left only the Palmaine to make the case for empire.

Still the governor-general looked entirely unperturbed. Not once had he tried to call for order. His face remained dour and pitiless no matter who joined their voice to the cause.

The truth hadn't changed. The natives might have had an edge in the numbers, but the Palmaine had something far more persuasive in this room — raw power. One unspoken threat from any of the Palmaine nobles and the council would put an end to all their nonsense. Wittadere and Zaza could have the effrontery to speak in favour of independence but how would the lesser councillors who owed everything they had to Palmaine patronage vote? Or the chiefs from far-off villages who had developed a taste for butter and only got to have it when they were summoned for council meetings? Or the native Palman priests who had risen high condemning the gods of their forefathers? Coldwater's eloquence would not wean them off the teat. Their loyalty was bought and paid for.

The governor-general cleared his throat when Wittadere was finished and gestured towards the lectern with a lazy finger. 'Anyone else?'

The words were spoken without a hint of concern. He feared nothing. Why would he? But it was not the first time Mama Ayeesha had been underestimated.

There was still skin to shed and another branch to her flowering plan. As the Chief of Wittadere settled back into his seat, a young Kuba man made his approach.

Governor-General Paru straightened in his seat, his eyes suddenly alive. The crowd held its collective breath as they watched the newcomer mount the dais.

The young Kuba walked with the quiet authority of a man who had servants as a child. His chin never seemed to droop, every step was a masterwork in unspoken power. If this was to be their champion, they had chosen one who looked the part.

An announcer, who until now had been an idle spectator, cleared his throat and remembered his manners. 'I... I now announce the High Secretary to the Governor-General, son of the honourable Chief Tubo. Shotuga Tumini.'

Shotuga raised a hand in greeting and heads bowed in reverence. Though he was young, he occupied an old and lofty office. More importantly, his father was perhaps the most important native in all of Basmine. The respect he commanded was total.

Shotuga gripped the lectern with both hands, lifting his gaze to slowly inspect the crowd. He nodded to himself, drew in a short breath and then he spoke into the silence.

'My name is Shotuga Tumini. Some of you may know my father – Chief Tubo Tumini. A loyal Basminian. He built the first native school in the Citadel. He has served under every governor-general this land has ever known. I make no exaggeration when I say my father's were amongst the hands who built Basmine.'

There wasn't a single hint of objection. It was the truth whole.

'I have seen first-hand the truth of this nation. I know our strengths. I have seen our growing pains. I believe, as others do, that we are a people who have come to full maturity. While we recognise and thank the Palmaine for their instrumental role in guiding us to this juncture, the time has come, as it does with every person, to face the world for ourselves.'

There were gasps in the crowd.

Shotuga raised his voice. 'I have heard from my dear colleague Kola Coldwater and today, before this esteemed council – I lend my voice to his own. Let native hands...'

A tall man rose to his feet amidst the crowd. His long kaftan had a slit just right of centre. Alangba glanced at Ladan who awaited his signal.

'...till this—'

A woman screamed as the tall man revealed a rifle from the slit in his kaftan and aimed it at Shotuga. 'Die, you native scum,' he shouted as he opened fire.

Ladan moved with terrifying speed. As the gun pellet whizzed, Ladan moved ahead and took the shot in his shoulder as he tumbled to protect Shotuga.

Blood spread across the floor as Ladan lay there, still as stone. Kola Coldwater stormed onto the dais, his face turning into a picture of shock.

A guard subdued the tall shooter in the crowd but that hadn't stopped the room from turning to total tumult. People streamed towards the too-small door, funnelling through like a colony of ants.

'Assassination!' Coldwater snarled. 'Have the Palmaine fallen so low? Is that your true weapon against us? You have killed our innocents but have failed to kill our ideas. Native hands will till this land, whether you like it or not.'

Alangba appeared at Ladan's side and inspected his shoulder. There was no wound and the blood was a well-executed ruse.

Ladan's eyes snapped open. 'That was a close one,' he said with a wink.

Alangba concealed his smile as Coldwater started to milk the attempt on Shotuga's life for all it was worth. 'We will not be silenced,' he said, saying things he wouldn't dare to say at the lectern. 'Justice! We demand justice!'

Shotuga, who had not been made aware of this part of the plan, played his part to perfection. He looked utterly terrified and outraged all at once. He pointed at the still-flailing assassin. 'You dare to make an attempt on *my* life? Me? After everything?' he shouted.

'Native hands!' someone snarled from the crowd.

The theatre descended into total pandemonium. Alangba watched it all, wishing that the old Odu woman could see it for herself.

Ayeesha played high stakes seraiye. It would be at least a month before a new vote could be arranged but in that time the stories would swell — the Palmaine tried to kill Tubo Tumini's son. They never wanted a vote — there was no chance they could win. What they wanted was more subtle and particular than that. *If you want to defeat a nation, first defeat its stories.* War was coming, whether Basmine was ready for it or not.

49
The Art of War

LETHI

It was cold at night in the village. Lethi tasted blood in his mouth as he again stared up at Loba. The big man stood over him, skin black as gunpowder, teeth white as bone. He had put a beating to remember on Lethi, but it had been less memorable than the one from the night before. He was improving, painful as it all was.

Loba grinned. 'And you are meant to be the superior race. Perhaps in this you will learn that all men are equal.'

Lethi placed a palm on the sand and managed to get back up to his feet. Lethi shuffled back and tried to find his fighting stance.

Loba shook his head. 'No. You don't set your feet like that.' He gestured with his feet to indicate the correct stance to Lethi.

Lethi wagged a finger at him. 'Perhaps if we were fighting with swords. My army will have rifles, and for those, you stand like this.'

He faced Loba head-on, shoulders square and back straight.

Loba groaned his irritation and raised his chin. 'Why do you want to learn how the shadowmen fight, if you are just going to use guns?'

Lethi licked his teeth. 'Contingencies Loba. If I end up in a fist fight with one of these shadowmen, I want to stand a chance. But hopefully it won't come to that. The shadow makes us faster, stronger, quicker on the draw. We can run leagues without fatiguing, carry fallen comrades without much trouble. Do everything better. We will become better gunmen than any army before.'

Loba furrowed his brow. 'That is your way, isn't it? You can never respect the art in things. You want to tear everything down for efficiency. Burn a garden to build a barn.'

'When this war is over, you can say you trained one of the greatest armies ever.'

Loba's head jerked back. 'Do you think I would ever admit to anyone that I taught you anything?' He pointed at Lethi's feet. 'I am not responsible for that.'

Lethi took a backwards step and let out a breath. 'All right then – show me how you would like me to do it.'

Loba gave him a long, appraising look, then took Lethi by the shoulders. He turned him ever so slightly so that one foot was set behind the other.

Lethi glanced up. 'A spearfighting form?'

Loba blinked. 'You know how to fight with a spear?'

Lethi rolled his shoulder. 'My father taught me with a bayonet when I was young.'

Loba frowned. 'Crude but manageable,' he said, raising his hand. A thin spear of shadow materialised in his open grip.

Lethi narrowed his eyes. 'How do you do that? Make things appear like that?'

Loba lowered the spear. 'It is called conjuring but you are not ready for it.'

'Why not?'

'It requires great command of the mind. True self-realisation. Acceptance of what you truly are. Incorporation of the darker elements of your being.'

'You still are not telling me why I am not ready for it.'

'You cannot see the truth of yourself because you hold too closely to the lies. It will break you to admit who you truly are.'

'How could you possibly know what I truly am?'

'I know what all the Palmaine are.'

'Not me.'

Loba laughed. 'That is the problem with you Palmaine. You are all hypocrites. You lie incessantly and do all you can to avoid the truth. You cling to collective lies because it releases you from personal responsibilities. You run from your inward shame and run into the arms of religion, patriotism and false piety where all you have to do to be a saint is to proclaim that you believe. Every Palmaine person is contaminated by one great lie.'

Lethi raised his chin. 'And what lie is that?'

Loba bared his teeth. 'That you are good. Perhaps if you could accept that you are evil, you would find some peace in this world.'

'And let me guess, the natives are all saintly?'

'Oh no, we are horrible, greedy, wicked, spiteful in all things, hateful and violent, but no one can ever accuse us of that great Palmaine crime of hypocrisy. You tell us all the time how bad we are and we accept it, but we are tired of you telling us how good you are. That, we cannot accept.'

Loba turned away from Lethi, but the soldier took him by the wrist. Lethi spoke slowly with a subtle air of command. 'Show me how it works.'

Loba glanced down at Lethi's grip, then snatched his wrist away. 'I cannot show you anything. You are a slave to your own ego.'

'Aren't we all? Or were you not like me once?'

Loba blinked. 'What?'

Lethi narrowed his eyes. 'If you truly believe all men are equal then why can't I be taught – just as you were?'

Loba gave him a long look, as his lips curled into a smile. 'You Palmaine are cunning as snakes.'

Lethi grinned back. 'I accept the charge. Now show me how it works.'

Loba scratched the side of his head, then let out an exasperated breath. Stretching out his hand he conjured a small ball of shadow. 'You command the shadow, but it will not listen until you have acknowledged the deepest, darkest emotions that your mind has always chosen to ignore. You have to reconcile with the parts of your being that you have ostracised. You have to tell the truth.'

'I am ready to tell the truth.'

Loba's smile was like a knifeslit. 'Then call your shadow... and prepare your mind for pain.'

The big man did not exaggerate. The work of straining the mind to face the shadow brought Lethi into confrontation with every single emotion he had run from. The hurt from his father's wordless rejection; the pain of his brother's death. The shame for abandoning his mother. His darkest thoughts took their turns on him and had their way but when they had done their worst, Lethi found there was power within him.

After an hour of silent focus on the shadow, Loba moved through a short choreography of stances to get Lethi's body acquainted with how he was expected to move to use his shadow. They were sharp, taxing manoeuvres that asked a lot of his soldier's knees and long-suffering forearms.

Loba adopted his fighting stance. 'Show me *shepherd holds the crook*.'

Lethi set his feet and began the choreography. As he did,

tendrils of black mist formed around his hands. He gave a start as he realised what was happening.

'Don't lose focus,' Loba snapped. He placed his hand on Lethi's arm and moved him into the same position. 'Start again and don't get distracted.'

Lethi drew in breath. Positioned his hands to restart the sequence. This time, he was committed to not letting anything break his concentration. No matter what strange things he saw in his mind, he would see the session to the end.

Later at night, when he lay alone in his room, he stood staring at the ceiling when he was struck by an idea so sharp that he jolted up alert. He grabbed his rifle and opened the box magazine, pulling back the bolt handle to test his theory was correct. He smiled as he stretched out his hand and began to conjure the shadow, forming a crude replica of the weapon. Satisfied with the effort, he let it dissipate and then started again. Practice, for Lethi, would make perfect.

50

The Shadow Thereof

RUMI

Sleep seemed just out of reach. Though they had a roof over their heads, the jungle watchfulness of Erin-Olu wouldn't go away. No matter how often Jarishma told them they couldn't be harmed in Dara's Tarry, Rumi couldn't put his mind at ease. They were in what must once have been a grand dining room. The ceiling was impressively high and the canopy was painted with an image of Xango with a sword in one hand and his double-axe in the other. Beside him stood his wife, Oya; she wore a necklace set with a single black cowrie and held a flute in her left hand – dark as coal. A table fit to host dinner for twenty was illuminated by two torches perched at perpendicular corners of the room.

A chubby rat scrambled over Rumi's foot as though it owned the place. Rumi glanced at it and the rat glared back with the proprietary air of a landlord to a tenant. Hagen growled and the rodent flitted down a small crack between the bricks at the corner of the room.

Nataré raised an eyebrow. 'If there is no one else here, why are there rats? What have they found to feed on?'

Jarishma narrowed his eyes. 'Get some sleep.'

Miselda, to her credit, had no trouble sleeping. Rumi thought if the mood came, the woman could sleep on a sailboat in a sea storm. With her feet propped up on the table, she sat on the grandest chair in the room. Listening to her snore, one would think she was in a bedroom and not a forgotten city in the bush of ghosts. Ahwazi too found sleep, though it was fitful. Sameer, who had helped Jarishma stitch his wound shut, was taking his time to look over the various paintings. The witch doctors preferred to stay outside.

'I only sleep with the clouds over my head,' Agbako had said.

Nataré was bolt awake. She took Rumi by the hand and led him to a cushioned chaise lounge beside the door. No one could hear them and only Sameer and Jarishma stood a chance of seeing them.

She leaned on Rumi's shoulder and lifted her chin so her breath brushed his neck. 'We are almost there. We are going to make it.'

Rumi stiffened. He was trying to make himself believe it but was struggling at that precise moment. They were no true match for the creatures in Erin-Olu and now even Jarishma was wounded. If the Obayifo attacked in numbers again, it was almost certain that someone would die. There were other things this high in Erin-Olu too. Things far worse than Obayifo.

'I am sorry for bringing you here,' Rumi whispered.

Nataré gave him an admonishing look. 'Can you explain to me why you have not apologised to the others for bringing them here, but have come to me to ask forgiveness?'

Rumi winced as the fire hissed and dark ash crossed his view.

Nataré drew her shoulders up. 'Is it because I am not a shadowwielder? Because you think I am easy prey? Because you think I am weak?'

'Nothing like that,' Rumi protested.

'Why then?'

Rumi glanced at the fire. 'Because...' But he had no easy answer.

Nataré drew close. 'For some reason I cannot understand, you feel it is all right to put your life at risk but not mine. I thought it was chivalry at first but now I see it is something else – something I don't entirely understand. What is it, Rumi?'

Rumi drew in a breath. An acrid sting bothered him at the eyelids and it was as though he had stepped too close to woodsmoke. Before he knew what was happening, a tear had rolled down his cheek.

'Are you... crying, Irumide?'

Rumi lowered his gaze. A harsh cough cut off in his throat as he cleared it to speak. 'I am in love with you, Nataré. I always have been and now that we are here – facing the threat of death – I am terrified that I will lose you. It frightens me so much that I hate myself. I hate myself for bringing you here. For risking your precious life. Risking what we have built. I could live with death. I couldn't live with losing you.'

Nataré was quiet for a long moment, then she touched his chin and raised it till their eyes met. 'Love is all about risk, Rumi. It comes with terror. So many times in my life I have run away from a chance at love. Abandoned my feelings to save myself. But you asked me if you were in this alone and it changed everything. Our bond is real. If it is ever severed it will rip parts of us along with it but that cannot be cause for fear. Not now. Death is all around us all the time Rumi, but it isn't here right now,' she said, tracing a finger over his thigh. 'Let us revel in the truth that tonight, we are more alive than we've ever been and we are in love, and nothing can take this moment from us.'

She pulled his chin towards her and their lips met. Her kiss was frighteningly gentle. Lips so soft that Rumi almost felt like he would crumple them if he kissed too hard. His grip found the second button of her tunic and he dragged her close. Her mouth tasted of apple and cocoa beans. Equal part sweet and strong. She lay in his arms after that and for a long moment they sat in complete stillness; safe in the all-conquering silence that they filled with unsaid words of love. The fear fell away as Rumi embraced something more hopeful. They would make it to the summit alive because they had the courage and determination to do it. Every one of them could have been somewhere entirely different and yet here they were on the precipice of the most dangerous parts of Erin-Olu. Sameer, Ahwazi, Nataré and Hagen were there because they loved him, and the only way he could love them in return was by fighting like a dog to see them home safe. Perhaps they should have never come to Erin-Olu – that too could be true. But Zarcanis said it best – 'yesterday is gone forever, you can't build anything with regret'. There was no time for regret now – only to face up to his fear and give it all he could. Even if he died, he would give everything before it happened – and who can blame a man for dying if only that his friends should live?

The nail-scratch sound of a child screaming broke his concentration.

'What was that?' Nataré asked.

Jarishma straightened. 'A bush baby.'

Miselda was up, sharp as a knifepoint. In her hand, a weapon of pure shadow was already materialising.

Sameer motioned to call his shadow but Jarishma raised an admonitory hand. 'Wait.'

Two pitched screams came again, one after another.

'Sounds to me like this isn't the sheggin' time to wait,' Miselda hissed.

'They are coming closer,' Sameer said.

'This shouldn't be happening,' Jarishma said again. 'Not here.' It sounded like he wasn't convincing himself.

Through the large open window, shapes moved in the darkness. Rumi heard the quick parting of leaves and stomping of grass.

Jarishma cleared his throat, accepting at last the threat of danger. 'Barricade the doors.'

Rumi and Nataré pushed the chaise lounge across the room and lodged it so it barred the door. As they edged it shut, Rumi saw a figure crawl into view. Though Rumi wanted to shut his eyes, he couldn't help himself but steal a peek. The bush baby's skin was the pallid grey-white of the long-dead and its hair was ashen and straw-like. From its lips spilled a pinkish white drool and its nails were a sickly yellow. Rumi managed, with some effort, not to look at the eyes but he could feel them watching him. He slammed the door closed and pressed his back to it, breathing hard.

'Did you look into its eyes?' Jarishma asked.

Rumi shook his head. 'No.'

'No matter what you do. Do not look into their eyes.'

Sameer pushed another chair to bar the door. 'What happens if you look in their eyes?'

'You die,' Jarishma said simply.

'I thought you said we couldn't be harmed in Dara's Tarry,' Sameer said.

'I said our blood could not be shed. Bush babies do not need to shed blood.'

The sound of the bush babies rose as Sameer moved the long table to bar the window.

Jarishma pulled at a small inset ring placed along the far wall and a drop-down door fell to the ground. 'Quickly, through here.'

They wasted no time to obey, rushing through the unexpected opening down a darkened staircase. Hagen flew out in front, barking at the top of his lungs as he sprinted down. At the bottom of the stairs, Jarishma summoned his shadow and brought a hanging torch to life, illuminating a wide corridor.

'Follow me,' he said, taking off at an easy sprint.

The sound of the creatures rose behind them as more bush babies joined their voices to the cacophony of noise. They followed the corridor to a broken gate. Jarishma pulled it aside and hurried through an open door. The others followed after, but something gave Rumi pause. His cowrie necklace was running scorching-hot. The cowrie was his kukoyi talisman. His light in the darkness. Whenever it ran hot, it meant there was something he needed to do.

'Where is Agbako?' Rumi said.

Jarishma glared at him. 'The witch doctors made their bed – we don't have to lie in it with them.'

'Let's go!' Miselda shouted.

But Rumi's cowrie was scalding hot now. 'I'm going back to get him.'

Without waiting for their affirmation, he took off running. Someone shouted his name but he wasn't turning back. Hagen sprinted alongside him – together until the sweet or bitter end.

The makeshift barricade in the room they had abandoned was nearly broken through with screaming bush babies. With the shadow, he kicked through the small crack in the wall where the rat had squeezed through. As he had hoped, a gap large enough to poke his foot in opened up. He broke through the stonework and burst into what must have been some approximation of a kitchen. The smell of the place was an act of abuse. Long-rotted flour was set beside thick sacks of rice. From the far wall hung thick cuts of rotten meat like something from an abandoned abattoir. Rumi covered his mouth, feeling the urge to vomit. Fat, pot-bellied rats scurried about at the intrusion, fleeing into different holes and crevices. In an act of pure will, he sped through the far door and found himself in an open courtyard. A tall figure lurched out from the darkness.

Rumi raised his halberd and the figure stopped.

'Agbako?' Rumi said

The giant witch doctor stepped into the light. One side of his head was spattered with blood and a large lump like someone had hurled an anvil at him. The other was carved with a sharp wound at his cheek. In one hand, he held the ruined corpse of a bush baby, in the other his bloodstained cutlass. His companion, Horse, stood hunch-backed behind him, breathing hard astride his horse.

'You came back for us?' Agbako asked.

'We broke kola nut.'

Agbako let out a sharp breath and for a moment just stared. Then another blood-curdling scream ripped through the night. The bush babies had found their way through.

'We need to get to the other side,' Rumi explained. 'The bush babies have flooded the inside. There's a—'

His words cut off as Horse muttered a chant in Mushiain and broke through the wall with his charging horse.

They stepped through and found themselves in another room, cold as a crypt.

'There!' Agbako snarled.

Ahead there was a gap in the wall with moonlight spilling through the crevice. *A way out.*

Rumi's cowrie flashed hot again and his stomach lurched. He glanced halfway over his shoulder as a flicker of dying torchlight illuminated a stone sarcophagus. *So it is a crypt.*

He squinted, trying to make the stone coffin out. It was

fashioned in the image of a man and something about it struck him as deeply familiar.

'Rumi!' Agbako hissed.

He wasn't listening. He had been in a burial ground of gods before – he knew this presence. It called out to him, plain and clear as a long familiar voice shouting his name.

'What are you doing?' Agbako shouted.

He was answering a different call. He stepped towards the sarcophagus, his eyes narrow and his stomach tight. Hagen's tail thumped against the ground with earnest anticipation. The bush babies' wail grew louder. Rumi's eyes widened as he noticed the words etched into stone around the coffin. *Here lies the Shadow thereof.* On the face of the coffin was a series of names. *Daraniju, Elesekan, Alabelowo, Kekererin, Tahinta.* Five names and Rumi knew who one of them belonged to. A shiver of realisation ran through him like a cold wind.

The ceiling trembled, producing a shower of dust as there came the distant sound of the bush babies breaking through their barricade.

He heard Agbako's voice. 'Let's leave him!'

Then came the clatter of hooves as the witch doctor's galloped away.

Time was no friend, but his commission was of a more urgent order. This was – he knew down to his bones – no time to run.

'Xango,' he breathed, staring at the stone likeness on the sarcophagus. Not the Alaafin himself but one of his descendants for certain. An ancestor.

He raised a hand and easy as blinking, a hammer of pure shadow materialised in his grip. He brought it down once, twice and then with a third blow shattered the age-old stone. Rumi's heart thumped as he stared into the broken coffin. The remains of what could only be vaguely described as a man were visible through the cracks. A bulbous skull, with a lower jaw crumbled to pulp. The spine still shocking white. Strangely, nothing about it made Rumi uncomfortable. It seemed as normal as staring at his reflection. The one thing that stirred his soul was clutched in the corpse's broken fingers. A flute of pure obsidian, shiny in its blackness.

It isn't stealing if you take it from an ancestor.

He reached down and grabbed the flute. As his fingers brushed against the spout, he felt a song of power chime through his veins. The cowrie at his neck ran hot enough to scald his skin. He stared at the flute. *This was it.* He almost laughed recalling Baron Saturday's joke.

A cry behind him made him whirl, shielding his eyes. A bush baby lunged at him spraying gobs of green-white spit as it screamed.

Rumi heard the whistling of an arrow before a bolt took the bush baby at the throat, pinning it to the wall. The scream was cut to instant silence. Another arrow flitted past his ear as another bush baby dropped dead merely a yard in front of him.

'Let's go, Rumi, now.' It was Nataré, standing at the edge of the room. Her voice was dark and cold as a cellar.

He was running before he had seen her face. He caught up with her in four strides and they sprinted as fast as they could manage in the near darkness, pursued all the while by the shriek of chasing bush babies.

Hagen rushed ahead as they sped through the broken wall and felt the exultant hiss of wind in their ears.

'Come on,' Jarishma shouted ahead, beckoning them forward.

He stood spotlit by a small rectangle of light at the end of the corridor.

They reached him in a matter of moments and he pushed an iron gate open to see them through. As soon as they were on the other side, he slid an iron bar across the gate mere moments before a thrum of bush babies thudded against it.

'Let's go,' Jarishma said. 'Dara's Tarry is compromised.'

They sprinted after the others who were waiting ahead. Rumi slid the flute into his satchel as Nataré ran up close.

'What did you take from there?' she asked.

Rumi narrowed his eyes, balling his hand into a fist. 'My inheritance.'

She gave him a searching look then kept running. 'I guess you will explain that one later.'

51

The Yellow Masquerade

RUMI

The whispers seemed to rise as they crept around the edge of the sixth level. Now they were whispering obscenities about Rumi's mother. He bunched his hands into fists and let out a heavy breath, knowing there was nothing to be done but to ignore them. If the day ever came where he walked the spirit realm, he had a list of them he would thump lumps out of.

The air felt thinner this high up. As though it would break in their mouths when they inhaled. The waterfall, on their left-hand side, was more beautiful here than perhaps it was at any level prior. The grass was tall enough to lose a person in.

Rumi's hand returned often to his satchel, where he kept the flute found in the grave of an ancestor. It could only be one thing – Saturday's joke made sense now – *I'm known to draw quite the crowd with this one. A three-of-a-kind instrument.* With that flute, he could summon the *egun*. The army of the dead. The time to use it had not come. He would likely only have one chance to use it. A chance he could not waste. He had told Nataré what he thought it was for and they had agreed it would only be used at the point of imminent death.

The five names he had read along the stone coffin seemed to burn in his mind. *Daraniju, Elesekan, Alabelowo, Kekererin and Tahinta.* The true names of the five Priests of the Son.

The foul smell, which had followed them right from the fourth level, seemed to deepen and thicken as they reached the sixth. Plainly they were getting closer to the source of the awful aroma. Hagen gave a low, disapproving growl as a sharp gust of wind blew the full stink into his face.

'Remind me to never, ever follow you anywhere,' Miselda said, pinching her nose. 'Worst mistake of my life, and I'm an addict.'

Jarishma raised a hand, gesturing for them to be quiet. They all took heed. The jungle mage had gone very quiet the moment they reached the sixth level. His sure confidence seemed to have deserted him and been replaced by a quiet anxiety.

Rumi glanced ahead and saw that the bush was thickening. A thick hedge lay a few metres in front, overgrown with yew, carpus and barberries. They would have to cut a path through the bush to forge ahead. Jarishma pulled a curved cutlass from his side and slashed away at the grass. Miselda formed a sickle of pure shadow and did the same.

Sameer hesitated. 'Does anyone else hear that?' he asked quietly.

Rumi could. Not just the whispers of the spirits but a low, deep groan. Like the earth clearing its throat for a great speech. *Something just woke up.*

A spirit's voice rang clear and sharp at his ear. 'Ojuju is coming.'

The whispering spirits stopped all at once – as though summoned to attend to some other task. That all-conquering silence returned and suddenly it felt as though grave danger was near. The stench grew worse. Hagen gave a low grunt of panic and rubbed his neck along Rumi's shin. His message was clear. *Go back.*

Rumi raised the halberd and hacked away at the hedge. *No going back now.* The branches and leaves were thick and gnarled from years without disturbance. More than once he had to hack at a branch two or three times to cut his way through. The bush seemed to slink away from the halberd with each axe-blow as though its metal reviled them. This, more than anything, was an act of great trespass. Deep down, they all knew that the forest would react to their hacking through the hedge.

They cut through to the other side and came onto a wide lawn. Rumi stared at the nearest tree and it made his heart sink to his stomach. The tree was bent over itself and the bark was a sickly yellow.

Latan's voice rang in his head. *If you see yellow trees – run.* He recalled what Agbako had said just days before about the signs of the one thing he feared. *Trees gone rancid yellow. Water running blood-red. A flock of dead birds arranged in a circle.* The signs of the Yellow Masquerade.

As though to provide a deeper confirmation, a bird dropped directly from the sky and hit the ground in a bloody thud. Rumi glanced up and saw that there was no obstruction. The bird had simply dropped dead of its own accord. Another loud squawk sounded above as a second bird dropped from the sky.

Hagen started a low growl, leaning back on his hind legs as though to pounce on some unseen enemy.

Rumi reached into the bond. 'What is it, Hagen?'

Hagen's only response was a feral bark, his ears perked up and tail thumping the ground. Horse's steed rose on its hind legs, sending him flying back. The beast whinnied and snorted then took off at a full gallop leaving Horse cursing from the floor. The creature had felt what they all felt.

Horse watched it leave, let out a breath and rose to his feet again. 'Good riddance.'

A hot flash of light burst through a chink in the forest canopy above. It was a yellow-white brightness that did not come from the sun or the moon. *Lightning.*

A moment later, a crashing retort of thunder reverberated through the forest. Something struck the ground a few metres ahead with force enough to produce an almighty spray of mud.

Miselda frowned and rolled her wrists. Her eyes were grave and calculating. Fighters were a superstitious bunch and Rumi knew what that roll of her wrists meant to her.

'What is that?' Sameer asked, pointing.

It was a building of some sort, stretched across their path. Rumi refrained from taking a step. He turned to Jarishma. 'Do we have to go *through* that building?'

Jarishma nodded. 'There is no other way. Our only hope is that we find it vacant.'

'Why? Who might be there?' Rumi asked.

Jarishma shot him a warning look. 'Let us hope that we find it vacant.'

An ominous answer, no doubt, but they were in the throes of fatigue madness, where fears seemed to fall away in favour of progress.

They walked with bated breath as the pathway led down to the large stone patio before the building. Rumi drew in a deep, resigned breath as he stepped past the curtain and continued inside. Though the limestone had cracked and crumbled in part, it was plain to see the room had once been the entryway to a great palace. Rumi thought of his mother then and the sacrifice she had made to see him live. He thought of all that had been done to bring him to this precise moment.

He took Nataré by the hand and cleared his throat. 'Let's go.'

The sudden grind of stone peeling from the roof made Rumi's heart lurch in his chest. Every step they took felt like a horrible decision.

The cavern opened at last into a massive throne room arranged around an open-air courtyard.

'Gods above have mercy on us who rest beneath, Dara's might, guard me from the terrors at night,' Ahwazi whispered frantically.

'Cover me with your wings and let me rest under the protection of your shadow,' Sameer whispered.

Rumi had not brought them along for their piety but Erin-Olu made priests of all people. Even Agbako must have made a belated appeal to the gods.

Here and there about the room there were dried yellow bones that were undoubtedly human remains. Rumi saw a hollow bowl on the far side of the room which looked to be a pit for musicians designed to produce the best acoustic effect. Inside were instruments of wood and brass left behind by the departed. Ahead was the courtyard filled with thick yellow trees that had sprouted and outgrown the ceiling. There was a time, no doubt, that this had been a beautiful place – a throne room to some mighty king of the forest, perhaps – but now it was dead and corrupted.

At the centre of it all, a wide stone staircase led up to a palatial dais made entirely of bones. Rumi lifted his gaze to the summit and froze.

'Godsblood,' he breathed. 'Blood of my every hope and salvation.'

Miselda cursed beside him in a broken cry of pure disbelief.

Atop the dais of bones was a masked figure clothed in yellow. Even though the figure was kneeling and wore a flowing loose kaftan, it was gigantic. Broad at the shoulders with arms that must have run thick with knotted muscle. Taller than Agbako and wider too. Its yellow apron was threaded with seeds and coral beads of white and red and extended part-way over a raffia kilt that ran from the waist to the ankle. Its ankles, which were each larger than a normal man's elbow, were girded in beaded anklets of black cowries. Its long mask was made from the skull of a Shinala with a nose that extended all the way to the chin.

Though the hooded cloak and mask kept its face a mystery, you could see from the shape of its head that this was a thing not all the way human. It moved as lizards do: extreme stillness was followed by sudden twitches of movement that were as sharp as they were unnatural. At its waist was a sheathed sword, bigger than any Rumi had ever seen, with a cruciform pommel.

Sameer stared in open-mouthed awe. 'It cannot be.'

And yet it is.

'This cannot be happening,' Nataré added.

And yet it is.

Ahwazi let out a shuddering breath. 'Ojuju Calabar.'

A name called to inspire terror.

As though responding to his name, the hooded figure jerked its head sharply towards them and gave a loud, exultant sigh.

It was Ojuju. The Yellow Masquerade. The star in every nightmare; a figure of horror's myth. A creature of entire darkness. Rumi recoiled as Ojuju straightened to his full height and spoke aloud.

His voice was deeper than any grave. Deeper than hell. Deeper than all the sin in the world. The impact of it reverberated through Rumi's legs and made his knees buckle. The voice alone was an affront to everything sane in the world. A voice that could cause things to break.

'You dare?' the creature asked.

It was subtle but Rumi caught a hint of amusement in the voice.

'Dara's might,' Ahwazi breathed.

The figure drew its hood back and turned to face them directly.

'You dare?!' it asked again, this time seeming more incensed.

Rumi was terrified and yet he couldn't look away. Hagen barked hysterically, spraying foam. The lionhound sounded hoarse and strained as sheer terror flashed through the bond. Ojuju took a single slow step into the small splash of light and lifted the mask – allowing them to catch a glimpse of his face. It was like staring at pure corruption. His face was that of a jackal except with the skin of a man, covered in scars that oozed blood and pus. His eyes were circles of yellow that were almost childlike in their misdirected innocence. Atop his bulbous head was a crown of forest bramble, twined with seashells. His hair fell like tree vines over its cheeks.

'Aren't you going to run?' he asked, almost mockingly.

Rumi felt many things. Weak. Helpless. Terrified. His mouth was bone-dry and a part of him wanted nothing more than to find a safe hole he would never leave. He knew that this creature was not only having this effect on him. He could almost feel the horror that radiated from his companions. Running seemed the logical thing to do but Rumi knew where that would lead. The moment they turned their backs to flee, Ojuju would give chase – and judging by the thick slab of muscle at his calf, he would catch them one after the other. Sameer would be the first to die – of that, Rumi was sure. He wasn't going to let that happen. Not a hen's chance in a wolf cave he would let that happen. *I'd rather die.* He hefted his halberd and called his shadow. The power flooded him and he drew in a deep breath. Prepared as ever to meet his end with all the fury and purpose of his late mother.

To his eternal pride, everyone held their ground. Not one of them had turned to run. Nataré nocked an arrow to her bow, Sameer and Ahwazi lifted their blades. Miselda twisted her wrists and summoned her shadow as a spear materialised in her grip. Jarishma set his feet and revealed his weapons. Even Agbako stood his ground, beating the shell of the tortoise as he chanted his abominations and Horse took up position beside him.

A smile curled at the corner of Ojuju's blasphemy of a mouth. 'You mean to fight me?'

Miselda raised her spear and thumped the ground. 'We'll do a lot more than fight today, demon.'

Ojuju tilted his neck until it made a sharp crunching sound. '*Demon?* I am no demon. Demon is a puny word for what I truly am. I have eaten more demons than you have lived days. Demons would have run if they stood where you did. I am all the sorrow of mankind returned. The swallower of hope.'

'Couldn't give a sheg what you are, to be honest,' Miselda said. 'But you should know that I am of the Kasinabe. And if you think I am going to turn down a chance to make a story out of you – you know nothing about the Kasinabe.' She twisted the spear in her grip. 'Now unless you have some agbo on you, I intend to get this over with quickly.'

Ojuju threw back his head and laughed. It was a sound so sharp and sudden that one of the nearby trees collapsed against itself. He slapped his knee as the raffia swayed, baring his legs, shaking with laughter.

In the thundering clamour of Ojuju's laughter, Rumi could almost taste the fear in his compatriots. But there was something else there in the bitterness of terror: resolve. They had spent the entire journey fearing death. The executioner can only hold the axe above your neck for so long before you start daring him to swing. Death had gone stale and lost its power over them. They were good and ready to get it over and done with. What will be, will be. When the music plays it is better to dance than stand still – or run, in this case. *The music is sheggin' playing now and we are going to dance.*

52

The Fraternity of the Fallen

RUMI

Rumi reached out in the shadow for Hagen's emotion and found it pure and full. *Fear, devotion, love.* His shadow swelled as he drew it in. He thought of his friends and how they had stood beside him to face a creature of nightmare and his shadow swelled the more. Moments like this, of the highest leverage, were where stories were made. If they died there and then, their story would only be another cautionary tale of the many troubles of Erin-Olu. Perhaps they would make a great drama of it about their doomed quest for the Door of Testimony.

Ojuju's laughter finally came to a stop as he let out a few, last wheezes of mirth. 'It has been a long time since I had a good laugh. I am glad of it.'

The voice of Horse, the witch doctor, rose in pitch as he chanted a curse in deep Mushiain. He leaned on his right foot and reached into his cloak. 'Die!' he snarled, hurling two daggers at Ojuju's bulb-yellow eyes.

The creature gave a look of stunned surprise as it dodged the first spiralling dagger. The second dagger it caught between two fingers, barely an inch before its face. With a look of utter disappointment he thrust the dagger into the ground and responded with a shift so sudden and violent that Rumi had to blink his eyes clear. In one moment, Ojuju was standing on his throne, in another his fingers were wrapped around Horse's still beating heart, ripped clean from his chest cavity.

Horse's body gave a terrifying twitch, then he fell to the ground, muscles still spasming as he died. His entire chest had been punctured through, exposing all his blood, guts and innards. Agbako gave his comrade one last look, then worked his mouth as his face hardened.

Winged Obayifo flew down from the trees, ecstatic with the scent of blood.

Ojuju bared his teeth and ripped Horse's spinal column from his body, as though he were de-boning a fish. Blood and guts were left further exposed in its wake. Ojuju ate Horse's heart in much the same way that anyone else would eat an apple. The Obayifo clapped their wings in a parody of applause for what was clearly their master. Ojuju bade them to join, sharing his food with them in a way Rumi might have done with Hagen.

Rumi's grip on the halberd slackened and now he was trying to work out whether running would be a good idea after all.

Jarishma jerked back as Ojuju's free hand whipped out to pull half a leg from Horse's body. Wiping blood from his lips as he finished the heart, Ojuju set his teeth to the leg and stripped it of meat with a single, sucking bite, the same way one would do a chicken bone.

They all stood watching – paralysed by horror.

'It is too late to run now,' Ojuju said as he gorged on Horse's body.

The Obayifo's howling rose to a frenzy. They were not attacking because they knew there was more blood to come. There was no rush.

Ojuju sucked Horse's femur clean and gestured to Miselda with the biscuit bone. 'Your comrade insulted me with that pathetic attack, but you amused me when so many others have failed. For that, I will offer you an unbeatable truce – give up three of your friends as a sacrifice to me and I will let you and two others leave in peace.'

Sameer raised an eyebrow and turned slowly to Rumi.

Rumi shut the notion down. 'Miselda, you cannot—'

'I speak for myself, Ajanla,' she said, raising a hand to cut him off. She turned to Ojuju. 'I may be a degenerate, but I am above all things a Suli.' She turned to Rumi and pointed. 'He is a Suli too. That's always been enough for me.' Rumi met her gaze and she touched her chest and pointed to the sky. A gesture of eternal trust. Then she turned back to Ojuju and beat her chest with a clenched fist. 'If you think I would sell my friends out to run from a fight – you know nothing about the Kasinabe.'

Ojuju gave an impressed smirk. 'Say your prayers then and prepare for your last stand, while I finish eating.'

Rumi glanced at Sameer with the thinnest piece of hope that the little man had a plan. Something that could level the playing field against an unimaginable foe.

Sameer met his gaze and slowly shook his head. He had nothing. He clasped his hands together and made a gesture of prayer. That was all they had left – a prayer.

He turned to Jarishma who stood staring at Ojuju, his face a picture of resolute purpose. He looked, in every way, like a man ready to die. To give everything for this one last chance at reviving his daughter. There was no tact or subtlety to his stance. Just two blades, gripped tight, ready to fight.

We are doomed.

The cowrie necklace grew hot at his neck as his free hand went to his inner pocket where the flute lay. He gritted his teeth, looking for some guidance in making his decision. *What if this isn't the time to use it?*

Dread came then as Ojuju rolled his shoulder and touched

the hilt of his massive sword. Rumi noticed it was formed in the shape of a winged Obayifo with its fork-like tongue curled around the pommel. 'It's time,' Ojuju said. He sniffed at the air in the direction of Jarishma and gave him a questioning look. 'Have we met before?'

Jarishma grinned and replied, 'You could say that.'

Agbako glanced at Horse's mangled remains and then up at Ojuju. The big witch doctor came closest to the abomination in height so when he met his stare it was almost at a level. 'You killed my friend. I am going to kill you in return.'

Ojuju snorted and drew his sword. It took a full five seconds to pull it completely out. 'I would like to see that.'

He swung the behemoth sword in a vicious practice swing. It was no ornamental blade – the creature knew how to wield it.

Teeming with the shadow, Rumi closed his eyes. 'Dara, Father of All, hear my voice. Precious Jahmine, listen to my heart. Gods of my ancestors, lend me your strength... please.'

The cloud rumbled above once more and rain fell through the open-air courtyard. Ojuju raised his face to the clouds, basking in it.

Nataré glanced his way, Miselda did too. They had the same imploring look – they were looking to him to lead.

Something about that long-extended moment of complete terror seemed to spark something inside Rumi. Something deep and intuitive far beyond the grasping reach of seeming reality. He saw that moment, clear as water in a glass. He could sense Ojuju's dominating power – they were no match for him, not even with the jungle mage. The Obayifo hung from the trees and watched with wide-eyed interest. They weren't joining the fight because they didn't need to – this was a rare opportunity to watch their master work.

If now was the time to die, they would not go quietly. Rumi

raised his weapon and his voice. 'Shadowwielders attack his sword side. Everyone else attack the left hand. Ahwazi, I need you to defend us from that sword with all you have. Miselda, punish him for every swing of the sword. Sameer – use that brain of yours to find a way for us to win.' Rumi turned to Nataré. 'You stay out of range and rain arrows down on him. Agbako, you take up his free hand and Jarishma... do what needs doing.'

Rumi didn't entirely know what he meant but Jarishma gave a nod of understanding.

'Enough talking,' Ojuju said suddenly.

A tree snapped in half at the sound of his voice as he suddenly darted forward. He attempted the same manoeuvre he had killed Horse with, but Ahwazi was equal to it, forming a thick shield of shadow to block his grasping attack on Sameer. Nataré fired off two arrows aimed for the head. Ojuju batted the first away with his hand and caught the second between his teeth. Agbako charged into him with a shoulder, causing Ojuju to blunder backwards. As he stumbled, the jungle mage launched his attack.

Jarishma moved in a blaze of shadow with his twin blades raised high. Ojuju raised his sword to block him but was not quick enough for the jungle mage. The first of Jarishma's blades bit into Ojuju's side. The second cut into Ojuju's raised arm. Rumi expected a scream of pain but Ojuju made no sound. Without giving a moment, Jarishma raised both arms as spears of pure shadow materialised in his hands and he plunged them deep into Ojuju's chest.

Still Ojuju gave no sound. Instead, the creature glanced at the cut, raised his arm with the jungle mage's blade still lodged deep, then pulled the blade free and tossed it harmlessly to the ground. He glanced down at his chest, pierced through with two spears of shadow. Pulled them out like pins from a board and flicked them away with his fingers. Before their eyes, the blood backtracked into the wounds as the skin sealed itself back up.

Jarishma stood stunned for a small eternal moment. He had cut the Yellow Masquerade almost to the bone and it had left no mark. He had stabbed through his chest and now there were no holes.

'Gods above,' Agbako whispered.

Ojuju let out a skittering laugh as he backhanded Jarishma. The force of the blow sent the jungle mage back ten metres where his flight was stopped when he struck the wall.

Rumi's heart thumped so hard he couldn't hear a thing. He raised the halberd and tried to grip the shadow but an overwhelming emotion had robbed him of his focus. *Hopelessness.* That was how he felt now – hopeless. Jarishma had nearly severed Ojuju's arm in two and the attack had done less damage than a mosquito bite. He had called himself the 'Swallower of Hope' – the name was apt.

He reached into his pocket for the flute – he had no other choice now. One whistle on it and they would all know exactly what the flute was for. If he was right – it would summon the *egun.* The army of the dead.

He gave Ojuju one final look. The creature was revelling in their imminent destruction as a child would revel in their chance at play.

The Swallower of Hope.

A thought occurred to Rumi then. Jarishma had told him that the emotions of others were what gave the agbara their power. Mandla had explained that it was the stories that made the temporal become eternal. *Maybe that is what Ojuju is – not a demon but an agbara. The agbara of hopelessness.*

The more he reasoned it, the more it made sense to Rumi. Who in the world had more stories than Ojuju? His name was one that stood on the infamy of ages long gone. He *was* the swallower of hope. He watched the Obayifo yip and yapper for him and saw it to be true. *Even in hell there is solace in the fraternity of the fallen.* Surrendering your hope to Ojuju was to worship and nourish him. But there was one thing that he prized above all. Chief Karile's words came back to him all at once – 'If there is one thing all gods love, it is human praise.'

How could anyone praise a creature such as this? He had likely been starved of it. Save for the praise of fear, which is a low praise. In that moment, he understood Ojuju completely. Down to the centre of his bone marrow. An angry child, feared but never loved.

Ojuju stretched out his arms, inviting all comers. He would play with his meal before he devoured them all.

'Sheg that,' Miselda hissed, stepping back from Ojuju. 'It's time to run.'

Agbako agreed and turned to take flight. Jarishma, who had managed to get back to his feet, offered no objection.

Nataré, Sameer and Ahwazi looked to Rumi. He could see they too wanted to take their chance at running. But the time to flee had passed.

As his friends stepped back from the Yellow Masquerade, Rumi stepped forward. The only thing he had to hold on to were his words. *Put love first. There is no greater power than to turn an enemy into a friend.*

'Swallower of Hope,' Rumi shouted. 'I have an offer for you.'

The thump of thunder shifted the earth as the Obayifo circled above. Ojuju hissed, spraying spit and foam at Rumi, but he stood his ground. Confidence in the shadow returned as he took another step towards Ojuju.

'What could *you* possibly offer me?' Ojuju said.

'The only thing that a man can offer a god. Praise.'

Ojuju's yellow eyes bulged and then narrowed with what Rumi could only understand as contemplation.

'You are not the first to beg me,' Ojuju said.

'But am I the first to acknowledge you as a god?' Rumi asked.

Ojuju gave no answer.

Rumi took another step towards him. 'Let me be the first to offer you a song. A song that will change how the entire world sees you. A song to change your story – to let you drop the mask. A song that will make people love you.'

Ojuju's jackal nostrils flared and his breath came in short gasps like a dog under the peak of sun.

Ojuju waved him away. 'A nice try, boy.'

Rumi pressed on. 'Or are you afraid? God of Hopelessness? Have you lost hope in yourself? Are you afraid that my song might enchant you, that a youngster like me might take you back to when you were a little boy yourself, dreaming of boy kings and warrior princes? Are you afraid to go back there? Before the world was poison. Before all was lost. Is that your true terror?'

Rumi caught an unmistakeable glimmer of wonder in the eye of the Yellow Masquerade. The faintest hint of curiosity. The creature tried to mask it – but was too ravenous for praise, for a new kind of worship. Not the worship that fear brings but the worship of awe and adoration. He wanted, desperately, to be loved.

'Just one song and I can promise you will dream again,' Rumi said. 'Listen to this one song and you can do with us as you please.'

Ojuju gave Rumi a long look, then folded his arms and nodded. 'One song,' he said, 'just one song. And then you die.'

Rumi drew in a breath. 'I will need a drum.'

Ojuju pointed to the pit at the far side of the room. The one that had been hollowed out to create the best acoustic effect. Rumi walked over and climbed inside. He found a crude drum – likely made decades before the dundun drum had even been dreamed up. He thumped it once, testing the pitch. The sound was lower than he needed it to be, but hollow enough to fingerbeat. He tested it with his forefinger and the sound made his heart stir awake. He beat a few more times to be sure and his hands came alive again.

'I'm ready,' Rumi said, climbing out from the player's pit. His voice was cool again, focused, confident.

Ojuju cleared his throat. 'Let us hear you then.'

Rumi glanced at Nataré and she gave him a single, solemn nod of entire trust. He exhaled and closed his eyes, waiting for silence. Not silence in the forest, but in his mind. He retreated to the dark corners of his mind, where the pain was, the demons he had pretended to forget. There was silence there – a place of total understanding, where empathy for even a murderous god could be found.

He started to play. Slowly at first, gently, but soon he was at work, feeling something he had almost forgotten. His hands battered the wood-formed drum with mourn-broken, elegiac energy. In his head, Rumi saw Morire nodding, enchanted, impressed and he beat the bust of wood with scattered intricacy, throwing cascades of sound at Ojuju and the Obayifo. He flashed a look at Ojuju, spellbound, now *his* prisoner. *I will take you back to show you the future. I will make you cry from the inside.*

He swore it to himself as he played. There is a place for violence, even in music – a place to unleash the torrent within and let it spill out in song. He beat the drums telling that story, showing that pain. The truth of a person condemned as an effigy of hopelessness. Rumi was no swallower of hope but he knew what it meant to have none. To play drums to drown out your stomach's grumbling. To hide the pain when told it's not your turn yet, when your turn should have come long ago.

The forest was still now. Rumi was liberated. His fingers danced across the drum, beating it in parts that had power. His chest took off and he summoned his shadow, transforming the drums into an entirely new instrument of acoustic bliss.

Hagen gave a low groan of candid awe. *When the music is good, even the birds stop singing to listen.*

Ojuju tapped his feet, trembling as Rumi fingerbeat those smaller parts of the drum. Then from the lonely shadow of sound, someone started to sing. Rumi did not recognise the voice at first, for it had been so long since he had heard it, but by the second line he knew it.

It was beautiful, pained and powerful, singing with no real words. Nataré's voice was as brittle as glass, yet as resonant as a hammer. Rumi stifled a broken gasp of emotion as he beat the drum to join Nataré at the crescendo of the note and she sang with no restraint, her voice soft and blessed. They had an understanding that only music could create. Rumi saw beyond the mask of her betrayed heart to things eternal in her. Though her singing had no words, it had deep, unavoidable meaning. There was pain in it, regret, failure and betrayed hope. All the things that any person who had trodden ten steps on the earth could understand. In his mind he saw the ghostly apparition of a face, strong and soft. Though he had never seen her before, he knew instantly who it was. Shirayo – Dara's champion. The *Sakosaye* said, 'wherever there is great music, surely Shirayo has been known'. She nodded to him, smiled and then disappeared.

Rumi drew in a sharp breath as he came to the close of the song and then he ended with a riveting flourish of pure emotion. For his family, for Nataré, for his friends. For Ojuju. Then he smashed the drums to utter pieces for there would be no encore.

For a long moment there was silence. Then Ojuju rose to his feet.

Jarishma flinched, his eyes glistening with tears.

'Promise me this,' Ojuju said, producing a red kola nut as a single tear rolled down his cheek. 'That if you make it to the summit and return to your people, you *will* play that song for them and tell them it was in dedication to me. Tell them it is…' his voice cracked. 'Tell them it is Ojuju's song.'

Rumi stretched out a trembling hand and took the kola nut, then he broke it and bit down on the broken half. 'I promise.'

Ojuju snorted a blast of putrid air then slid his sword slowly into its sheath. 'Go forth then, drummer boy, and bring my song back to humanity. No creature in the forest shall harm you. I will send the Obayifo to go with you to the summit; they will carry you down when your business is done – I want you to return safely. You have a cleared path to the summit.'

Ojuju stepped aside and pointed down the path. 'Go now… friend.'

53

A Bedevilled Mind

RENIKE

Renike led N'Goné down the hallway and took the turn towards the men's dorms.

As they crossed into the narrow catwalk between the men's and women's dormitories, Renike reached into her pocket for the dreamwalker bracelet. Kharmine, they had determined, slept at the edge of the second dormitory along the corridor. To get to him, they would have to climb into the men's dormitory through the rear window of the bathing chamber. It was no secret that people did this. There was a similar entry point to the women's dormitory with a shadow-wrought step ladder at the base. The dorm wardens turned a blind eye to it for the most part, but it still felt a little wrong to be sneaking around.

They crept along the wall and out into the corridor before turning into the corner of the second door on the left. It was quiet as they stepped inside – everyone was fast asleep. In the morning was another fighting day and no one was casual about a good night's rest before fighting days.

N'Goné huddled into a dark corner and pointed towards a bed. Kharmine lay with a leg dangling and half his bedcovers on the floor. He slept like a drunk, which Renike thought was an excellent condition for a night of dreamwalking.

N'Goné raised a thumb in a gesture that said, 'Are you sure you want to do this?'

Reniké drew in breath and gave a firm nod. 'I've been in his mind before — it will be slightly less resistant to me. It's better I do it.'

It was only half the truth. Though Reniké did have the advantage of knowing Kharmine's mind a little better than N'Goné, she was annoyingly nervous and that made her prone to mistakes — stubborn pride would not let her admit that to N'Goné. Her heart was beating hard, not because she had to dreamwalk but because the last time she had tried to peek into Kharmine's mind she had seen a demon. The images you saw in another person's mind had a way of returning to your consciousness over and over. She had seen that demon's face so many times in her mind that she wondered if it had some deeper resonance.

N'Goné gave her a questioning look. 'Are you all right?' she whispered.

Renike let out a breath and gave her an affirming gesture. 'I'm fine.'

She closed her eyes, called her shadow and slipped the bracelet on. 'Let's go.'

Renike closed her eyes and called her shadow. When she opened them again, she was in what looked to be a market square. The sky above was the pinkish red of a goat's innards and the trees rose high as the clouds. White orbs of memories drifted through the air like balloons dancing on the wind. She avoided the memories for now — not worth the risk with a demon lurking around.

The market square was teeming with people who looked — for the most part — perfectly normal. Tents and canopies arranged in huddles around an open square with a quadrangle of dead grass at its centre. Further ahead was a large yellow tent with a conical tip that Renike reasoned must have been their equivalent of the spice and rice market. The sizzle of still-cooking food hissed beneath the urgent thrum of music, which told her that this was still early in the market day.

Renike passed by a wagon laden with pan-fried beancakes and touched her lip. Kharmine never struck her as the sort whose mind would idly dream of beancakes.

'You've touched it now boy, you have to buy!' came an old man's ragged voice.

Renike glared up at him. 'I'm a girl and I didn't touch anything,' she protested.

'You did too!' cried the old man. 'That honey-dusted beancake. I saw it with my own two.'

'You're a liar and a fool,' she said. 'I didn't touch your—'

She stopped herself short. The man had said the beancakes were honey-dusted. Honey-dusted beancake sounded like something from the very best sort of dream – her stomach groaned a desperate plea. *I like honey. I like beancakes.*

She glanced up at the old man. 'Did you just say honey-dusted?'

He grinned, nodded then stuffed a beancake into a fold of card for her. 'Dusted them myself.'

Renike licked her lips as she reached into her pocket and – amazingly – found a single gold coin which could only have come from the dream world. She handed it over to the man and his eyes gleamed with delight.

'Enjoy,' he snapped as he wheeled his cart in the opposite direction.

Renike glanced down at the beancake. Gaitan had warned them not to make a scene but had said nothing about eating in the dream. *It must be harmless, otherwise he would have warned me.* She took a bite from the beancake and something strange happened. In one sense, it was the most delicious thing she had ever tasted, the perfect blend between sweet and spicy. In another sense, it was utterly tasteless. It was as though someone had merely touched her tongue with the flavour but when she tried to bite and savour it, all the taste was gone. She was reminded, of course, that she was only as good as a ghost in this dream. Of course the food was tasteless. She hissed and tossed the beancake aside.

Dreamwalking was not as dangerous as mindwalking – Kharmine was only part-way conscious and she would need to make an almighty blunder for him to become aware of the fact that she was an intruder. She spotted a man scurrying past a column of coloured spices with his hooded cowl drawn up. She could tell from his gangly frame and the clog-stepped way that he walked that it was the dream world's iteration of Kharmine.

Renike narrowed her eyes, watching him cross the market square. He checked his shoulder every third or so step. He drew his cowl tight more than five times in the short walk across the square. If he wasn't the traitor, he was certainly acting like one.

Renike grinned to herself. Though this was the market of a dream world, it followed largely the same rules. Renike had been a market girl once and knew the entire song and dance of it. There was a time when sneaking about in the market had come as easily to her as passing wind. Market people were almost always looking for something – all you had to do to slip beneath their notice was to make it clear you were not what they were looking for. She rolled her shoulders and arched her back, the way any urchin of tenured experience would do before a bout of begging. People loved to avoid eye contact with the dirt poor and playing that part ensured no one would hold her stare long.

She folded herself into a swathe of people passing by and found herself pointedly avoided. People of the dream were almost identical to those of the real world – so much so that after spending time in the dream world it was easy to forget it wasn't real. Renike had even wondered once whether the dream world was true reality whilst theirs was the parody.

She kept her eyes on Kharmine as she followed him from a distance. She was certain it was him, more than once she had caught a glimpse of his profile as he checked his shoulder. She had seen the sidelong scar that ran down from the base of his skull which she knew all too well.

She jerked with surprise as a horn blared from ahead, startling her. It must have been some call to dream prayer, for people seemed to rise and turn towards the sound. Suddenly the streets were alive with movement.

Renike stepped close to Kharmine. Close enough to reach out and touch him. With people huddled so close, she was still in no great danger of being seen. Though he seemed conscious of being followed, Kharmine seemed barely to notice her. They slipped past the spice market into what looked to be Kharmine's dream version of the meat market. A man waving a large butcher's knife gestured to his collection of hanging meats and hissed something in a language Renike could not understand. She paid him no mind as she kept her eyes on her moving target. He cut off down a sharp path and drew his cowl even tighter as he walked down a tight alleyway.

Renike hesitated. The market was busy enough to hide in plain sight but an alleyway was something different. If she went after Kharmine, she ran the risk of being discovered. She glanced at her quarry. He was already halfway down the alleyway and soon she would lose her chance to follow him entirely – as soon as his mind was not on that alleyway it could dissolve into something entirely different. Gritting her teeth and tapping her foot, she followed.

The alleyway was dark but a building at the far end of it was illuminated by two hanging lanterns. She followed slowly as Kharmine strode towards the building. Closer up, Renike noticed the sign above the door. A sharp spark of panic ran up her spine as she realised what it was. *A four-point star – the symbol of the Palmaine church.*

A part of her wanted to shout traitor and leave the dream. Perhaps if it had been before she met Zarcanis that would have been what she had done, but the Viper had told her many times before she called her shadow – 'wait until you are sure what you want to do'.

Kharmine pushed the door open and stepped inside. Renike drew in a breath and mouthed her father's words. 'Dara gives orders to the morning and shows the dawn its place. I stand with him and stand against fear.' She drew in breath and followed Kharmine inside.

Renike found herself in the anteroom of what must have been some sort of grand hall. The scent of rotting meat was thick in the air, but it didn't linger in her nose. A small, still-open door at the far end of the room shone with a rectangle of light. *Kharmine must have gone through there.*

She stepped past a mosaic on the wall that depicted a man in the throes of utter torture. A great beast was using him as its footstool and his face was painted in an expression of total anguish. Her heartbeat quickened. Here and there were the rotting remains of men or beasts that had likely served as something's supper. *What sort of place is this?*

The thought occurred to her to leave. She had seen enough – Kharmine was worthy of suspicion and there was no need to follow further. She had every reason to go and yet her feet refused to move. There was – she knew – more to see. If she left now, she would never get to the bottom of why there was a demon in Kharmine's mind. She kept going.

Her heartbeat pounded against her chest as she closed in on the door. Soon, she knew, N'Goné would pull her from the dream but she pressed forward. She had to know.

She got to the door and peeked her head through the gap glancing into the room. For one small moment, her heart stopped. Kharmine knelt, his head bowed in obeisance before a golden dais. Standing on that dais was a creature born in a nightmare. Its face was red as blood, with white tribal marks carved into each cheek. Instead of a nose, it had a snout with two slanted slits for nostrils. Its mouth was like a corrupted scar, with all canines for teeth. Planes of pure muscle corded its arms with every cut of definition visible beneath its ink-black fur coat. At the top of its monstrous head were two horns that protruded like those of an Adamawa bull.

Kharmine pressed his forehead to the ground. 'Ibilé, Blood of the Desert, Demon of Vengeance. I am here to beg you once more – give me the strength to kill my enemies. Give me the power to murder the entire Palmaine clan. Sharpen my blade that it may drink the blood of those who took my family.'

Renike's eyes widened with realisation. Kharmine had found a way to summon a demon. He wasn't looking for a way to betray the Eredo; he was looking for something that Renike deeply understood – vengeance.

Demon of vengeance. Its name resounded in her mind. *Ibilé*.

Just then, as though her act of simply thinking its name was a summons, the demon's head jerked sharply towards her. Startled by the sudden terror of it all, she let out a sharp gasp. Kharmine rose from his bow and slowly turned towards her. Instincts returned and she turned to flee before he could meet her eye. For a moment, she saw the open door of the anteroom that led out from that forsaken place. She lunged forward with every instinct now committed to run. Then a hand closed around her wrist and pulled her back with a violent jolt. She glanced up at the grinning demon with its eyes red as any fire. It leaned close, its smell foul as death and spoke a single word. 'Dreamwalker.'

A part of her wanted to scream but a deeper, more feral part told her to kick out with both legs, the way her father had taught her to do if someone too strong ever tried to climb over her. She obeyed her instinct, kicking the demon in its too-broad chest. It was like striking out at a wall. She knew she didn't hurt it but she had startled it enough to loosen its grip on her wrist. Ripping her hand free, she bit down into her arm, trying to free herself of the dream. The demon reached out for her again, then she was hit with a force that drove all the breath from her.

She opened her eyes and saw N'Goné standing over her. She sat bolt up, her heart still thudding against her chest as though asking to be let out.

'What is it?' N'Goné asked. 'Did you see a demon again?'

Renike gave a weak nod, breathing hard as she tried to gather her bearings. 'I did.'

N'Goné's face hardened. 'Good thing I pulled you out when I did. It could have hurt you.'

Renike closed her eyes and let out a relieved breath. 'That was close. Too close.'

'Did it touch you?' N'Goné asked.

'Only for a minute, grabbed me by my wrist but I managed to pull myself free.'

N'Goné's eyes widened with terror as she went silent.

'What is it?' Renike asked.

N'Goné brought up a shaking hand and pointed to Renike's wrist.

She glanced down. The dreamwalker bracelet was gone.

54

Traitors

RENIKE

Reniké drew in a breath as she stared up at the door. It had been four days since she had lost the dreamwalker and all efforts to get it back had failed. She had to tell Gaitan.

She knocked twice and the big man answered.

He raised an eyebrow. 'Rain? What brings you to my door?'

Renike frowned. 'It's about the matter we discussed.'

He beckoned her inside and closed the door. 'Take a seat,' he said, gesturing towards a vacant chaise lounge.

Renike exhaled sharply as she sat. 'I lost the dreamwalker,' she said.

Gaitan's eyes went wide. 'How?'

'I was walking through Kharmine's dreams and something in his mind recognised me.'

'What do you mean something in his mind?'

'A demon,' Renike explained. 'He had a demon in his mind. He was pleading with it to give him vengeance on the Palmaine.'

Gaitan seemed unsurprised. 'What does that have to do with losing the dreamwalker?'

Renike bowed her head. 'The demon spotted me. It knew what I was and took the dreamwalker.'

Gaitan gave her a confused look. 'What?'

'The demon took the dreamwalker from me. In the dream.'

The crease at his brow seemed to thicken as he rose to his feet and called his shadow. 'Renike – that's not possible. Nothing, demon or otherwise could steal the dreamwalker from you in a dream.'

Renike raised her chin. 'But then how did I lose it? When I woke up it was gone. I had N'Goné right there watching—'

The realisation hit her hard. 'No.'

Gaitan raised his chin. 'Does she know you were coming to see me?'

Renike nodded. 'She convinced me to take some time before telling you – so we could try to find it.'

Gaitan left the room.

For a moment, Renike stood there in stupefied silence. N'Goné – who she had trusted with her life – a traitor. As the tears filled her eyes, she called her shadow and sprinted after Gaitan.

By the time she got to the dorm, N'Goné's locker had already been broken open. It was empty save for unwashed bed linen and a small golden chain with an ornamental four-point star – the symbol of the Palmaine god. Seven words were inscribed upon the chain – *The Eye of the Light sees all.*

The horn sounded. An alarm heard throughout the Eredo – the place was being locked down.

Renike was reminded of the day the Priest of Vultures attacked. No one knew how an Obair had got into the Eredo – and yet, N'Goné had been the first to check what the commotion was all about, just moments before the Obair appeared. *She did it. Toshane is dead because of her.*

Hate swelled in Renike's chest. She balled her hands up into fists as all N'Goné's small betrayals paraded through her mind. How she spent so long in the bathroom. Times when she awoke to find N'Goné not in her bed. When she would disappear sometimes before breakfast. All this while – she was working for the enemy. And yet there were other memories too – how she had fought the Obair in the corridor. How she had nursed Renike back to health after the fight. How she had encouraged her and made her feel less alone. *What was real and what was a ruse?*

It was enough to make anyone break. Every friend she had was either lost, a traitor or dead. Nothing – not even her father's death – had ever caught her so unawares. Overwhelmed by it all, she dropped to a knee – allowing wave after wave of emotion to give her its best shot.

Someone touched her shoulder. She glanced up. It was Zarcanis.

For a long moment, the Viper just stared. Then she raised her chin and said, 'I once heard that you were not a flower. That you are an iroko.'

The tears blurred Renike's vision. Zarcanis's hand didn't leave her shoulder. She was struck by a strange but familiar feeling. Like someone tugging against your skin from the inside. *Mindwalking.* She glanced up at the Viper.

'We will need you in the days to come,' Zarcanis said. She gestured at Gaitan who stood just a few metres behind. 'She's clean.'

'I suppose I owe you two barrels of firewine, Zarcanis. Correct on both counts.'

Zarcanis's expression was solemn. 'You do.'

Gaitan rolled his shoulders and they made a clicking noise. 'How did you know?' he asked her.

'Know what?' Renike said.

The Viper looked away.

Renike's stomach dropped. The Viper's words from days

before resounded in her head. *Oh, I already know why you are here, Nagode. I know what you are, down to your bones.*

'You knew she was a traitor,' Renike said.

Zarcanis didn't meet her eye. 'I only suspected. I hoped I wasn't right.'

'That was why you said you knew what she was. That day at training – you were taunting her.'

'I thought she would try to escape that night, but she didn't. She's good – I'll give her that. That kind of discipline is rare for someone her age.'

'Then why not just arrest her and read her mind?'

'We would only rob ourselves of an opportunity to watch our enemy up close. See how they think. What their tendencies are.'

'But why give us the dreamwalker? Why put me through all that?'

Gaitan cleared his throat. 'Because—'

'No,' Zarcanis said, cutting him off. 'Let her figure it out herself.'

Renike furrowed her brow, recalling the feeling that someone had just been mindwalking on her. She glanced up at Zarcanis. 'N'Goné wasn't the only one you were watching. You were watching me.'

'For what it's worth, I knew you were not a traitor,' Zarcanis said. 'From the very beginning.'

'How?'

'Flowers have shallow roots but the roots of the iroko run far deeper than that. The iroko tree does not break in the wind. Though it might sway – it does not fall,' Zarcanis said. 'You and Rumi are the kind with deep roots. You will not fall from this. It is a setback. It is a lesson. But it is not final. The time for fighters is here, Renike, and how you react to this will tell you everything about how the rest of your life will go. You are the only student I have left. The only one who knows what I need. Tell me, Renike, will you fight?'

She had known her answer long before Zarcanis arrived. Even in her pain she was plotting her resurgence. This was no time to be cowed. There was too much she had to do. Too many wrongs she had to right. She would find N'Goné. She would make her pay for every deception. For Toshane's death. For the betrayal. For the pain. Renike would not break in this strong wind for she was not a flower. She was an iroko tree. Born beneath a bloodwood tree in the sight of her ancestors.

Renike met Zarcanis's gaze. 'I am Odu. We always fight.'

Zarcanis beat her chest and pointed to the ceiling.

Renike cleared her throat. 'I have a question – if you knew she was a traitor and were watching her – how did she escape?'

Gaitan frowned. 'Because she had help from the highest level of the Eredo. Only one of the chiefs could have got her out.'

Zarcanis nodded. 'Chief Karile has joined the other side. They left together. Our very best mindwalker is a traitor. The time for war has finally come.'

55

A Time for Fighters

FALINA

Falina wanted to scratch her scalp beneath the beaded crown but in front of her war chiefs, she had to look the part. Maka Naki stood at her side and she stole some of his confidence. He had become to her something of a pillar in the bedraggled settlements of her mind. He was a man of straight lines, clear and direct. She liked that about him. When he was hungry, he ate; when he was happy, he smiled; when he was excited, his lips curled at the corners like a cat's. He could be that way, of course – he was a soldier. Leaders, she was beginning to realise, could not be people of straight lines. They had to be flexible.

The doors at the other end of the room creaked open and three people stepped into the room. The first of them was tall enough to headbutt the hanging lantern, broad at the shoulders and possessed of a fighter's bearing. He wore a red tunic with an extended, upturned collar that covered his neck. The tail of the coat was covered in decaying leaves. He bowed low, pressing his forehead to the ground. 'Ka-Biyesi O.'

The figure who followed him was a short, squatly woman, who looked as though she knew the ins and outs of giving a good slap. Her expression was the old, wizened one of a person who was going to watch a village play for the hundredth time. She bowed low but said nothing, for she was mute.

The third person was thin as a drunkard's patience, with two curved blades fixed to her waist belt. She had a twitch to her that made Falina raise a brow, though with Maka Naki by her she was as close to fearless as was possible in these troubled times. The third visitor too bowed low and pressed her forehead in the highest prostrate salute.

Mandla tapped the edge of the table with his head still tilted in a bow. 'Your Majesty, from the village of Korin, Toro Hoba and his mother Mama Toro, and from the village of Tadjorah, Temi Jon.'

All three bowed again.

Falina inclined her head, letting the beaded crown fall to be caught in her waiting grip. She had got good at it now – one nod was enough to remove the crown with all the easy grace of a monarch at jubilee. She sat alongside Lord Mandla and her six chiefs – ready for a meeting that would make or break the war effort.

'Let us begin,' she said, meeting Mandla's gaze.

He gave half a grin and nodded towards Toro Hoba.

Toro cleared his throat as he rose to take a seat at the table. 'Your Majesty, it is a great honour and privilege to see you again. My mother and I were blessed to receive your summons.'

Temi Jon of Tadjorah joined them at the table. 'I too am honoured to be here.'

Falina quietly drew in breath. 'I thank you all for your gracious attendance. It is my honour to have you here.'

Mama Toro made a gesture of what Falina thought was pride by tapping her chest and pressing her hands together as though in prayer.

'My mother says you are a stream in the desert. A sight for crying eyes.'

Falina gave a smile she had perfected in her months as queen.

Not a free, gushing smile but a tight, respectful one. A smile that was dexterous as a knife — like she had seen the Palmaine use. In diplomacy, a smile or a frown could do the work of a decree if you knew what the whole business was about. Though she was no veteran practitioner, Falina knew the business.

'The time for crying eyes has come to an end, Mama Toro. The blood of our beloved will cry out from graves no more. War is coming and I have asked you here to know where you will stand.'

Mama Toro shot her son a pointed look and his face hardened.

'The people of Korin have suffered more than most. My mother is a reminder of the injustice that was done to us. An entire generation with tongues cut out; we cannot forget that pain.'

'Nor should you,' Falina said.

Toro rolled his shoulders. 'But sometimes, even we have learned that we have to put survival before satisfaction. As much as we would want nothing more than to march on the Palmaine and drive them from our land, we must be realistic in all things. We are a small village of proud people. Sending what little fighting force we have to join a doomed effort will only weaken our defences and make us easy meat for our enemies thereafter. We cannot be part of a doomed expedition.'

Temi Jon nodded. 'Tadjorah feel much the same. Though we have not suffered in the same ways that Korin has suffered — we too must put our people first.'

Falina gave a slow nod, allowing the room to take in all that had been said.

She met Toro Haba's gaze. 'I read about your father,' she began. 'Sani Hoba.'

Toro narrowed his eyes at the name. 'Your Majesty, we cannot—'

'I thought you would have learned from his legacy by now. He sacrificed himself to lead an entire army away from the village of Iseyin, am I not correct?'

'It's not so simple as that. He—'

'If I recall, the people of Iseyin were enemies of Korin. You'd had several skirmishes before.'

'This isn't about that,' Toro snapped. 'We—'

His mother raised a hand, cutting him off so Falina could continue.

'Your father sacrificed his life for his enemies. What will you do for your friends?'

Toro lowered his head.

'The people of this nation have never been ones to dig a hole and hide in it. We have allowed ourselves to become an ugly parody of what we once were. Of what good are our lives when our brethren suffer in Basmine? The day soon comes when the Nyme is cut down and the Palmaine will come to our gates too. Of what good will our fortifications be then?'

Temi Jon looked away.

'Just a few months ago, I was almost a stranger to this land, but it took no time at all to see that its people are worth fighting for. We are not going to war for ourselves. We are going for all the precious people in this land who are waiting for someone to come out of hiding.'

'Sentimentality,' Toro said.

Falina shrugged. 'Perhaps, but that has always been the strength of our people. Our emotion. Our will. Our passion. Without it, we are nothing. Let me ask you this, Toro – what will you say when we defeat the Palmaine? What part will you tell your children you played? You are the son of a proud father. What will your child say of you?'

It was pointed and manipulative, Falina knew, but these were times of desperation. Every hook and handle had to be pulled with all the force she could muster. If it meant beating Toro's pride like a drum, so be it.

'When my father, King Olu, needed Korin's courage, all he had to do was blow a horn. Times have changed I suppose.'

Mama Toro made a gesture to her son that she could not decipher, then he let out a resigned breath. 'What chance do you stand of winning?'

Falina bit down on her lip to stifle any hint of a smile then glanced at Chief Gaitan, who sat beside Mandla.

The big chief cleared his throat and rose to his feet. Though there were barely a dozen of them there, he spoke as though to a larger crowd. 'We have managed to double our fighting force. The Shadow Order now boasts more shadowwielders than we have ever had in our history.'

'And what is the most recent count?' Falina asked for the benefit of the visitors.

He blinked. 'Nearly eight hundred.'

Falina gave an approving nod. It was a good number, but she knew that most would be new recruits – many of whom perhaps would not have got a chance to join the Order in years gone by. But these were desperate times.

She gave Zarcanis a questioning look. 'What do you think of the Order?'

The Viper scratched a collarbone as she let out a breath. 'What most lack in natural skill, they have made up for with passion. I have been in the Order many years and I have never seen such commitment. Not a single lesson skipped – not even languages, which has always been a neglected course. No one is taking shortcuts. They know what lies ahead and they are courageous in their efforts to try to meet it.'

It was a political answer. That a person was committed did not mean they were competent. Zarcanis had managed to answer the question without truly answering it. Perhaps a more direct response was not what the council needed at that time.

Falina furrowed her brow. 'And our efforts in Basmine?'

Okafor, the First Ranger, answered. 'Better than expected. The Third Ranger reports that the natives are building a formidable rebel force in the South of Basmine. All the tribes are behind it.'

Toro raised a finger. 'All the tribes?'

Falina tucked a lock of hair behind her ear. 'All the tribes,' she said.

Mandla gave her a cautioning look. She knew, of course, that the people of Korin were no friends of the Kuba, but if she was going to have their allegiance she would not hide the truth to get it.

'Our victory shall be one for all the natives, including the Kuba,' she said.

Toro smiled and gave his mother a smile that said, 'I told you'. His look was one of a person who had finally seen that his opponent at seraiye was actually a novice.

'The Kuba cannot be trusted. They will do anything to have the power. They sold us out before, what makes you think they won't do it again?' Temi Jon said.

'I believe that there is good in the Kuba, albeit a goodness that is touched with self-interest. I will make them see that our victory serves them too.'

'How?' Temi Jon asked.

Mandla coughed loudly and made a gesture, shaking his hand. His eyes met hers and she saw that though he did not like the idea of what she was willing to do – he trusted her completely.

'I will give them the crown, although only for a period of time.'

Toro Hoba slapped the table as though she had just revealed she was a lunatic. 'They will *never* give it back.'

'Yes, they will,' Falina said, her eyes level and sure.

'Why?'

Falina glanced at Gaitan and blinked once at him. A column of pure shadow rose up behind her, so sudden that it made Toro Hoba jerk back in his chair.

Falina rose to her feet and spoke aloud, her voice reverberating with the strength of Gaitan's shadow. 'Because they shall see what all others will see when we topple the Palmaine. That I am the blood of my ancestors. That to stand against the Kasinabe is to stand on the side of death.' She glanced at Maka Naki. 'That we love this nation and that we fight for the things we love.'

Gaitan beat his chest. 'Until the last Kasinabe heart stops beating.'

'The very last one!' someone shouted.

Another shadow had been called and a spiralling pattern of black oscillated across Mama Toro's face.

'We die in defiance,' Gaitan said, thumping the table with a fist.

Falina hadn't meant to rile him up, but it didn't take much with Gaitan. The man believed in her and that made her believe in herself. She met Toro Hoba's eye and saw in that moment that he had not seen her as a queen when he walked in. Now he did.

She leaned close. 'The bird on a branch does not fear it's breaking. It trusts its own wings. When we strike, it will be as one.'

There was a small lull of silence and then Toro glanced at his mother. She gave a grim, purposeful nod. He looked at Temi Jon. Her look was much the same, on a younger face. Brass and purpose. Toro closed his eyes and let out a breath then he dropped to his knees and pressed his forehead to the floor.

'Ka-Biyesi, blood of our forefathers. Kora, Tadjorah Bieni and all the villages of the Nyme will stand with you. It was never in doubt.'

Falina ignored the lie – he was waiting to see if she was a queen worth following. They all were.

Now was the time to press home the advantage. A question, though unspoken, was heavy in the air. *When do we strike?*

It was a question that had addled her mind for days. *When do we strike?* If they struck too early, they would be crushed by overwhelming Palmaine force, but waiting too long gave the Palmaine time to strategise, reinforce and strike first. They still had the last vestiges of the element of surprise; with traitors on the loose, the Palmaine would surely soon hear of their plans. Worse still, the threat of the Palmaine breaking down the Eredo walls still lingered – Zaminu was a famously cunning man and he knew they were there fomenting rebellion. He was not the type to let a threat such as theirs have time to breathe. The envoy from Basmine had told them the rebels were ready. Falina had made her decision.

Falina formed a line with her lips, thin as a blade. She worked her jaw as though chewing then drew in a deep breath and raised the crown to her forehead. 'I have made a plan with the leader of the rebel force in Basmine. Ten days. On festival day we march on Basmine.'

Mandla's cheek tightened but he said nothing. No one else moved or said a word.

Then someone started to sing. It was a new song, written to the music of the drum. Maka Naki had told her that people thought it was an even better song than 'Furae Oloola'.

Gaitan's singing voice was not a pretty one, but it was thick and strong as the iroko tree. A voice from the stomach and chest that gave Falina gooseflesh across her arms.

> 'Arise the heroes of tomorrow. The day for bravery is now!
> Put aside for now, the painful sorrow of those who made their earthly bow.
> Our ancestors offer us a bargain, that none who walk the Way shall spurn
> To fight beside the Golden Eagle and watch their holy temple burn.
> So wet your hands and pick your mortar, prepare to take hold of your clay
> For the building plans will need good hands, the promised tomorrow has come today.
> We are taking back our land. The soil, the grass, the sand. And if the soil is dry?'

'We water it with blood!' came the refrain.
'*And if the soil is dry?*'
'We water it with blood!'
Falina was not fond of the song at all. To her, it was crude and it lacked all the poetry of 'Furae Oloola'. It spoke of vengeance and violence but said nothing of the Skyfather's salvation. It was a fighter's song, not a leader's song. But perhaps that was what the Eredo needed now. They were going to need fighters, after all. Fighters who had the fortitude to wage war against an enemy that was feared; avoided but never faced.

Gaitan's voice sounded again. '*And if the soil is dry?*'
Falina watched through the beads. *We water it with blood.*

56

The Seventh Level

RUMI

Rumi gave Nataré some semblance of a smile. She blinked and stared at him, plainly unable to return the gesture.

'I still do not believe what just happened,' Sameer said. 'You spoke to Ojuju Calabar as though he was a village salt-seller.'

Rumi's jaw tightened. 'Everyone wants something. If you can understand what a person wants and find a way to give it to them, you have a subtle kind of control over them. Ojuju just wanted to feel a little *hope*.'

'Sometimes I wonder just what sort of story I have got myself into,' Sameer said.

'A long one still,' Rumi said.

Still Nataré said nothing.

Rumi glanced at her. 'What's wrong?'

She cut her eyes towards him with a look of reserved rage. 'You throw yourself into danger every time. It's like you have some sort of death wish that you aren't telling us about.'

'I brought you here, it is my job to make sure you return safe – even if it costs me my life.'

'Did it ever occur to you that the reason we are all here is because we don't want *anything* to cost you your life?'

Rumi met her gaze. 'Nataré—'

He reached out for her hands but they were balled into fists.

Her eyes — he noticed for the first time — were lidded with fury. 'This isn't just your story, Rumi. It is all of ours.'

He blinked at her. 'I know.'

'Then sheggin' act like it,' she hissed. 'Sheggin' act like it.'

Rumi's stomach tightened at those words and he straightened to his full height.

A crowd of Obayifo flapped their wings above, singing and chattering in their unknown tongue.

Sameer glanced ahead. 'We are here.' He gestured with his chin. 'We made it.'

They walked under the shade of the forest past a bent-backed tree with the face of a man carved into the bark. Down a dust-covered path they went twisting around what they hoped was the way to the source and the Door of Testimony.

After an hour of walking they came to another tree carved with the face of a man.

Rumi gave a start. 'Is that the same tree?'

Sameer glanced at the tattered map and then back at the tree. 'It can't be, it says here that we should...'

'It looks just like that first tree,' Miselda said.

Jarishma blinked and frowned, then he glanced around at the trees. He rubbed his palm along a tree's bark and glanced down at it.

A wrinkle formed on the bridge of his nose. 'It *is* the same tree,' he said.

'How can that be?' Ahwazi asked.

Sameer rolled up the map. 'A damudamu charm. It warps our sense of direction. We will never find our way around here. Not without a guide.'

They took a different path, cutting across the marshy soil till they came across a clearing where the water came cascading down a flight of stairs. A thin spray of sunlight shone through a cleft in the trees.

'Who is that?' Nataré asked, pointing.

Only then did Rumi notice the small figure standing right beside the stairs. A man from the look of it, old and bent-backed with a walking cane in his hand.

'The guide,' Jarishma said, his eyes wide. His voice was so thick with emotion that Rumi thought the jungle mage was going to sob. 'The guide to the Door of Testimony.'

They moved to meet the guide at the side of the riverbed. What they noticed up close gave Rumi a jolt of surprise.

The dark of the guide's eyes had been glazed over with the cloudy white that came from only one condition. His mouth had been stitched shut in a criss-cross pattern of straw-like string. Across his chest was a single word in Mushiain: *Alaabo.*

'He's blind,' Ahwazi said, stating the obvious. 'He also can't speak.'

As though to confirm this, the guide made a pained, muffled sound that came from the end of his throat.

'How can a blind man be our guide?' Miselda said.

Sameer stepped close and took the guide by the hand as he called his shadow. 'The blind leading the blind.'

Rumi narrowed his eyes. 'Mindwalking.'

That was how the guide would show them the way: with his mind.

They followed without opposition. Hagen was not particularly fond of water but even he waded after them. The water rose above their ankles as they climbed the stairs. Rumi realised then that all the ghostly whispers from the levels before were gone. In their place came the saintly hum of heavenly hosts in a tone thick with encouragement. They were being serenaded.

They stepped past the highest trees and a column of light

sprayed out from above, illuminating the path before them. It was as though they had passed the threshold of some lower world and were being welcomed into the palatial fore-gardens of the higher one. Ahwazi jerked his sword belt straight and Miselda combed a hand through her hair to scrape out the dirt. Jarishma dusted himself down and dry-washed his hands.

'Remove your ghost stones.'

They all obeyed.

Sameer directed them up over a ledge of rushing foam and they came to a wide expanse of water that stretched out ahead as far as the eye could see. Towering rocks stood on either side, making it feel as though they were being watched by ancient giants as they strode through.

The water ran high as their knees but not more than that. They removed their shoes as they waded slowly through, their feet tickled by fish of bright and lively colours. Painted along the rock walls were words in a language none of them could recognise.

The heavenly hum seemed to rise and for the first time since they had stepped into the forest, Rumi realised that his fear had receded. He let out a breath of utter relief. *We made it.*

Agbako was the only one who seemed a little uncomfortable. He kept checking his shoulder as though expecting some great fish to jump out at him.

'This place is beautiful,' Nataré said.

There was no denying that. Even the Obayifo had grown quiet and respectful. A statue ahead depicted Precious Jahmine with a just-born babe in each hand. Water flowed down the sides of her dress.

'Who built these?' Rumi asked as they walked past.

Agbako spoke for the first time. 'The first jazzmen, jujumen and witch doctors. Before the first schism of gods. When things were still whole. They were mostly just priests then.'

Rumi wet his lips. 'Perhaps things will one day become whole again.'

Agbako groaned and looked away, quickening his pace and splashing through the water as he strode ahead.

'There it is! There it is!'

Rumi lifted his gaze. Squinting against the river breeze, he brushed an unruly tress of hair away from his face.

Erin-Olu ended in a deep bowl shaded by a canopy of trees, with the water current stirred by the pressure from deep beneath the surface. It was the source of Erin-Olu – of all Oké water.

There are times, when even cynical men must bow their heads in awe and acknowledge the superiority of greater creative forces. This was one such time. As they stepped up to the source of Erin-Olu, the only expression was awe.

The water was clear as glass and seemed to run deep as the stomach of the earth.

Miselda stared at the source with a look of utter reverence. She smiled for a moment then stripped to her underclothes, setting them beside the trees. With a triumphant smile, she dived head-first into the water. For one terrifying moment, she disappeared beneath the surface and Rumi feared the ghost frogs had started the work, then she emerged with a smile and laughed.

It didn't take long for everyone else to disrobe and jump in after her. The restorative power of Oké water extended beyond just the body. Pains of the mind seemed to fall away as Rumi revelled in a perfect peace.

'It's incredible,' Nataré said as she waded up to him with a smile. Even Agbako was smiling and laughing.

After a half hour of swimming, they climbed out and sat

on the edge of the water. Their bodies thrummed with fresh invigoration.

'How do we collect it?' Nataré asked.

Miselda stepped forward. 'Leave that to me.'

She summoned her shadow and raised her hands. A thick slate of shadow materialised in the air as she narrowed her eyes in concentration. It took a moment to realise what she was doing but when Rumi saw it — he was awed again. *The superiority of greater creative forces.*

She began by conjuring a perfect spherical tank, then she spread her hands and it split perfectly across the middle creating two halves, each with the curve of a calabash shard.

'Incredible,' Ahwazi said.

'Ingenious,' Sameer added.

Miselda lowered her hands thrusting the two halves into the source, collecting the water as one would with their empty hands and bringing the sphere perfectly back together. With a deep breath she lowered the sphere back to the water surface where it bobbed across, seeming light as a feather. Finally, she conjured little hooks into the hard shell of the tank so it could be dragged or carried.

'That should do it,' Miselda announced, dusting down her hands. 'Our work is done.'

In a sense she was right. They had collected enough Oké water to heal half the Eredo for the best part of the next ten years. With the help of the Obayifo, they could return safely to the Eredo and receive a hero's welcome. But for Rumi, there was still something more he needed at the summit.

'I can't go, not yet,' Rumi said.

Jarishma nodded. 'Neither can I.'

'Nor I,' Nataré said.

'Or us,' Ahwazi said.

Miselda shook her head. 'What about you, witch doctor?'

Agbako shrugged. 'We've come this far, might as well see what the Door of Testimony is all about.'

Miselda nodded. 'I'm not going further than this. I won't take the chance.'

Rumi nodded. 'We wouldn't ask you to. Take the Oké water with the Obayifo and return to the Eredo. They will give you a hero's welcome.'

Sameer nodded. 'So, it appears this is farewell, Muriel.'

'Only for now. we will certainly meet again at the Eredo,' Rumi said.

'Good,' Miselda said, spinning the tank so the Obayifo could take hold of the hook handles.

'Dara be with you,' Miselda said, and she took his hand and kissed it.

Rumi blinked at that and met her gaze. 'And also with you.'

He kissed her hand in return.

'It has been a pleasure, friends,' she said with a grin, then she called the Obayifo for aid, weaved threads of shadow through the Oké water tank and climbed on the shoulders of the largest Obayifo.

Rumi watched her fly off – hoping it would not be the last time they saw each other.

'To the Door of Testimony, then,' Sameer said.

And so, they continued. They filled their waterskins with Oké water, wrenched their clothes as dry as was possible and left the source of Erin-Olu with the guidance of Sameer. As the sun lulled, they came to a wide grassland before a stone pergola.

Jarishma shouted from behind them. 'Dara, Skyfather of All. Blood of my ancestors! The Door of Testimony.'

The stone pergola lay a few metres ahead and inside, they could see what they had come all this way for. It looked more like a window than a door, for there was neither handle nor hinge. Just an open rectangle of total blackness that seemed to suck and hiss at the world around it. There was unspeakable power there – even a baby could see that. You could taste it in the air, feel it on your skin.

Hagen barked frantically. A choking bark, so hard and raspy that he was spraying foam.

'Relax, Hagen,' Rumi said.

The lionhound didn't let up. That was the first sign that something was amiss. The second sign was the music in the air; the heavenly hosts were still singing but there was something dark and ominous in it now.

Nataré's voice shot out from behind. 'Agbako, what the sheg are you doing?'

The big witch doctor ran up to the stone pergola and blocked the entrance. 'Leave now, while you still have the chance. Run, Rumi! Run, all of you!'

Something was moving behind him. Coming from the other side.

'Run, Rumi!' Agbako snarled. 'Run!'

A slender hand reached out and cuffed Agbako around the neck. It was done with the gentle attention of a lover, yet Rumi heard the loud crack of broken bone as Agbako went down clutching his shoulder.

A woman with two golden cats stepped over Agbako as he fell away. Rumi couldn't see her features at that distance but the sheen of her eyes was unmistakable. Gleaming, yellow eyes. Though her face was young, hers were the ancient, knowing eyes of a cat.

This time, there was no hesitation. They took off running. They could feel the swollen corruption on the air.

Rumi turned to Nataré. 'Run.'

She obeyed, as did Sameer and Ahwazi. The two cats darted forwards and gave chase.

Rumi was set to turn himself when he saw Hagen still barking at the woman with the yellow eyes.

'Hagen!' he screamed.

The lionhound kept barking.

The woman was getting closer to Hagen now. Rumi reached deep within the bond and tugged hard. Hagen didn't respond.

Shege. Shege to my father's balls. He ran after the lionhound and grabbed him around the neck. 'Let's go,' he hissed. Finally, his lionhound gathered sense.

The cowrie at Rumi's neck flared with a sudden explosion of heat. Nataré let out a sharp shout of pain and something hit the earth hard. Out of pure instinct, Rumi moved his hand up. A silver garrotte wire curled around his fingers, biting into the skin at the side of his neck. He gasped as he was hauled off his feet. That single instinctive act of raising an outstretched hand was the only thing between the garrotte and his throat stone. Pulling desperately at the wire, Rumi came to terms with what was happening.

It was a trap and Agbako had tried to warn him.

Straining, Rumi angled his head trying to see who was holding the wire. He couldn't turn his head enough. Not with the garrotte wrapped around his fingers and his assailant standing directly behind him. At the edge of his vision he could see Nataré, slumped face-down on the ground. He tried to call her name but could only manage a wordless hiss.

He brought his other hand up to clutch at the wire, blood dripping down his wrist as it cut into his skin.

He strained his neck and saw Ahwazi wrestling with one of the godhunter's cats. It had tripled in size – now just as big as Ahwazi as they struggled for dominance.

The woman with the yellow eyes stepped out from the stone pergola. Her face was utterly perfect. No artist's masterwork could match even the slant of her neck or the curl of her lips. Thin as a blade, she had an affecting, inevitable beauty. The boubou she wore was cut out at the sides over wide-leg trousers in patterned black and yellow. She moved with a sinuous rhythm; her walk so dancerly that if you set it to music, she would be on beat. It was like watching water poured from a glass; a seamless, jointless movement that was as inhuman as it was perfect. The same way the Priest of Vultures moved. When she stood in the light, she cast no shadow.

Her name came to his mind immediately. *Pretty Yelloweye.*

'Hello,' she said. Her voice was soft as a baker's dough, warm as an oven; but there was something cutting in it.

Fear had returned and was making up for lost time. Rumi's heart thudded against his chest so hard that it hurt. The garrotte was cutting into his fingers as he tried to hold it back.

He tried to call his shadow but could not manage the words with the wire inching towards his throat. A second thought came to him. *Go for the flute.*

If he did that, the garrotte would get to his throat but before he died, he could blow one good note out. *Summon them.*

Pretty Yelloweye glanced at Agbako, who lay broken on the floor. 'Did I just hear you telling them to run? I would say that was a breach of our agreement, wouldn't you?'

Agbako shrank back from her, muttering curses.

She put a heel on the shell of the tortoise. 'Who would have expected a witch doctor to grow a conscience?' Her teeth flashed as she stamped down on the tortoise shell. It shattered as the tortoise exploded, spattering blood and innards. Agbako screamed as though he had been the one to die. He had not screamed for Horse or No-Horse, but he screamed for his tortoise.

Pretty Yelloweye glanced past Rumi. 'Good thing I had a failsafe plan.'

The garrotte tightened against Rumi's hand as blood spilled down his palm. The force was incredible. Before long, the wire would sever his fingers and then bite into his neck.

Hagen was barking at Yelloweye but she paid him no mind at all.

Agbako stumbled to his feet and stretched out his good hand. A sword materialised in his grip as he turned to face the godhunter.

She blinked at him. 'Are you quite mad?'

He dragged a foot back and set himself. 'I came to a new understanding, godhunter. You know my work. I've drunk blood enough to turn Erin-Olu red. Killed too many men to count on a hundred hands. But I like the boy.' He pointed his sword at her. 'And I don't like anyone.'

Pretty Yelloweye threw back her head and let out a deep, guttural laugh that made the grass ripple. It was a sickening sound. Unsettling as a scream. Soft tremors of panic ran along the hairs on Rumi's skin as she cackled.

Agbako, not one for ceremony, lunged at her while her guard was down. For a moment it seemed he would stab her through the stomach, then there was a sharp flash of light. Agbako's sword flew spiralling along with what Rumi first thought was a glove. Only when he saw blood fountaining from Agbako's severed hand did he realise what had happened. Agbako made no sound, until with a move of horrible speed Yelloweye snatched him by the neck and flung him away. He flew, like one of the twigs Rumi would toss in the Thatcher for Hagen to run after. Rumi watched his body soar till it hit the ground and his screaming was cut off.

'Let that be a warning,' Yelloweye said, dusting her palms.

A sick feeling curdled in Rumi's throat. This was it. The cowrie was burning a mark into his neck, the garrotte had cut into bone. His assailant put a heel to his back and pulled hard on the wire, more determined than ever to put an end to the struggle. He had no escape. He tilted his head towards Nataré. If it was to be the end, let her face be the last thing he saw. *Get up. Please.*

Hagen screamed from deep in the bond making Rumi's entire body shudder.

A thought hit him then. Frantic, he bit down on his tongue until the copper-salt taste of blood filled his mouth.

Before he ever called his shadow by name, he had called it by blood.

The shadow came and he moved his focus, slipping into the mind of his dog. Through Hagen's eyes, he saw who stood with the garrotte wire and his stomach tightened like a balled-up fist. *Jarishma.*

The jungle mage was trying to kill him.

Rumi closed his eyes and gritted his teeth, aiming for one impossible strike. Through Hagen's eyes, his vision was keen and sure. He clutched deep at that well of emotion. The feelings that had driven him here. Brought him to a place that so many had died trying to reach. Love for his family. Love for his friends. Love for Nataré. Love for himself. With a spattering of hate and outrage, he lashed out in the shadow, sending a conjured spear right for Jarishma's throat.

The conjured spear flew true and instant, destined for its indelible mark.

Somehow, by some incredible joinder of luck and skill, the

jungle mage brought an elbow up to block the attack. It cut through flesh and bone, sending Jarishma off his feet.

The garrotte slackened and Rumi fell forward, sucking in precious gulps of air.

Rumi could scarcely believe it. He had put all his focus into making the strike instantaneous, giving Jarishma no chance to react, but the man had somehow seen it coming.

'Impressive,' Jarishma said, raising his ruined, bloody elbow to take a look at it. 'I had forgotten you could call the shadow with blood alone. An old technique.' He glanced at Hagen. 'You used the dog to make your aim. Clever. You would have been a great shadowwielder in the end.' He grinned. 'You nearly killed the jungle mage.'

Rumi doubled over, stealing breath. 'You are a traitor to the Order.'

Jarishma moved to stand on the side of Yelloweye. 'The Order was a traitor to me. What happened to my daughter never should have been allowed. After all I gave.' He shook his head and looked up at Yelloweye. 'I brought him here,' Jarishma said. 'I held up my end of the bargain. You get to kill him on sacred ground.'

She made a nonchalant gesture towards the stone pergola. 'I have unlocked the Door of Testimony. It is yours to explore.'

Jarishma ripped the broken spear from his elbow and ran straight for the Door of Testimony.

Rumi ran to Nataré's side and pulled her neck, cradling her head. 'Nataré.'

She gave no response. Something hard pressed against his knee. He turned her onto her side. A dagger was lodged deep into the back of her spleen.

'Shege,' Rumi breathed. Nataré let out a low groan and spasmed. She opened her eyes, her breath short. 'Irumide.'

His name on her lips. An eternal gift he could never repay in kind. Her breath was faint, her eyes were narrowed. Her condition was clear. *She's dying.*

Ahwazi managed to overpower the cat and get back to his feet. The two cats recoiled and started to circle him, hissing and spitting. He raised his sword, covered in dirt, blood and muck. 'I will not have my story end by being killed by a sheggin' cat.'

Rumi lifted his halberd, breathing hard as he faced up to Pretty Yelloweye. *Where is Sameer?* She stretched out a hand. A thin rapier materialised in her open grip. She spun it over her wrist and smiled.

Rumi pointed at her. 'This is between you and me, god-hunter.'

She grinned. 'I quite agree. Allow me to rid you of the distractions.'

The heavenly hosts stopped their song.

Pretty Yelloweye moved in a blur to Ahwazi. He raised his blade but she slapped it aside and pushed her rapier through his mouth till it broke through the back of his neck.

Rumi gasped.

Ahwazi raised a hand in a desperate plea for mercy.

Pretty Yelloweye offered him none. She kicked him off his feet and when he hit the ground, she stamped down on his chest crushing it. Blood spattered. Innards sprayed.

The effortlessness of the slaughter was sickening to watch.

'No!' Sameer screamed, throwing himself from a tree with his blade raised.

Pretty Yelloweye snatched him out of the air, holding him up like a troublesome puppy. 'Aren't *you* going to beg?'

But Sameer's eyes were vacant. As though he had already abandoned ship.

Yelloweye put her hands to his temple and crushed his skull.

Rumi screamed but he didn't hear himself. All he could hear was his shallow, powerless breathing as he watched Sameer's ruined corpse fall to the ground. *Sameer and Ahwazi dead.*

Yelloweye dusted her palms and smeared blood along the sides of her dress. Her expression was that of an excited house-cook. She turned to Rumi and picked her rapier back up.

Rumi could hear a ringing sound in his head as his heart thumped his ribs. Silently, he moved to stand between the godhunter and Nataré.

'Godhunter! This is between me and you. Leave her alone!' Rumi roared.

Yelloweye didn't respond, instead she just kept walking towards them.

Like a candle in the wind, hope guttered out. Rumi gripped his halberd, trying to think.

'I had forgotten just how much fun you mortals can be,' Yelloweye said as she stepped closer.

Rumi raised his weapon, his mind frantic. 'Wait! Wait! I have an offer for you godhunter.'

Yelloweye stopped. 'What is your offer?'

'Leave my friend. Spare her life and let me face you once in a circle. Like the old days.'

'Why would I save her when I could kill you both with far less trouble?' she asked.

Rumi met her gaze. 'Because I know your name. Your true name. And if you don't help her, I will scream it till all the spirits in the forest know it too.'

Her smile faded. 'Lies.'

'Was I lying when I called the name Tahinta? When I broke him from the inside out? I wonder how far the Blackfae will carry your name when they know it true.'

Her face gave an ugly twitch and she glanced over her

shoulder as though someone had called her name. 'No,' she breathed, her eyes narrowing till they looked like yellow-gold moon crescents. 'Fine.'

She broke kola nut and tossed it at him. 'We are agreed.'

Rumi chewed the kola nut, then walked up to Nataré and pulled the waterskin from her side. He poured her entire waterskin along with half his own of Oké water down her throat before the broken skin curled against itself. The dark stain of blood slowly lightened to a spritely pink as her wound healed. Nataré let out a ragged cough, then breathed hard. Her closed eyelids seemed to tighten for a moment, then stretched wide.

She sat up, gasping – as though waking from a hideous dream.

Pretty Yelloweye frowned as she raised her hand. 'She will live.'

With a wave of her hand Nataré was flung back as a circle formed around Rumi and Yelloweye. 'But you won't.'

Hagen lunged towards them but hit something thinner than air yet harder than stone. Pretty Yelloweye had set unbreakable wards around her circle. She let out a declarative sigh and twirled her rapier as one would a dancing wand.

'You have my word, Son of Despair. I'll take you and you alone. But even to you I offer a choice, tell me, will you serve the Son.'

Rumi considered it for a moment and felt the strength leave his front leg. Then he remembered the way this servant of the Son had crushed Ahwazi's skull.

He raised his halberd. 'Never.'

57

Festival Day

LETHI

It was hot in the south. It always was – but that day it was as though the sun had grown a little spiteful. Lethi wrung the sweat from his handkerchief and gave his forehead another wipe. 'How long till we get there?'

Attem pointed down the path. 'We are there already,' he said.

Lethi glanced up. A few hundred yards ahead, buildings had come into view. Atop the roofs and hanging out the windows were people – hundreds of them, all desperate to get a view of the governor-general. It had been a good seven years since any governor-general had come this far south. Most of the people in Alara had only some vague notion of who the governor was. He was an idea to them, rather than an actual person.

The one they had come to see was at the centre of the procession in an open-topped carriage – waving at the masses like some angel just down from heaven.

Lethi searched the streets with his eyes – high and low. The Black Hammer Clan were there – he could feel it. They couldn't waste such an opportunity. The question was – what were they going to do with it?

'They are here,' Attem said.

'You see them?' Lethi asked.

He shook his head. 'I just know.'

Lethi stared at the people as they passed through the village gates. These were sun-toughened, hard-bodied folk with looks that went from mollified to murderous as quickly as one might blink. Any one of them could be part of the Black Hammer Clan. There were others amongst the crowd too. Dressed like villagers but trained by Attem. They were just as ready as everyone else. *If this plan doesn't work, Zaminu will have me killed.*

His horse whinnied and snorted as the scent of frying pepper and tomato hit them. It was a smell that transported Lethi almost directly to a long-forgotten time. He could almost hear his mother's voice. *Let the rice cook slow. Don't lift the lid even if it starts to hiss.*

He stiffened as they came to the centre of the village square, where an ornamented dais had been set up for the governor-general to address the gathered crowd. The people there must have numbered in the thousands. Not just from Alara but from all the villages in the South.

A dozen or so goats were crowded into a small pen set beside an open grill where the first of them was roasting on an oscillating spit.

'Festival day indeed,' Lethi muttered

He glanced up at the Palmaine standard at the head of their parade, slapping against the wind. The four-point star – a symbol of their faith. In God. In King. In country. Lethi looked away from it, a little ashamed.

Banasco pulled his horse up beside them and spat at the ground. 'If they are not dogs, how can they live in such squalor?' he asked, staring at the pit latrine behind a bungalow.

Lethi gave no answer. Squalor meant different things to different people and Banasco was no authority to speak on the matter. If ever a man could be said to be of utter moral squalor, Banasco was that man.

Banasco raised his rifle. 'Those Black Hammer bastards are here. Tell you, I can't wait till we start on them. Can't wait.'

Lethi gave Attem an almost apologetic look.

Roadie gestured ahead. 'See that?'

They looked up. It was a rooftop about a hundred metres from the dais. It wasn't the perfect vantage point but it might have been possible for a very skilled archer or gunman to take his shot from there.

Lethi nodded. 'Go take a look.'

Roadie nodded and peeled off from the procession.

Attem had spent the week before covertly scouting every point of attack and blocking them off. The placement of the dais had been the work of one month of careful planning. If their trap was to succeed it had to be precise.

'Are we ready?' Attem asked.

Lethi looked over the consular guard who had come with him. Nearly three hundred of them – armed as though for war. He nodded to Attem. 'As we will ever be.'

Their horses parted in a choreographed pattern around the dais, allowing the governor-general's carriage to come forward. The man stood, flawlessly straight as the door was pulled open for him to mount the dais. His wave was like an actor's in a perfect drama – firm but not harsh, humble but not pandering. Lethi had to admit he played the part well.

He rose to the top of the dais and the crowd couldn't help but cheer.

Lethi looked at the man's face. He did bear some resemblance to Governor-General Paru, but anyone who had seen the face of the real governor would have known this was an impostor. But of course, hardly anyone in Alara had ever seen the real governor.

Lethi's heart thumped hard in his chest. Now was the moment. He glanced up to the far-off roof, squinting to get a good look – a single head bobbed up above the parapet. Just as they had expected.

'Who the hell is that?' Banasco snarled.

Lethi turned. A big man dressed in a blue and red ankara had stepped onto the dais. How he had managed to get past the guards was a mystery.

'Stop that man!' Lethi snarled.

Everything happened in a few blinks of an eye. The sharp report of gunfire rang from the rooftop. The false governor went down, clutching his chest. The stranger who had run onto the dais stamped down on the wood and it broke apart like paper. A hole opened in the dais, dragging everyone on it down like a sinkhole.

'The governor has been shot!' Banasco snarled. 'Treason!'

Light flared at the corner of Lethi's vision. The shooting had started. The consular guard had drawn their weapons and people were already screaming. A keen eye might have noticed that some consular guard had had their weapons aimed before the governor fell but amidst the chaos, there was no time for keen observations.

Lethi cleared his throat and spoke aloud. 'By the powers invested in me under the Collective Responsibility and Punishment Ordinance I give the officers of the consular guard to use any means necessary to bring this insurrection to order.'

It was a farcical measure. Lip service to justice. But Lethi was beginning to understand that lip service was a big part of what it meant to be Palmaine. Punishing an entire village for the alleged transgressions of an unknown few was quintessentially Palmaine.

The ground trembled and there was a shower of discharged earth ahead as a cannon was fired into a building. Something thudded into the ground a few yards ahead. Looked like the sort of thing that would be found hanging in a butcher's window. Lethi didn't take a second look. He coughed, choking from the gun smoke as the trample of boots and barefooted flight scattered all around. A fire went up from a building in front of him. There was always fire.

'Stop killing us!' someone shouted.

They won't.

'You cannot do this!' another person screamed.

They will.

There was no running from it now. They were in the midst of a massacre and Lethi had been at the centre of planning it. Chaos ensued as guns blared and people ran here, there and everywhere. It was forbidden to shed blood on festival day but they were no respecters of pagan custom. *For the Son sees our hearts and brings peace to those who resist evil.* Lethi had accepted that his heart was dark as coal and there would be no peace for him, for he had not resisted evil. *No peace for me now, only war.*

A white and yellow cat crept amid the chaos. The sharp and sudden splintering of wood made it lurch in surprise as it crept up to the dais. It looked frightened and alarmed at everything happening to its village.

Someone pleaded behind him. 'Help me.'

But Lethi only had eyes for the cat. It arched its back in a stretch and came to the broken wood by the hole where the dais had fallen. It stared down into the breach and then hopped over the ledge.

Lethi gasped. Without hesitation he walked over to the hole himself. *Why did a hole open up?* That had never been a part of their plan. How was it there? Who was that strange man on the stage and why had they dragged the false governor-general down that hole?

Attem was staring at it too. Wordlessly, Lethi tightened his sword belt and strapped his rifle close to his chest. Attem stepped up beside him.

Coming up to the lip of the hole Lethi glanced down. His eyes nearly popped at what he saw. It was a tunnel. He dropped to his haunches and leaned to get a better look. There was a walkway down there – he was sure of it.

Attem's hand fell on his shoulder. 'Dangerous.'

Lethi remembered the last time an officer of the Meladroni had gone down a strange tunnel and stopped.

A man screamed behind him, running to get away from a chasing guard. A rifle applauded and the man fell dead. Lethi grimaced. 'Sheg staying up here, I'm going down.'

He jumped down into the tunnel. It was deeper than he had judged but he fell in a crouch to avoid any injury. Attem landed right after him.

The tunnel was illuminated by torch lanterns that hung from the wall. This wasn't something newly built. It had been there for a long time. The dais collapsing had been no accident.

'What is this place?' Lethi asked, looking at the tunnel walls. A flicker of movement ahead cast a shadow in the dancing light.

On the floor, in a pool of blood, was the man they had dressed as the governor-general. His uniform had been taken away and he had been left dead with nothing but his underclothes. Lethi glanced up and caught the faintest afterimage of dark ankara rounding the corner.

'Stop,' Lethi said, giving chase. 'Stop in the name of the king.'

He took off after the man, Attem close at his side.

'I said stop,' Lethi yelled.

He had rounded a corner and saw the tunnel kept going for at least a mile. The big man from the dais was far ahead but there was only one way he could run.

Lethi narrowed his eyes. He looked back up towards the hole. 'Who was responsible for building the dais?'

Attem's hand moved in a quick blur, stabbing him behind the knee. Hard and quick. Pain exploded behind Lethi's right kneecap.

He dropped to one knee, gasping desperately for air. 'Shee ... shege.'

The hilt of a dagger protruded from the meat of his thigh as Attem stood above him with his rifle aimed at Lethi's forehead.

'Attem,' Lethi gasped. 'Attem, what are you ... what are you doing?'

Attem's face was cold and grim. 'I tried to give you a chance, but you just refused to listen.'

Lethi winced and blinked, the wound making his entire face heat up.

'You are a traitor?' he gasped.

Attem ignored him. 'You have the potential to be a good man, Lethi, that is the only reason I won't kill you. In another life, we would have been friends, fighting on the same side.' He dragged Lethi along the floor and set him beside a pillar. 'But the life we have is this one and here we cannot be friends.'

He pulled his collar down and raised his neck so Lethi could see the underside of his chin. A single black hammer was tattooed to his neck, just below his beard.

Lethi's hope fled. 'How could you do this to me? After everything I have done for you?'

Attem frowned. 'You did me no favours. Everything I got in your employ I earned thrice over. If you want me to applaud you not for being a turd like the others...' He raised his rifle. 'Consider this my debt repaid – I won't kill you today but if I ever see you again, I will. Stop fighting for a cause you don't truly believe in, Lieutenant.'

Lethi reached out for the native. 'Attem, how could you?'

Attem gave him a disgusted look. 'My name is not Attem. It never was.'

Lethi lifted his chin to meet his gaze. 'Who are you?'

The man he had once called Attem rolled his wrists and straightened to his full height. 'My name is Kwame Elaro Damascus. First son of Kojo Damascus.' He drew in breath through his nose and rolled his shoulder. 'It has been good knowing you, Lieutenant. I hope you are remembered as a good man.'

With that, Attem raised his rifle high and smashed the buttstock into the side of Lethi's head. He went down with a grunt, losing his grip on consciousness.

★ ★ ★

When Lethi woke, the noise of violence above was still exceedingly loud. Attem had blown out the lantern light and the tunnel was dark as pitch.

Lethi shouted every name under the sun, but no one came to his aid. They were hard at the work of a slaughter where their enemies offered little resistance. No time for a broken man down in a hole. He thought for a moment that he might die there on that cold tunnel floor. An impressive amount of blood had leaked from his leg and there was no chance of him climbing out. The only thing he had was... He straightened. *Why didn't I think of it before?*

Closing his eyes, he drew in breath and called his shadow. Power filled him as slowly, carefully, he rose to his feet. He shuddered as he glanced up. There were small clefts in the interlocking stone that he could climb.

His eyes widened. He forced his mind under control and

focused on a climbing axe materialising in his hand. Dark blood trickled from his nose as the memory of his father slipped into his mind. With a strained effort, he managed to form a crude shiv that he could use to scrape his way up the wall.

He glanced up. It was like he knew without thinking – this would be the hardest thing he'd ever had to do in his life. He was no mountaineer; he was a soldier.

There was nothing to find but death in the tunnel. The only way to live was to climb. It was only about ten metres high but in his condition it would be hard work.

He felt three emotions most of all. The first was sheer terror. Terror in the knowledge that his resolve could break and the shadow-wrought climbing shiv would shatter like struck glass. Terror in the knowledge that one small mistake and he would fall to his death. The second emotion was rage. Fury that Attem had betrayed him. That he had managed to be fooled for so long. That the men above didn't have the good sense to glance down the hole. The last emotion was gratitude. He was still alive. Attem – whatever his real name was – had let him live, despite it all. He still had a chance, and he meant to take it with both hands.

He drew all that emotion in, filling his mind with the far-off prospect of seeing the sun again.

He swung the climbing shiv and stabbed into the stone. It cut deep and stuck true. *It will work.* Gripping hard, he pulled himself up. His leg was raw with burning pain but adrenaline had him firmly in its grip now. This was a raw, desperate fight for his life. As close as one could come to knowing the true depth of their desperation. As the darkness pressed down on him, he considered that this was a fitting metaphor for life; alone and in a pit; shrouded in darkness and struggling towards the light. Slowly drifting away from everyone around him and trying to scale an impossible height. He gritted his teeth and stabbed the blade into the next fold of stone. *Just keep climbing.*

Memories in the shadow flashed through his mind as he climbed; things that he had forced himself to forget. The night he had found his aged father spasming in a pool of his own piss and blood. How he had swung into instantaneous action to ride him to a surgeon who saved his life. How he'd kept his eyes on the man the whole time – fearing that if he looked away, his father would die. He remembered how he had nursed his father back to health; holding his hand to the chamber pot and waiting him out. Helping him learn how to walk again. Seeing him through it all. He remembered the pain when one day, his father had pissed himself at night and – when Lethi tried to change the bedsheets – he had spat at him and called him the son of a Zarot whore, threatening to have him flogged. How his father had burned every garment that Lethi had touched. How he ordered that Lethi be cast out.

Strange thing was, it didn't even feel like a betrayal. It felt like something entirely expected. Perfectly in keeping with the theme of his life. The days caring for his father had been the dream but the hate was the reality.

In that moment, Lethi considered letting go. Of giving himself to the darkness and letting his body fall to perish. *Why not die? End the pain now.* He had no heir – no one to continue the cycle of hate. *Best to end it now.* His hand slipped from the shadow. Attem's words flashed through his mind. 'I hope you are remembered as a good man'.

His eyes snapped open, his pupils wide. This was not where it would end. He would not have someone else telling his story. The lieutenant who led the massacre of Alara. The man who butchered innocents to maintain Palmaine control. That was not how he was going to be remembered. Not a kitten's chance in a foxhole. He snarled as he stabbed at the next part of the stone. Pain spread like heat up his spinal column. *Just keep climbing.*

Memories came but he ignored them. This was a test of will and want, and in that, he had no superior. Pain and fear were long-time companions, but no one had the passion to keep going like he did. No one. *Just ... keep ... climbing.* He *was* a good man, and if he lived, he was going to prove it.

He saw the faint light from the opening above. The remainder of the tunnel loomed below like a dark adversary but he kept his focus on that small glow above.

His whole body ached under the strain and weight of the climb, but he wouldn't give up. Not when he could quite literally see the light at the end of darkness.

He pressed forward for the final charge. His body screamed a rebuke but his mind kept him going, inch by precious inch. The faint light grew brighter and brighter until it hurt his eyes. Then, finally, his hand touched the edge of salvation. Triumphant.

He swung his good leg over the lip of the opening and hauled himself up. He allowed a few breaths of relief before he sat up and looked around. The consular guard were still killing the natives. As far as massacres went they had done an eager job. But Lethi saw no sign of dead members of the Black Hammer Clan.

Narrowing his eyes, he looked back into the hole. *Where were they going?*

He looked around again, trying to see what he was missing. A horse whinnied at the front of the dais and Lethi saw what he had missed before. The carriage of their impostor governor-general was gone. Lethi turned towards the village gates. For some strange reason, they were shut.

His eyes widened. 'Stop, you fools! This is a distraction! Stop!'

Some of the men glanced at him but no one stopped. They were too busy killing innocents.

'They want us trapped here. They are going for the House of Palman!'

No one heard him over the noise.

He remembered what the leader of the Black Hammer Clan had told him in captivity. *You kill ten of us, we kill one of you and count it as victory. We will outlast you because we fight for something you will never understand.*

He watched the people who were dying. They were fighting back but not with the same gusto he had seen in Oké-Dar. It was as if a bell rang in Lethi's head – they were stalling them. These were not victims, they were martyrs. A sharp tingle of realisation shot up Lethi's spinal column. *How long had Attem been one of them?* He recalled how Attem had been the one to rescue him from their captivity. How he had even killed one of the Black Hammer guards to see him free. *All martyrs.*

It was so intricate. So delicate that he almost wanted to applaud. But this was no time to marvel – he had to stop them. They had lured half the Palmaine force to the South and had immediately moved North. *They are going to strike tonight.*

58

Power Mighty in the Blood

RUMI

Rumi circled Pretty Yelloweye with *egret crosses the river*.

The godhunter smiled. 'A bit dramatic. It has been a long time since someone had the stones to fight me alone.'

Rumi did not respond. His mind was deep in shadow. He saw Nataré at the ward, trying to intervene — her face a picture of utter despair.

'Don't worry about her,' Yelloweye said. 'I want your eyes on me.'

Rumi felt himself a little taken in by her then. A part of him wanted to press his stomach to the tip of her rapier.

She smiled at him and for a moment, he wanted her more than he did his next breath. He was overrun by a sharp desire to worship her. Kiss her feet and call her what she was. A woman singular and apart. Perfection. He dropped his halberd and took one step forwards. A sharp pain stung his mind as he glimpsed Nataré past the ward. Just the faintiest glimpse but it was enough to give him the cleft of space to remaster himself. He fortified his mind, knowing this was all part of her effect. She was more nettle than rose.

'That won't work,' Rumi said as he spun the halberd spear-wise. She gave the weapon an indifferent look as though it had a blunt edge.

Rumi considered, as he circled her, what Sameer would have done. He was the one who knew best how to handle a more powerful opponent. *And now he is gone.* The memory of it made him almost buckle.

Yelloweye held her rapier low and to the side in an almost unaggressive stance, inviting him on.

'Come on, let me see what you have,' she said.

Rumi didn't move. He was in no hurry to engage – watching your opponent was an essential part of the craft. His emotion was ready and available, but he would not explode until he had to.

She glided towards him and their weapons kissed once. She turned his halberd aside with her rapier then spun over his back and landed on her feet. She grinned at him when he turned to face her again. It was a manoeuvre similar to *fox enters the henhouse* but faster and more relaxed. She didn't use the forms, of course, she was older than them. She fought with the liberated freedom of a fighter like Zarcanis. Fighting, to her, was as music was to Rumi. There were some who followed the rules in music, but the great ones remade them.

She laughed as realisation hit his eyes. It was plain she was just testing him, watching him as much as he was her. Playing with her food before devouring it. She was faster, stronger, more experienced and seemingly immortal. He had no chance. *Think Rumi, think.*

He had her name, but she would be waiting for him to use it. If he slipped inside her mind, she would crush him.

He looked her full in the face. 'You don't happen to be a lover of music, do you?'

She blinked and raised an eyebrow. 'Sheg no.'

Rumi swallowed as he hefted his halberd. 'Didn't think so.'

The word 'doomed' fluttered about Rumi's mind like the Blackfae. He stood no chance against a godhunter. Not on his very best day. The only thing he could do was fight honourably. Fight like a dog. Be the struggler. Maybe leave a mark on Pretty Yelloweye that she would never forget. Punish her as much as he could for that she had done.

She lunged at him again, feinting left then lashing out right. He dodged just out of reach as she slid a finger from his wrist down his forearm until his elbow. Her touch was cold as the mountains on his skin.

'Don't worry,' she said, smiling as she sucked her finger. 'I will make this last.'

She stuck out her rapier and he parried and darted out of range. Then, without preamble, he went for her. Her eyebrow rose for a moment as he lurched forward. Before then he had acted only in defence. Now he had jolted into sharp attack. Her hand shot out, turning aside his halberd with her thin blade. If she were a normal person, Rumi's blow might have sent the blade spinning from her grip but she was – of course – a godhunter. Her wrists were strong as steel, her thin arms powerful and firm.

Rumi lurched forwards, like a battered prisoner finally turning against his terroriser, swaying wild, abandoning any particular adherence to the forms. *Sometimes you just need to sheggin' hit someone.* He brought his halberd up in a wicked flailing arch and nearly cut open the cleft in her chin. She shifted at the very last moment, bringing her elbow up to send Rumi back.

She grinned. Her smile was like a loaded rifle or a drawn dagger. A weapon – make no mistake about it. 'They didn't tell me you fight like this,' she said.

Rumi paid her no mind. He only wanted to scar her. Cut her once. Mark her with a forever memento. Let her know that he was no easy meat. Not in this life or any other to come. He was lost to the fighter's high now. Surrendered himself in soul and body to the shadow within. The darkest part of himself that would kill everyone, everything, just to have one rushed minute with Yami again. Power flooded him as he thrust the halberd spearhead.

'I will kill you,' he snarled. *And he meant it.*

Her eye flashed a moment of recognition as she saw something in him that made her take a backwards step. He was no easy meat. He was Irumide Omo-Xango. Son of Adunola. Of the darkman. Trained by Zarcanis the Viper. He had walked through the Arakoro with his head whole. Killed the Priest of Vultures. He was a story. Living, breathing, swinging, singing. Every sinew of Rumi's body was tight with rage.

His halberd hissed as it clashed with Yelloweye's rapier. He brought it up and chopped again, once, twice, a third time. She turned it aside each time, stepping out of his murderous range.

This was no longer about Yelloweye. No longer about the Door of Testimony. It was about drawing a line. Saying enough was enough. Screaming in the silence.

He spun after a swing, aiming a backfist for the side of her head. She caught him at the elbow – her grip tight as the coiling snake.

'Enough,' she said, in a cold whisper.

She squeezed against his joint, her eyes dark with irritation.

Strangely, the pain was not instantaneous. First came the sound – the sharp crack of breaking bone with the meaty glob of battered innards. Pain like fire flared up at his elbow and shot up to his wrist.

She slapped him open-handed. The way a stern-faced tutor might his trouble-minded ward. He spun a full circle as his jaw jerked sharply right. Before he could steady himself, her fingers curled around his neck and she lifted him off his feet.

She looked up at him with a look of disappointed affection. 'You are no Son of Despair,' she whispered. 'Just another angry shadowwielder.'

She reached into her pocket and pulled something out. It gleamed in her grip like an ingot of silver. At the edge of his vision, Rumi saw Nataré pounding at the ward. He saw Hagen staring at him with ears drooped and his tail flat on the ground. Though he was just a dog, Rumi saw Hagen's depression. He saw the end. Rumi was going to die.

Yelloweye raised the silver object high. It was a four-point star. She held it above Rumi's head and chanted. 'And the Son shall strike them down, erase their names, their seed in the land. And so sacrifice was made of the blood of the godless.'

Rumi had no seed in the land. His family were dead already and now he would join them. He closed his eyes and lowered his head. Defeated.

Through the bond he felt an urgent pulse from Hagen and mindwalked into his lionhound's head for the very last time. 'I love you Hagen. Take care of Nataré for me. See that the darkman lives. Finish my story.'

Rumi heard a familiar voice in his head. Sameer. *I'm still here.* He lowered his head as the memory of his dear friend washed over him.

Hagen gave a low nod and barked his agonised understanding. Through Hagen's eyes Rumi saw himself. Broken and beaten, beneath a raised four-point star. The spectacle, he realised, reminded him of something. The great symbol of the Palman religion – the one inscribed on the cover of their holy book. The Son beneath a broken noose and a four-point star.

The story went that Palman called fire at the point of his death and all other gods were cast into the flames of hell.

A cold shiver ran from Rumi's chest to his ears. *Sora o, awon toni ikulapo wa nile. Pe ara.* Death in their pocket. Call thunder.

Yelloweye was chanting something that Rumi could not understand but it didn't matter now. He had raised his eyes to the heavens where dark clouds were roiling above in wait. A flicker of lightning flashed above and Rumi knew then exactly what he had to do.

He closed his eyes and spoke at the very height of his voice. Loud enough for all the forest to hear. 'Some call him the Skyfather, some call him the Dumaré-Adandan. I call him Dara, the Dancing Lion. He still lives. *Ara*, hear my voice!'

A sound like ripped parchment tore through the air and the wind stopped all at once. Yelloweye stopped chanting and stared up to the sky. The clouds parted and a single bolt of white lightning struck her directly. She screamed, spasmed and roiled as the grass hissed away around her. The rapier shook in her trembling hand before falling from her grip. Her eyes went white as eggs as the bolt cooked her from the inside out. Black foam drooled from her mouth as she tried to reach out towards him.

Rumi stepped back, watching. His eyes level, his arm cradled, his mouth tight in a frown.

The lightning ceased and for a moment, she seemed herself again, her eyes clear and lucid. Then she fell flat on her face.

A cat screamed as the wards were broken and Hagen came bounding towards them. Rumi didn't need to check. He knew she was dead.

Nataré approached him with dead caution, walking as though she were afraid he would call lightning down on her too. He let out a breath, trying to relax, but she kept her distance.

Hagen rolled Pretty Yelloweye's corpse over and they saw her rolled back eyes.

'She's dead,' Nataré said.

Rumi nodded.

The cats fled, cutting through the grass like snakes.

Nataré's eyes bulged. 'How did you... what are you?'

Rumi reached out for her hand and pulled her close. 'Tired.' He kissed her lips, then her throat and collarbone. Her hands curled around the back of his kaftan as their embrace tightened around one another.

'Godsblood, Rumi, how in all the earth are we here right now?'

He kissed her hair. 'Dara only knows.'

A dark shadow fell over them and Rumi whirled with his good hand going to his halberd. Agbako stood with the smashed carcass of his tortoise tucked underarm. He looked broken in ways that only a man who has tasted despair can look.

'I tried to warn you,' he breathed. 'I tried.'

Rumi met his gaze. 'What did she promise you in exchange for bringing me here?'

Agbako frowned. 'The only thing I ever cared about.'

Rumi gave a slow nod. 'Power.'

'Beyond my imagination. She said you had to be brought here. There was something significant about you dying at the seventh level. She kept saying... *and the seventh must fall at the seventh.*'

'What does that mean?' Nataré asked.

Agbako shrugged. 'Spirits are always talking sheg.'

Rumi's temple throbbed. 'What made you change your mind? Why did you try to warn us?'

Agbako was quiet for a long moment, then he shrugged. 'I don't know.' He heaved in a deep breath. 'Your stupid speech got into my head. All the way here I just kept asking myself — what if this idiot is right? What if I haven't gone too far to turn back? Then I thought, I want to turn back. I ... want to change.'

Rumi's lips flattened into a line. 'That small decision. That moment you gave us. I am certain that you saved our lives, Agbako. Thank you.'

He blinked and his eyes went almost childishly wide. 'If you say so.'

A declaratory chime rang behind them and the earth shook with thick ripples. The light from inside the stone pergola shone brighter and the sound it emitted was like something from some great, celestial instrument.

Rumi turned towards the stone pergola, his face hardening as he drank Oké water from his skin. The pain in his hands and elbow receded as he drank the skin dry. He took in the last drop, flexed his grip and hefted his halberd — Jarishma was still in there.

He glanced at Nataré's quiver, silently counting the arrows she had left, then he looked up at Agbako.

'Do you have one more fight left in you?' Rumi said.

59

Prelude to War

ALANGBA

Alangba wore the uniform of a dead officer of the consular guard. The worst things about it were the socks. He hated wearing socks. His feet curled uncomfortably in his boots. 'How do they walk around in this nonsense?' he asked.

Ladan laughed. 'It makes them feel Palmaine – they'd pay any price for that.'

The carriage slowed and Alangba glanced out through the window to see why. 'What's this?' he whispered, narrowing his eyes.

A small patrol of consular guards had waved for their carriage to stop.

Alangba opened the door and stepped down, urging Ladan to stay put. An ash-haired consular took his helmet off in a gesture of respect and stepped up to speak to him. He was in his middle years and had a kindly face. Like a caring shopkeeper or a humble priest. Alangba gritted his teeth, hoping he wouldn't have to kill him.

'Good evening, sir,' the man said.

Alangba stepped close. 'Good evening.'

'We didn't mean to stop you, sir, just to pass on a warning. Our orders are to let every carriage that passes this post know.'

'Know what, exactly?' Alangba asked.

The man lowered his voice. 'Bandits, sir. Dangerous ones. Rumours say they are led by two men. More demons than men. One who runs with a lion and another with one hand who moves in darkness.

That Alangba didn't sputter in laughter at that moment was an act of incredible discipline. With a smile purpling about his lips, he asked, 'Is that so?'

The consular gave a certain nod. 'My cousin Tasin saw them with his own two eyes. Said he had never seen anything like it.'

Alangba turned back towards the carriage. 'We'll be sure to keep our eyes out for anything strange. Don't you worry — they won't get us.'

The man gave them a long contemplative look and then bowed low and gestured to the mainland road. 'May God go with you,' the man offered.

Alangba nodded and turned towards the carriage relieved not to have found cause to kill the man.

Hinges on the carriage door whined as he pulled it open. The consular's voice cut through the night air.

'Were you trained in the Citadel sir?' the consular guard asked.

Alangba glanced over his shoulder. 'Why?'

The consular narrowed his eyes. 'You didn't offer an official salute.'

What salute?

Alangba turned slowly to face the man. Taking a chance, he raised his right hand in the four-finger salute and lowered his head. 'Long live the King.'

The consular stared at him for a long moment, like a predatory pawnbroker examining an old heirloom. 'You're not—'

A knife flew through the open carriage door and struck the consular in the throat. He went down clutching at his neck as though he could stop the death from happening. Ladan moved at frightening speed. Before the consular's compatriot could raise his weapon, Ladan had gutted him twice in the stomach. Another consular made an effort to raise his weapon but Alangba was faster, pulling his wrist down, snapping it and then snatching his rifle and breaking his nose with the buttstock. A flash of metal, a spatter of blood and the deed was done. Others from the carriage moved with the same speed, killing the consular in seconds.

As the first, kind-faced consular lay dying, Ladan stood over him, raised his stump high and grinned. 'I believe the correct salute is Debari reigns.'

After killing and discarding the corpses of the consular, they stepped back into the carriage. As they took off down the mainland road again, Ladan glanced out of the window and smiled. 'Tonight, we change our nation for good.'

Alangba kissed his fingers. 'For good.'

The plan was one of immaculate design. How Mama Ayeesha had known that the Palmaine would not check the hole, Alangba could not guess. It had seemed a risky plan when he'd first heard it, but it had gone off without a hitch. *Almost too well.*

They turned off from the mainland road just beside the Citadel and came to a small farmhouse – a mere stone's throw from the Citadel gates.

They pulled up outside the door and Alangba went in with Ladan. It was dimly lit but even in the dark, it was hard to miss the precious stones draped around the beaded crown.

Alangba fell forward pressing his forehead to the floor. 'Ka-Biyesi O.'

Falina inclined her head and set down the beaded crown. It was death to look upon a monarch crowned, but with the crown set aside, they could talk face-to-face. Beside her sat Lord Mandla, the First Ranger and three other Eredo chiefs.

The queen smiled wide and beckoned him forward. He took a step towards her, sheepish at first, then she rose to her feet and gathered him in her arms.

'I am so glad to see you,' she said, pressing her head to his chest.

Alangba squirmed, struck flush by a sharp pang of emotion. 'It is good to see you too, my Queen.'

Maka Naki, who stood just behind the queen, raised his chin and smiled. 'Looks like you have brought quite the army with you, brother.'

Alangba touched his chest and pointed to the sky. 'We did what we could, but true praise rests with Mama Ayeesha. That woman is a miracle.'

Queen Falina drew back. 'I hear she has raised a troop of five thousand?'

Alangba nodded. 'At least.'

Mandla smiled. 'I am looking forward to meeting this Mama Ayeesha.'

The door creaked open and Ayeesha stepped into the room. She walked with a limp but had a sure-footed air. 'I know how to make an entrance, no?' Ayeesha said.

Falina laughed. 'You certainly do; glad to finally meet you in person.'

Ayeesha dropped to her knees and bowed her head as low as she could manage. 'My Queen, the pleasure is entirely mine.'

Falina gave a slight nod, graciously accepting the praise. 'I saw a statue in your stronghold of a woman I am told is Adunola Voltaine.'

Ayeesha nodded. 'All of my authority in the Black Hammer Clan flows from her. When people in Alara prayed, it was Yami who answered. It is said that when you build a shrine for your dead, you open the door for them to become an agbara. Our prayer is that door is opened for her.'

Falina touched Ayeesha's shoulder, helping her to her feet. 'A good omen then, that her son Ajanla rides with us.'

Maka Naki cleared his throat. 'The boy had not returned to the Eredo before we left.'

Falina frowned. 'Then his spirit rides with us.'

Maka Naki nodded. 'Too true.'

Ayeesha raised an eyebrow. 'May I ask, my Queen, how many rode with you from the Eredo, not including spirits?'

'We have a force of about four thousand. Nearly a thousand of them are shadowwielders,' Maka Naki said.

Alangba tapped his shoulder. 'A good number.'

'Their leader is a battle-tested warrior. She will be—'

'Since tonight is about entrances,' came a voice as the door creaked open. A woman stepped into the farmhouse with an iron helmet fashioned in the image of a Viper. She pulled the visor open and bowed low to the queen.

Queen Falina inclined her head. 'I greet you, Zarcanis.'

The Viper straightened. 'We are ready to move, Your Majesty. The hour has come.'

Ayeesha took a step forward. 'I was told you had six chiefs, but I only see five here.'

Falina blinked. 'One of our chiefs has ... defected – seduced by the promises of our enemies.'

Ayeesha grimaced. 'How much information did the traitor have?'

'A lot of it. Chief Karile was the finest mindwalker we had amongst us; we must assume they know everything.'

Falina glanced at Okafor Blaise then at Toro Haba of the

Village of Songs. 'Except, of course, for our strategy. Which we have only communicated in the hand-signals of Korin.'

Okafor cleared his throat. 'We breach the Citadel gates and move directly for the House of Palman. The governor-general is there; the real one. If we can take control of the House of Palman, Basmine is ours — for the night, at least.'

'Zaminu knows that as well as we do. The House of Palman has always been the most heavily guarded place in Basmine,' Ayeesha said.

Okafor nodded. 'We expect robust opposition. There is no getting around it. We will face the finest of the consular guard within those walls. They will be armed in ways we cannot match and will know the terrain better than we ever could.'

Alangba sniffed. 'They have the better ground, they have the numbers, they have the experience, they have the weapons.'

'We have the Viper,' Gaitan said.

Alangba glanced up at the big warrior and nodded. 'True enough.'

'And some of us have experience too,' Mandla added. 'Isn't that right, Gaitan?'

Gaitan rolled his shoulders. 'I was born with soldiers battering down my mother's door. War is a homecoming.'

Okafor cleared his throat. 'We must not forget Zaminu. He is a ruthless man who knows how to win a battle.'

'So, we don't make it a battle,' Falina said.

Alangba blinked. 'What do you mean, my Queen?'

'They will be expecting a fight and we cannot beat them at their own game.' She glanced at Maka Naki. 'If we go to battle with the Palmaine tonight — we will lose.'

A sobering word that, but someone had to say it. Better a queen that says it how it is than one who hides from the truth.

'So what do we do?' Alangba asked.

Mandla stared at Falina with an intensity that gave the impression of a silent conversation taking place. He nodded once as though giving her a final note of encouragement. 'Long live the golden Eagle.'

Falina bit her bottom lip and stared up at the ceiling. 'Every strong tower has a back door.' Slowly, she picked up the beaded crown and placed it at the centre of her head. Everyone bowed their heads. Her voice came out in a whisper that carried throughout the farmhouse. 'We do what they always do to us.' She glanced at Alangba and started to sing.

'And if the soil is dry?'

'We water it with blood.'

60

Testimony Time

RUMI

Through the gaping door of the stone pergola, Jarishma stood with his back to them. His arms were raised high and his calves were marbled with veins. The Door of Testimony was a whirlpool of black, purple and blue, shifting this way and that under a torrent of celestial wind.

The jungle mage spoke in sharp Mushiain and thrust his hand into the Door of Testimony. 'Molewa, my precious daughter, I call you forth.'

The Door of Testimony seemed to quiver and swoon around Jarishma's hand and his body went taut as though pulled by an invisible string. Then, like a fish from the river, a figure leaped out from the Door of Testimony.

It was a little girl, her hair tangled about her head like an underused play doll. Her eyes were big and wide, and her mouth was a perfect facsimile of her father's.

Rumi stood transfixed as Jarishma dropped to his knees and gathered his daughter in an embrace. 'Molewa,' he breathed. 'Oh, precious Molewa. You are mine again.'

Rumi, Nataré and Agbako seemed to stop at the same time. Though they had come with plans to kill the man, there seemed something especially wrong about contaminating that moment. Even Hagen went perfectly still.

Molewa pressed her mouth to her father's ear and spoke. Her voice was clear as glass but strong as iron. 'I watched you, Father.'

Jarishma gave a start as though taken aback with the weight and timbre of her voice. Though she was a little girl, she spoke with the voice of a grown woman.

'I watched everything you did,' Molewa said. 'You killed people. You drank their blood. You broke every natural law and vow. You betrayed every friend. You sought the assistance of demons and now, you have broken kola nut with those who killed the gods of your ancestors. You did all this in my own name. I knew no peace in the Higher World. Watching you and seeing what you have become was a pain far worse than death to me. I blamed myself ten thousand times.'

Jarishma's reply was a broken whisper. 'I did it all for you.'

Molewa drew back from him. 'It was *never* about me. Never. Not once did you visit my resting place. Never did you speak my name in prayer.'

'It was too painful, it hurt too much to see your grave,' Jarishma insisted.

Molewa's voice fell like a hammer. 'Lies! Be honest with yourself for once, even if never before. What will you do now that I have returned? What tortured cause will you adopt as a camouflage? What will you tell them in the Eredo about how you brought me back? You think I will support your lies?'

'I did it all for you,' he whimpered.

'You revelled in your story – the jungle mage whose mourning drove him into the forest. Tell the truth now. Your crusade was not because you loved me; it was because you felt insulted by Dara.'

A long moment of silence passed, then Jarishma rose slowly to his feet. 'Dara let you die. After everything I gave to the cause. Every sacrifice that I made. He is no god of mine.'

His voice was deep as the grave, with a tremor in it that prophesied violence.

Molewa met his gaze. 'There we see you. The mask has fallen. You couldn't become a god, so you decided to become a devil.'

Jarishma snatched her by the throat with both hands, raising her off her feet. 'There are no gods, Molewa, only devils who pretend.'

With that, he threw her back into the gaping Door of Testimony.

Rumi stood, still as a statue, horrified by what he had seen, then he drew breath and stepped into the stone pergola.

Jarishma stood with a look of shameless triumph. Now dispossessed of his mournful disguise, he looked every part a thing of the dark.

Hagen lunged at the jungle mage but Jarishma waved his hand and the lionhound flew sidewards. His howl cut off as he hit the wall with a wet thunk and slid broken to the ground, leaving a smear of blood.

Nataré nocked and loosed an arrow so fast that Rumi heard it before he saw the movement. Jarishma caught it between his fingers and broke the stem in two. 'Arrows?' he asked with a sneer. 'No.' He shot out a hand and a thick shadow blow to the stomach folded her over.

Rumi swung the halberd just as Agbako hurled a dagger. Jarishma dodged the dagger and brought a sword of shadow that sent the halberd spinning from Rumi's grip and landing a few paces away.

Rumi lunged for his weapon but Jarishma jumped at the same time. They ended in a rolling tangle and Jarishma gained the upper hand. He raised a fist and brought it down in a shadow-encrusted hammer blow.

'What did you think would happen here?' Jarishma snarled.

'That you and your friends could defeat me?' He brought his fist down again and Rumi blinked out of consciousness for a moment. 'I gripped the shadow before you were even an idea. Even a possibility.' He punched again.

Nataré stumbled to her feet, loosing two more arrows. Jarishma blocked them in the shadow and struck her down with a blow hard enough to kill. Agbako screamed something but Jarishma sent him flying through the door of the pergola.

Rumi shouted the name of thunder and lightning but no answer came this time.

Jarishma wiped blood from his mouth, grinning as he reached for the halberd. 'You know,' he began, 'a part of me would have never wanted this to end this way.'

'You don't have to kill us,' Rumi breathed. 'It's not too late to stop now.'

Jarishma gave the Door of Testimony a long look then closed his eyes as his shoulders drooped. He turned back to Rumi, his eyes dead and cold. 'I don't have the story I want, Rumi. Not while you still live.'

Rumi rolled onto his side. 'I will tell anyone whatever you want, just, please – let us go.'

Jarishma let out a breath as he gripped the halberd. 'I am sorry it has to be this way.'

He raised the halberd high with his face one of colourless determination. Then he brought the spike down on his own chest. The point broke through his sternum in an explosion of blood and Jarishma's eyes seemed at once shocked and elated. With the axe wound still gaping, he lifted the weapon again and brought it crashing into his own face, splitting himself to the skull from his forehead all the way down to the cleft of his chin. He let out a sound like a gargle of laughter as he fell for the very last time.

Rumi stared at Jarishma's skull as his shadow pooled and a black, inky substance returned for the final time to its master. He twisted the halberd, wrenching it free and saw then the powdered dust of a charm along the handle. The same thing that had killed the jungle mage's daughter. The isakaba charm.

Rumi drew in breath. He thought back to what Sameer had told him before they left Jarishma's grove. *I added a personal touch to your halberd. You'll laugh when you figure that one out.* He smiled but didn't laugh – not without the author of the joke there. 'Dara, thank you for my friend, Sameer.'

As though in response to his name, Hagen barked.

Rumi moved to help Nataré to her feet and found her hair matted to her head in blood. His heart shuddered as he noticed the flattened cheeks; the vacant eyes.

'No,' he whispered, pulling her close. Her clothes were soaked through with blood, too. His heartbeat quickened. 'Please... please... Dara, please. I've lost too much. I can't lose her. Not now.'

'Then bring her back,' Agbako said.

Rumi glanced up at the big witch doctor. Agbako met his gaze and pointed at the Door of Testimony. Marked along the frame were words in ancient Mushiain.

'It's your choice, you have one name to call.'

He stepped close and raised his hands high, just as he had seen Jarishma do. He spoke the first words of prayer that his mother taught him. 'Awon mimo Alaini!'

The Door of Testimony bucked and rippled as though in reaction to his words. He lifted Nataré up and carefully pushed her through the Door of Testimony. It accepted her without protest.

Seven words granted a soul passage to the Originate. Rumi spoke them clear. 'No man can kill a true ghost.'

The Door of Testimony stopped writhing and settled into a pool of clear midnight blue. He dipped his hand into the pool and it was like reaching into thick custard. He had come here to bring his mother back but now was given an impossible choice. *Nataré. Ahwazi. Sameer. Yami.* Their faces flashed through his mind and he could only call one back. Abruptly, a hand closed around his wrist. He pulled against it, but it pulled back harder, dragging him into the door.

'Rumi,' Agbako called out, but he was already being dragged inside. 'Rumi!'

He was pulled all the way in. The transition was immediate, but still sickening. For a fraction of a second, he was horribly sure his stomach was going to fall out, but before he could puke, it was all over.

He opened his eyes as a wall of heat struck him in the face. The sun in the sky seemed low and close. As though this world was nearer to it than the one from which he had come. A towering ivory gate lay just ahead, through which was a stream of endless, manicured lawns. The smell of grilled pineapples was heavy on the air. He felt... no pain, only... rapturous bliss, joy overflowing.

'You should not be here,' came a very familiar voice.

Rumi's heart dropped to his stomach and he pressed his hands to the floor in obeisance. 'Yami.'

She stood, proud as a warrior. A light to her dark face like the moon glinting on a pool of oil. Though she was the same woman he had always known, there was something unknowable in her countenance that had not been there before.

She smiled at him. 'My son.'

He lunged at her, pulling her into an embrace. 'I knew you would come back to me. I knew it.' Hot tears ran down his face as his grip tightened and he pressed his head into her neck.

She scratched the back of his neck and drew back from him. 'I cannot return with you to the Lower World, my son. Things are different now.'

Rumi looked up at her. 'What do you mean?'

But he saw it in her stare. Saw it in the way her hair didn't move even when the breeze touched it. Saw it in her eyes most of all.

'I am an agbara now,' she said, 'and the time of the brave cometh again for the gods. My place is here in the spirit lands. Do not call me back.'

'Then let me stay with you,' Rumi said.

She shook her head. 'You cannot. Besides, that isn't what you truly want, is it?'

She gestured with her chin, towards the Door of Testimony. Through it, he saw Nataré's face – warm and inviting as always.

'I like her,' Yami said, with a smile.

'I cannot do this without you,' Rumi said. 'I cannot keep doing this all without you.'

'And who said you are without me? Do you think you would have come this far without the favour of your ancestors?'

Rumi thought back to his fight with the Priest of Vultures and lowered his head. 'No.'

Adunola touched his chin. 'You have never been alone.'

She turned towards the gate and pointed. 'Look.'

A tall figure was approaching. As he stepped into the light, Rumi took in his face. His jaw had thickened and he walked with his shoulders thrown back. His eyes were calm and thoughtful and his chest was marked with the blue and white paint of a spirit.

Morire beat his chest four times and pointed to the sky. *Always with you.*

Rumi closed his eyes, lowered his head and repeated the gesture to his brother.

The Door of Testimony made a shrieking sound and Adunola's smile faded. 'You have to leave, now,' she hissed. 'Let us go, son; you have our permission to move on with your life. You have different priorities now and I need you to take that responsibility. Now, get back to the Eredo, all of you.'

Rumi blinked. 'Yami, why do—'

'Now!' she hissed and she threw him through the Door of Testimony.

That sharp, sickening feeling followed as he hit stone on the other side – back in the Lower World. Agbako stood over him.

'What happened?' he asked.

Rumi wasted no time. He reached back into the Door of Testimony and called the name that few but him knew. 'Nataré, the woman I love, I call you forth.'

A hand gripped him about the wrist and he pulled with all his force. Nataré fell through the door, whole again. Her eyes knowing and serene. She looked at him for half a moment, then she turned and pointed at the door. 'Close it!'

A thick bull horn emerged from the Door of Testimony. Yami swirled into view, grabbing the bull horn with both hands and pushing it back into the door. 'Leave this place now, Rumi,' she hissed.

Rumi stared in horror as she tried to force the creature back, shouting, 'Elesekan, this is not your place.'

Agbako grabbed Rumi, pulling him out to leave. The earth shook. Showers of sand, peeled off from the stone pergola, trickled from the ceiling.

'I am Iyaloja, agbara of commerce and trade,' Yami snarled as she wrestled with the horned beast. 'Protector of women and children.' She turned towards Rumi. 'Irumide, I give you authority to read my book.'

The horned beast knocked her back, nearly goring her to the wall. Rumi caught a glimpse of the creature's shadowed face. A man with eyes dark as mud and the horns of a bull.

'Run, Rumi, now,' his mother breathed.

That put the fear of Dara in him like nothing before. 'Let's go.'

Nataré obliged. Rumi lifted Hagen into his arms, gave Yami one last look, then he turned and ran. The pillars of the stone pergola shook as they fled. The struggle between Yami and the beast would bring it all down for good.

'Did you find what you came looking for?' Agbako asked.

Rumi gritted his teeth. 'Yes. Then I lost it forever.'

61

War Begins

RENIKE

'They are opening the gates,' someone whispered.

Renike's jaw throbbed. The plan had worked. They were crouched down in a caravan halfway down what the Palmaine believed was a royal convoy. The ornamented blue carriage of the governor-general ran at the centrepiece of their procession and the Citadel welcomed them in as though to do them honour. *Big mistake.*

Crouched down beside her was Jaja, coiled tight as a snake, ready and willing. The caravan just ahead of them had the Viper waiting just so.

Renike watched through a crack at the window as they filed in. She had been allowed into the Citadel before but never welcomed. A part of her wanted to laugh.

They kept moving until the very last caravan was through the entranceway and then came to a stop.

'What do we do now?' someone whispered.

'Wait for the signal,' someone said back.

'What's the signal?' Renike asked.

A lion exploded from one of the caravans, pouncing on an unsuspecting watchman.

Renike drew in breath. 'Signal enough for me.'

Fighters spilled out from the caravans like bees from the hive, launching themselves at the guards who had let them in.

A great shout came from a Citadel watchman as a shadow-wielder emerged from what he'd thought was a caravan laden with gifts.

'Close the gates!' someone shouted. It was far too late. A campaign after the election.

Zarcanis's voice reverberated through the wind. 'Shadow-wielders, call your shadows!'

Renike's eyes snapped open as she called her shadow and was struck sharp by a thick vein of awesome power. She pulled her long blade slowly from its sheath, frowning as the steel scraped against the leather. Something about that sound had always made her a little afraid. Some Seedlings obsessed over their weapons. Spent hours cleaning and swinging them but Renike had always kept a healthy fear of her sword. Fighting with a blade raised the stakes. It was one thing to risk a bloodied nose, it was quite another to risk an opened throat. She had dreamed of this day, half a hundred times and now here it was.

'It's time,' Jaja said with a grin.

What a time indeed.

They sprang out from the caravan with weapons raised. Shadowwielders were already killing the Citadel watch while civilians ran and screamed. Against the shadow, mere men were no match. They wilted in minutes and before long, the Shadow Order stood unopposed.

'To me!' Zarcanis shouted.

They moved as one. The Viper didn't have to shout for her voice to carry. Her voice was the closest thing to god on the battle field.

The Viper thumped a spear on the ground as the unsuspecting

people of the Citadel screamed and ran. No one else could be so calm in chaos.

'First-year Seedlings must stay here and guard the gate,' she said. 'The men coming from outside the Citadel are not likely to have guns. They are no match for you in a fight of blade on blade. Make sure they learn that.'

She gave Renike a pointed look. 'This is no time to prove yourselves. There will be plenty of time for that. Nothing fancy. Just survive.'

The Viper turned back to the rest of the shadowwielders. 'The rest of you know how this ends – death or glory. No retreat. No surrender. Anyone caught running and I will…'

She didn't finish the sentence, just raised her chin a little and frowned. Everyone got the gist of it.

A few Truetrees beat their spears on their chests in understanding. There would be no retreat or surrender. Better to die fighting than risk having to explain to the Viper why you ran.

Zarcanis arched her back in a stretch and limbered up. 'We fight in threes. Break their spirit. Show them that they have no monopoly on terror.'

The Sulis shouted their affirmation and with that, Zarcanis straightened and slammed her helmet shut. 'When this is all said and done, may we be remembered.' She raised her gaze to the skies and called her shadow. Neat and fine as a cape – an almost perfect synthesis of shadow and substance. A few gasped in awe. Newcomers to the spectacle.

She pointed her blade at the House of Palman. 'Stop at nothing and victory is ours.' Then she took off at a run headed for – to Renike's surprise – the Golden Room.

Renike watched her go, awed and afraid all at once. Someone running past knocked her shoulder and her blade clattered to the ground. She moved to pick it up and stumbled over a loose cobblestone.

'Sort it out,' Jaja hissed, helping Renike back to her feet.

Her heart pounded against her chest as she joined the gathered Seedlings. Their orders were simple – stop anyone from coming through the gates. Easy enough to understand – but it was unclear what they would come up against. The most dangerous fighters were within the Citadel but there were still blade-wielding soldiers to fear on the other side of the divide.

Two men of the Citadel watch lay dead and discarded just ahead. Renike looked away. There was something raw and real about seeing a dead body up close – you never got used to it. A question flared up in Renike's mind. *Are you ready to kill?* Her answer didn't matter, she'd find out soon enough.

'Here they come,' Jaja said, gesturing forward with his chin.

A gaggle of armour-clad consular guard boiled out towards the gates, screaming the name of their god and king. Renike gritted her teeth and hefted her blade. In that moment she had an answer. *I am ready to kill.*

Strange how that happens. One minute you are considering death, the next you are considering murder. Worryingly instinctive.

The Citadel grew quieter, but for the rising patter of boots on cobblestone. The Seedlings stood in a scattered huddle ready for a night that might be their last. No one spoke.

Kharmine was down on one knee. His eyes closed, head bowed. More than likely, he was praying to the demon that lived in his mind.

Jaja swung his sword in an arc of practice – his breathing loud and heavy.

Renike closed her eyes and whispered. '*I am not a flower. I am an iroko tree.*' Her voice was hoarse but she clung to those words as though they were life itself.

A voice bolted out from the gathered mass of seedlings. Unmistakable in its depth and pitch.

'They are here,' Kharmine said.

Renike's eyes snapped open. The enemy had come into view. Moonlight gleamed against their silver-white swords as they marched forwards with weapons raised high. There were at least thirty of them, likely more. At that distance, she could pick out faces. They almost didn't seem human. Just a nameless, soulless enemy.

Drawing in a breath, Renike raised her sword.

'We fight in triangles. Same as every other shadowwielder. The triangles don't break. They never break,' Kharmine said.

Renike glanced up at the tall Seedling and he stared back at her. 'I'll join your triangle,' he said.

'Watch out!' Jaja shouted.

An arrow hissed past, barely missing Renike's head. The guards had closed the gap. Another arrow nicked at Jaja's ear as they returned fire with a volley of their own. A screaming man crashed into them and Renike gasped as she batted his sword aside, his shoulder went down at an awkward angle and her sword bit into his clavicle. He let out a shrill cry and tried to bring his shield around with his other hand. Renike was equal to it. Wrenching her sword free from his shoulder she ducked beneath his failing swing and stabbed him in the stomach as hard as she could.

'Sheggin' bastard,' she yelled as she stuck him through. Where had that come from? She didn't know. She had always been the one to warn those around her against such language. Her dead father's words resounded in her mind. *Sometimes you need bad language to talk about bad things.*

She drew in shadow as another soldier came at her. Their swords clanged thrice before she kicked his kneecap to knock him off balance. He swung wildly at her with a back-fist, missing by a hair. As he tried to straighten, she pulled her security knife free and buried it to the cross-piece in his armpit through the gap in his gambeson. He let out one sharp breath and the strength went out of him as he dropped.

She glanced up as an arrow, destined for her forehead, shot towards her. Kharmine stepped in front of it with a shield of shadow. She whirled as another man, big bastard, jumped forward with an upraised warhammer.

'Native sheg,' he hissed. 'Die you b—'

Jaja's sword skewered his cheek and came out from the other side, cutting off his insult. Renike saw the moment death touched him. A flutter of the eyes and the hammer fell from his lifeless hands. Through the wound in his face, she saw stark-white teeth closed in an eternal grin.

One of their own, stuck through with arrows, kicked at the air — spasming as he died. Renike looked away.

Kharmine's voice cut through the night. 'Keep going!'

The clouds above belched with thunder and rain fell. Just what they needed. Not enough that they were in a bloody melee, but now there was water enough to make you slip and fall.

Renike squinted through the crowd of bodies when she heard a sound unlike any that had come before. The report of a gunshot was so stark and sudden that, for a moment, all the noise of battle seemed to fade into silence.

A Seedling lay dead beside her, a hole the size of a kola nut cratered on the side of his head. Another gunshot cracked and a Seedling went down. She saw another Seedling turn, run and get gunned down.

The men here were not supposed to have guns.

'Hold,' Kharmine screamed. 'Do not let them break our will. Stand this once and face them down.'

Renike lowered her chin as a soldier lunged at her. She brought her sword down like a hammer, splitting his face in two. A spatter of blood hit her eyes, blinding her. She cleared her sight just in time to see a heavy sword spit out at her. She hissed and dodged as the weapon whistled past. Another figure moved at the edge of her vision but Jaja moved faster, parrying the first blow and then driving his sword through his chin. Renike brought her sword round in a backhand and slapped a man aside, making him stumble forward. Biting down on shadow she kicked him down and hacked away at him. A uniformed soldier came for Jaja's unguarded side but Kharmine flung his sword sidearm and it opened a line of red across the man's neck. He went limp and fell over sending both Jaja and Renike stumbling back.

Ahead a man aimed a rifle and fired. Kharmine shifted his head and the shot whistled past. Before the man could aim again, Kharmine's sword whipped out at him, lashing his head from his shoulders.

He leaped over a waiting corpse and pressed forward on a lone watchman with a gun. He was too slow in aiming his weapon and lost his life trembling to try. His companion a few yards behind screamed the word 'Demons', dropped his weapon and fled.

'A gun doesn't make a man a warrior,' Kharmine snarled. 'Test for the warriors!'

You didn't need N'Goné's knack to see what emotion he was burning. *Rage, clear as day.*

The soldiers, overwhelmed by the Seedlings' vicious defence, started to retreat.

'Press them,' someone shouted over the din. They were of one mind. They pressed the soldiers until they took off at a total run.

'I told you!' Kharmine shouted, his arm and blade wet with sticky blood. 'They are cowards in disguise.'

Renike's heart was pumping like a Shinala at the races. The rain bucketing down did nothing to blur her vision. She saw the entire battlefield in shocking clarity. Fear and excitement had mingled till they were completely indistinguishable and her whole body throbbed with every heartbeat. There were dead bodies everywhere. A wounded Seedling behind her was screaming his lungs out but Renike barely heard it.

Renike gritted her teeth, refusing to let her mind linger on the thought that had just crossed it. *Run – you should not be here. Run while you still can.*

Jaja spat a gob of blood out and sheathed his sword.

They had won. Done what they needed to – broken the Palmaine resolve and driven them into the bushes. A heroic effort – that much was clear. *So why don't I feel heroic?*

Kharmine slapped Renike's shoulder and squeezed her neck. 'Try not to think about it now. You'll have time enough for that. For now, just thank the gods above that you are still alive.'

Renike did just that, silently, as she let out a heavy breath.

Her shadow squirmed as she sensed a large host of shadowwielders rushing towards the gates. She glanced over her shoulder. 'We have reinforcements?'

Something struck Jaja and his head exploded like a burst tomato.

Kharmine turned slowly and narrowed his eyes. He drew in a sharp breath and then slammed his helmet shut again. 'Not reinforcements. Enemies.'

Renike stared in horror at Jaja's ruined corpse. What sort of weapon could kill a shadowwielder from that distance? As though to give her a taste, something whistled past her ear and struck the man behind her – sending him down and spattering blood. Her ears were ringing so loud the only thing she could hear was her pounding heart.

In a matter of seconds, seven shadowwielders were down. Whatever was firing at them was no normal weapon. A part of her wanted to fold. To drop her weapon and run for cover; but a deeper, more essential part of her stood firm. Her days of running and hiding were long behind her. No longer was she a flower.

Kharmine snarled something and prepared to charge. She glanced up, steadied herself, and then she was running too. Weapon raised, eyes wide, ready for anything.

★ ★ ★

Lethi was alive with the shadow. The sounds of fighting were in the air and his heart pounded like a war drum. With the shadow in him, the fire of pain burning behind his knee had receded to a dull ache. So long as he held the shadow, he could bear the pain; the more he accepted the pain, the easier it got.

Behind him were a battalion of fighters, under his command. 'Soldiers of the Light' he called them, despite the fact they had all touched the dark.

'There,' Lethi said, pointing towards the Citadel gates. Fire cast the night into brightness ahead.

A group of screaming men ran towards them with weapons raised. Lethi stretched out his hands and a night-black rifle formed in his grip. He grinned, drawing in breath as he squinted over the crosshair.

He gave a start. The men running were not enemies. They wore the uniforms of the Citadel watch and had the four-point star pressed on their chests. His eyes widened. They were not running to fight — they were running for their lives. Lethi lowered his gun.

What are they running from?

That was when he noticed the small party who stood at the gates — about a dozen of them. From the way they stood in defensive triangles, he recognised exactly what they were. The rebels had left a small force to guard the gates into the Citadel — *clever*.

Lethi took a step forward and raised his rifle, aiming at the biggest target amongst them.

'Goodnight,' he said, pulling hard on the trigger.

His aim was perfect, his release pure. Yet, somehow, he missed. It wasn't quite that he missed. More that the figure had moved with such sudden speed that the bullet missed its mark.

'Shege,' he breathed.

He drew back and raised a looking glass to his face, peering through. Thick wisps of black smoke oozed from their skin as they stood with storybook calm. In their hands were long black blades and spears that did not resemble any steel you could make with hammer and iron.

He lowered the looking glass, his heart thumping. *Shadowmen.*

The fleeing Citadel watchmen darted past them.

'Demons,' someone screamed. 'Demons!'

Lethi's jaw tightened. This was it — their first encounter with real, fighting shadowmen. If he had to guess, the shadowmen at the gates were the newest recruits — likely close in training and experience to his own group, who had followed him on the merest whim. He was excited and terrified all at the same time.

'Soldiers of the Light,' Lethi shouted. 'Call your shadows.'

Lethi's men obeyed as he tightened the knot on his gambeson. 'Darkness can *never* triumph over light.'

He trudged forward and spoke under his breath. 'Aim your weapons.'

His men raised their rifles. Each was black as pitch with a bolt that didn't move when you fired. Loba had said Lethi didn't respect the art in things – how wrong he was. With just one small, ingenious use of shadow, Lethi had created a rifle with a single tubular magazine that you never had to reload – bullets of shadow that could burst a man's head from two hundred metres away. *Innovation is an equaliser.*

The shadowmen saw him coming but didn't move. They were as ready as the sun for its rise. As they drew closer he saw them set their feet and take up their fighters' stances. They meant to dance their blades with him. He laughed as he stopped short, raising his rifle.

'I'd sooner shoot you than stab you,' he whispered to himself.

He raised his weapon; the trigger so soft that it was almost teasing him to shoot. He fired hard. The head of one of the shadowmen exploded as a pellet of pure shadow perforated his skull.

Someone screamed as Lethi fired another shot. It hit another one of them in his chest and he went down in a spatter of blood.

One of the shadowmen, a tall one, waved a hand, beckoning him forward.

Disbelieving, Lethi aimed his weapon at the tall shadowman. 'Darkness flees in the presence of light.'

He fired again and missed. *Impossible.*

There are barely twenty of them. He told himself. *They are mere recruits.*

Nothing served to stop his heart from thumping. Even as they went down, they kept coming. The tall shadowman screamed in the Common Tongue. 'What a blessing it is to kill our torments.'

Then – sudden as the storm – the shadowmen were running towards them. His men who had been firing without reprive, seemed to hesitate.

'Keep shooting!' Lethi screamed.

They obeyed but the shadowmen didn't stop running, even as their comrades fell. *They are going to get to us.*

Lethi raised his blade just in time as one of the rebels made an effort at knocking him down. Their blades kissed and he drew back, adopting the old soldier's form that his father had unknowingly taught him. He swung his blade and tried a side-step but slipped in a puddle of mud. His assailant stood over him with blade raised high. He stared up at her. *Only a girl.* Barely twenty if his guess was right. About to kill a man in war. No winners all around.

She met his eyes and for a moment he saw hesitation in her. It was just enough, the small splice of time he needed to kick out at her lead leg. She jerked back, slipping in the mud as her sword fell from her hand. As she fell, Lethi kicked himself up onto his feet and then he was running.

'Don't let him get past,' someone shouted but he was already through. He had left his men behind to fight for themselves. He had to get to the House of Palman. That was the only thing that mattered. If the holy temple fell, then all was lost. As he ran he recalled the words of Belize's last dialogue. *And so he dived into hell; for the angels offered sanctimony and the devils offered exculpation.*

★ ★ ★

Alangba smiled as a tall, slender man opened the barred dungeon door. 'Good evening. We were told to bring a new prisoner down,' Alangba said, gesturing to Ladan who he held roughly by the collar.

The slender man gave Alangba an unimpressed look and glanced down at the grubby state of his uniform. 'I wasn't told about any—'

Alangba stabbed him in his stomach, hard and fast. The man gave a shocked groan that reminded Alangba of a dog barking, then he fell into Alangba's hands spilling blood down the front of his shirt.

'Let's go,' Alangba said, beckoning his men inside. The Chainbreakers streamed into the dungeon carrying burlap sacks, full to bursting.

It was a long, dark cellar with iron-barred cells carved into the wall. The stones in the cobbled ceiling looked ancient and strong. Why a music theatre needed a dungeon was something he could not understand.

'Lay them down everywhere,' Alangba said. 'Be generous with it.'

The men obeyed, setting down the small black orbs in clusters around the dungeon, throwing them into the empty cells and along the dungeon floor.

Alangba unfurled a long black rope of straw and lined it around the edge of the wall before slinking it around the central pillar.

'No Music, where are the matches?' Ladan asked.

No Music touched his pockets, then the inner lining of his jacket, then slapped his forehead and made an apologetic gesture to Alangba. *I forgot.*

Ladan shook his head. 'I don't know why we always trust you with bringing the matches.'

Alangba produced a match box of his own. 'We don't.'

Ladan smiled and gestured for the others to leave as they filed out of the dungeon.

'I'll be right behind you,' Alangba said. 'Get everyone out.'

Ladan kissed his forehead and chin. 'I will.'

When the dungeon was empty Alangba struck a match to flame and set the straw alight. He was about to leave when there was a rattle of chains from the darkened cell at the corner of the dungeon. *I thought they were all empty.*

The flame was burning through the straw, edging closer to a cluster of orbs. Alangba turned once more to leave but the chains rattled again.

'Shege,' he breathed as he ran towards the sound. A man was inside, dressed in rags and huddled in the dark corner of his cell. His face was dark as gun smoke with blisters around his lips and ears. His arms bore the pink-white marks of torture. The smell of him made Alangba want to break his own nose.

'Don't leave me here, please,' the prisoner begged.

Alangba tried to force the padlock open but it wouldn't budge. He glanced down at the slowly travelling flame as it burned through the straw.

'Dara's might,' Alangba breathed.

The prisoner clutched at the bars, pressing his face to the iron. 'Please,' he begged. His eyes wide.

Alangba let out a sharp breath. 'I'm sorry... I can't help you.'

The flame had almost reached the orbs now. Alangba tried to stamp the fire out but the flame had gone to the core of the straw. There was no stopping it now.

The prisoner pulled against the bars. 'Please! Please! Please!'

Alangba winced as the prisoner howled. There was nothing to be done – he had no time. He was at the door when he spotted the golden gleam of keys on the dead doorman's belt hole.

He gritted his teeth. 'Shege... shege...'

Ladan screamed his name from the top of the stairs. 'Alangba! What the sheg are you doing?'

Alangba grimaced, tried again to stamp the flame out, slowing it for the moment, snatched the keys from the floor and darted to the cell. He fumbled for the keyhole and turned twice, ripping the gate open. The prisoner stepped out from the cage into the light. A big man; taller than Alangba by far with eyes dark as a vulture. His entire body was covered in torture marks and his scarred knuckles bore the tell-tale marks of a lifetime's worth of bare-handed brawls. Across one side of his chest was the big, ugly tattooed imprint of a single word; *Freedom*. A killer, make no mistake.

'Let's go!' Alangba hissed.

They took off at a dead run. For a big man, the prisoner was surprisingly quick. They were halfway up the stairs when there came a sound that could only be from the pits of damnation. Hell's scream of triumph. A ripping, snarling, biting sound like all the world was being ripped apart. The floor beneath them gave way as the building collapsed. A brick from the ceiling struck Alangba at the side of his eye and he stumbled forward. The prisoner paid him no mind and offered no assistance. He just kept running up the stairs. *Serves me right for being a bloody idiot.*

Smoke was everywhere now and Alangba could barely see, let alone breathe. He coughed up flecks of blood as he climbed on all fours up the stairs. A hand grabbed him by the wrist, hauling him up.

He glanced up, expecting Ladan. 'I knew you would—'

His sentence cut off short. It wasn't Ladan.

Zaminu smiled down at him, with a rictus grin. 'We meet again Alangba.'

Alangba gave a start. 'How?'

Zaminu only smiled. 'And the Son of Despair shall cast down the holy temple and declare himself Lord of All.' He grabbed Alangba by his collar and dragged him up the last of the stairs – his expression utterly triumphant. 'Let the tribulation of gods begin.'

A TESTIMONY OF BLOOD

★ ★ ★

Lethi raced past the gates of the House of Palman. It was quiet – no signs of fighting at all. He was approaching the door when something fell from the sky. It landed with a metal thunk, biting four inches into the cobblestoned street. The four-point star. Flames sprouted from the foundation of the House of Palman and the building was crumbling.

'No,' he breathed, staring up.

The holy temple had fallen.

A voice from behind made Lethi freeze.

'Do not despair, my child – all things work together for the good of the Light.'

Lethi glanced back at the bishop of Basmine. He wore a golden tiara beset with jewels, over a white kaftan and golden chasuble. Seeing how he was dressed, Lethi's stomach fell.

'You knew this was coming. You let it happen.'

The bishop nodded. 'It is part of our plan.'

'What sheggin' plan?' Lethi hissed. 'This will lead to war. Thousands will die.'

'Destruction is another form of creation,' he said, spreading his arms wide, and Lethi saw shadows in the shapes of men appear. A slice of moonlight illuminated the glint of steel and the glares of stone. Soldiers, hundreds of them – all wearing the uniform of the Meladroni.

There was something strange about the bishop. The way he stood, the way his chasuble didn't seem to move in the wind. The moon fell on him and Lethi realised what it was. *He has no shadow.*

The bishop's grin widened. 'Seven is the number of completion. Seven days. Seven sins. Seven books in our holy scripture. And now seven priests of the Son. Welcome to a new beginning.'

62

The Old Dog Never Dies

RUMI

Rumi heaved out an exhausted breath as the Obayifo set him down before the wall-gate of the Eredo. A journey that had cost him much more than he had hoped to ever pay. He winced, recalling the two fresh graves at the summit of Erin-Olu. The softborn clan was no more. He drew in breath as he touched the cold metal of the flute again – reassuring himself that it was not a total expedition in failure.

A figure stood ahead as the Obayifo beat their wings to depart. 'Miselda?' he called out.

Relief flooded him as a familiar voice shouted back. 'Ajanla Erenteyo.'

They walked towards each other and met under the shadow of a tree. She pulled him into an embrace and he was so startled that he forgot to return the warmth.

'Did you find the Door of Testimony?' she asked.

Rumi gave a grim nod. 'We did.'

She glanced at Nataré and Agbako. 'What happened to the others? To Ahwazi and Sameer.'

Rumi felt like he'd been punched. 'We lost them.'

His voice came out in a ragged croak, his throat dry as bones. The three words were like new knife wounds. *We lost them.*

Miselda lowered her gaze and frowned. 'Then summon the

Obayifo – let us return to the Door of Testimony. Call them back.'

Rumi shook his head. 'The Door of Testimony has been destroyed now. There is no coming back for them.'

Hagen growled and their bond pulsed. He glanced at his lionhound and narrowed his eyes. A voice sounded in his head that nearly made him jump.

'I already told you – I'm still here.'

Rumi's heart lurched. It was Sameer's voice, sharp and clear – coming from the bond with Hagen.

'Sameer? How?'

'Mindwalking,' Sameer responded. 'When I knew my fight was lost, I hopped into Hagen's mind – figured it was a safe place to throw my consciousness. Body is gone, but I always thought the best thing about me was my mind. I have cheated death and I have access to Hagen's thoughts too – a translator for your little bond.'

Rumi laughed.

'What are you laughing at?' Nataré asked.

Rumi beamed. 'It's Sameer – he's in Hagen's mind. I can hear him through the bond.'

Nataré gave him a confused look.

'He threw his consciousness into Hagen's mind.'

Nataré smiled and let out a relieved breath, then narrowed her eyes. 'Does that mean Sameer can hear everything you think? Feel everything you feel? Know everything you know?'

Rumi realised what she was getting at and something shifted in his stomach.

'Don't worry, I can shift my consciousness to one of Hagen's blindspots whenever I need to give you some... privacy,' Sameer said. 'And the bond is only strong enough to link minds when we are close together.'

Rumi turned to Nataré. 'There are ways to close the link.'

Nataré narrowed her eyes. 'Good.'

They turned towards the Eredo. 'It's time we returned,' Rumi said.

Agbako raised a hand. 'Before we do.' He carved five thick marks into the bark of a tree and smeared them with blood. 'For those who fell.'

Ahwazi. Sameer. Horse and No-Horse.

'Who's the fifth fallen?' Miselda asked.

Agbako touched his chest where his tortoise used to be. 'Ijapa. He was my friend.'

Rumi touched the mark in the tree and as he did, it struck why he cared so much about his friends. 'Ahwazi and Sameer gave me the greatest gift I could ever receive – they made me a part of something.' He choked up as he spoke. 'The softborn clan. They were everything I couldn't be and made me everything I am. Took the hard steps. Faced the tough battles. Never ran. Never turned their backs. It won't be the same without you here.'

Sameer was silent in the bond, though Rumi could sense he was there. *Pain.* Regret flashed in his mind.

Miselda touched his shoulder. 'The softborn clan is forever.'

After a few moments of silent prayer, they turned towards the Eredo. It took Nataré a while to find her markings in the wall-gate and when they finally made it through the Thatcher, the Eredo was strangely quiet.

A sentry caught them as they made their way down but lowered his bow when he saw Nataré and Miselda.

'Where is everyone?' Rumi asked.

'Gone to war.'

They made their way towards the botanical ward. At the top of the tunnel, the large tank of Oké water that Miselda had brought back was being decanted into small skins. Uroma stood at the centre of the effort directing the others on how to make sure every drop was properly taken.

'Uroma,' Rumi called out.

She looked back at them, her eyes wide.

'Ajanla,' she breathed.

Rumi closed his eyes as he asked his question. 'Does the darkman live?'

Uroma lowered her voice. 'He does. He was the first to receive the water. He's been asking for you.'

Rumi smiled, and turned directly towards his father's room. Sprinting down the stairs, it took him only a short while to reach the botanical ward.

Griff was on his feet when Rumi walked in. When their eyes met, a look of true pride touched his face. 'You did it.'

Rumi nodded. 'The Old Dog Never Dies.'

Griff blinked. 'And Adunola?'

Rumi lowered his head. 'I saw her... and she told me to move on.'

Griff closed his eyes for a long moment. 'We had better get some rest then. I let my love fight alone once before – I won't do it again. We've got a battle to get to.'

Epilogue

The newest book in it was marked in fresh ink. The *Book of Iyaloja*, the agbara of the market. Rumi muttered a quiet prayer, then turned the page and began to read.

In my life, I made three great mistakes.

I was born on a market day in the hour when the sun and moon kissed. The year before I was born, an oracle came to our village and prophesied that an accursed child would soon be born with a preference for its left hand. The oracle's instruction to the council of judges was to kill the left-handed child. A child who would be sad when others were happy and quiet when others would speak. The oracle's description of me was accurate. My parents tried to stop me from using my left hand – but they couldn't teach it out of me. I tried to laugh when the other children did, but acting was never my gift. In the end, my father and I had to leave the village in the dead of the night to save my life.

Those were hard days, running from the judges. Sleep was short and light, food was scarce and small. My father taught me the Darani way – how to walk in it and to understand the power in a name. He taught me how to use a sword, battle-axe and spear. Taught me the ways of business and commerce. He was preparing me for the days to come.

The judges' assassins caught up to us in the end. My father killed all of them, but suffered a fatal wound in the process. Before he died he taught me one last thing: how to call my shadow. I was twelve.

I went after the judges. Found every single one of them and put an end to their hunt. Though I had sated the fires of my vengeance, I had committed an abomination against my own people and sought refuge in the only place that would accept me – the Darani Temple. I lived with the holy women of my time for eight years, learning their ways. I hoped to become a priestess myself but that was not the path that Dara cleared for me.

I met a man and he changed my life. He was Kasinabe and kind, two things I have always been soft for. We fell in love, and after I had been ordained as a priestess, I abandoned the holy temple. For a season, I had everything I wanted. But seasons come and go.

Palmaine ships had always come to our shores. At first as a venture of commerce. Then in the trading of flesh. In the final analysis, their business was blood and conquest. When war broke out, my lover wanted to go into hiding. He urged me to think of the children; our first had been born with a challenge in speaking and I was still heavy with the second. I had so much rage then. I could not see what he was trying to say. I wanted to fight. To protect people.

I named him a coward and took his name. That was my first mistake.

He never forgave me. He abandoned me and the pain of that decision made a home in my heart. I nurtured it, even as I continued in life.

My second son, a kukoyi child, was born soon after the father left. The boy was quick to both laughter and anger. He had the most marvellous gift of music that I made every effort to nurture. Music, I now understand, has a way of sanitising our banal emotions. It speaks for us with words that do not sting.

One day, while I prayed, an agbara appeared to me. It was Ilesha, agbara of crossroads and chaos. He brought troubling news. A war amongst the gods was coming to its crescendo and a Sixth Priest of the Son had arisen. Their Champion. Dark of hair and eye, with a double-axe wrought of light. The Sixth Priest, it was said, would bring an end to the last of the old gods. Ilesha asked me to learn the true name of this Sixth Priest – for I have always had a gift for names.

So, I followed the signs of this Sixth Priest. Journeyed as far as the spirit lands to know his work. He was more powerful than all the others and seemed to know the true names of all our gods. He knew their strengths and weaknesses and took them down one after the other. Though I saw his work, I came no closer to knowing his name. He was as subtle as he was severe.

Life went on and Ilesha appeared to me a second time. He told me of how my children would stand at the centre of the war of gods and that they had a special part in it. I denied it and did all I could to hide them from that world. I wanted to keep them safe. To protect them from it all. When a man called Tinu offered to take my children to the Eredo, I refused – for I feared if they knew their father and everything I had done to keep him from them, they would never forgive me.

That was my second mistake.

Destiny arrives whether we welcome it or not. I should have known that. Should have made better preparations. Should have told my sons their name. They are Omo-Xango. Descendants of the Alaafin. The agbara of thunder and lightning.

When I learned that the Priest of Vultures was coming for my son, I panicked. I sought help from all the places one never should. Not only the agbara of the light but also the agbara of the dark. I make no excuse for myself – I knew the difference between a dog and a wolf. This was my greatest mistake.

I made a deal with Ilesha. He gave me a kola nut to visit the spirit lands, where I could make my petition to Dara himself. I journeyed into the spirit lands – going as far as the hellmouth where Dara himself holds Billisi. I knew as soon as I arrived that something was not right but something stubborn in me urged me to keep going. I had come too far to turn back.

When I spoke into the hellmouth and called Dara's name, it was Billisi who answered. Her voice was strong, and though Dara held her back, his grip on her was weakening for the Son's hold on the world grows ever stronger. Desperate and afraid, it was to her I made my petition. When I realised what a mistake I had made, I fled, for Billisi spoke with the voice of terror.

I learned the name of the Sixth Priest on the day that I died. It was something the Priest of Vultures said that stirred the cauldron of my mind – 'Join the Light'. Only as I stared into the face of death did I realise who the Sixth Priest must be – a new convert. An agbara of old who had knelt before Palman and become a patron saint of the Son. The old agbara of lightning and thunder. He who was once shunned by the other gods. He who broke kola nut in his dream. Xango, the great ancestor of my children.

Rumi closed the book slowly, still reeling when the cowrie at his neck burned into his flesh. The walls shuddered as though being thumped by a giant's fist and the horns of the Eredo began to sound. Once. Twice. Three times.

We are under attack.

Acknowledgements

Thank God for this beautiful journey.

To my mother. To my sister Demi and brother Shore. To my father, my younger siblings, GC, cousins and all my family who have supported me all the way. Thank you – I could not have done this without any one of you.

To my agents Jordan and Rachel, who supported me through everything. To my editors Marcus and Claire, who believed in my story and made it the best it could be. To everyone at Gollancz and the Blair Partnership who worked to get this book out. Thank you.

To my good friend Maro, who saw the vision and ran with me. To Eniola (and Fo) who believed in me. To Clair who was instrumental in all of this. To Sekemi and Olaolu. To Omo-B, Olaedo, Erin, Richard and Martin. Thank you all for your everything.

To Sayo, most of all – for without you there would be no words.

Credits

Rogba Payne and Gollancz would like to thank everyone at Orion who worked on the publication of *A Testimony of Blood*.

Editorial
Marcus Gipps
Claire Ormsby-Potter

Copy-editor
Abigail Nathan

Proofreader
Patrick McConnell

Editorial Management
Jane Hughes
Charlie Panayiotou
Lucy Bilton

Audio
Paul Stark
Louise Richardson
Georgina Cutler

Contracts
Dan Herron
Ellie Bowker
Oliver Chacón

Design
Nick Shah
Rachel Lancaster
Deborah Francois
Helen Ewing

Finance
Nick Gibson
Jasdip Nandra
Sue Baker
Tom Costello

Marketing
Hennah Sandhu

Publicity
Jenna Petts

Operations
Group Sales Operations team

Sales
David Murphy
Victoria Laws
Esther Waters
Karin Burnik
Anne-Katrine Buch
Frances Doyle
Group Sales teams across
Digital, Field, International
and Non-Trade

Production
Paul Hussey
Katie Horrocks

Inventory
Jo Jacobs
Dan Stevens

Rights
Rebecca Folland
Tara Hiatt
Ben Fowler
Alice Cottrell
Ruth Blakemore
Marie Henckel

First published in Great Britain in 2025 by Gollancz
an imprint of The Orion Publishing Group Ltd
Carmelite House, 50 Victoria Embankment
London EC4Y 0DZ

An Hachette UK Company

The authorised representative in the EEA is Hachette Ireland,
8 Castlecourt Centre, Dublin 15, D15 XTP3,
Ireland (email: info@hbgi.ie)

1 3 5 7 9 10 8 6 4 2

Copyright © Rogba Payne 2025

The moral right of Rogba Payne to be identified as
the author of this work has been asserted in accordance
with the Copyright, Designs and Patents Act of 1988.

All rights reserved. No part of this publication may be
reproduced, stored in a retrieval system, or transmitted
in any form or by any means, electronic, mechanical,
photocopying, recording, or otherwise, without the
prior permission of both the copyright owner and the
above publisher of this book.

All the characters in this book are fictitious, and any resemblance
to actual persons, living or dead, is purely coincidental.

A CIP catalogue record for this book is
available from the British Library.

ISBN (Hardback) 978 1 399 61266 1
ISBN (Export Trade Paperback) 978 1 399 61267 8
ISBN (eBook) 978 1 399 61269 2
ISBN (Audio) 978 1 399 61270 8

Typeset at The Spartan Press Ltd,
Lymington, Hants

Printed and bound in Great Britain by Clays Ltd,
Elcograf S.p.A.

www.gollancz.co.uk

A TESTIMONY OF BLOOD

ROGBA PAYNE

A TESTIMONY OF BLOOD